BULLET UP THE GRAND TRUNK ROAD

Jonathan Gregson was born and raised in Calcutta. He read and taught history at Oxford and Queen's University in Canada before entering financial journalism. After a stint on the *Sunday Telegraph's* City Desk he moved on to travel writing, and returns each year to the subcontinent. He writes for the *Daily* and *Sunday Telegraph*, the *Independent on Sunday*, the *Observer*, the *Globe and Mail* in Toronto and the *Gulf News* in Dubai.

Jonathan Gregson is married to the food writer, photographer and strategy consultant Sarah Woodward. When not travelling, they live in East London.

Jonathan Gregson

BULLET
UP THE GRAND
TRUNK ROAD

SINCLAIR-STEVENSON

First Published 1997

1 3 5 7 9 10 8 6 4 2

© Jonathan Gregson 1997

Jonathan Gregson has asserted his right
under the Copyright, Designs and Patents Act, 1988
to be identified as the author of this work.

First published in the United Kingdom in 1997 by Sinclair-Stevenson
Random House UK Ltd, 20 Vauxhall Bridge Road, London SW1V 2SA

Random House Australia (Pty) Limited
20 Alfred Street, Milsons Point, Sydney
New South Wales 2061, Australia

Random House New Zealand Limited
18 Poland Road, Glenfield
Auckland 10, New Zealand

Random House South Africa (Pty) Limited
Endulini, 5A Jubilee Road, Parktown 2193, South Africa

Random House UK Limited Reg No 954009

A CIP catalogue record for this book is available from the British Library

Papers used by Random House UK Limited are natural,
recyclable products made from wood grown in sustainable forests.
The manufacturing processes conform to the environmental
regulations of the country of origin.

ISBN 1 85619 660 7

Typeset in 11 on 13 point Bembo
by Deltatype Limited, Birkenhead, Merseyside
Printed and bound in the United Kingdom by
Mackays of Chatham PLC

To Hugh and Mollie
for
The land of my birth

Contents

List of Illustrations

The illustrations are by Sarah Woodward, unless otherwise stated

Bullet on the Grand Trunk Road
'Hell on Earth': Durgapur
Weaponry for sale beside the GT Road, Bihar
Mending the Bullet's tyre near Bodh Gaya
Grim determination, Bihar
A dhaba in UP
A pilgrim takes the easy way up Mount Parasnath
Sher Shah Suri's tomb at Sasaram
The bathing ghats at Varanasi
Godmen afloat on the Ganges, Varanasi
A guru and his followers at the Margh Mela, Allahabad
A devotee of Lord Ram near the former site of the Babri
    Mosque, Ayodhya
Mirza Nazim Changrezi at the Jama Masjid, Delhi (*Jonathan
    Gregson*)
The Golden Temple, Amristar
Pakistani minibus driver, Rawalpindi
An impromptu cricket match beside Jahangir's tomb, near
    Lahore
The riverbed road to Rohtas Fort, near Jhelum
Sher Shah Suri's caravanserai beneath Attock Fort
The Khyber Pass, with bodyguards Momin Khan and Zar
    Khan

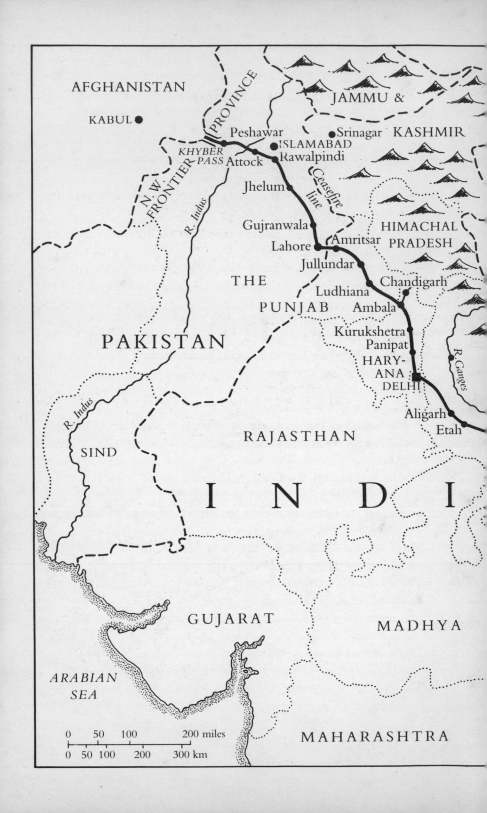

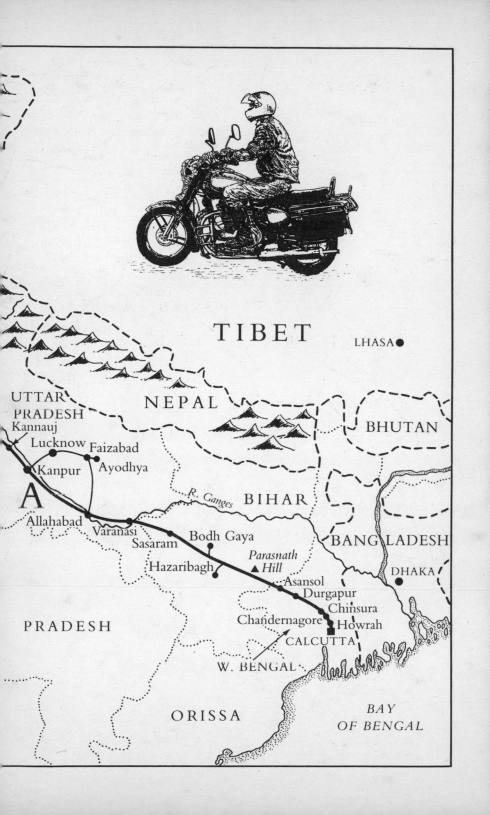

TIBET

LHASA●

UTTAR
PRADESH

NEPAL

BHUTAN

Kannauj

Lucknow   Faizabad

Kanpur   Ayodhya

A

R. Ganges   BIHAR

Allahabad

Varanasi

Sasaram   Bodh Gaya   BANG LADESH

Parasnath
▲ Hill   DHAKA

Hazaribagh

Asansol

Durgapur

Chinsura

PRADESH   Chandernagore   Howrah

CALCUTTA

W. BENGAL

ORISSA   BAY
OF BENGAL

PROLOGUE:
BRIEF ENCOUNTER WITH A BULLET

'So you want us to lend you a Bullet?'

The voice down the telephone line belonged to Praveen Purang, managing director of Royal Enfield Motors Ltd. I had been badgering him for months to loan me a bike. Obviously my latest letter had arrived in India.

'Yes, please,' I replied, trying to sound calm. The Enfield Bullet motorcycle hasn't been built in England for twenty-five years. Mr Purang's factory near Madras still turns them out by the thousand.

'I have read through your request.' His voice was guarded. 'You propose to ride one of our machines from Calcutta to Peshawar, correct?'

'The entire length of the Grand Trunk Road,' I declared with enthusiasm, 'through the heartlands of India and Pakistan. It's almost fifty years now since both countries gained their independence from Britain.'

'I see.' He sounded unconvinced.

'And the Enfield Bullet is almost exactly the same age,' I blundered on regardless. 'The prototype was being developed here in England, at the Redditch works, while these momenttous events were happening in India. It would be a noteworthy expedition,' I added hopefully, all my ammunition now spent.

There was a long silence. I could hear him breathing 5,000 miles away. 'Are you familiar with the Bullet?' he asked.

'Of course,' I replied. 'I've ridden one of the import models here in England.' So I knew that the Bullet's technology goes back to another era, that it has a kick-starter only, and that the gear change is on the right-hand side – the opposite to all modern motorcycles. It shares with other classic British bikes a tendency to leak oil and demand constant attention. The 350 cc Bullet is heavier than some of today's 1000 cc machines. Compared with most modern bikes its performance is sluggish.

For all that, the Bullet has a grand style which has been lost somewhere along the way to making bikes lighter, faster, more efficient. Its single-cylinder engine produces a low, steady thump that is a delight to hear. The old-fashioned riding position allows you to sit up and look around. And its solid build was up to the battering meted out by Indian roads. As for its looks – the elegant teardrop tank, the wire spokes, all that chrome . . . I fell in love the first time I saw one in north London.

'You see, what appeals to me is that it's a British classic still manufactured in India. I feel it is absolutely the right machine to ride up the Grand Trunk Road half a century after Independence and Partition.'

'Very well,' said Mr Purang. 'We will provide you with one of our models. Also, full support from Enfield dealers along your route. Of course, that applies only within India. We can go no further than the border. In Pakistan, we have no presence whatsoever. To my knowledge, there are no Bullets in Pakistan.

'There is one condition only,' he continued. 'You will come and visit us in Madras. Also, could you please tell me why, out of all the places to go in India, you have chosen the GT Road?'

How could I explain? I knew the modern GT Road – the abbreviation is universal in both India and Pakistan – would be no joy-ride.

I had few illusions about this road. Rudyard Kipling may have written about 'the green-arched, shade-flecked length of it, the white breadth of it speckled with slow-pacing folk'. But that was before the internal combustion engine.

Today's Grand Trunk Road is a very different kind of beast. It is dangerous and noisy and clad in grease-grey tarmacadam – for the most part torn and buckled and wreathed in diesel fumes.

I had already travelled by bus or car down short sections of the GT Road. It had been horrific. So why was I now going to ride all sixteen hundred miles of it from the Bay of Bengal to the North-West Frontier?

Well, for one thing, the Grand Trunk Road is one of the world's great historic thoroughfares. For more than two millennia it has served as the country's lifeline, drawing together peoples of different culture, religion and language. Over the centuries it has carried along its broad path countless pilgrims and scholars, ambassadors and merchants, soldiers and adventurers, some of whom left vivid accounts of the road itself and the cities it passes through.

As early as 1500 BC it was being used by the Aryan invaders from Central Asia, who called it the Uttarpatha or Great North Way. It is far older than the fabled Silk Road, or, for that matter, any of the other transcontinental trade routes. There may be stretches of modern highway in China, in Anatolia or in the Peloponnese that follow equally ancient roadways. But there is none in all the world that pursues the same route over so great a distance or has been in such constant use as the Grand Trunk Road.

The road was already there when Alexander the Great's armies crossed the Hindu Kush and descended into the Punjab's debilitating heat. The Greek ambassador Megasthenes travelled down it in the fourth century BC on his way to see the Emperor Chandragupta Maurya, who founded the greatest of India's home-grown dynasties. But perhaps his most enduring legacy was that he reconstructed this already ancient highway as the Royal Trunk Road. The reformist religions then emerging, Buddhism and Jainism, naturally spread along this central axis. And while Europe was plunged into the Dark Ages, the same road was trodden in safety by Buddhist pilgrims from as far afield as China and Java.

Yet the Grand Trunk Road was never intended primarily as a trade or pilgrim route. A military road, its purpose was the maintenance of unity and empire. Ever since Chandragupta's time, all the dynasties which aspired to rule over northern India spread out from its central backbone. The road was rebuilt and furnished with caravanserai during the Mughal period and again improved by the British as their armies advanced inland from Bengal.

As a symbol of unity and order imposed from above, there is nothing in the Indian subcontinent to equal the Grand Trunk Road. The abandoned cities and grandiose mausoleums scattered across the country may reflect the personal glory of former rulers; but the road represents the real sinews of power. It outlasted more than a dozen imperial dynasties.

But when the last of these, the British Empire, finally quit India in August 1947, new borders sprang up. Now there were two countries, India and Pakistan. The Grand Trunk Road no longer served to unite the peoples of the subcontinent. The main artery had been cut.

The British left a country divided as it had never been before along religious or communal lines. The end of empire and foreign domination was a cause for much rejoicing; but Independence came at a terrible cost.

During the final, frantic months leading up to the 'transfer of power', the age-old unity of this vast subcontinent, which had, it's true, always depended on imperial rule, was allowed to dissolve. India was to be partitioned. Red lines were hurriedly drawn across maps. Communities that had lived peacefully side by side – Hindus, Muslims, Sikhs – were set at each other's throats.

The bare facts I gleaned from reports and eyewitness accounts of that era. Somewhere between 500,000 and a million killed. Fifteen millions uprooted from their homes and forced to flee across the new borders.

Those are only estimates. There are no precise figures available. All the same, the scale of these events defies comprehension. Fifteen million people . . . It was the greatest mass exodus in history. And unlike the coldly planned campaigns of mass-genocide or 'ethnic cleansing' that will forever blot the twentieth century, the killings across the subcontinent almost always arose from mob violence.

During the Partition of India and the creation of Pakistan, the GT Road once more came into its own, this time as an escape route for the fearful and homeless masses seeking safety on the other side of the religious divide.

Kipling once described the Grand Trunk Road as being 'truly . . . a wonderful spectacle', for along it flowed 'such a river of life as exists nowhere else in the world'. In 1947 it was turned into a river of blood.

Even now, fifty years on, communal bloodletting breaks out sporadically in cities along its length. The most notorious flashpoint is Ayodhya, but Hindu–Muslim tensions have also erupted in Varanasi and Lahore. The scars left by Partition have not healed over.

Along the way I hoped to discover what has been Partition's real legacy. The GT Road it is still the main road artery in both India and Pakistan. It still draws in peoples of different language and creed, mixes them up, takes its toll and spits them out again when they have reached their final destination. That is why I chose the Grand Trunk Road. For that is how truly great roads have always behaved.

I didn't tell Mr Purang all of this down the phone, just in case it scared him off. But I did go first to Madras, as agreed, to meet him at the Enfield Factory.

Mr Purang was a northerner, sent down from Delhi to sort out the old reliability problems and develop new models. I was given a tour of the factory and told to take my pick of the gleaming new machines.

'Personally, I would advise the 350 cc model,' said Mr Purang. 'It is more economical and spare parts are easier to come by.'

But I decided to go for the 500 cc version, not so much for the extra power but because it has a much larger front brake. Local driving habits ranged from the eccentric to the downright anarchic. I wanted something that could stop fast.

Mr Purang was occupied with running the business, so I spent more of my time with a marketing man who 'had been assigned to my case'. He was a different kettle of fish – always willing to please, but somehow always incapable of delivering. As Enfield was only lending me the bike, it had to be registered and insured through a local dealer. A roll bar and side panniers needed to be fitted. Inevitably, there were delays. The more he smiled and waggled his head, the longer the delays.

I spent a lot of time studying the advertising posters on the walls. One carried pictures of six identical Bullets. Beneath each was a different date: 1955, 1963, 1971, 1979, 1987 and finally the current year. That spelled out most of my own life. At the bottom of the poster was the motto: *Tested, Trusted, Timeless.* Another declared: *The Enfield Bullet. If you are not a bike lover, we are really not interested.*

The sun shone every day. It was nearly Christmas, but the temperature hovered around eighty. Palm trees rustled in the ocean breeze. I'd left behind a hard winter in Europe and should have felt ecstatic. Instead, I felt like death. Not because of any malignant microbes invading my bowels. No, it was a bad dose of flu I'd brought out with me from England. This particular strain flourished mightily in a tropical climate. It loved it in Madras.

I was introduced to the Bullet that would carry me up the Grand Trunk Road. It had pearl-grey paintwork and I loved its classic looks. The only problem was that I was so weak I could barely hold the damn thing upright. I almost dropped it on a test-run; so it was with mixed feelings that I watched it being wheeled into a wooden crate and packed with straw for the rail journey up to Calcutta.

The rest of my time at the Enfield factory I underwent a basic mechanic's course meant to assist in 'roadside trouble-shooting'. My instructor was an ex-military man equipped with a booming voice, splendidly upswept moustaches and a wooden rod with which he pointed to different parts of a demonstration bike. I would have to identify each component and then take it to pieces and reassemble it. I learned how to remove wheels, tighten drive chains, adjust tappets.

At least, he showed me how to do it. How much I actually took in was another matter. I was still running a fever and my powers of concentration were blown. At the end of one day I collapsed over the work-bench and fell to the ground. So, instead of manhandling the bike, we moved on to a session of theoretical on-the-road diagnosis.

I answered his first two questions adequately. Number one, fouled spark plug; number two, blocked fuel line. 'Number three case,' his voice boomed. 'You are going at 60 kilometres speed. The vehicle stops abruptly as if some thirty–forty peoples pull your vehicle from the backside. What is this signifying?'

'Instant death?'

He chose to ignore this. 'This indicates,' he solemnly declared, 'your vehicle has been seized.'

'Seized?' I queried. 'Stolen? Confiscated by police?'

'Goodness, no,' he laughed. 'Only engine is seized. So, you see, in number three case also you should not panic.'

CALCUTTA:
THE KILLING TIMES

At the front of the older Calcutta telephone directories, among the usual instructions and dialling codes, there is an unusual request: *Please do not bribe the telephone operator.* It is there because that is precisely what most Calcuttans know they must do in order to get a 'decent line'. As I redialled the same number for the twentieth time I regretted that the telephone I was using was obviously not a 'priority line'. Then, to my surprise, I got through.

'Ah, Jonathan, so you have arrived,' said Jahar Sengupta. Jahar has what is known as 'clout'. *He* wouldn't have problems getting a telephone connection.

'So what mad plans have you this time?' he chuckled. 'Walking over the Himalayas into Tibet like your father? Or do you still want to visit those headhunters up in Nagaland? I must warn you, permission is still impossible to get.' Jahar knew of some of my wilder schemes and had helped out in the past.

'Oh, nothing so unusual,' I replied. 'This time I'm going up the Grand Trunk Road on a motorbike.'

'I knew there would be some madness involved. Have you ever been driven on this GT Road? Every day there are so many terrible accidents. And what about Sarah? Is she also going with you on this motorcycle?'

I assured Jahar that I'd be alone on the bike. My wife would follow by car up to Kanpur only, together with an artist friend who was flying out to join us in a few days' time. It's difficult to fit three people on a bike – though in Madras I'd seen families of six going short distances on a two-wheeler.

'Well, that's some relief, anyway,' Jahar sighed. 'And everything's all right with the flat? There should be enough room for three of you.'

'Everything's fine,' I said, looking around the spacious apartments. Normally they were used for putting up visiting executives from one of Jahar's companies. 'And thank you for arranging everything.'

'Not at all, not at all . . . But tell me, why the GT Road?'

I told him about the Road and Partition.

'I see,' said Jahar. There was a long pause. 'In that case, why don't you come round for a chat. My own family came over from East Bengal.'

It felt good to be back in Calcutta. I was born here in August 1953 – just six years after Partition – and grew up in this bewildering city. I won't call it 'home', for I have no family here and am not a Bengali. But I feel as much at home in Calcutta as I do in London.

I have known Jahar since those early days when he had worked with my father. After my family left India in 1966 he took over running the company. Since then he had gone on to greater things.

At 7.30 p.m. the doorbell rang. Jahar had sent his car to fetch us. As we drove through the darkened city I saw pavement dwellers bedding down for the night in front of fine mansions, crumbling palaces with foul bustees jammed in between them, the very rich and the unimaginably poor living cheek by jowl. Not in Delhi – not even in Bombay – is there such a juxtaposition of poverty and wealth.

I opened the car window and breathed in the heady cocktail of vegetal, animal and industrial fumes which only in Calcutta seems to attain such ripeness. This may be because Calcutta was the first place where the Industrial Revolution collided with the tropics. The smoke from its Victorian factories and untreated fumes from smaller workshops combine to produce an odour reminiscent of burnt-out brake linings. Then there is the smell of natural decay rising from the stagnant lakes around it, the stink escaping from its hundred-year-old sewers or the slumland bustees which have no sanitation whatsoever.

During that ride across town I picked up more pungent local odours. Each time the driver slowed for a road junction or to overtake a bullock cart, the smells rose up and triggered one set of unexcavated childhood memories after another. Bumping along in the back was like being in a mobile cinema, each odour unleashing another rush of eight-millimetre home movies which had somehow survived the last thirty years in the cerebral attic.

The driver honked his horn, a chowkidar unlocked the gates, and we moved carefully down a private lane to the house that Jahar had built for his retirement. It reared up like an ocean liner squeezed into too small a berth. He had only been able to acquire a small plot – land prices in overcrowded Calcutta are astronomical – so all the features he was used to, such as a veranda, were tacked onto different levels. The downstairs reception room was sumptuously furnished and smelled of newly burned incense.

'That's on account of the wedding coming up,' Jahar explained. 'Roma's so busy arranging things. Bhikari! Make whisky-sodas for our guests!'

As the old servant shuffled about we talked about my plans for the journey ahead.

'This motorcycle, where precisely is this machine at present?'

'On its way from Madras by train, I hope.'

Jahar looked unconvinced. His expression triggered a whole load of my own doubts and fears. Not that I was worried about the bike turning up in Calcutta as promised. I knew I could trust Enfield on that score. It was what I was going to do with it that made my stomach flutter.

Even the short ride over to Jahar's house through Calcutta traffic had made me aware of how unprepared I was. Indian road manners, I knew, are different from those that prevail where there are hard-and-fast rules. In the West, if a driver caused an accident by pulling out without first looking or indicating then it was their fault. Witnesses, the police, insurance companies, would all agree on this. But in the subcontinent it is always the responsibility of the following vehicle to take evasive action – no matter what madness has been committed up ahead. To ride a bike in these conditions requires a different approach, a whole new set of responses. So while sitting in the back of Jahar's car I had imagined I was on the Bullet and fed in what my responses to various potential disasters *en route* would have been. In half the cases I had got it wrong.

Jahar broke up this dismal line of speculation. 'You wanted to ask me about Partition. Have you not asked your own father about this? He was here in Calcutta at the time.'

'Yes, he's told me about the dead bodies in the streets and how the killings went on all through 1947.'

'Any specific instances?'

'There was one about the old godown in Entally where they used to assemble storage batteries. Some of the Hindu workers were attacked by a Muslim mob. He said five were killed. The rest either fled or ran into the godown and hid among the wooden crates used for transporting battery containers. They didn't dare come out, so some of their Muslim workmates smuggled in food for them.'

'Amidst all these tragedies,' Jahar interrupted, 'there were many such examples of kindness – Muslims helping Hindus, Hindus helping Muslims.'

'My father went to the godown to speak with them, but they still wouldn't budge. There was a lot of looting and arson going on in Entally at the time. He was worried the godown would be attacked, so he went to the police and told them this and that there were tankfuls of concentrated sulphuric acid inside.'

'He was always a resourceful man, your father. You know there were many acid-bomb attacks at this time?'

'The police put a guard on the front gate immediately.'

'But nothing untoward happened to himself – or your

mother?' Jahar's concern was such that, if anything had occurred, he himself would somehow share in the responsibility.

'Some goondas, criminal types, tried to force their way into the house. Unsuccessfully, otherwise I wouldn't be here to talk about it. No, as Europeans they weren't the main target. But what about yourself, Jahar?'

'I myself have seen people hacked to death in front of me,' he exclaimed, 'but was powerless to intervene. It was right here, in the middle of Calcutta. At that time I'd just completed my examinations and entered the Government of India Service, so I opted for India. But as I told you, my family came from East Bengal. My father was already a pensioner. He was given the choice of either moving to India or staying in East Pakistan for his pension. Nobody really knew what would happen. So he said to me: "I'll stay put; let us split the risk."

'It became impossible for me to go and visit him. If I'd tried I would have been killed, being a Hindu, just like that.' He made a cutting gesture across his throat.

'Not in our village, mind you. In our village there was never any trouble. It was called Panditsar, a very isolated place, so in the wet season you could only get there by boat, and in the dry season they took you along unmade paths by palanquin. It was that kind of village – very peaceful, very traditional.

'Most of the villagers were Muslims. They were wonderful people. Never would they have harmed anybody. It was the politicians who stirred up the trouble, sending threats to Hindu families. The situation in the East grew more tense, and after four years I made special arrangements to bring my family out.'

This fitted well with what I knew of Jahar. If anyone could have organised 'special arrangements', it was he.

'My father,' he remembered, 'was in tears when we left the village. "Look at these people," he said to me. "They are so kind, such good people." And the villagers cried out to him: "You're like a father to us. Why must you be going?" Everyone was sad that we were leaving for good, but we had to. At such times you hold your life in your hands.

'That is my own experience of Partition,' he sighed. 'We were only one family out of millions.'

The winter months in Calcutta are a busy time. For the wealthy, it is the peak of the 'social season', a non-stop whirl of parties and weddings to be enjoyed before the rising heat and humidity put an end to such entertainments.

Everyone was enjoying the cool weather. Across the maidan, the open expanse at the heart of Calcutta, there were cricket matches and open-air poetry readings.

The New Year was looming, so I went out to celebrate. There were parties in houses of unimaginable opulence where I met Bengali painters and poets and industrialists. On New Year's Eve, I danced with sari-clad ladies adorned with dark sapphires the size of pigeon's eggs at the Bengal Club, before going out into the street to join the noisy celebrations.

The downtown area around Park Street was jammed with cars tooting their horns in joy rather than habitual anger. Bands of revellers wearing party hats or blowing whistles wished me 'Hah-pi Nu-Yargh' and shook my hand repeatedly. Firecrackers were going off; people were cheering; even the policemen on duty were fooling around, any pretence at keeping the crowds in order abandoned long ago. Calcutta likes to celebrate the New Year in style.

It was odd to see how an old pagan ritual from Europe had recreated itself in Bengal. The crowds were as dense as in Trafalgar Square or Sauchiehall Street; but without the drunkenness they seemed less threatening. The only problem was 'Eve-teasing'. I heard several women screaming about having their bottom pinched or some other unwanted attention. When a foolhardy youth tried it on Sarah, she turned on him and yelled, 'Suar ka bacha!' – which implies an intimate family connection with a pig. The boy was struck dumb; but I decided to move on before he could call up his friends.

Calcuttans delight in the art of conversation – or chit-chat, as they say with typical self-deprecation. The older generation had all been around at Partition and had stories to tell. It seemed unreal, as I sat there in the plush houses and clubs of Calcutta's seriously rich, knocking back imported whisky, to hear eye-witness accounts of servants being murdered, houses burned down, rickshaw-wallahs having their throats cut in broad daylight.

On New Year's Day it continued out at the racecourse, courtesy of the Royal Calcutta Turf Club. In between races an impeccably tailored and well-spoken industrialist told me how as a boy he had witnessed the first outbreak of violence during the infamous 'Calcutta Killings' of August 1946.

'We were living in a block of apartments, fairly high up,' he began. 'But we could see from our verandas cars being stopped, people being pulled out and beaten up, their cars then set on fire. We even saw a number of cases where large mobs attacked houses, ransacking them before they too were set on fire.

'I vividly remember this, though I was quite young in those days. We stayed put for six days before we were moved out under military escort. We happened to be in a predominantly Muslim area, and the Muslims were killing the Hindus; but in other parts of the city Hindus were killing Muslims. This continued off and on for months, flaring up and dying down again.

'That was many years ago now. At least here in Calcutta we haven't seen communal riots for decades. Of course there are still communal tensions elsewhere in India; but very little compared with what we had before . . .' His melodious voice trailed off. Over the loudspeakers an excited race commentator was following the progress of the 2.30 handicap. 'It doesn't sound like I backed the right horse,' he laughed, before waving across the room to some late arrivals.

Jahar and Roma were there as well. We looked out from their box across the maidan to the shining marble dome of the Victoria Memorial and the occasional high-rise office block along Chowringhee Road. Jahar seemed deep in thought. I studied the kites wheeling high above us. Eventually he turned to me and said: 'You know, this ought to be a great city. In some respects it is; but all it's known for in the West is its poverty and its problems.'

I nodded. I'd often been told by Calcuttans how they resent their city being labelled a hopeless case. It doesn't matter if it's known as Mother Theresa's City, the City of the Dead, or the City of Joy – they feel insulted and point out that there is more to Calcutta than its notorious bustees. I'd had an earful of this from an indomitable old lady the previous evening. 'Tourists don't go to New York to see all the povery and vice in Harlem,' she exclaimed. 'Why should they seek out only these things when they come to Calcutta? Do they not know that Calcutta is a city of palaces and poets, that we Bengalis have an immensely rich culture?'

Jahar's thoughts ran on different lines. 'It was Partition that killed this city,' he declared. 'It was built for a maximum of three millions. Now there are maybe 15 millions. It has had to absorb surplus population, not just refugees but economic migrants, for fifty years. And most of these people have come from East Bengal.'

'Look at these Bihari Muslims,' he went on. 'They emigrated from Bihar to East Pakistan in 1947. Then, after that country became Bangladesh, the Banglas didn't want them. So where do they go? They come here. Nowadays in Calcutta there are three or four millions of them. As soon as one group begin to progress and leave the bustees, more immigrants take their place. And because we have had a Communist government here in West Bengal, the Congress government in Delhi wouldn't lift a finger to help.

'I wouldn't blame any one party for Partition,' he warned me. 'But for Calcutta the price of Partition has been enormous. And not just here. In the Punjab, on the other side, the people paid a terrible price.'

Those of a generation too young to remember Partition itself had since witnessed outbreaks of communal violence. Like Mrs Malabika Sarkar, who teaches English Literature at Calcutta University and lives in a predominantly Muslim area near Park Circus. 'This family has lived here a long time,' she said, 'and when there were riots in the 1950s we gave shelter to Muslims who had been chased out of their houses.

'Nowadays Hindus like us are living between two Muslim bustees. It is worrying, that all these people without education are so communal. There are exceptions, of course; but so many Hindus are unreasonably anti-Muslim, while the Muslims are very sensitive to what they think is an insult and straightaway come out wielding their lathis.'

We had been warned against going into this Muslim area, particularly after dark. 'If you go to Park Circus when there's a cricket match on and Pakistan side is winning, then they are throwing crackers in the air. But if India is playing and look like winning, then the houses are in total darkness.'

India's 120 million Muslim minority is often charged with being unpatriotic or 'anti-national' over such issues as Kashmir. But a cricket match? In England it's considered perfectly normal for British Asians to support India or Pakistan or Sri Lanka. For Indian Muslims to support Pakistan against England or Australia hardly seemed adequate grounds for suspicion of treason. But then I hadn't yet realised that, in the subcontinent, cricket has become a form of war by proxy.

Calcutta's cold season isn't a blessing for all of its inhabitants. As the night mists descend, the pavement-dwellers shiver under their threadbare blankets and the cold creeps in through the cracks in the makeshift 'temporary dwellings' that spring up beside roads and railway tracks. Yet, for all Calcuttans, the winter months are considered a favourable time of year for weddings.

The courtyard outside our flat in Middleton Row had been festooned with tired-looking marigolds when we first arrived – the left-overs of a wedding party the night before. A week later the garlands were going up again for another wedding. A white horse was hired for the bridegroom and a raucous wedding band put in an appearance. I watched the festivities, wondering when my own charger – the pearl-grey Enfield Bullet I had last seen in Madras – would arrive in Calcutta. On the practical level, I badly needed some experience of riding in local traffic. But I also harboured a romantic or childish urge to ride that thumping great machine around the same streets I had once trudged as a young boy.

Rising from the courtyard below, the smell of wetted-down marigolds and winter roses reminded me of when I was six or seven, and of the old flower seller doing his rounds. Usually I met him, with his pannier of puja flowers and tuber roses piled high on his head, during my early morning walk around the local tank – a man-made lake just opposite our house in Loudon Street.

I decided to visit the tank. It was only a ten-minute walk away through backstreets I knew well.

Soon I found myself in Loudon Street. The faded Palladian mansion was still there. It had been built by Warren Hastings to house the dispossessed heirs of Tipu Sultan and their tutor. For nearly twenty years my family had rented the ground floor. And it was here, squatting on the steps to the servants' compound, that I picked up the vile concoction of languages known as 'Kitchen Hindi'.

I crossed the road and went through the wrought-iron turnstile. The tank is surrounded by gardens and tall trees which shield it from the din of Calcutta. The only sound came from the dhobis as they slapped their washing against wet stones. It was still a peaceful place.

I sat down on a stone bench. The old flower seller used to rest his load just here, beside the sunlit waters, before continuing on his morning rounds. Occasionally he'd give me a single bloom to take home. It was during one of these desultory conversations that I first learned of the tank's dark secret; that some ten or twelve years earlier, at the time of the 'great killings', when the flower seller's hair hadn't yet turned white, this peaceful lake had been used for dumping dead bodies. They would be weighted down with stones like those the dhobis used, but for some reason they would always float to the surface later. The flower seller pointed to the tranquil waters of the tank. I nodded solemnly. It was my first knowledge of the horrors of Partition.

Even aged seven, I was curious rather than horrified. By then I had already seen dead bodies lying in the street, registered the flies swarming around upturned eyes before my ayah could drag me away. Growing up in Calcutta it's hard to avoid seeing death and disease. But when I reported my latest discovery about the tank opposite my parents were not best pleased.

My father explained that those had been difficult times, before I was born, when people had been killing each other. Now it was perfectly safe to walk around the tank. Then, for some reason, he added that he'd only known one person who ended up there – a Bengali theatrical impresario.

The mystery of the tank was added to other inexplicable events. As when a swarm of locusts descended on the city – so many that the sky was dark at midday and the scavenger crows gorged on the brown insects until they were unable to eat any more. Or the time that I tried to give a few annas to a street-boy my own age and all the other beggars started fighting over it so that I was lucky to escape with just a few scratches to my arms and face.

Only later did I understand that the boy had been operating on another beggar's patch. Or that in big cities begging is highly organised with pavement rights passed down through families who must often pay protection money to the local goondas. What I did appreciate was the frightening speed with which an ordinary crowd can transform itself into a violent mob. It scared me rigid then; and it's still the thing that scares me most about the subcontinent.

As a child I was completely innocent of the politics of Partition. I knew only that India was a great and independent country; that Nehru was Prime Minister and always talked to hugely cheering crowds; and that I didn't know all the Hindi words when I sang the national anthem. The consequences of Partition, the sprawling slums and bustees packed with refugees from East Bengal or Bihar, were an accepted part of the urban landscape. I knew there was another country called Pakistan with which India would sometimes fight a war. And I knew there were times when it was dangerous to go through certain areas in Calcutta because of communal riots between Muslims and Hindus.

I'd had my brushes with violence. Like the time when the Muslim butchers in the New Market went on the rampage, pursuing some unfortunate with their blood-smeared cleavers raised high. Or the day when our driver was taking me home from the cinema and we ran into a demonstration. The crowd started pointing at the car. Or rather at the driver, whose beard and astrakhan cap marked him out as a Muslim. I remember him winding up the windows and the look of pure panic on his face as the crowd closed in, beating with their fists against the windscreen, trying to wrench open the doors.

The driver was as scared for my life as much as for his own. Somehow he managed to reverse out of there without running anyone over. A couple of brickbats were thrown after us, but we got clear of the crowds and accelerated away. I couldn't understand why it happened or how anyone – Hindus, Muslims, whatever – could hate each other so much that they'd attack people they'd never seen before, against whom they could bear no personal grudge, but purely because of what they stood for.

The Great Calcutta Killings of August 1946 marked the beginning of a new phase in Hindu–Muslim riots. Not just because of the scale of the massacres – official estimates give four thousand dead and ten thousand injured, though unofficial figures are more than twice that – but because it was the first real trial of strength between the two communities over what would happen after the British left India.

There was nothing new about communal violence on Calcutta's streets. There had been clashes between Muslims and Hindus before – over religious processions or labour disputes, or about one side's objecting to the other's not joining in *their* protest against British rule. But this time the British were left out of it. Everybody knew they would quit India sooner or later. No, this was a strictly communal affair: Muslim against Hindu and Sikh.

The protagonists were driven by a whole new set of aspirations and fears. Should there be a separate Muslim homeland called Pakistan? Would this mean India must be physically divided? If so, would Bengal be sliced in two, with a Muslim majority in East Bengal and a Hindu majority in the west? These questions were of vital importance to Calcuttans, many of whom had family or properties in rural areas. On which side of the border would they fall?

And where would Calcutta fit into this? It still prided itself on being 'the Third City of the Empire' after London and Glasgow. It had most of the industry and capital in Bengal. But if the province was divided, all the jute factories would be in the mainly Hindu west and most of the jute fields in the Muslim east. Big money was at stake. If India was to be divided, there must also be a division of spoils.

These were some of the tensions building up in Calcutta during the summer of 1946. Within the city Muslims were in a minority. But in Bengal as a whole they formed the majority, and it was the Muslim League which ran the provincial government. The chief minister, H. S. Suhrawardy, was a political tough with a weakness for night clubs and champagne. He wanted Calcutta to remain capital of a united Bengal. But at this stage he was in awe of Mohammad Ali Jinnah and followed his call for a separate Pakistan.

It was Jinnah who issued the call for a Direct Action Day on 16 August. There was to be a hartal, a general strike, which all Muslims were expected to observe. Jinnah exhorted 'the Muslim nation to stand to a man behind their sole representative organisation, the Muslim League, and be ready for sacrifice'.

In Bengal, Suhrawardy was ready to back this to the hilt. Although not the most sophisticated politician, he knew he had to stake his claim to Calcutta. Unfortunately he believed that a show of force would strengthen his hand. The Muslim National Guard was put in readiness; student organisations mobilised; transport arranged to bring in Muslim League supporters from outside the city. Inevitably there was talk of Jihad. The League didn't accept Gandhi's creed of non-violence. Muslim pride – and their legendary martial spirit – was stirred up through mass meetings and inflammatory articles in the press. On the eve of Direct Action Day a Muslim leaflet boasted: 'We shall see then who will play with us, for rivers of blood will flow. We shall have swords in our hands, and the noise of Zikr. Tomorrow will be doom's day.'

Calcutta's Hindu majority made their own preparations. The right-wing Hindu Mahasabha and its militant arm, the Rashtrya Swayam Sewak Sangh, stepped up recruitment and armed their followers. Hindu shopkeepers were urged to stay open and ignore the general strike, because 'to join the hartal is to support the demand for Pakistan'. Both sides wooed Calcutta's gangland bosses and their strong-arm men, the goondas. If it came to street-fighting and arson, these were the real experts.

On 15 August, the Muslim-led Bengal Government declared Direct Action Day was to be a public holiday – ostensibly to prevent provocations to violence. In fact, it released thousands more onto Calcutta's streets. Everyone expected bloody clashes. But nobody anticipated the scale of the massacres, nor where they would lead.

To discover what had happened next I set off for the offices of Calcutta's most venerable newspaper, the *Statesman*. Somewhere in its archives there had to be old copies from Partition days. If nothing else, the shock of what was then happening to the city should come jumping off the page.

I walked along Chowringhee, eyeing its six lanes of anarchy-on-wheels with some trepidation. Soon enough I'd be out there on my bike. Then I stopped in front of the tall Doric column which used to be known as the Ochterlony Monument. It was here that chief minister Suhrawardy called a mass meeting of Muslims on Direct Action Day. They turned up in their tens of thousands. The place has always been a favourite for holding big political rallies, and I noticed preparations for another one were in progress – Communist, to judge from the red-and-white bunting. When they came to power in the late 1970s, the Communists renamed the monument Shahid Minar – 'The Martyr's Memorial'.

The *Statesman*'s offices lay at the far end of Calcutta's main thoroughfare. I was taken up several floors to a room filled with racks of brown-edged newspapers. The editions of August 1946 were soon fetched.

'Over 270 killed, 1,600 injured, in two days of communal riots in Calcutta', ran the headline. 'Stabbing, arson, looting and destruction were widespread on both days . . . Curfew from 9 p.m. to 4 a.m. was imposed . . . Section 144 promulgated prohibiting assembly in public of five or more persons . . . Calcutta Fire Brigade attends to 900 fires . . . crowds barred access . . . Mullick Bazaar completely gutted . . . as were a Bengali newspaper in north Calcutta and several bustees . . . *Statesman* office attacked Friday p.m. by a mob of hooligans who set fire to a number of doors and windows.'

The note of panic is thinly disguised. What mattered to the *Statesman*'s English-speaking audience was the threat of anarchy overtaking the city. There were reassuring stories of successful army sweeps in north Calcutta. But the scale of the massacres in the bustees wasn't yet recognised.

By the end of the third day of rioting the death toll had leapt to between two and three thousand. Though it was 'impossible to obtain any accurate estimate of the number of injured', they were known to run to 'many thousands'. Now there were eye-witness accounts – as when 'a mob surrounded and set fire to a bustee. As the inhabitants rushed out they were seized and hacked to death. The whole bustee, with all its residents, was wiped out.'

The streets of Calcutta were full of corpses and there was danger of an epidemic. In Upper Chitpur Road 'about fifty bodies had been thrown haphazardly in two heaps and were being devoured by vultures', while near Park Circus, 'beside the burnt and looted remains of a two-storeyed house, lay the remains of two men and a dog'. The staff reporter noted that the 'vultures had attacked the former, leaving the dog alone'.

It made grim reading. Many of the victims were tortured or mutilated. Sir Francis Tuker, then head of Eastern Command, recalled that 'in one particular place a man had been tied by his ankles to a tramway electric junction box, his hands were bound behind his back and a hole had been made in his forehead so that he bled to death through his brain'. Some of the most brutal killings were committed by professional criminals; but just as many were the result of local people settling old scores.

The mainly British troops detailed to remove putrefying corpses had to be issued with gasmasks and capes. They called it 'Operation Grisly'. A Major Dobney described how 'handcarts were piled high with bodies and had been left abandoned at the kerb-side, the arms and legs sticking out grotesquely like a load of large, broken dolls. On doorways and shop fronts bodies had been dumped from the houses themselves. Once it was known that the mad Englishmen were collecting the dead, more bodies appeared from the labyrinth of houses and hovels that comprised the area.

'All night,' Dobney reported, 'the horrible task went on. Most of the bodies were foully mutilated and nearly all in an advanced state of decomposition and were impossible to lift up on to the trucks without bursting into a sickening pile at the feet of their collectors, so that often officers and British Other Ranks would turn away and be quietly sick before returning to their task.'

The great Calcutta Killings were just the first wave to break. News of the atrocities spread across the subcontinent. The first large-scale retaliation broke out around Noakhali, in East Bengal, where Muslims formed a large majority. Then the storm centre shifted to Bihar, whose Hindu majority wreaked terrible vengeance on the Muslim population, before moving up through Uttar Pradesh to the Punjab – the greatest killing ground of all.

Back at the flat in Middleton Row, I spread out a map of the subcontinent and stared at the thin red line representing the Grand Trunk Road. With the exception of Noakhali, my route would follow the epicentres of communal violence as they spread across India in the year leading up to Independence and Partition. It would also pass near the main flashpoints of Hindu–Muslim conflict today – Ayodhya, Varanasi, Mathura. The old fears and animosities have not completely gone away. For most Indians, Pakistan is still the whipping boy, the necessary 'external evil', just as the Soviet Union was for Middle America during the Cold War.

I had three more days before setting out on my journey. What I needed was someone to help me through all the historical controversies and political minefields which surround the subject of Partition. Was it inevitable? Who was responsible? Has any good come out of it for the peoples of the subcontinent? Not the kind of questions likely to go down well in either India or Pakistan.

I folded up the map, poured out a whisky-soda and prepared to wrestle with Calcutta's antiquated telephone exchange.

The next morning I was again stuck in the grid-locked traffic, but I had a smile on my face. I'd managed to track down Amales Tripathi, an eminent and reputedly impartial Bengali historian.

Though now retired, Professor Tripathi has written learned histories of the Congress Party and of the more extremist 'freedom fighters' such as Aurobindo Ghose. He gave me tea and Bengali sweets, which I devoured as he discoursed with authority upon the different strands that resulted in Partition.

'It is often said that it was the British who brought this about, through their policy of "Divide and Rule". There is some truth in this.'

'So Partition was primarily the result of British policy?'

'Not so quickly,' he chuckled. 'The British sought to separate the Muslims from the mostly Hindu extremists who called for an armed struggle. But the extremists were outflanked not so much by the British or the Muslims as by Mahatma Gandhi. He realised India was so vast that an armed struggle was impossible. Non-violence was the only practical method of carrying on a mass struggle.'

'What went wrong then? It didn't end peacefully.'

'That is certainly true. I'm a great admirer of Gandhi,' he declared and then sank into silence. A full minute passed. I poured myself more tea.

'However,' he resumed, 'I think when he launched the "Quit India" movement in 1942 it was a terrible mistake. Why? Because it was certain to become violent. Gandhi himself was in jail. He couldn't lead it or control it. And look at the timing. You British had your backs to the wall. How could it be expected you would tolerate derailing of trains and suchlike?

'The British reacted against Congress mainly by supporting Jinnah and the Muslim League, who were more willing to co-operate in your "war effort". Politics became more communal now – Muslim pitted against Hindu rather than a united struggle against the British. Now there were two protagonists.

'After the War the British knew their time in India was limited. The pressing question was should it be divided or not? Gandhi was strongly opposed to Partition. But the other Congress leaders, Nehru and Patel, were slowly worn down by the constant friction with the Muslim League. In the end they wanted a settlement, even if it meant dividing India. To this the British agreed. From there it was only a question of how to partition India.'

I'd sipped my tea down to the dregs. 'What about Calcutta?'

'Just before the date set for Independence tensions were running high. Calcutta was like a time-bomb waiting to explode. Then Gandhi came and stayed in this place of miracles, Hydari Mansion. Have you been to this place?'

'Not yet,' I confessed.

'But you must. If Gandhi hadn't come there would have been another riot as in 1946 and not one Muslim in the city would have lived. On the night of Independence, Gandhi fasted rather than celebrating India's freedom. His example prevented great bloodshed. But he himself was at the end of his tether. Right to the last moment he had opposed division. Now all his work had fallen into dust.'

Professor Tripathi removed his glasses. Clearly he was still moved by these distant events. 'That is the history,' he said. 'But you asked who was responsible for Partition? It was not just the British – although they are always being blamed for it. Divide and Rule? It was we Indians who divided amongst ourselves so that the British could rule.

'I tell you, all of us were responsible – Hindus, Muslims, Sikhs . . . It may be that we are all too much rooted in our own culture and religion. Why, even today these same conflicts which led to Partition have not been solved. Still we are at loggerheads – and not just with Pakistan and Bangladesh, but with our own minorities. The blame must be apportioned to all of us. We should hang our heads in shame.'

As I made to leave, he held up his hand. 'Yours,' he said, 'is a difficult quest. You will find most people willing to cast the blame elsewhere. Do you know this saying, "the fault lies not in the stars but within ourselves"? Then keep that always before your eyes. Now let me give you directions to Hydari Mansion.'

I had no problem in finding the big cinema in Beliaghata. As the Professor had suggested, it was a well-known landmark among the surrounding bustees. But when I asked local people in the street where Hydari Mansion was, not one out of fifteen had heard of it.

I tried out 'Gandhi's house?' Again, the same blank looks. The inhabitants of Beliaghata seemed to suffer from collective amnesia over Gandhi's ever being among them; which is strange, because by coming to this unprepossessing corner of east Calcutta the Mahatma certainly saved thousands of lives – the parents and grandparents of those I was asking included.

Gandhi had arrived in Calcutta a week before Independence Day. There had been terrible communal riots all through the previous month and worse was expected. What he proposed was extraordinary. He suggested to the Muslim chief minister, Suhrawardy, that they both move into a deserted house in Beliaghata, a mainly Muslim bustee badly hit during previous riots. There they would live together, hostages to the city's good behaviour, until peace was restored.

It was a high-risk experiment. Suhrawardy was loathed by

Hindus for provoking the original Calcutta Killings, and on the first day a Hindu crowd broke into Hydari Mansion demanding why Gandhi was with such a man. Why had he come to succour the Muslims when it was the Hindus who had suffered? Gandhi replied: 'How can I, who am a Hindu by birth, a Hindu by creed, and a Hindu of Hindus in my way of living, be an "enemy" of Hindus?'

The hostile crowd dispersed. From then on, processions of Hindus and Muslims made their way to Hydari Mansion, where they swore to keep the peace. The fear of communal violence that stalked the city was miraculously released and on Independence Day both Muslims and Hindus joined together in celebration. While the Punjab was aflame, the streets of Calcutta rang to the shout of Jai Hind! – 'Long live India!'

Through his personal example, Gandhi had done what thousands of troops could not achieve. He had tamed Calcutta's communal frenzy. Mountbatten told him he was 'a one-man boundary force'. Hydari Mansion became known as a 'miracle place'.

Surely the local people had not forgotten?

It was a man from outside Beliaghata who eventually helped me out. The house was down a side lane not sixty yards away. I found an old, yellow, slightly Italianate mansion, set in a small garden. The house was shut up. A frangipani tree was in full bloom, its stained white petals scattered across the gravel. A chowkidar arrived but he had no keys. Together we went off in search of the caretaker who lived several streets away.

Mr J. C. Ghosh was surprised to find an Englishman at his front door. 'Foreign visitors are most unusual,' he said, before disappearing to find the keys. He re-emerged with the keys, carrying an umbrella with an elaborately carved handle like some staff of office. He told me he was eighty-three years old.

The doors of Hydari Mansion had to be wrenched open. At the end of the entrance hall was a mural in sombre greys and browns depicting Gandhi, cross-legged, at the centre. Around him were scenes of communal fighting and processions of grateful citizens. The artist had gone easy on the violence.

'This house belonged to the widow of a Mohammedan cloth merchant,' Mr Ghosh explained. 'Every day Gandhi held a prayer meeting and 50,000 came from all over Calcutta – Hindus and Muslims both.'

I learned that the 'miracle' lasted only a fortnight. At the end of August, a crowd again invaded Hydari Mansion, carrying a Hindu they said had been knifed by a Muslim. This time not even Gandhi could calm their frenzy. His entourage was attacked and he himself was injured. Calcutta erupted with uncontrollable violence.

Against this Gandhi applied his 'ultimate weapon'. Unless peace was restored he would fast to death. On the first day the rioting continued; but from the second day of his fast calm gradually returned. Mixed processions marched through the city. Gandhi told them to go out together and patrol the troubled areas. Calcutta's police force – both Indians and Europeans – fasted for twenty-four hours while remaining on duty. Hindu militias surrendered their weapons to Gandhi. A notorious gang of Hindu goondas submitted themselves to whatever penalty he chose. He told them to go out among the Muslims and assure them of protection. Only when he was convinced that peace had returned did he end his fast.

A second 'miracle' had come to pass in Hydari Mansion. I stared at the dusty relics: the wooden sandals Gandhi had worn; the earthenware cups from which he took water; the stuffed figure of a white goat which had provided his milk when he visited England. Mr Ghosh busied himself in plumping up cushions and beating the dust out of old armchairs. 'Only very few people are coming,' he apologised. The house has become a sadly neglected shrine to a half-forgotten ideal.

The countdown to departure was now really on. Tyrel arrived from England. He too had been born in Calcutta, but his family left when he was just three months old. This was his first time back in India and he was intoxicated by the clamour and vitality of it all. As a professional artist he revelled in the saturated colours of women's saris, the hand-painted billboards outside cinemas, the intricate decoration on rickshaws. He would be sharing the car with Sarah as far as Kanpur. It was good having him with us. He had a different way of seeing things and he knew a lot about bikes.

Last-minute purchases needed to be made. Road maps were one problem. Few were available, and those that were looked hopelessly outdated. Accommodation was another. There aren't many hotels beside the GT Road in either West Bengal or Bihar. I would need somewhere with at least a locked gate so that the bike didn't disappear overnight.

Sarah sallied forth to the West Bengal Tourist office and returned several hours later with chits guaranteeing rooms in state-run guest houses at Pandua and Durgapur. Only later did we realise there are two Panduas in West Bengal, or that the one we had booked into was a hundred miles north of our route. Mr McDonald D'Silva – a kindly man who had worked for the Calcutta Port Authority – gave us a letter of recommendation from an electoral commissioner. 'Never know when it might come in handy,' he said. It was to prove invaluable on several occasions.

I went down to Enfield's offices on Camac Street to go through the paperwork. I discovered from the local manager, Mr Chakrabarty, that I was to have some grand send-off. He told me to look up his brother-in-law when I arrived in Durgapur. He also put me in touch with a company that could provide a car for Sarah and Tyrel as far as Varanasi. The car was a Hindustan Ambassador. The driver's name was Misri Lal Ram.

Events were gaining a momentum of their own. Mr Sil arrived from Patna. He was in charge of Enfield's operations throughout north-east India and had even grander ideas than Mr Chakrabarty. I was to be 'flagged off' by a senior police officer. There was to be press coverage.

The bike had arrived by train and was being checked over. I desperately wanted to get my hands on it – if only to notch up a few miles in local traffic conditions. But first I had to go off with Mr Sil and scout the best location for the 'flagging-off ceremony'. We settled on the Lion Gate in front of the Victoria

Memorial – a grandiose monument to the permanence of British rule in India.

The Bullet was only handed over to me the day before I was due to leave. When I asked to take it for a test run they insisted a mechanic ride pillion – just in case. I felt like a child who couldn't be trusted with an expensive Christmas present. Was all this fuss really necessary?

Finally I was allowed to go off on my own. I slipped into gear and moved out into the traffic. Sarah and Tyrel would be waiting for me back at the flat. I turned down Park Street, slicing through the traffic, the big single cylinder thumping reassuringly. Here I was on a Bullet, riding past the street where I was born.

My mistake was to stop for some cigarettes. I pulled over and started to dismount, when my right leg caught on the side-pannier. The next thing I knew I was on the floor with 400 lb of shiny new motorcycle on top of me.

Christ, I thought. This is really stupid. I've only had the keys for five minutes, and what do I do? I drop the bloody bike. When I'm not even moving.

At first I was so angry with myself that I didn't notice the pain. A crowd immediately gathered around and pulled the bike off my leg. Was I was all right? 'Tik hai, tik hai – I'm OK, thank you.'

Even as I said it I knew I was lying, like some drunk driver slurring his protestations of innocence through a three-quarters-closed car window. No, I was not all right. The pain around my groin was spreading. I prayed it wasn't serious; otherwise I'd have to postpone the entire trip. Besides which, my self-confidence was in shreds. If I couldn't pilot the bike safely across three miles of familiar streets, what was I doing setting out down the most notorious road in all of India and Pakistan? It was madness.

I checked out the bike for damage, running through the routines on automatic-pilot. Nothing serious, thank God: only a broken rear-view mirror and a few scratches on the chrome-plated crash bars. Then check the fuel tap is on, gears in neutral, pump the kick-start a couple of times to build up compression. The routine keeps you going, makes you feel you're still in control.

At least I made it back to Middleton Row without further mishap.

Sarah was waiting impatiently, a cigarette in one hand and what looked distinctly like a gin-and-lime in the other.

'What kept you?' .

'I'm sorry, things took longer than I expected. And besides,' I decided to get the confession over and done with, 'I dropped the bike on the way home.'

'You did what?' she shrieked.

'You heard me,' I said. 'And this leg's killing me.'

'Well, you're obviously still up and walking, so don't expect any sympathy from me.'

'What about the bike?' asked Tyrel. He'd been riding motorcycles most of his life and knew even a minor accident might cause all kind of unforeseen problems.

'Just a cracked mirror,' I said. 'But I think I've strained my groin somehow. It hurts like hell when I try to move.'

'Just slap on an ice pack,' was Sarah's advice. 'Pretend you're a cricket player. As for tomorrow, what a glorious bloody farce that's going to be. You should see yourself. You look more like Hopalong Cassidy than anything out of *Easy Rider*. Let's just hope no journalists turn up for your grand departure.'

'Why?' I asked weakly. I knew Mr Sil at Enfield would drum up some coverage.

'Oh, I can see the headlines already,' Sarah was laughing. '*Groin-strain up the Grand Trunk Road*. It just sums it all up.'

I must have fallen asleep clutching the ice pack to my balls. What else could explain the sodden sheets? I felt around and, sure enough, there was the handkerchief into which the night before I had crammed half a dozen ice cubes. They'd melted overnight, but for a while they had numbed the pain. Add aspirins and whisky in equal measure and I'd even managed to get some sleep.

I tried moving my leg. All the muscles around the hip and groin area shrieked out in unison. I collapsed back against the pillows and stared up at the overhead fan.

The Muslim bearer was surprised when I asked for ice at this hour. I made up another ice pack and waited for the numbing to take effect before getting dressed.

From outside came the sound of morning puja at the little temple in the courtyard. I had listened to these same muted sounds of devotion every morning since arriving in Calcutta. Today would be the last time.

The early light was flat and grey. A town crow alighted on my windowsill and began cawing in the way that only town crows do. In its shiny beak it held a crushed marigold, a fragment left over from the wedding party. The crow looked at me sideways before flapping off with its unprofitable prize. Hardly an auspicious omen.

I tugged on my boots and picked up my helmet. Was I ready for this? I could hardly have been in worse shape. But as I hobbled down three flights of stairs I knew I was as ready as I'd ever be.

2

WEST BENGAL:
'A VERY FEARFUL MAN'

If I was going to be at the Victoria Memorial by eight, as promised, I had to leave immediately. The Bullet was cold and wouldn't start. I tried half a dozen kick-starts – a sequence that got my groin-strain going but nothing else. I was going to be late.

'You may well have flooded it,' was Tyrel's verdict. 'Come on, let's try a push-start.'

So it was that Tyrel ended up pushing the bloody thing down Middleton Row, me on top with legs flailing.

When the engine finally roared into life, I was so relieved that I forgot all about filling the near-empty tank with petrol. Instead I turned left into Park Street and rode straight down Chowringhee. Just as I swung right towards the maidan I saw that there was a barrier across the road. An armed policeman stepped out in front of me.

'Today is no entry,' he shouted.

'But I must go to the Victoria Memorial,' I protested.

He would not be moved. 'Today is practice for Republic Day Parade. Only military and official vehicles permitted.'

'But I am an official vehicle,' I declared. Bluffing looked like the only way of getting through. The policeman was unimpressed. Then I tried my trump card. 'I have special permission from the Deputy Commissioner of Traffic Police.'

This was not strictly true, but it did have the desired effect. The policeman called over one of his colleagues to discuss what to do with me. After five minutes they waved me through with the warning that I was to proceed no further than the Victoria Memorial.

I arrived to find just one member of the Enfield team, Mr Singh, already there. The marmoreal bulk of the Victoria Memorial glowed in the flat morning light. All around us detachments of infantry and naval ratings were forming up in preparation for the big dress-rehearsal. The rumble of tanks and military transports came from the Racecourse perimeter. I had planned to set off that way, towards the new bridge over the Hugli. This was obviously no longer an option.

The Enfield contingent turned out in force. Some came with their families by car or taxi. Others arrived on their own Bullets, including several with sidecars. A banner was unfurled between the two stone lions that guard the Victoria Memorial's main entrance, wishing 'Happy Ride to Mr H. J. Gregson on Bullet 500 cc.' Clearly, this was going to be quite a tamasha.

Sarah and Tyrel finally arrived on foot, having being turned back by the same policeman who'd let me and all these other vehicles through. A garland of marigolds was draped around the handlebars of my bike. Then all three of us were called forward and had garlands placed around our necks. Bouquets were pressed into our hands. I was beginning to feel embarrassed, but Mr Sil, as master of ceremonies, was determined I should have a grand send-off.

I was introduced to a tall, smooth-looking man dressed in a blazer and cricket whites. This was the Deputy Commissioner of Police who was to 'flag me off'. But before that there were the speeches to be made and a little ceremony to wish me a safe journey. It was performed by Mr Chakrabarty's daughter, a shy young girl who was as uncomfortable about her role as I was about mine. But the senior Enfield managers beamed encouragement. The oil lamp was lit and passed in a circular motion above the Bullet's headlight. A tray containing coloured pastes, flower petals and rice was produced, and the young girl dabbed me three times on the forehead – first with yellow, then with red paste, before adding a grain of coloured rice as the finishing touch.

As I leaned forward to thank her she dropped some of the rice. From the immediate hush, and the way that the onlookers then tried to make light of it, I gathered this was inauspicious. But there was no stopping the ceremony now. One of the Enfield mechanics kick-started my flower-bedecked bike and led it before me. It reminded me of the way the ceremonial horse is brought to the bridegroom at the outset of a wedding. As I mounted my charger, two other Bullet men started their bikes and drew up alongside. It seemed that I was to have a motorcycle escort, whether I liked it or not.

Mr Deputy Commissioner stepped forward and raised a green flag. Engines roared in unison, the flag was lowered, and we were off – moving in slow formation around the statue of Sri Aurobindo, which looked down unsmiling from its pedestal in the middle of the traffic circle. I would have liked to have just ridden off there and then, to get started on my journey. But my outriders had different ideas. Apparently we had to complete a second circuit, to wave at all the well-wishers.

It was then that the unthinkable happened. The engine coughed a couple of times. It spluttered. And then the bike just died on me.

Mr Sil rushed forward. 'Mr Gregson, Mr Gregson! What is wrong?'

'I am very sorry, Mr Sil, but I think I have just run out of petrol.'

'But did you not check?'

'I knew I was low, Mr Sil, but not that low. I was going to fill the tank straight after the ceremony.'

It was hard to tell which of the two of us was more embarrassed. Mr Sil had all his honoured guests to think of. But it was I who had fallen before the first fence.

'Not to worry, Mr Gregson,' he said unconvincingly. 'This thing can be sorted out.' At which he issued commands and the Enfield mechanics started scurrying about.

Five minutes later they had procured a length of plastic tubing and petrol was being siphoned from one tank to another. I was still smarting from such public humiliation, and I had no one to blame but myself. Why hadn't I stopped to take on petrol? I'd let everyone down.

'Take two' of the grand departure was effected without further mishap. A motorcycle and sidecar was dispatched to follow me as far as the petrol station. 'Christ, they really don't trust me,' I thought, 'and probably with good reason after that débâcle. But then how do they expect me to get up the Grand Trunk Road?'

That was a question which, at that moment in time, neither they nor I could answer with any confidence.

I still had to reach the start of the Grand Trunk Road. It begins not in Calcutta itself but on the far side of the river, outside the Botanical Garden.

I filled up the tank and headed warily towards the new suspension bridge over the Hugli. Delhi's drivers may be more addicted to speed (they have the roads for it); Bombay's may be more flamboyant; but for grim determination, unpredictability and serpentine logic, Calcuttans win hands down.

Previously I had observed this anarchy-in-motion from the back of a car or taxi. Now I had to deal with it myself, and it made me a very fearful man. Mr Chakrabarty had told me, 'In Calcutta traffic, you must move like a snake.' Sound advice – except that others were much more adept at it than I was. Constantly nudged this way and that by snub-nosed Ambassadors and overburdened buses, I felt like an innocuous grass snake in amongst a nest of king cobras.

Once clear of the Racecourse – and the congestion caused by the army parade – the way ahead was clear. As I accelerated up a series of ramps towards the new Hugli Bridge, I had the sensation that I had left India and all its chaos behind. It was like rolling down a US Interstate. I peered at the rusting barges and country boats two hundred feet below, and then at my speedometer. It registered 80 kph, but after our snail-like progress through Calcutta this was really flying. And where was all the other traffic? Perhaps, after waiting so many years for their new bridge to be completed, Calcuttans preferred to ignore its existence. Or maybe the planners had put it in the wrong place. It didn't matter to me. That brief burst of speed took me across the river and almost to the gates of the Botanical Garden.

I got off the bike and threw myself down on the grass. It was time to take stock. My progress so far had not been an unmitigated success. In the last twenty-four hours I'd dropped the bike once. I'd given myself a groin-strain that made walking an agony but fortunately didn't affect riding the bike. I'd screwed up the grand departure by running out of petrol. And now, having reached the Botanical Garden, I had to work out where the Grand Trunk Road began.

Some traditions have it that the great banyan tree in the middle of these gardens is the proper starting point; others that it begins at Gate No. 3. Curiously, there is no official monument or plaque marking the precise spot from which India's main road artery begins or ends, or why it should be here. But then there are hundreds of ancient monuments in India that lack any public recognition. If they're lucky, there's a rusted blue sign erected several decades back by the Archeological Survey of India declaring them a protected monument.

Just outside the gardens is an old milestone. Its message is cryptic and uses Roman numerals. III Miles, it declares. But whether this is three miles from the original start of the road is unclear; and, if that was its intention, it rules out the banyan tree, which is less than a mile distant.

I never solved this puzzle. Obviously the road has to start somewhere. But before the building of Howrah Railway Station there was no real focus to the scattered settlements across the river. The Road had always clung to the west bank of the Hugli, and before the completion of the massively solid Old Howrah Bridge in 1943 travellers crossed on floating pontoons. It could have started anywhere opposite Calcutta.

Perhaps the choice of the Botanical Garden was dictated by military considerations. It lay downstream of Fort William and drew some protection from the old defences on the west bank known as Charnock's Fort. But the real reason, I think, is this.

Before the present road was built in the 1830s, its immediate predecessor – the New Military Road, as it was called – had followed a more southerly route, cutting straight across the rocky outcrops and jungles of South Bihar rather than the flatter, more populous regions traversed by the modern GT Road. The New Military Road has long since fallen into disuse; but on old maps its starting place is marked close by the Botanical Garden. It made sense, therefore, to begin the new road-building enterprise at the same spot. From this junction, the armies of the East India Company could choose between two lines of advance.

Given this uncertainty, I decided to cover my options. I headed first for the banyan tree, past stagnant tanks where egrets padded across giant water lilies. The banyan is the most revered of all trees in the subcontinent and shrines are often built into their trunks. They also offer shade and protection to the traveller. As I was about to discover, there are some fine specimens up and down the Grand Trunk Road, in both India and Pakistan. The Botanical Garden banyan is more than two hundred years old and has spread over an enormous area; it is a self-contained forest rather than a single tree and the roadway actually passes between its thousands of secondary trunks. I felt that this grandfather of banyans is where the road should begin.

From there I continued to Gate No. 3. I paused before riding through the gates and out into the traffic. It was a moment to savour, the beginning of my journey. Then I left the gardens behind me and the reality of where I was, and what I intended doing, sank in.

Kilometre one of the GT Road is an unearthly place. The air was filled with exhaust fumes and the low growl of slow-moving trucks. Traffic hardly moved at all because the road was up for repairs. A blackened steam-roller sat in the middle of the road. It was a satanic contraption, its tar-bucket belching dark and viscous smoke that mingled with a fine grey dust rising from the loose chippings that were being raked over by a small army of coolies. Only fifty yards separated the Botanical Garden's lush serenity from this infernal scene. It was like passing from the left-hand panel of the Hieronymous Bosch triptych *The Garden of Earthly Delights* straight into the sulphurous world depicted on the right, without any transition whatsoever.

For the next two hours, as the day's heat grew, I struggled through the unredeemed industrial wasteland that is Howrah. I was so scared I hardly noticed anything apart from what was on the road ahead of me. Not that I was moving fast. The sheer weight of traffic prevented anything from travelling at more than ten miles an hour, and there was no point in threading my way through it as I'd have left Sarah and Tyrel in the Ambassador far behind. No, what was so terrifying was the unpredictability of it all. The way the bus in front slammed on the brakes for no apparent reason, forcing the passengers hanging from its sides to cling on for dear life; or the rickshaw-drivers' habit of swinging out right in front of you. Pedestrians were a constant menace, stepping out into the road without so much as looking.

It was a crash-course in urban driving, Indian-style. Occasionally I looked up from the road and saw I was riding past blank factory walls plastered with cakes of cow-dung, or through the cloth vendors' section of some bazaar. These first miles of the GT Road are lined with workshops and huddled stalls, off which narrow lanes with open sewers running down their middle gave on to what I knew were some of Calcutta's worst slums.

Fifty years earlier, during the Calcutta Killings, these same slumlands had furnished many of the goondas and migrants from upcountry who went on the rampage across the river. There was killing and arson in Howrah but it was spared the worst of the carnage, the Hindu and Muslim communities maintaining an uneasy and heavily armed truce.

It was hard to judge what progress I was making because Howrah is not so much a town as a sprawling industrial belt. The jute mills and high-walled factory compounds lining the Hugli belong to an earlier phase of the Industrial Revolution. Linking these factories are hundreds of railway lines which the old road has to negotiate; and squeezed between the factory walls and the branch lines are the notorious bustees. If there is such a thing as a centre of Howrah, it is probably its railway station – the great, Gothic main-line terminus on the west side of the river linking Calcutta with the rest of the country. Its platforms are among the most crowded in the world.

I knew from the build-up of traffic that I was getting near Howrah Station. Taxi- and rickshaw-drivers attempted the most desperate manoeuvres to break through the gridlock, egged on by passengers fearful of missing their train. I sat it out, trying to control my mounting sense of panic. In two hours I'd covered less than ten miles. The bike was overheating. At this rate we wouldn't be clear of the metropolitan area before dark. Where the hell were we going to stay the night?

Then suddenly I was riding over the bridge which spans the main railway line, the road ahead was clear, and I finally picked up enough speed to shift into fourth gear. From there on the traffic eased, though the state of the road itself – an amalgam of ruts and potholes, worn down in places to the original red brick of the old Grand Trunk Road – still kept my speed down. 'Now I'm really off,' I thought.

I should have known better. A few miles down the road, the engine cut out completely.

I hauled the Bullet over to the edge of the road, leaving just enough room between the bike and a drainage channel to kneel down and check for obvious faults. Everything seemed OK. A shopkeeper offered me some tea, which at that point I needed badly. One of his friends, an elderly man wearing round, Gandhi-style glasses, decided to engage me in conversation. Although dressed in a threadbare singlet and dhoti, he was well educated and obviously commanded authority. One word from him, and the young boys who had been fingering the bike took fright.

'Good afternoon,' he began, smiling effusively. My hands were covered in oil so I just waved a greeting.

'I am a schoolteacher here, recently retired. Where are you from?'

'England.' The inevitable opener; the inevitable response.

'But today you have not come from England,' he beamed.

'Er . . . no. I started in Calcutta.'

'And what, if I may be so bold, are you doing here?'

'I'm going up the GT Road.'

'This thing is self-evident. But where, may I ask, are you going?'

'Tonight to Chinsura, I hope . . .'

'No, no, no.' He wagged his finger at me like a recalcitrant child. 'I am asking where are you going?'

It occurred to me that this could be the beginning of a long philosophical debate. Stupidly, all I could think of saying was 'the end of the road'.

'Ah, but where is this end?'

'Peshawar.'

'Peshawar in Pakistan?' he queried.

'Yes.'

'Then it is true what my father told me,' he said, shaking his head. 'All Britishers are mad.'

Having discovered what he sought, he walked off down the road. I stared at the dead Bullet and decided he was probably right. Here I was, not even clear of Calcutta's suburbs, a hopeless case if ever there was one. I cursed myself for not running in the damn thing before setting out. I felt like kicking the bike. Instead I tried another kick-start. It fired first time.

Twelve miles up the road the engine cut out again. The industrial sprawl had gradually petered out and I was on an open stretch of road, enjoying my first glimpse of the lush water-landscape of Bengal. As I pulled out to overtake a lorry, the motor coughed a couple of times and packed in. I yanked on the clutch to prevent a skid and freewheeled onto the road's dusty shoulder.

I was baffled. I'd been travelling at speed, the engine wasn't too hot, everything working fine, and then . . . nothing. This time there was room for the Ambassador to pull off the road behind me. Sarah sat down disconsolately in the shade of a neem tree while Tyrel and I tried to diagnose the problem. Twenty minutes later, and none the wiser, we heard the distinctive thump of another Bullet as it went thundering past us. Then we heard it coming back again. Whoever was on that other bike had wheeled round and come to see what was wrong.

It was a 500cc machine, like mine, but its owner said he'd had it for more than ten years. His name was Tufail and he'd worked in America for a while and been through London.

'What seems to be the problem?' he asked airily.

'Can't say,' Tyrel replied. 'Spark's good, fuel line's clear, distributor looks OK. We were wondering whether it might be an air-lock in the petrol tank . . .'

'Let's see,' said Tufail, pulling out his own tool kit. He looked like he knew what he was doing.

'Look, if you're in a hurry . . .' I started.

'Not at all. I was on my way to a small factory of my father's, not five kilometres from here, and am in no special hurry. We Bullet Men in India, we stick together.'

It took him five minutes to locate the problem. See here,' he said, holding up the spark plug cap for inspection. 'There is a clip missing. Look, I will show you.'

He walked over to his own bike, disconnected the cap and came back with it. Before I could say anything he was fitting it onto my machine.

'Really, you shouldn't,' I protested.

'No matter, we will exchange. Yours will serve the short distance I have to go. Now let's see if this works . . .'

With practised ease he pushed down on the starter pedal. On the second kick the motor roared into life. 'Now, if you don't mind, I'll just run up and down the road a little way to check that everything is in order.'

He returned and handed the bike over to me. 'Everything's fine. Now I must be on my way.' All three of us competed in trying to thank him. As he rode off with a casual farewell wave, Sarah turned to me.

'You are a lucky sod,' she pronounced. 'That's not a Bullet Man; that's your guardian angel.'

My belief in divine intervention lasted all of five minutes, which was how long I had been back on the road before the engine started coughing again. Clearly the replacement cap hadn't done the trick.

Not that this is any way diminished my gratitude towards Tufail. But the motor cut out three times in a row over the next ten miles. The third time I managed to freewheel as far as a roadside scooter repair shop. A mechanic who looked about sixteen checked it over — carburettor, distributor, fuse box, the lot. Again, he could find nothing wrong. And again, after ten minute's rest, the bike started easily.

Whatever was causing the problem was obviously an intermittent fault. Probably it had something to do with the engine running hot. I'll never know, because we never located the problem or had it corrected. The next day it just disappeared. Even when I got the bike to an Enfield dealer nothing showed up. It remained a mystery.

That didn't help me as I nursed the Bullet through that first afternoon. We were headed for Chinsura, a former Dutch trading post. There are virtually no hotels outside of Calcutta, but there was a Government Circuit House in Chinsura. These are intended for civil servants doing the rounds, but I'd been told we might be put up for the night. We'd just have to chance it.

The River Hugli lay over to the right, a vision of serenity. I myself was far from serene as I struggled to keep the engine from stalling, using every combination of throttle and clutch control in the book. There was no way that I would stop or switch off the engine unless it was absolutely necessary, so we had to go hurtling through the Bengal countryside which grew more beautiful with every mile.

I had occasional glimpses of red-tiled houses sheltering beneath graceful palms, of bamboo groves and dark-leaved mango topes, of still backwaters or tanks crowded with water-hyacinth. But most of the time I had to concentrate on keeping moving, and these images of rural tranquillity became all mixed up as though seen through a kaleidoscope.

The evening light was fading by the time we reached

Chandernagore, a former colonial enclave which remained French territory until 1950. The kaleidoscope whirled again and I saw images of once-stately mansions, their ornate Corinthian columns now stained by a hundred monsoons. A gateway bore the legend *Liberté, Egalité, Fraternité*. That apart, nowadays there is nothing particularly Gallic about the place, the old French street names and shops having given way to Bengali. Still, I would have stopped over if the bike wasn't so troublesome and there was somewhere to stay.

As it was, I pushed on to Chinsura, arriving just before nightfall. The Circuit House was down by the river. To reach it we had to go through the old Dutch settlement with its seventeenth-century church and central maidan. I stopped to ask the way outside an imposing building which now housed the offices of the Superintendent of Police, though in former times it had been one of the East India Company's barracks. A restrained neo-classical façade stretched away into the evening gloom. It struck me that all these old colonial buildings were built on a palatial scale. What on earth would the Circuit House be like? I worried that if it were too grand they wouldn't take us in.

I dug out the letter of introduction from Mr Dutt, Electoral Commissioner (retd), and stuffed it inside my shirt like a talisman. I had no idea whether it would work or not.

The appearance of the Circuit House was hardly reassuring. A well-kept drive lined with flower pots led to a porticoed mansion – not as large as the barracks buildings, but substantial nonetheless. A pair of official-looking Ambassadors were parked in the drive. Somebody else was staying the night.

A glum-looking caretaker appeared from nowhere, listened to my request in silence, took the letter, and went upstairs to find the District Commissioner. We waited for ten long minutes. When the caretaker reappeared he was looking slightly less glum and carrying a heavy ring of keys. The Commissioner sahib had granted permission. With a sigh of relief I set to unpacking the side-panniers.

We had been assigned two suites of rooms with interconnecting doors. The place was enormous – the ceilings were more than thirty feet high, and you could have held a winter ball in the living room. Two rows of overhead fans descended from the ceiling on tubular steel supports, so designed that they would agitate the air immediately above head-level. Electricity was obviously a late addition to this venerable building. The light and fan switches looked as if they had been borrowed from the control panel of a 1930s power station. By the time I'd worked out how to get half of the eight fans in the main room working there was a power cut. I explored the further recesses with a torch.

The bedrooms were cavernous and I kept bumping into sharp-edged furniture, confused by the layout and by the way the torch's beam reflected off old and mildewed mirrors. Then I realised the beds were positioned in the middle of the room, under an overhead fan, to maximise the circulation of air. The beds turned out to be four-posters of the no-frills variety, with a plain wooden frame for hanging mosquito nets. There were two bathrooms with massive porcelain thrones – those most enduring legacies of Empire – but not a single bath between them. Wallowing in a tub of warm water is one European custom which never really caught on with most Indians, who are fastidious in the extreme about their toiletry. I tried the shower head, which was rusted and emitted only a thin trickle. There was a plastic bucket so I filled this with cold water and doused myself. The whole set-up was typical of state-run facilities in the provinces: a colonial cast-off, hugely impractical and only semi-functioning. All the same, it was rather grand.

Sarah and Tyrel were camped in the middle of the drawing-room, sharing a bottle of warm beer and the light from a single candle. I shut the double doors to keep out the mosquitoes, which even at this time of year came up in squadrons from the nearby Hugli.

'Christ, it's still hot,' observed Tyrel, staring ruefully at the unmoving phalanx of fans. 'Imagine what it must be like in summer.'

'It's not so much the temperature as the humidity,' I said, childhood memories of the debilitating hot season in Bengal rising before me. 'It drains every ounce of energy.'

We sat in silence, listening to the whine of the mosquitoes, and I thought of the generations of Dutchmen with long names and short life-spans in the cemetery behind the church, laid low by cholera, dysentery, malaria . . . Then I reached for the malaria tablets.

This stretch of the Hugli has been the unwilling host to practically all the maritime powers of Europe. The Portuguese arrived first, in the sixteenth century, and settled just a few miles upstream at Bandel. Then came the Dutch, who built their Fort Gustavus at Chinsura in the early seventeenth century. There they remained until 1825, when it was handed over to the British in exchange for trading posts in Sumatra.

The French presence in Chandernagore goes back to 1673. Though captured several times during the Anglo-French wars of the eighteenth century, it was always handed back. In fact, it remained French territory for three years after the British left in 1947. A little further downstream the Danes set up their factory at Serampore. All these nations were trading in Bengal by the time that Job Charnock established a British factory on the east bank of the Hugli at Calcutta.

It was the prospect of trade that brought all these Europeans to this dank and disease-ridden stretch of river. Bengal has always been one of the richest provinces in India. It produced fine cotton and muslin, for which there were ready markets overseas, and its rivers were a gateway to the interior. Indigo and opium, saltpetre for making gunpowder and jute for backing carpets – these were the staples of the Bengal trade.

The Europeans were constantly fighting over the spoils. Even after the battle of Plassey, when British supremacy in Bengal seemed assured, the Dutch sent a powerful squadron from Batavia to try and wrest back control. On 24 November 1759, a numerically superior force of Dutch and Malaya troops advanced against the British commanded by Colonel Forde, who wrote to Robert Clive in Calcutta for official orders.

The victor of Plassey was then engaged in a game of cards. Without leaving the table he wrote in pencil on the back of a letter: 'Dear Forde, Fight them immediately, I will send you the Order of Council tomorrow.'

The next morning the two armies met on the plains of Bedara, not four miles from Chinsura. Clive's own report is as follows: 'The engagement was short, bloody, and decisive. The Dutch were put to a total rout in less than half an hour; they had about one hundred and twenty Europeans and two hundred buggoses (Malay troops) killed, three hundred and fifty Europeans and about one hundred and fifty wounded. Our loss was inconsiderable.'

The battle of Bedara is generally forgotten; yet if the outcome had been different the Dutch might have become the dominant European power in northern India, and Chinsura grown to become as great a metropolis as Calcutta. It was, as Clive noted, a decisive engagement. And as with so many decisive battles in India's history, it was fought beside the Grand Trunk Road. In fact, I had unknowingly motored through the Dutch army's line of march earlier that afternoon.

Sitting in that old colonial mansion which was now the West Bengal Government's Circuit House, it struck me that there was nothing predestined about the rise of the British in India. Nor, for that matter, was there anything inevitable about the way in which they abandoned their Indian empire.

Who would have imagined in August 1945, as the British Empire and its allies celebrated complete victory over Germany and Japan, that in precisely two years' time the British would voluntarily leave India? Not even the nationalist leaders thought independence could be achieved within that time-frame. And who in all of Bengal then believed that the age-old unity of their homeland would be shattered, that in future there would be two Bengali-speaking nations, divided by religion and an undefendable border? Jinnah may have privately followed through the logic of a future Pakistan; but the Muslim League's leadership in Bengal most certainly had not.

The unforeseen result: there now existed, not forty miles to the east of where I sat, another country, called Bangladesh, which had come into being thanks only to India's military intervention against the other 'successor state', Pakistan. Anyone in post-war Calcutta who had suggested that Dhaka might in time become the capital of an independent sovereign state would have been considered stark raving mad. Back then the 'two nation' principle was difficult enough to digest. To imagine a third nation in the subcontinent arising out of the rural backwaters of Bengal, stripped of their capital and industry in Calcutta . . . It was unthinkable.

Before Calcutta was founded, all the European trading posts stood between the Hugli and the old Grand Trunk Road. Of these two arteries, the river was by far the most important to a maritime power, for when the Portuguese arrived the Hugli was the main channel through which the Ganges emptied into the Bay of Bengal and was navigable far inland. But slowly the Ganges shifted its course eastwards, so that today most of its waters flow out through the River Padma and its innumerable side channels in Bangladesh.

Then the Hugli started silting up, making it increasingly difficult for sea-going ships to reach Calcutta – let alone the older trading posts upstream. As a child I watched the dredgers at work on the Hugli, clearing the channel which allowed merchant shipping to dock at Calcutta. It was an unequal struggle. Nowadays the big container ships put in at Haldia, fifty-six miles down river.

This gradual silting up of the Hugli means there is a curious pecking order among the old trading posts. The older they are, the further upstream. The Portuguese established themselves at Bandel, the Dutch a little down river at Chinsura, the French immediately below them at Chandernagore, the British at Calcutta. And they became redundant in the same order, as ocean-going ships grew larger and the channels they had to negotiate more hazardous. Whenever war broke out between the European powers, it was standard practice for the trading post further downstream to sink shipping in the main channel in order to blockade their rivals up river. By the late eighteenth century, the French and the Dutch colonies survived only on sufferance.

Nowadays these once prosperous entrepôts are provincial backwaters. After Calcutta's bright lights, downtown Chinsura was like something out of the Middle Ages. There were no cars, only bicycles winding their way down unlit alleys. Figures loomed out of the dark. The 'hotel' or eating place we eventually found was deeply provincial, its attempt at sophisticated decor running to a fibreglass waterfall garnished with plastic fish. Few visitors come here any more. The main road carrying most of the through-traffic now curls west below Chandernagore, leaving this older stretch of the GT Road free of heavy vehicles.

I enjoyed this calmer pace the next morning as I rode north towards Bandel. There has been a Catholic church here for nearly four hundred years, but the present structure is an unfortunate amalgam of styles. White pavilions and balconies perch incongruously on top of the main body of the church. The cloisters are more restrained, their walls lined with strip cartoon-style pictures explaining the meaning of the Lord's Prayer and other central doctrines. The artist seemed to have been in some confusion as to whether to portray the angels and saints, the sinners and devils, as Europeans or Indians, and ended up distributing the honours more or less evenly.

It was Sunday and the Bengali Christian community had turned out in force. I was soon informed of two miracles associated with the place. Both go back to the early days of persecution, when the Mughal Emperor Shah Jahan took against the Portuguese and their proselytising and sent an army to besiege Bandel. Only one of the five Augustinian friars then present survived the siege, and along with several thousand Christian prisoners he was taken to Shah Jahan at Agra. The man who built the Taj Mahal ordained that Friar Joãn de Cruz and his followers be left to die at the mercy of ferocious elephants. But, according to the legend, 'one elephant with its trunk raised and placed Friar Joãn on his back and slowly carried him in front of Shah Jahan and knelt before him, as if imploring for mercy'. At this, the Emperor set Friar Joãn and his followers free, their release being commemorated as the Miracle of the Elephants.

The second miracle also begins with the siege of 1632. A local man named Tiago, 'an ardent devotee of Mary', attempted to save a statue known as Our Lady of Happy Voyages from the Emperor's soldiers. He tried swimming with it across the Hugli, but was shot through with an arrow and sank with the statue. Ten years later Friar Joãn, by then safely back from Agra, heard Tiago's voice calling from the river. 'Over the water, illumined by a miraculous light, he announced our Lady was coming back.' The following morning a fisherman brought the statue to the priest with the words: 'Guru, Ma has come back.' This was cause for great celebrations, during which a Portuguese ship appeared sailing up the Hugli. It had narrowly escaped shipwreck in the Bay of Bengal and the grateful captain donated his mast to the church. The wooden mast still stands between church and river, a curious relic, now lacking solidity.

Directly opposite the church a group of party workers were preparing a rally for some political bigwig. Bicycle rickshaws arrived carrying horn-shaped megaphones, and overladen buses festooned with streamers with the colours of the Communist Party of India (Marxist) jammed all the approaches. It was going to be a big affair, with cadres being bused in from all over Hugli District. The Communists have been in power in West Bengal since 1977 and were a highly organised political movement for at least thirty years before that. It appears that every doctrine under the sun – Hinduism, Christianity, Islam, Communism – can flourish in the fertile soil of Bengal.

We stopped in a chai-house for a breakfast of cake and tiny bananas and enjoyed the chaotic spectacle around us. The sounds of political slogans amplified to the point of distortion competed with Hindi pop songs being broadcast at top volume by a bootleg cassette vendor. The vitality of it all was intoxicating and I began whistling along to one of the cassette-wallah's pop songs. The tune seemed strangely familiar, although the wailing actress and deep-throated male sounded pure Bollywood. Then it suddenly dawned on me. It was an Indian rendering of the theme-tune to a Clint Eastwood 'Spaghetti Western'. It was, unmistakably, *The Good, the Bad, and the Ugly.* I had to buy that tape.

Compared with the carnival atmosphere around Bandel, the neighbouring town of Hugli was a model of self-restraint and calm. But then there is a sizeable Muslim community here, for whom Sunday is no more nor less than an officially approved secular holiday – just another leftover from the British raj. There isn't much to show that this was once a busy port. Nor is it obvious that this was where the British first set up a trading post in Bengal some forty years before they started at Calcutta, for since then the town has been repeatedly sacked and burned to the ground.

By far the most imposing building today is the Imambara of Hazi Mohammed Mohasin, an important centre for Shi'a Muslims. A group of old men sat by the entrance, passing the time of day. The main courtyard, where the faithful assemble to pray, was deserted apart from a couple of young goats, one of them wrapped in a woollen cardigan. I guessed they were sacrificial animals being prepared for Id-ul-Fitr, the feast that marks the end of Ramadan.

Over the gateway there rose a massive clock tower flanked by what appeared to be twin minarets. As I craned my neck someone began speaking over my shoulder. 'May you be informed, good sir, this clock is 400 kilos in weight and cost 65 lakhs rupees.' I turned around to find I was being addressed by a slight man with a thin moustache.

'Please permit me to explain,' hc continued. 'I am Mirza Munna Ali, guardian of the Hugli Imambara.' And so began my guided tour. He was happy enough to show me the ornate chandeliers above the marble inlaid prayer hall, and the heavy tazias – one of them requiring eighty men to lift it when it is brought out at Muharram, when Shi'ites commemorate the martyrdom of the Prophet's grandson Hussain.

But when I asked about Partition he became evasive.

'Here in Hugli all peoples, Muslim, Christian, Hindu, all are living in peace,' he declared. Then, after thinking about it for a minute, he told me that, yes, there had been some communal violence and that in the West Bengal troubles of 1950 the madrasa or religious college had been evacuated from its old site to the west end of the Imambara, further away from the road. He then switched away from the subject, with which he was obviously uncomfortable, to the foundation of a new madrasa in 1984. 'Now we are having one hundred religious students,' he announced with pride. And just to make sure I'd got the message, he repeated, 'Now Hugli is a very peaceful place.'

I took one last look at the Hugli River. A few country boats moved across its glassy surface and the only sound was that of the boatman's paddle. Along the far bank was an unbroken line of trees. I knew this would be my last view of the Gangetic delta, as from here on my route turned west towards Durgapur and the 'Black Country'. At that moment I was an unwilling traveller. I didn't dare tell Tyrel, who was desperate to sit and paint. But there was no time.

Soon enough the rhythm of the road took over. The countryside grew drier, with greater distances between waterways and village tanks. Traffic was light and the going easy, maybe because it was Sunday.

At Pandua, I pulled off the road to look at the medieval Victory Tower, said to have been erected by the Muslim saint Shah Sufi-ud-din to commemorate his conquests over the Raja of Pandua in about 1340. It was unmissable, rising 120 feet beside a curve in the Grand Trunk Road. I parked the Bullet in the shade of an ancient tree whose gnarled and contorted branches suggested it had been planted not long after the tower and adjacent mosque.

It was obvious that few visitors bothered to come here. Around the perimeter of the old building complex a line of thatched cottages had grown up. Villagers were drying their washing in what had once been the central courtyard but was now just a grassy mound. A five-year-old was flying his kite. As it spiralled upwards, it seemed to mock at the massive tower opposite, which reminded me of the famous Qutb Minar in Delhi. But this version, erected about 150 years later, was squatly provincial, a vainglorious monument to a forgotten victory.

The nearby mosque is a ruin. What remains of its walls and arches are of thin, red brick, from which ferns sprout as in some tropical variant of a Piranesi etching. The free-standing basalt pillars, which once supported the mosque roof, are elaborately carved in the Hindu manner and have obviously been taken from some nearby temple.

There are hundreds of old mosques like this, going back to the times of the Muslim invasions, which incorporate pieces removed from Hindu temples – just as the early Christian churches in Rome or the great mosque in Damascus used pillars and capitals taken from pagan temples. But in Europe and the Middle East the old religion was superseded. Not so in India, where Hinduism always remained the majority faith. So, while it is not unusual for the buildings of one faith to use materials borrowed from another, the very existence of such 'provocative' mosques in India can make modern-day Hindu zealots see red and demand they be torn down.

I returned to the bike to find a group of farmers had assembled, along with some prize specimens of their cattle. They were engaged in a leisurely argument over the relative merits of this bullock or that milch-cow, either to pass the time of day or as a warm-up for more serious bargaining to come. When I expressed admiration for a tall, cream-coloured bullock, its owner immediately asked if I wanted to buy it. Foolishly, I asked 'How much?' 'Twenty thousand rupees,' the owner replied. By the time I had worked out he was asking nearly £400, his neighbour had drawn me aside and was trying to interest me in his highly desirable milker, which had extravagantly long eyelashes and came with calf attached. It took me five minutes, and much pointing at the motorcycle, to persuade them I was not in the market for either.

The rural interlude was soon over. West of Burdwan the countryside became bleaker and the sun was obscured by industrial smog. We were heading into the Black Country, the coal-and-steel belt which straddles the West Bengal–Bihar border. The road was crowded now with heavy trucks – mostly local traffic carrying loads of coke or chemicals to nearby factories. Some were so seriously overladen they could barely manage twenty miles per hour. Others, with their tailgates down, were running empty apart from the work-gang huddled in the back clutching their shovels and dragging on bidis, the rank-smelling local cigarettes.

Those trucks on the return run were trying to make speed and pulled out to overtake with little regard for whatever else was using the road. Two times out of three they'd get it wrong, slam on the brakes and pull back into their own lane. Anyone behind them had to brake hard and get out of the way. Which is exactly what I did, dropping off the tarmac onto the soft verge and then accelerating back onto the hard surface. Not a manoeuvre I particularly enjoyed, as there is all kinds of rubbish – broken glass, shredded tyres, discarded springs – in among the dust that lies beside the GT Road. But it was better than trying to play Russian roulette out on the tarmac, when I had the only Bullet on the road and they had all the body-armour.

Up ahead a pall of smoke spread across the western horizon, blotting out the sun. I was so busy trying to anticipate the next act of insanity I didn't notice the miles slip by. The next thing I knew I was staring at rows of cooling towers and smokestacks stretching out on both sides of the road like some mad industrialist's answer to the Maginot line. Dark plumes rose languorously towards a burnt-orange sky. It looked like one of those photographs smuggled out of the bad old Soviet Union by environmental activists.

So this was Durgapur. Somewhere in amongst my dubious papers I had a chit from the West Bengal Tourism Office in

Calcutta confirming our reservations at the state-run Tourist Lodge. Not that I could imagine Durgapur attracting that many tourists. Businessmen, engineers, metallurgists, visiting politicians, maybe. Even parties of schoolchildren, bused in on some educational tour organised by a bunch of unreformed Stalinists so that the younger generation could see for themselves the glorious results of Nehru's Five-Year Plans – that was just about credible. But tourists? I had my doubts.

As this is a planned city – or, at least, an example of post-war urban planning – it took a good half-hour to track down the Tourist Lodge. It was on the outskirts, towards the Durgapur Barrage, which I later learned is nearly half a mile in length and controls the waters flowing through fifteen hundred miles of canals (these kind of statistics are easy to come by in Durgapur). To reach it, we had to negotiate a complex grid of metalled tracks that wander off into the scrub. These serve as access to rows of functional and box-like bungalows which looked as though they had originally been intended for middle management and technical staff. Now they were run-down, their plots overgrown. But this 'colony' had been planned with space in mind; each residence was set in the middle of its own plot, completely divorced from its neighbours. It was sterile, quite unlike anything I'd ever encountered in India.

The Tourist Lodge was an Indo-modernist block – a style of building popular through the 1960s and 1970s, but one which doesn't wear well in India's climate. The concrete surfaces grow dark and irremovable stains, while the specifically 'Indo' motifs – in this case honeycomb screens added to the upper-floor balconies for the sake of privacy – soon become a breeding ground for all manner of things green and slimy. The garden, at least, was pleasingly traditional, with its beds of dahlias and marigolds, its scarlet poinsettias and protective screen of Ashok trees.

I took off my boots and washed some of the diesel stains from my face. I was hot, sweaty and tired, and the groin-strain hurt like hell. But at least the Tourist Lodge had cold Black Label beers. By the second one I felt about ready for the evening's social engagements.

Mr Chakrabarty, the Enfield manager in Calcutta, had told me that when I got to Durgapur I should look up his brother-in-law, Lion S. P. Mookherjee, 'an educated man whose views will be of great interest to you'. True to my promise, I'd phoned ahead from near Burdwan and arranged to meet him that evening.

He arrived promptly at eight with his wife and daughter, and we adjourned to a bare and cavernous hall which was occasionally used as a conference centre. It was not the most relaxing of atmospheres and all three of them accepted only non-alcoholic refreshments. I was running out of social chit-chat when Mr Mookherjee asked about the Bullet.

'I'm planning to ride it to Peshawar, in Pakistan,' I explained.

'Ah, that should be most instructive for you. I also went touring by motorcycle when I was a younger man.'

I waited, without much enthusiasm, for him to continue.

'It was an organised rally, of course. We were flagged off in Calcutta on 23 March 1979. I then proceeded from Calcutta to London on a Rajdoot.'

I sat up and regarded Lion S. P. Mookherjee in a different light. All the way to London, on a Rajdoot? Back then, the largest machine they made was, I think, a 175 cc two-stroke. It made my own journey across the subcontinent on a 500 cc Bullet suddenly seem unadventurous. 'We planned to go via Pakistan,' Lion Mookherjee elaborated, 'but just then their Prime Minister, Mr Bhutto, was about to be executed. Iran was in turmoil. So we crossed by ship from Bombay to The Gulf and proceeded overland. In Iraq there were many Indian nationals who were most kind to us.'

It was a remarkable story. But Lion Mookherjee wanted to turn to matters closer to home. He produced some pamphlets about the good works being done by the Lions around Durgapur district, such as funding a mobile eye hospital and immunisation centres. 'Last year, six hundred cataract operations were performed in one camp,' he said. 'At least a few of the sufferers are getting their sight restored. That's a choice we can give them.'

By now Sarah and Tyrel had joined us and the bearer was whispering that dinner was served. Though it looked distinctly unappetising, the Mookherjee family accepted my invitation to share the meal. This was a mistake. Mrs Mookherjee and her daughter had obviously agreed only out of good manners and played with their food. Everyone was relieved when the plates were taken away. Meanwhile, Mr Mookherjee was telling me how he'd followed his father into the law.

'I'm an advocate, working mostly in civil cases, for employees of the steel plant and other factories, industrial tribunals and such-like. My father was also a civil lawyer, becoming Government Pleader in Bankura, a district headquarters not thirty kilometres from here. My family was always from West Bengal, but my wife's family were from the East, near Barisal. Why don't you tell Mr Gregson about it, Kamala? He will, I'm sure, be most interested.'

Mrs Mookherjee, with the reticence typical of a Hindu wife and mother, had been talking mainly with Sarah. It took some gentle prodding from her husband to persuade her to explain how she had been brought up in East Pakistan, where her father had been headmaster of a school in Patuakhali, right down in the delta, where the combined waters of the Ganges and Brahmaputra empty into the sea.

'It is really not so very interesting,' she said modestly. 'We remained in the East until 1956. Then, because of the communal tensions, my father chose to retire over here. In East Bengal there was not this sudden mass migration as in the Punjab. Many Hindu families – professional people and zamindars, the landlord class who had properties there – stayed put after 1947. In the villages especially, everyone kept good relations. But then some mischievous people would keep sending threats, so slowly the Hindu people began to leave.'

'Which way did you come to India?' I asked.

'By the Bangaon border, near Calcutta. They didn't allow us

to take any valuables, not even what was to hand. All the landed properties they grabbed immediately. Some of my family, an uncle and some cousins, are still there.'

'So many refugees came from East Bengal,' interrupted her husband, 'who needed to be resettled. It caused a big headache for the Government of India, which had to provide them with land or loans to start up a new business. This migration was continuing from 1947 until 1956 at latest.'

'And did Muslims leave from where you were, Mr Mookherjee, in West Bengal?'

'Not so much, I think. Some communal trouble was always there. There were Muslims who resided near to us. They took shelter with us, and we provided them with food and clothing. Then the situation calmed down and everything was OK again.'

'Was this at the time of Independence?'

'No, some time later, I think. The day of Independence I remember well. People were celebrating and shouting "Jai Hind" and singing patriotic songs. At school we were told that Independence was coming and that we should put on a smart uniform for the special day ahead. Leaders would come and give lectures and patriots would sing patriotic songs, and there was a display of martial arts. All people were very much enjoying this day when India received its freedom after such a long time.'

Lion S. P. Mookherjee was beaming with joy at these childhood memories. I didn't want to drag him back to the darker events of those times. Besides, I'd already heard something of what it was like for Hindu families on both sides of the border. They had been kind to come out and meet me; and after the disastrous meal they probably wanted to get home and have some decent Bengali food.

As we said our goodbyes, their daughter was still telling Sarah that Durgapur was not such a bad place to live. It had its parks; there was a forest nearby. Then, out of the blue, she asked Sarah whether she'd ever been to New York.

'Why, yes. But not for a long time.'

'My friend,' declared Miss Mookherjee, 'tells me New York is just like Calcutta.'

I couldn't agree with that particular statement. But I would like to have agreed with the young Miss Mookherjee's views that Durgapur isn't as bad as first impressions suggest. Most countries have their industrial eyesores. Steel mills and benzol refineries aren't easy on the eye or nostrils, wherever they're situated. Durgapur just happened to be situated in the middle of India's richest coal and iron-ore deposits. It was a logical choice for building India's answer to Dortmund or Bethlehem, PA.

Yet it is not so much the scale of Durgapur's steelworks and heavy engineering plants that is inhuman, as the failed attempt at social planning, at creating a new Soviet-inspired order, which surrounds them. Even if you buy the dream of modernisation as an end in itself, accept the legitimate demands of an emerging nation to be self-sufficient in such vital materials as iron and steel, or recognise that in certain circumstances centralised state planning is the only way forward, what's happened at Durgapur still holds a peculiar horror.

It is an unholy union of yesterday's large-scale technology with the methods and labour practices of the early industrial revolution. It is a place where gangs of women scratch up loose coal into baskets and carry them barefoot across the treacherous slag heaps to be poured into jute bags which are then strapped to a specially adapted tricycle for further despatch. And while equally unproductive methods are applied all across India, in villages and building sites as much as in factories, the fact that they persist in the very shadow of these shining steel towers of progress is doubly depressing. For the planners of Durgapur back in the 1950s and '60s, from Jawaharlal Nehru down to the local sanitary inspector, the new industrial towns were not just about increasing production; they were about creating a Brave New India. That vision was probably false from the outset. It has certainly not been realised in Durgapur.

There are worse horrors in these parts. Coal-mines, where underground fires have been burning for half a century and which will continue to belch poisonous fumes in the foreseeable future, blight the land and lives of local villagers because they cannot be extinguished by any affordable technology. There are foundries dating back to the British period, which bear a much closer resemblance to 'dark, satanic mills' than anything that's gone up since. Yet these never pretended to offer anything more than jobs for the workers and profits for the shareholders. The new industrial centres of post-Independence India pretended to be something more than that, and that promise has been revealed as a sham.

I searched in vain for signs of hope. What I found was a grim determination to eke out some sort of living from this mineral landscape. Lines of men and women trudged miles down the road to their place of work (for Durgapur is planned and zoned, so everything is well spread-out). There were coke sifters and dhobi-men, scaffolders and factory hands, coal-carriers and self-regarding clerks. Many were first-generation migrants, still country people in their habits. They squatted among the roadside weeds, clearing their bowels or cleaning their teeth with wooden sticks, for they had nowhere else to perform their morning ablutions. The waste ground directly in front of the main steel works had become one vast public latrine.

Through the flat grey smog of morning I peered at bustee dwellings perched on slag heaps, where children played among the industrial spoil while their mothers bent over sooty pools of water, scrubbing out their cooking pots or trying to wash the family's clothes. A single tree survived among the coke fields, bearing silent witness to how recent these encroachments are. The great factories with their rows of chimneys and cooling towers loomed out of the mist like supertankers lost in a sea of blackness. Orderly, self-contained units of production, no doubt, but surrounded by the chaos of primitive and unregulated capitalism.

Jawaharlal Nehru once called the new steel towns of West Bengal and Bihar the 'temples of modern India'. And Durgapur, named after the goddess who is the destroyer of evil, was to be among the biggest and brightest of these 'temples' to material progress. In so far as it is a mighty centre of production it is a success. But I couldn't help feeling that if Nehru saw what has happened here he would have wept bitterly. All the promise of a New Age has gone. The worst of the old practices, including indentured labour, have simply been transplanted to Nehru's green-field sites.

Before I left Durgapur it began to rain. But it was no ordinary rain. The heavy droplets were discoloured by some infernal cocktail of coal-smoke and waste gases. I pulled down the visor on my helmet, but they left dark streaks across its surface. It appeared to be raining soot.

The concentration of heavy industry eased a little beyond Durgapur. For a few miles there were open fields and the sun nearly burned through the pall. Then more smokestacks reappeared and the road cut through great mountains of industrial waste. Each town along the way – Andal, Raniganj, Asansol – offered more scenes of blight and desolation.

The road was slick from the morning's rain, its dusty verges turned to mud. Potholes had filled with rainwater mixed with spilt diesel and coal dust. The spray thrown up by passing lorries was blinding. And it was more of the same, all the way to the Bihar border. By the time I left Bengal I was cold, dirty and thoroughly dejected. I had only one consolation. At least I could escape this hell on earth.

3

BIHAR (i):
BETWEEN HEAVEN AND HELL

The first sign that we were about to leave West Bengal was mile upon mile of parked trucks waiting to have their papers checked. I sped past them in the overtaking lane with Misri Lal Ram right behind me. The handful of uniformed officials manning the state border didn't seem interested in us and we were waved through.

We crossed the modern bridge below the Maithan Dam and over into Bihar. A thin trickle of water curled its way between the sandbanks below, and around this small knots of women were washing clothes. On the Bihar side of the border there were rather more policemen, some of them waving their lathis like swagger sticks. A long queue of heavy vehicles was waiting to leave Bihar. But Fortune was smiling on us that morning and again we were waved through without delay.

There is no immediate change after crossing the state border. We were still in the coal-and-steel belt. The sun was beginning to burn through the haze, but what it revealed was an industrial landscape every bit as desolate as the area around Asansol. Factory chimneys emitted dense plumes of untreated brown smoke and the few patches of greenery in between mountainous slag heaps were coated with a film of coal-dust and industrial effluent.

If anything, Bihar is less rigorous in enforcing anti-pollution laws than its wealthier neighbour to the east. Even by the standards prevailing in India, Bihar is a desperately poor state. The bare statistics tell their own grim story. Infant mortality in the countryside is above 11 per cent, almost twice that in the area around Delhi. Less than one in four women can read or write. Land reforms never really got off the ground here and the zamindari system – not far removed from feudalism – still prevails. Corruption is endemic at all levels. Whatever measure you care to pick, Bihar will come out pretty close to the bottom of the barrel.

Few out-of-state Indians – let alone foreigners – bother to visit Bihar. Smooth young Calcuttans were horrified when I told them I was going there. 'It's just one big cesspool,' commented an up-and-coming *Statesman* journalist. 'The corruption there makes all the doings in Delhi look whiter-than-white.' The 'doings' he was referring to were the 'hawala scandal', the uncovering of a series of back-handers worth crores of rupees which had been paid to government ministers and opposition politicians alike. But then Bihar had its own corruption scandal involving the siphoning off of massive funds intended for the purchase of livestock feed. 'In Bihar,' he told me, 'corruption is not so much a problem. It is a way of life.'

Judging by the condition of the GT Road in Bihar, not much of the central funding allocated to road maintenance got through to where it was supposed to be spent. Unlike West Bengal, where there were some good sections along with the bad, the road surfaces I encountered in Bihar were appalling. There was plenty of variety – subsidence, corrugation which produces a washboard effect, and every shape and pattern of pothole imaginable.

Most of the trucks using the GT Road are seriously overloaded and the continuous pounding meted out to their tyres and suspension inevitably results in casualties. In every town and village along the road, there is a ragged line of mechanics' shops and tyre repairmen who wait with the patience of vultures for the next broken-down vehicle to limp in. Some towns specialising in this passing trade avoid any pretence at road maintenance, since to do so would only reduce the likelihood of new business.

The same logic must apply to the positioning of 'speed-breakers'. Whereas in West Bengal there was usually some explanation for these axle-threatening bumps across the road – a railway crossing or the approach to a village – in Bihar they seem to be positioned at random and left unmarked so as to trap the unwary traveller. Sometimes they come one at a time; at others they lie in wait like U-boat packs virtually invisible in the dull morning light. And when you hit one of these 'sleeping policemen' at speed the bike's back wheel jumps up like a bucking bronco and you are left hanging on to the handlebars, knees desperately squeezing the petrol tank for grip.

Truck drivers have their own technique for dealing with potholes. Rather than risk another puncture or broken suspension they will zigzag across the whole width of the road, pushing lesser vehicles into the verge as they struggle to maintain possession of the smoother patches of tarmac. Their lumbering Tatas and Ashok Leylands have the advantages of size and weight, so most traffic will give way to them. It is when they challenge each other over who is going to hog the best line that things get serious.

The spectacle of these orange and blue monsters charging straight at each other, closing at a combined velocity of eighty-five miles per hour, with horns blaring and headlights flashing and pennants of black or red streaming behind them (a red flag normally indicates an explosive or toxic load), is about as close as you will get in modern India to the titanic clash of charioteers as described in the *Mahabharata*. The drivers, wild-eyed and gesticulating madly inside the cab, mouth obscenities through cracked and darkened windscreens, their plastic statuettes of Ganesh or Durga bobbing up and down above the dashboard in divine defiance, challenging the adversary either to hold his course or, by giving way, to accept that he belongs to some lesser race of mortals.

It is frightening to behold. Yet such contests occur every few minutes on the Grand Trunk Road, not just when trucks are overtaking each other, but whenever the road surface has deteriorated so much that most truck drivers prefer to hold the best line – even if this demands a head-on confrontation – rather than risk tipping over their grossly overladen and top-heavy vehicles by hitting a bad patch at speed.

I saw enough overturned trucks to know that this is a real danger. The continuous pounding to suspension and steering provokes even the less aggressive breed of truckers to try their luck on the smooth surface. Most of them carry passengers unofficially to earn a little extra money, and they might have had an earful of complaints or even had their customers throwing up from road-sickness. There are many, many good reasons why a life-threatening head-on charge might seem the lesser of two evils. All it requires, after all, is the right attitude. Hold your line, wait until you see the whites of his eyes and then flip the wheel over at the last instant, missing the oncoming fender by centimetres. Ninety-nine times out of a hundred it works.

But as I rode west I passed one terrible wreck after another. A Public Carrier and a State Transport bus still sat in the middle of the road where they had ploughed into each other. Their front ends had been raised off the ground by the impact so that they seemed to be grappling with each other like scorpions. Another bus had wrapped itself around a tree in such a way that there can have been few survivors, while just down the road two trucks had obviously just nicked each other at high speed. The entire offside front wing, including the wheel, had been torn away from one vehicle, while the other had ended upside down at the bottom of an embankment. Mostly they were not head-on collisions, showing that the driver had tried to move over – only he'd left it a fraction of a second too late.

Beyond Dhanbad the country started to open up. The fields were mostly dry paddy, though some mustard seed and winter wheat were being grown in places. The shade trees beside the road, which back in the 'Black Country' had been either stunted or had their branches stripped for firewood, now grew luxuriantly, at times overarching the road so that I seemed to be riding through a tunnel of greenery.

I could relax a little and take notice of how different things were from Bengal. The women wore brighter colours: even those carrying baskets of sand or lengths of bamboo on their heads were decked out in vivid reds, pinks and yellows. Those carrying the especially long bamboo used for scaffolding maintained a level, steady motion, to prevent their load from flexing too much. They kept their left arms outstretched for greater balance.

We passed through a village that specialised in making spears and axe-heads. Some were attached to bamboo poles, all ready to go. There were hundreds of them lined up for sale, and I hoped they were intended for decorative or ceremonial purposes rather than as weaponry. The half-moon axe-heads looked particularly vicious. I knew Bihar's reputation as a haven for dacoits – gangs of bandits who will turn their hand to anything from extortion to highway robbery – and decided to keep moving.

Rocky outcrops from the Chota Nagpur plateau started crowding in on the road. I thought we must be getting close to Parasnath, the mountain sacred to the Jains, which rises some 3,000 feet right beside the GT Road, but I had no idea where the turn-off was.

Still riding west, I saw what looked to me like Mount Parasnath. There were white-painted temples or shrines all along its ridge. But I couldn't find any approach road, and there was no alternative to riding right past the sacred mountain. An enforced stop at a railway crossing allowed me to consult the map. The road junction was at Dhumri, just the other side of the railway line, and from there we'd have to backtrack down country roads.

The moment we left the GT Road a blissful calm descended. There was no heavy traffic on this side route apart from the occasional pilgrim bus, so villagers treated the tarmac ribbon as their front yard. It was like stepping back to an age before the internal combustion engine. Village elders sat in the shade of a banyan tree right beside the road, discussing the community's affairs or just snoozing through the afternoon heat. The younger children of the village played on the verges while others, only a year or two older, drove the cattle or goats they had been placed in charge of right down the middle of the road. Practically all the houses were built of dried mud, their roofs covered with new thatch. It was absurdly picturesque, but such pristine rural scenes usually mask a life of unremitting drudgery. In India, what the eye appreciates most is often still there only because agricultural practices have not been improved and much-needed land reforms have been left unenforced.

At the next crossroads I stopped to ask the way from a group of itinerant labourers whose manner of dress suggested they were Muslims. This was confirmed by their foreman, who replied in Urdu rather than Hindi or one of the Bihari dialects. They had been working on an irrigation project and were waiting for transport to take them up north, where the majority of Bihar's Muslim population still live.

There has been a substantial Muslim minority in Bihar for more than 500 years. While communal tensions existed, they were not such a problem in this economically backward state as in UP or Bengal before Partition. Then, in the aftermath of the Calcutta Killings of August 1946, communal violence spilled over into Bihar, and here it was the Muslims who were the victims. Muslim shops and houses were burned down. Entire villages, thousands of men, women and children, were slaughtered in cold blood.

The Bengali Muslim leader, Suhrawardy, protested to Mahatma Gandhi that Muslim women had been subjected to the vilest atrocities in Bihar, their breasts cut off and their bodies mutilated. 'Do you know that they took – be it to our shame that we still live to say it – Muslim women naked with dance and song along the streets and then drowned them in the river?'

Jinnah was equally shocked by the Bihar massacres and sensibly urged Muslims not to retaliate in provinces where they were in a majority. But he also made political capital out of the 'sacrifice' of Bihari Muslims by declaring that 'the sufferings of the Muslims in minority provinces, and the terrific death roll and the butchery that has taken place, will not go in vain. This sacrifice will, I am sure, establish our claim to Pakistan.'

What happened in Bihar after the monsoon of 1946 brought out in sharp relief what everyone secretly knew all along: that any partition of India would almost inevitably result in massive bloodshed and in the exodus of several million people. Jinnah was more ready than most to accept this outcome. 'The exchange of populations,' he suggested, 'will have to be considered seriously [and] as far as possible, especially after this Bihar tragedy.'

For Bihar's Muslims the outlook was bleak. They lived in a landlocked state where they were outnumbered five-to-one by the Hindu majority. As the two-nation theory gathered momentum, they knew they would never be included in any future Pakistan. Many, especially the community's leaders, decided to emigrate. By far the largest contingent went to East Pakistan; but, once there, they found it hard to fit into a predominantly Bengali society, which was, in its turn, ruled as a virtual colony by an élite drawn mainly from West Pakistan.

Although officially welcomed by their co-religionists, these Bihari emigrés found it difficult to find jobs or settle down in East Pakistan. So a good number moved on – those with the money and connections to secure seats on a flight went to West Pakistan, many of them settling around Karachi. But most were left to slip back across the border into India, seeking work and anonymity among Calcutta's large Muslim underclass. Since Independence, they have been joined by hundreds of thousands of economic migrants from Bihar – both Muslims and Hindus – so that today Biharis constitute the second largest grouping in Calcutta.

The majority of Muslims in Bihar stayed put, keeping their heads down and hoping that the bloody events of the previous year would not be repeated after Partition. And, upon the whole, their hopes were justified. Bihar escaped the mass slaughter which afflicted the divided provinces of Punjab and Bengal in 1947. Since then there have been occasional outbreaks of communal violence, but nothing to compare with the tensions simmering just across the border in UP where Hindu fundamentalism and the BJP's dominance of state politics leaves the Muslim minority anxious.

Bihar's Muslim community has grown to around 12 million, or around 14 per cent of the overall population, an electorally significant grouping which has usually combined with low-caste Hindus to keep state government in the hands of a non-sectarian party. Until the 1990s the Congress Party ruled supreme, but since then a similar alliance of backward castes and Muslims has maintained in power the Janata Dal and its populist leader Laloo Prasad Yadav. Corruption, not communalism, is the main issue in modern Bihar. And looking around at the desperate poverty in which most Biharis live, the persistence of indentured labour, the arrogance of the local mafia and the general state of lawlessness, it is difficult to decide which is the greater evil of the two.

Just how far the rot has set in was brought home a few miles further on. There was a road block manned by a bunch of local kids who were demanding a 'contribution' from any vehicle passing down 'their' stretch of road. It was all very organised: the younger boys handed out tickets and collected the money, while their elders leaned on lathis and tried to look menacing.

I checked with Misri Lal Ram whether this was an official toll of some kind. 'These are not police,' he said, 'only village boys chancing their luck.'

I took him at his word and, steeling myself for an argument, rode straight through the makeshift barricade. Nobody attempted to stop me and Misri stayed glued to my tail. One of the boys tried waving a ticket at me, but there was no real attempt to make us pay.

Maybe it was because we were foreigners that we escaped scot-free. After all, who could guess what manner of important persons we might know, and if we lodged an official complaint their game was up. Yet other drivers were being hauled over and obliged to buy a ticket. How could this be going on in broad daylight, I wondered, unless the local police chose to turn a blind eye – presumably after taking their cut?

It was only petty extortion after all, and many of the vehicles on this road had out-of-state plates. That meant pilgrim traffic, and pilgrims spelt rich pickings. For the passengers would mostly be Jains on their way to Parasnath; and, throughout India, the Jain community is famous for two things – their wealth and their unswerving commitment to non-violence.

What I found worrying about this small-time scam was that it was considered perfectly acceptable, that it was just how things are done in Bihar. That, at least, was Misri's response when I asked him about it. 'Aieee, Bihar!' he spat with disgust. 'Here all police are corrupt,' he continued, before adding that 'such things cannot be happening in Bengal'.

Misri was born and bred in Bihar, up by the Nepalese border, and his contempt for such petty extortionists was borne out of experience and not just the usual big-city disdain for country people. I expressed my relief that we hadn't had to confront a policeman in person and he waggled his head affirmatively, repeating that in his opinion 'all Bihar police is corrupt'. Within twenty-four hours I was to have first-hand experience of their methods.

The pilgrim town of Madhuban squats like a postulant at the foot of the holy mountain of Parasnath. It is approached by a single track road from the north. First impressions are not favourable. There is only one main street and this is often blocked by herds of water buffalo. Stray dogs and the occasional cow roam the narrow space in between lines of makeshift stalls selling the usual mixture of vegetables and hardware. Half of the stalls were empty, and I guessed they only bothered to open on market day or when an important religious festival brought pilgrims in their thousands to Parasnath. But now the pilgrimage business was quiet and the townspeople wore a hangdog expression.

Only towards the upper part of the town, closest to the mountain's base, was there any sign of activity. Gangs of labourers were erecting bamboo scaffolding around a half-completed temple-cum-pilgrim hostel complex. It was being constructed on a vast scale. Among the Jain community there is no shortage of money for 'investing' in their holy places. Many of these are to be found in Bihar, the cradle of Jainism as well as Buddhism. A truck loaded with bricks nearly ran over my foot as it attempted to reverse through the new institute's gates.

My left leg was still hurting and I must have pulled another muscle while dismounting. There was no sign of any hotel in town so, cursing the persistence of groin-strain, I hobbled off in search of somewhere to stay. Maybe one of the pilgrim hostels would put us up for the night. I tried first at the gatehouse of one opposite the building site. There was nobody on duty, so I joined a couple of prosperous-looking gentlemen studying a schematic map of the pilgrimage route up Mount Parasnath.

'The circuit is 29 kilometres in total,' said the elder of the two. He was wearing a western-style sports shirt over a white cotton dhoti. Designer-framed and tinted spectacles shielded calculating eyes.

'For the full circuit you will be needing seven-to-eight hours,' he informed me, 'so you must start early in the morning, before the sun is coming. Also, you must be knowing that no item of leather is permitted on the holy mountain, no trouser belt or footwear. It is against our religion.'

The Jains, as part of their adherence to a code of non-violence, never willingly take the life of any sentient creature. They are strict vegetarians and particularly abhor the wearing of leather. This made me feel uncomfortable, since my jacket, boots and gloves were all made of the offending material. Unless I stripped off there and then, there wasn't much I could do about it.

'Tomorrow,' I said, 'when we ascend Mount Parasnath, we will make sure we are wearing nothing that may cause offence. But for now we are looking for somewhere to stay the night. Do you think we can stay in this hostel?'

'I do not think this thing is possible. Did you not see the sign as you entered? This is a place for Digambara people only. Look there!'

My eyes followed his pointing arm and there, wandering

through the hostel's gateway, were two men padding along without a stitch of clothing between them, looking completely unconcerned. Then it dawned on me – Digambara, the 'sky-clad' sect of Jains, whose austere rules forbade any material comforts or possessions, not even the warmth and modesty provided by a single article of clothing. In their hands they each held a water pot and a brush of peacock feathers with which they swept aside any minute insects which might lie in their path. By the state of their peacock brushes, which had been worn down to greyish stumps, they had obviously swept clear countless places along the way.

'I'm sorry,' I spluttered. 'I didn't know this was a Digambara hospice.'

'No cause to worry. But I think it will be difficult for you to stay here. Better to try the JSS hostel. It is only two minutes walking from here.'

I thanked him and set off for the JSS place, forgetting in my haste to ask what these letters signified. But, as usual in India, the letters alone sufficed. Tyrel joined me and soon enough we were descending through a series of well-ordered courtyards to the heart of the Jain Svetambara Society's complex in Parasnath. A young man called Praveen Jain showed us a bare cell, freshly swept but without any bedding. He explained that the Svetambara sect wore white clothes and, amongst other things, desisted from tobacco and alcohol. Any such 'narcotics', he said, were not permitted within the temple complex.

I had some misgivings about this, as my nerves were still ragged from the day's journey and my bad leg cried out for some form of pain-killer. But I had to agree with Tyrel that this was probably the best we could do. We followed Praveen through yet more courtyards to request permission to stay the night.

An aura of ordered calm prevailed, quite unlike any Hindu temple complex I had visited. A member of the JSS management committee read through the rules of the house, re-emphasising the ban on alcohol and tobacco. I signed various chits and handed over a deposit of 60 rupees. The charge for our rooms and food was five rupees each.

'You will find the charges here very reasonable,' announced an elderly man who was also waiting to conduct some business with the JSS supervisor. 'But then we Jains are expected also to make a contribution according to our ability to pay.' All very businesslike, I thought, and it avoided the barefaced pursuit of donations which makes some centres of Hindu pilgrimage seem driven by greed. Judging from the extent of the JSS buildings and their good state of repair, the wealth of the Jain community flowed in on a regular basis.

'I am now waiting to discuss my own donation,' continued the old man. 'My family, we are merchants coming from Ujjain. Have you already visited Ujjain? It is in Rajputana, a most beautiful city and a great centre of the Jain religion. But you must see this place, you must. Now, I think it is your turn.'

Praveen took it upon himself to show us around the vast compound. Meals were taken communally, in a canteen that could handle two thousand people at a sitting. Removing our shoes, belts and any other articles of leather, we entered the temple complex. White marble shone in the moonlight. I felt a sense of calm and openness, the architecture of these Jain shrines having nothing of the darkness and sensation of claustrophobia I sometimes experience when approaching the sanctum of a traditional Hindu temple. Here, there seemed to be no single focus of worship. The statues of the tirthankaras in white marble looked out in all directions, their forms human-like and unadorned, their gaze impassive in the flickering light given off by little lamps fed with ghee. I noticed one of the statues' eyes seemed to follow us wherever we went in the room. Praveen, meanwhile, was trying to instruct us in the basics of Jainism.

'For the Jain there are twenty-four tirthankaras, which are like gods to us. Lord Paravanatha, whose footprint you will see on the mountain, was the twenty-third. All Jains believe in the same God, but the style of prayer and ceremony is different with each sect. You know already the difference between the Svetambara and the Digambara, I believe?'

'Oh, yes,' I replied, thinking of my attempt to share lodgings with the naked ascetics just down the road.

'Because I am Jain,' Praveen continued, assuming a serious air, 'I will not be smoking cigarettes or drinking any whisky. My family is from Meerut in UP State, but my service is here. Because I am Jain I must do self-torture every day. It is my duty.'

'Self-torture?'

'Oh yes. Because I am Jain there is no marriage, no home, no comforts. For man to become like God he must be without all comforts. His life must be for prayer to God only. Sorry for bore!'

I assured Praveen that he was not boring us. And I was relieved that his definitions of self-torture had nothing in common with the practices of Shi'ite flagellants, but was only his way of describing the austerities of Jain ascetics.

'Our duties are written in the Jain scriptures, our examples in the *Kalpsutra*, in which book are the stories of the tirthankaras. Our Jain religion is so very old. Our tirthankaras have been with us for lakhs [hundreds of thousands] of years. In Parasnath there is devotion without stopping for thousands of years. And there are so many other Jain holy places in Bihar. Will you be going to Rajgir, where our chief guru Mahavir was making the fast until he died? So many of the Jain people who come here go also to Rajgir. It is not so far from Patna.'

I said that unfortunately we hadn't the time for such a detour. By now we were walking back across the moonlit courtyard. The visit was over and I desperately needed to get some sleep.

But Praveen would not be dissuaded from accompanying us back to our quarters. He seemed to be steeling himself to say something more.

'I am Jain, but I am the young generation,' he started, mainly for Sarah's benefit. 'For Jains there is no smoking, no drinking, no marriage. I am young. I am frank. You are not minding, please? Sorry for bore!'

'Think nothing of it,' I said, though I didn't like the drift of his conversation.

'We young Jains say: "Food is good; beer is good; God is excellent." ' He smiled, waiting for some response.

'Look,' I said, 'we're all very tired and—'

'Only last 31 December,' he interrupted, 'many smart girls are coming to Parasnath, from all over India and America also. I am being friendly with them. I am liking very much.'

I couldn't work out what his game was. It looked like he was asking permission to go off with Sarah. I decided to say nothing.

'For young Jains,' he continued, 'life is self-torture. For young Jains no women, no cars, no comforts. It is our duty.'

'Well, I'm very sorry for you, but that's your choice.'

'It is my duty,' he agreed, looking distinctly crestfallen. 'Sorry for bore.' At which he disappeared into the night.

We got up at four the next morning, long before the first glimpse of dawn, and struggled into jeans and sweaters for the ascent of Mount Parasnath. Leather belts and watchstraps were left behind. Footwear posed a more intractable problem, though we'd been assured that for non-Jains it would be all right to wear leather boots. After a cup of sweet tea bought from a market stall, our guide led us to a shrine for a brief puja before beginning the long climb.

The temples and smaller shrines sit on top of a steep ridge some 3,000 feet above the surrounding plain. It wasn't that stiff a climb and the path up had quite recently been laid with concrete blocks and steps to make life easier for the urban pilgrim. But if the climb wasn't too stiff, my bad leg most certainly was. Sitting on the bike it was the upper body that took most of the strain. All I had to use that leg for was braking. But now I had to drag it along in a stiff movement from the hip and as soon as we hit a steep section I started falling behind the others.

It didn't take long for the locals to notice I was the weak one in the group. Even in the darkness I became aware that I was being followed by a couple of dhooli wallahs. The dhooli is a simple palanquin, comprising a wooden pole balanced on the shoulders of two sturdy hillmen, from which is hung a lightweight chair in which the customer sits. For the elderly and the infirm, the corpulent and the downright lazy, hiring a dhooli provides a painless way of getting to the top of the hill. All you have to do is sit back and let the dhooli wallahs take the strain.

I didn't consider myself to belong to any of the above categories and wanted to get there under my own steam. The dhooli wallahs thought otherwise and hovered twenty yards behind me like vultures waiting for a stricken animal to collapse. The tap-tap of their sticks as they kept an even pace grew more sinister as the pain in my leg grew worse. And they were determined they would have me, arguing fiercely with other dhooli wallahs we met over their 'right' to snatch up the lame foreigner and charge a small fortune for carrying him the rest of the way.

As long as it remained dark I was turned in on myself. All I was aware of was my protesting muscles, and at times I thought I'd have to abandon the ascent. But as soon as it started growing light I became aware that I was climbing through verdant jungle and could try to focus my mind on other things: the song of unseen birds, a clump of orange and red flowers whose name I didn't know but which I remembered seeing as a child in Darjeeling, the bowed figures of other pilgrims making their way slowly up the mountain. The dhooli wallahs went off in search of other customers.

From then on the climb became easier and, reaching a gap in the forest, we stopped to watch the sun, flat red and corpulent, ease its way over the eastern horizon. The only things I didn't care to look at were the white temples on the crest of the hill, for they seemed as distant as ever.

At the half-way stage we stopped for tea at one of the many stalls lining the pilgrim route. High above us the main

Digambara temple clung to its rocky outcrop. The moon, still visible, seemed to hang just over its shoulder, giving the impression that on this holy mountain the great divide between heaven and earth was somehow narrowed. At this altitude the early morning air was sharp and pure. The plains stretched out before us towards the Ganges and the Himalayas far to the north. I felt as if I was rising above the struggle of life down in those plains, above the turmoil and worldly comforts that it offered. And those constant companions of the road, the sense of danger, the need to take rapid decisions, receded from me. Even the pain of my injury seemed to ebb away. The Jains had chosen their holy mountain well. It breeds detachment, just as the cities of the plain are the breeding ground of intrigue and discontent.

While I was still sipping my tea a pair of sky-clad ascetics came barrelling up the path. One was in the prime of life, the other a grey-beard. I felt it would be rude to stare at them, so I kept my eyes fixed on the far horizon. As they walked past the older man offered his greeting. 'Good morning,' he said in crisply enunciated English. 'And what a very fine morning it is, too.'

It came as a shock in this jungle clearing to be greeted in this fashion, and by a naked ascetic of all people. His accent and diction were those of a retired civil servant, which in all likelihood he might have been in his previous life, before taking his vows of renunciation as a Digambara monk to give up his family and all worldly possessions. Now, I couldn't help staring at them as they marched on up the path, arms clasped behind their backs like the Duke of Edinburgh. Except that each of them was clutching a peacock brush over his unclothed buttocks.

The main approach to Parasnath is on the north-west side of the ridge, so that in the morning almost the entire climb is in shade. The sun was already well clear of the ground haze when we reached the top and we found the cluster of white-painted shrines around us bathed in a golden light.

Family groups were rushing to and fro, relieved that the long climb was behind them and clearly exhilarated at having reached their goal. Dhooli wallahs, their leg muscles bunched into knots, were setting down passengers, among them a young mother who immediately set to suckling her infant. Her head was covered by a white bonnet and around herself and the child she had wrapped a scarlet shawl. Silhouetted against an azure sky, these two looked as if they had just stepped out of a 'Madonna and Child' by Giorgione or one of the other Renaissance colourists.

Some of the pilgrims went about their devotions in a calm, almost puritanical manner. With others, especially groups of young men, a more festive atmosphere prevailed. Not many foreigners visit Parasnath, and several times I was asked whether I was a Jain. When I told them I was not, they invariably asked me why I had come on this pilgrimage. To which I had no ready answer. My journey up the Grand Trunk Road was, I suppose, a pilgrimage of sorts. But the concept of a purely secular pilgrimage is not easily explained to the devout. In the end I decided to tell them I had come 'to find peace', which appeared to be acceptable and was at least truthful.

I looked about for a secluded spot. Eventually I perched myself on a rock overlooking the steeper, south-facing side, whose jungle-covered slopes glowed green and gold in the morning light. Down in the plains a heat haze was beginning to build up, and through this haze I could just pick out the silvery reflections given off by the Grand Trunk Road. From up here it looked so small and insignificant, a thin metallic ribbon lost in the dun-coloured vastness of the plains.

A gust of wind carried with it the faint sound of diesel engines and horns being blown. Then the wind changed and all was silent again. As my eyes grew accustomed to the glare I spotted lorries and buses making their way along the highway 3,000 feet below. They hardly seemed to be moving at all, so great was the distance between us. I knew what was going on down there. Only yesterday I had ridden that same stretch of road. But now I felt completely detached, as if I was looking down from a plane.

Tyrel was ecstatic about the quality of light and rushed off to do some painting. Sarah decided to follow the prescribed pilgrim route, clambering from one rocky outcrop to the next. I took an easy path down the southern slope to a large temple surrounded by a water tank, the Jal Mandir of Lord Paravanatha.

While crossing the causeway I bumped into the merchant of Ujjain. 'Ah, Mr Britisher,' he exclaimed and began shaking my hand with both of his. 'Remember, we met last night at the JSS. Is this not a most wonderful place? Such a peaceful place. You must also be feeling this.'

I assured him I was and that Parasnath was positively my best experience since starting out on the journey. 'Ah, but you have not been to Ujjain,' he said, 'where I come from. You must, you must. It is even more beautiful than here.' I left him still glowing with his peculiar admixture of civic and religious pride.

From within the temple came the low hum of prayer and the reading of sacred texts. Then a lone voice, a young girl's, started singing. It rose and quavered, shifting up and down unfamiliar scales. I sat in the temple's south porch staring out at the sky, one portion of my mind observing how its lustrous blue took on a darker hue as it merged with the hazy horizon, the other filled with nothing but this girl's voice.

It was quite unlike the group devotional chants I had heard in Hindu temples, or the strongly masculine call of the muezzin. In fact, it was unlike anything I had heard in the subcontinent; and it struck me that I knew very little about these Jains. Their strict ethical code I understood was built upon the doctrine of ahimsa, the belief that all life is sacred, that even the smallest insect has an immortal soul, which accounts for the Digambaras' careful brushing before they sit down, while other Jains wear a gauze mask to prevent them from inhaling microscopic insects. Gandhi's non-violence was based on the same principle.

Jains have also avoided those occupations, from soldiering to cultivating the soil, where it is difficult to avoid harming other creatures. Instead they became merchants and financiers, middlemen who stood at one remove from the suffering caused by their investments. They kept outside the mainstream of Indian society and many of them amassed enormous wealth.

The Jains do not figure large in the history of Partition. Relatively few lived in those areas of the subcontinent that became Pakistan, the largest Jain communities being in Rajasthan, Gujarat and southern India. Those which were caught on the wrong side of the new borders left along with the Hindus; and in many ways it was easier for Jain families to pack up and leave. They had none of that attachment to the soil which kept Hindu and Sikh cultivators hanging on until it was too late. Their assets were more easily cashed in, their wealth could buy a safe passage, and in India there was a tight-knit community ready to welcome them.

Sitting there in the temple porch, I was aware that I was in the presence of a very ancient religion – older than Buddhism (which also first emerged in Bihar) and far less changed during the intervening centuries than Hinduism. Of all the world religions only Judaism and Zoroastrianism adhere so tenaciously to traditions from so distant a past.

The singing inside the Jal Mandir stopped and I gathered my energies for the final ascent to the main Digambara temple. Again, it would have been an easy climb if my leg wasn't playing up. As it was, I sweated up the hill and had to crawl on hands and knees up the temple's stone-clad staircase. Sarah, who suffers from vertigo, was also on her hands and knees, for there was a sheer drop on either side. In fact, the temple occupies a rocky outcrop apart from the main ridge, so that from some angles it appears to float between heaven and earth. It was here Lord Paravanatha is believed to have set foot on earth. A temple guardian ushered us into a low chamber beneath the main temple to see the footprint left in the living rock. As an unbeliever all I could think was, 'What little feet he had.'

The descent of Mount Parasnath soon became a forced march through the jungle. If anything, I found going down put a greater strain on my bad leg and I had to drag it along like Long John Silver. What's more, it had been decided we'd move on to another town for the night, which meant I'd have to ride the bike after clambering up and down this mountain all day. Sarah and Tyrel went on ahead to pack up our bags and load the car while I lurched after them, alone amidst the silent forest. A stray dog accompanied me for the last two miles. It waited at each bend in the trail for me to catch up, and soon I started talking to the animal. I found this helped to ease the pain; at any rate, it was better than swearing at each and every tree I passed.

By the time I fetched up at the JSS hostel the others were ready to go. A crowd had assembled. Their mood was not friendly. A small boy approached me and demanded money for parking fees. Another wanted money for cleaning the bike (which Misri told me he had done himself). Evidently it had been agreed that the foreigners should pay some dues before leaving town.

I wasn't having anything to do with this petty extortion. I fired up the Bullet and turned to face the crowd. I'd been told that throughout India, and especially in Bihar, the Enfield enjoys a certain notoriety as the preferred mode of transport for goondas, dacoits and other varieties of hit men. Now we'd put its reputation to the test. I revved the engine. The crowd parted. I eased through them and out onto the road. A kid threw a stone after me as I rode down the main street, but otherwise I experienced no problems in leaving town.

Not so the occupants of the Ambassador, who I imagined were following close behind. Just beyond the town limits I pulled over and waited for them. Ten minutes passed. Maybe they'd left something behind at the hostel. I decided to check the bike's tuning, since on my last run the engine had almost cut out a couple of times. But after twenty minutes I suspected something had happened to the others and headed back towards Madhuban.

We almost ran into each other on the bridge into town. Misri was driving like a bat out of hell and Sarah and Tyrel were waving their arms about. As I pulled alongside Sarah screamed out, 'Those bastards. Those vicious, thieving bastards.'

Apparently, the moment I disappeared the crowd had closed in around the Ambassador. A man claiming to be police, though he wasn't in uniform, came forward and demanded, 'Car inspection, car inspection.'

'A fat, greasy individual,' commented Tyrel.

'And he kept sticking his head through the window, trying to look down my tits,' Sarah added.

Whether he was in fact a policeman or not, Misri Lal Ram was convinced he meant trouble and, switching to English, suggested he'd better be paid off with 50 rupees. 'He tried to grab the note from me,' Sarah said, 'but I wouldn't let go until he'd told us "OK, you go now." But as soon as he'd pocketed the money he started demanding whisky and said he'd have to search for the stuff.'

'Avaricious bastard,' said Tyrel. 'That's the bottle I brought out from England. And he knew exactly where it was. Kept pointing and shouting, "Whisky, whisky".'

'You handed it over?' I asked in dismay. It was our only bottle.

'Never!' Sarah was outraged at this suggestion. 'I told him he'd got his bribe and that was it – bas, finish, hogya. Misri drove on and we left him gawping.'

'Until we hit the second road-block,' Tyrel interrupted. 'Kids this time, some of them with lathis, saying we had to pay some religious tax. There was no way out so we handed over our small change. Which took us another fifty yards before we were stopped by another bunch of kids.'

'And this time I'd really had it,' Sarah broke in. 'It was daylight robbery with the whole bloody town conniving.'

'So?'

'So I got out of the car, clapped my hands at them, and whooshed them out of the way. When the road ahead was clear I signalled Misri to drive on.'

'He was grinning all over his face when you sorted that lot out,' Tyrel added, 'weren't you, Misri?'

A contented chortle came from the front seat. 'Madam Zara,' he declared, 'is doing this thing like a pukka memsahib.'

'Now that's what I call a compliment,' said Sarah. And she had reason to feel proud. In the last resort she'd refused to give in to all this petty racketeering. She'd brazened it out and won – probably because the would-be extortionists were so surprised that anyone, let alone a woman, would confront them head-on rather than wheedling about how much to pay.

Yet if just one of them had tugged at her clothing it could have gone horribly wrong. Confronting a crowd anywhere in the subcontinent is a high-risk option. Which is why most times a wealthy Indian will bribe his way out of trouble. The same applies when dealing with the police and the judiciary on more serious charges. The only problem is this: that as long as this compliance continues there will be corruption and extortion and miscarriages of justice. And while practically everyone moans about corruption at all levels, very few are willing to lift a finger against it. Easier by far to pay people off – just as we had done back there, two times out of three.

There was no time for congratulation; we had already lost an hour's daylight. Corrupt policemen and street gangs operating within the town precincts were one thing; running into armed bandits out on the open road after nightfall was a more disturbing prospect. I'd read enough in the newspapers about bands of dacoits operating in Bihar and I didn't relish trying to outface them. With less than two hours to nightfall and close on a hundred miles between us and where we planned to stop near Hazaribagh, I knew we would have to put on a turn of speed.

With an effort I forced myself to concentrate on the road. This time I was really pushing it, trying to cover as much ground as possible before darkness came and I'd have to slow right down. But my mind kept switching back to all the stories I'd heard about dacoits. I imagined the scene: the tree trunk across the road; a dozen men armed with home-made spears and cutlasses surrounding the car, shouting in some local dialect; Misri Lal Ram being forced to explain that sahib and madam would have to 'step down'; and me on the bike, arriving twenty seconds later and having to decide whether to intervene or to high-tail it out of there and seek out the local constabulary. On a bike you might be able to accelerate out of that kind of trouble, going off the tarmac to get around the road-block. But an Ambassador would be a sitting duck.

As the afterglow spread across the sky I had to accept I wouldn't make it before dark. It was the cow-dust hour, when the cattle and goats are led back to the village, kicking up a fine dust haze which catches the sun's last rays. Evening fires were being lit inside thatched cottages, thin trails of wood-smoke adding to the haze. It all looked so voluptuously peaceful, and I wished I didn't need to hurry on.

By now the villagers were out in force, buying vegetables or paan in marketplaces that sprang up around crossroads at this hour. Many more were just walking intently along the road. Where they had come from, and just where they were going to, it was impossible to tell. Usually there were no houses for miles down the road in either direction. But these country people trudged through the twilight, making for home or on a visit to relatives, their destination hidden behind a tall-growing canefield or clump of mangoes. Their human forms grew indistinct in the gathering gloom.

I had just swerved to avoid an unlit bicycle-rickshaw when I saw a formless black mass spread across the entire road. The headlight picked out a cluster of yellow pinpricks in the dark, around knee level. They looked like eyes but were much too large and wetly reflective to be human.

Water buffalo! I slammed on the brakes. I'd seen what happens to the front end of a bus when it runs into one of these lumbering beasts and knew I had to lose speed fast. The next moment I was in among the herd, travelling slowly through them, wary of their long, backswept horns. The cowherd waved and shouted something as I inched my way past his sleek-skinned animals.

A greeting, or was it some warning? I dared not stop because by now I had fallen a long way behind the Ambassador. There was no trace of its tail-lights up ahead, only the sudden blackness of rural India after nightfall. Like it or not, I was now travelling alone in the dark through the backwoods of Bihar.

The next stretch of road was quite straight and evenly surfaced. I piled on the speed, straining to catch sight of some light which might be another vehicle up ahead. But Misri Lal Ram was obviously not hanging around either. I didn't catch up with the Ambassador until the streetlights of Hazaribagh shone on the horizon. At a junction just before the town proper I drew up alongside.

'What the hell kept you?' shouted Sarah.

'Water buffalo!' I yelled back, revving the motor whenever my headlight beam started fading. The Enfield had a nasty habit of cutting out completely when the lights were on and you let the engine drop to normal idling speed. If it cut out, I'd have to switch off all the lights and kick-start it in the dark. Then I'd be as invisible as all those bicycles and pedestrians I had so narrowly avoided back down the road.

'Where do you want to stay?' Sarah bellowed above the rattle of hot machinery.

'How the hell should I know?' Here I was, perched on a motorbike, in near total darkness, on the outskirts of some provincial town in Bihar I hadn't even heard of the previous day, and here was my wife asking for some recommendation as though I had the Michelin Guide in my lap. 'Just find some hotel in town,' I shouted. 'Anything's better than sitting out here on the road. You lead, I'll follow.'

And so began our multiple circumnavigation of Hazaribagh. There was supposed to be a government-run guesthouse in town. But every time we stopped to ask the way, the new person offering directions had a different idea about where this guesthouse was located.

We honked our way through the main bazaar in one direction. Then we about-turned and had to negotiate all those same potholes and shadowy bicyclists a second time, since our latest informant was 'one hundred per cent positive' that the guesthouse was in the cantonment area, right over on the side of town we had first arrived.

All the hazards of riding a bike through crowded streets were magnified by the darkness. In Hazaribagh functioning street-lights were a rarity, and the spirit-lamps inside stalls set up by street-vendors did not spread their yellowish illumination so far as the edge of the road. As we crossed and recrossed the maidan, repassing the Gothic outline of the old Anglican church for what seemed like the hundredth time, the very idea that we would ever find this mythical guesthouse, or that I would be able to switch off this over-heating engine and get out of the saddle, assumed an unreal quality.

Somewhere in the cantonment area Misri Lal Ram turned down a side road. There were no lights whatsoever, and soon the road degenerated into a bumpy track choked with coarse grass and weeds. I wondered about snakes moving around in the dark. If I ran over a krait lying in the dust, would it curl itself around the wheel spokes and retaliate when I drew to a halt? And if one struck, how much protection was afforded by my heavy riding boots?

Such morbid thoughts were interrupted by voices up ahead speaking in English. The guesthouse was nearby and some kind soul had offered to guide us there on foot. Misri Lal Ram and I were to stay with the vehicles. I switched off the engine and put the bike up on its centre stand. It seemed we had come an awful long way since Parasnath and this morning's sunlight among the Jain temples.

The search party re-emerged from the darkness. 'We can stay there if you want, but there are no sheets, no electricity, and nothing to eat. In fact, it looks like nobody's used the place for years. It's some sort of Gothic mansion and there are cobwebs everywhere. Our friend here says there are hotels in town and has offered to show us the way. What do you think?'

All I wanted to do was to remain still, wherever it was, for a while longer. But I was too tired to argue, so I kick-started the motor and wheeled the Bullet round. At least now there would be some sense of direction in our wanderings. But the first

hotel we tried was full. There was some government conference going on, and I had to look on enviously as huddled civil
servants downed their chota pegs of whisky on the veranda.

The next place was a Hindu businessman's hotel. I knew this
probably meant there'd be no alcohol – and I needed a drink
badly – but the rooms were large and clean. As I tried to wash
away some of the dust and half-burnt diesel from my face,
Sarah suggested I go downstairs and talk to the young man
who'd so kindly shown us the way. 'His name is Ratandeep
Sharma, and he's really very interesting. Did you know that
Tagore used to stay in Hazaribagh and wrote some of his poems
here?'

No, I did not. But armed with this new information I limped
down the stairwell to find Ratandeep waiting for me in the
lobby.

'You are a writer,' exclaimed Ratandeep, enthusiastically
pumping my hand. 'That is very good. You see, I am a teacher
at DAV Public School here in Hazaribagh. I teach English to
14–15-year-olds but I have so very few chances to converse
with English people and to discuss literature.'

I didn't feel up to an in-depth discussion of world literature
at that moment. But Ratandeep's enthusiasm couldn't just be
turned away. Already he was firing off the names of English
authors – Dickens, Aldous Huxley, George Bernard Shaw. It
seemed to me rather a dated miscellany, probably reflecting the
set texts he'd taught in school. I suggested we took some tea
and steered Ratandeep towards the hotel restaurant.

This was an open hall filled with aluminium frame tables and
chairs. The room was bathed in an unearthly purple glow
emanating from the strange combination of blue and red
overhead light bulbs which the hotel's management obviously
felt provided a relaxing atmosphere. A blaring colour TV was
propped up in the place of honour, and the few local
businessmen and travelling salesmen who were eating had
gathered like moths around it. Some Hindi soap opera was in
progress.

I chose a table as far away as possible but the volume control had been set so high it was hard to carry on any form of conversation. 'I understand that Rabindranath Tagore used to live here,' I shouted above a wailing musical interlude.

'Oh yes,' replied Ratandeep. But whatever followed was drowned out by the high-pitched stage-screams of a Bombay starlet.

When our teas arrived I asked the waiter to turn down the volume a little. 'But this is new TV,' he protested.

'I don't give a damn if it's new or not, just turn down that noise so we can talk.'

The waiter sauntered off and entered a lengthy discussion with one of his colleagues, who in turn called upon a third party – apparently the only one authorised to approach the holy of holies – to turn down the volume. He accomplished this task so delicately that there was no discernible reduction in decibel levels. 'This TV,' Ratandeep shouted across the table, 'it is the only source of entertainment for these people.'

I decided to give up on cutting the background noise and tried instead to pick out what Ratandeep was saying about Tagore coming here when one of his children fell seriously ill because Hazaribagh was considered to have a healthy climate. After the shit I'd been through on the Grand Trunk Road, with all those chimneys and exhaust pipes belching unregulated volumes of poisonous fumes into the atmosphere, I wasn't quite prepared to accept Hazaribagh as the subcontinent's answer to Baden-Baden. But then everything is relative.

'What about your own family?' I ventured. 'Have they always lived in Hazaribagh?'

'Oh no. We used to live in Lahore before Partition and all that. I am much too young to remember, and my father doesn't want to talk about it much. You see, there are still people from my family, uncles and suchlike, who we've never found.'

'Your family are Hindus, then?'

'My great-grandfather was a Hindu, but my grandfather converted to Catholicism. He studied in Burma under the missionaries, and when he came back he converted other members of the family to the Church. My father was a

Christian, of course. He used to work at the TB hospital in Calcutta, and previously with the Indian Army in the Andaman and Nicobar Islands. My mother was from Calcutta, from a Hindu family. They worshipped Siva. But when she entered our family she also converted.'

I was becoming rather confused by this multi-generational saga of the Church triumphant over Hinduism. Instead, I wanted to get back to Lahore and Partition – if he'd let me.

'My father still thinks of Lahore as the family home,' he said, 'even though he was only a small boy when all these events happened. He was three or four years old, and one of the family's maidservants took him with her when she went to market to buy vegetables and suchlike. Then there was much rioting in Lahore city and it became impossible for this maidservant with my father to return home. So placing my father inside her basket, the maid fled from Lahore and came over to India.'

The soap opera had given way to commercials, but now I was tuned in to what Ratandeep was saying. 'We lost so many members of our family because of this Partition. Some we know are now living in Bombay, but we have never met them. Yet there are still four or five of our family whose fates we do not know, who we still have to find.

'With others we have been more fortunate. Maybe fourteen or fifteen years after Partition, my father met by chance one of my uncles. They were standing in a railway station at Rourkela Steel-Town in Orissa State and recognised each other. There, on the railway platform, they embraced each other, with so much joyous weeping. But some members of his family he has never seen since. God knows what happened to them. My father only met another brother of his after so many years, when this uncle of mine was on his deathbed.'

I sat up, all my fatigue forgotten now, listening with rapt attention. What was unusual about this tale of lost relatives and starting out anew in another country – a story that I knew could be repeated countless times by Hindus and Muslims and Sikhs – was that it concerned a Christian family.

I asked Ratandeep what he felt about more recent outbreaks of communal friction, such as the riots following the destruction of the Mosque at Ayodhya. 'These communal tensions,' he explained, 'are still felt by my father's generation. Younger people don't have that problem. Everybody is nowadays too busy earning enough money, so they are not too concerned about whether this person is Hindu or Muslim or Christian. And if anything does happen – violence and suchlike – they'll help each other. But older people, they are often angry about what has happened to them. My father's an old man, an angry man, and he won't listen to anyone. I can never discuss this kind of subject with my father.

'With our generation, some of these attitudes are changing. I have one friend, a Muslim, who used to keep only with his family, but now he has friends who are Hindus or Christians. Also, as a traditional Muslim family, they wouldn't allow their daughters to study beyond primary level. Now they are admitting his sister to High School. Likewise, before Muslims used to have twelve or fourteen children each; now they have just one or two. Population control is so much popularised on TV and elsewhere. Education, also, is very important and now much improved.'

Sarah and Tyrel arrived, eager to get on with ordering dinner. 'I don't know whether you've read this before,' Sarah said, dropping a paperback copy of George Orwell's *Homage to Catalonia* on the table, 'but if you haven't, then please take it. It's about an Englishman fighting against the fascists in Spain. Autobiographical, mostly, but very well written.'

'I will read it in my class,' said Ratandeep, leaving me wondering how a bunch of fourteen-year-old Biharis would respond to Orwell's bitter analysis of Spanish republican politics and the betrayal of youthful idealism. Probably familiar enough territory in this blighted state of Bihar, where attempts at social reform have been repeatedly squashed and the levels of corruption are legendary.

'Our generation,' Ratandeep declared, 'we are capable of much but we don't get the opportunities. I joined teaching for other reasons, but for most people teaching is not considered an important job. All young people want to do today is business or marketing, and for this they must go outside Hazaribagh. I myself worked for one year for the *Indian Express* newspaper in Delhi, for the circulation and market research departments. But I wanted to become a teacher, to improve people's education. Conditions are very different from my father's generation. He was very strict on discipline. It used to be that everyone in the family had to be back home before 7 p.m. at latest.'

This memory made him look instinctively at his wristwatch. 'Time is getting on,' he said. 'I promised to be back more than one hour ago.' He began leaving hurriedly, wondering how he was going to get home. But Tyrel had agreed with Misri Lal Ram to drop him back at his house, down that same dark lane where he'd emerged like some saving angel.

Once he left we set into our first meal of the day, the usual curry and dal and rice. But after climbing Mt Parasnath and then riding the Enfield through the night, any form of sustenance was welcome. I don't even remember going to bed. As soon as the food hit the system I was unconscious.

4

BIHAR (ii):
BLOW-OUT BY THE BODHI TREE

Another morning, another early start. Until setting out on this trip I hadn't realised how precious daylight is. That morning we didn't permit ourselves the luxury of bed-tea. 'We'll have breakfast in the game reserve,' Sarah declared. So I crawled into my exhaust-stained jeans, pulled on my boots and was out on the road before I really knew what was happening.

It was becoming like second nature now and I knew I wouldn't stay on automatic pilot for long. In the chill dawn of Upper India, before the sun has dispersed the morning mist, you don't need artificial stimulants to wake up in a hurry. About half a minute on the bike travelling at 50 mph does the job nicely.

This is just as well, since the road we now joined was not some little side road but the main link between Ranchi and the southern end of the coal-and-steel belt − home to such massive, Soviet-inspired production centres as Rourkela and the Tata Iron & Steel works at Jamshedpur − and our old friend *cloaca maxima indiensis*, otherwise known as the Grand Trunk Road.

Even at this hour there was plenty of heavy traffic moving. But the road surface was better than anything I'd grown used to and we sped past the early morning convoys and out into hilly, well-wooded country. This is part of the Chota Nagpur Plateau, a northerly extension of that basalt mass known as the Deccan which accounts for most of central and peninsular India.

Hazaribagh wildlife sanctuary was a peaceful enough spot to have breakfast. When we arrived it appeared to be deserted of

animal, as well as human, life. The forest rest-house looked as if
it had been shut down for decades.

While Sarah went looking for someone to brew up some tea,
I bumped into a grizzled gentleman wrapped in a threadbare
cloak. He was poking at the embers of a wood-fire and turned
out to be one of the game wardens. I asked him about the forest
area and he recited to me a list of official statistics he had
obviously learned by rote: park area, 182 square kilometres;
number of dams, eight; mammal species – sambar, nilgai, deer,
chital, leopard . . . he even claimed there were three tigers.
Before Independence, he told me, all this forest belonged to the
local Raja. It was he who had dug the old tiger traps I'd seen by
the side of the road.

The game warden's assistant took me down to the deer
breeding centre. A family of half-tame sambar, the dominant
stag looking like a moth-eaten subcontinental copy of 'Monarch
of the Glen', came to his call and nuzzled my fingers with wet
noses through the wire enclosure. It was more like being in a
zoo than a wildlife sanctuary.

Misri Lal Ram got it right when he declared, 'This is a
cheating park.' The fact that Misri knew a word like 'cheating'
was a surprise to Sarah and Tyrel, who had mistakenly thought
he spoke no English at all. They had been discussing matters in
the back seat of the Ambassador which, on reflection, would
have been better left unsaid.

The breakfast tea was good and strong. The view from the
canteen across the confluence of two streams was soothing; and
the large papaya Sarah had bought two days earlier was sliced up
and served with fresh limes and salt. But although sitting around
a wildlife park, looking at the occasional fishing heron and
flocks of egrets, was a pleasant enough diversion, it was no more
than that.

I actually wanted to get back on the GT Road. It had
become for me that 'river of life', as the ancient rissaldar
describes it in *Kim*. And having spent only an hour on that road
during the previous two days, it was for me, as it had seemed to
that old soldier, 'as a river from which I am withdrawn like a log

after a flood'. But as soon as I rejoined the main artery at Barhi junction, I wished I could be back on some nice, quiet country road. Anywhere, in fact, rather than that hellish ribbon of buckled tarmac and hot exhaust gas.

A quick lesson in Indian road etiquette. Sudden changes in direction or speed are accompanied by a languid arm movement. An outstretched arm on the driver's side generally means he intends to keep hogging the middle of the road, though it could also mean a right turn is imminent. When the palm is raised and waggled about the driver is asking 'What the hell do you think you're doing?' A downward wave means stay back; though if you see the driver's mate doing this through the nearside window it means they're cutting in on you and you'd best slam on the brakes or get right off the road – or both.

The signal for 'road clear, please overtake' is the same as anywhere else, but don't trust this one. Too often I pulled out to find a snarling Tata or Ashok Leyland bearing down on me. This is considered a monstrously good joke by regulars on the GT Road. Whenever I finally overtook the offending vehicle I noticed the driver and everyone else in the cab were laughing.

Playing chicken is another time-honoured part of the great road-game. This one is open to all comers, regardless of size. For, while the universal law of the road is that might is right and that it's up to the smaller, more vulnerable vehicle to get out of the way, when it comes to playing chicken all normal rules are suspended, all sense of natural hierarchy dissolved. It is a game at which even the weakest and most downtrodden can win. All that is required is a total disregard for human life, especially your own.

Most fearless of all are the children. They have been raised beside the river of life-threatening metal. They have played in its potholes and muddy verges, only inches clear of the massive wheels that rumble past their roadside dwellings day and night. Since they first began to walk they have been dodging between buses and rickshaws, tongas and trucks, scooters and bullock carts. They must run this gauntlet every day just to fetch a stem of sugarcane or to see a friend on the other side of the great divide. Their toys are the worn-out parts of vehicles which can no longer be recycled. Such children know the ways of the road, how sharply a laden truck can brake and why passenger buses are especially treacherous, as if by instinct. They know also that if they do get their timing wrong as they dart between vehicles, if there is an accident one day, that within seconds a lynch-mob will surround the driver who knocked them down. From there on his only hope is that the police will arrive in time.

Most drivers in India would rather cause a multiple pile-up than run over either a child or a cow, retribution for either offence being similar and immediate. For the children of the road this is their only insurance policy; but it is an effective deterrent nonetheless.

I was terrified of many things on that road, but the thought of running over a child held a particular horror. And it very nearly happened that morning.

Just west of where we rejoined the GT Road a young boy practically leapt under my front tyre. I slammed on the brakes and in my frantic efforts to avoid him almost collided with an auto-rickshaw. I ended up in a cloud of dust by the side of the road. Looking back I saw this ragged child, hands on hips, staring with cool superiority at the idiot motorcyclist who had lost his nerve, who didn't know how to play the game. Behind him stood a motley band of bazaar children; and I saw they were laughing at me.

Then, as if by some unspoken agreement, another boy launched himself into the path of a truck, staring the driver down, forcing him to swerve into a deeply potholed section of the road. I looked down at the dry earth and saw that it was sprinkled with metal shavings, the left-overs from some axle-grinders or bodywork repairers, and I wondered whether these kids were paid a few rupees to force through-traffic into this minefield.

There were enough mechanics' shops and second-hand tyre

merchants on the strip. Most of the population seemed to make their living by attending to breakdowns and recycling the discarded bits. So perhaps these children were actually doing a job of sorts: touting for business, encouraging the worn-out tyres and overladen axles of passing vehicles into the worst part of the road, so that more of the through-traffic would have to stop for repairs in this village and not one fifty miles up the road. Then there would be more work for the tyre-wallahs and gearbox-strippers, from whom, of course, the young daredevils would later claim their commission, taking care that they had been positively identified (but not caught) by the angry driver for having caused the accident in the first place. Such is the serpentine logic of 'job creation' in India, and nowhere is there such pressure to earn a few extra rupees as in Bihar.

Yes, these kids are naturals when it comes to playing chicken. They show no fear. And this is a massive advantage in a game where indifference to life is critical.

Most are from low-caste, landless families, who have settled in the no-man's-land between public road and private property. Their homes are so-called temporary dwellings, roofed over with an amalgam of corrugated iron, tarpaulin and thatch, which have existed beside the road for decades. And the road has an appetite for cheap labour. It needs coolie gangs to fill its gaping holes, laying in the inadequate mix of tar and rubble by hand and finishing the rejuvenated surface with a rolling pin. It needs stonebreakers, and the women who carry the broken fragments in wicker baskets on their heads for miles down the road.

All the shoddy, unplanned, unfinished development – the garages and tyre-shops, the godowns and pawnshops and brothels which spring up beside the road – also requires labour. In Bihar, especially, this is usually furnished by smiling contractors who know they can undercut the opposition because they actually own all the muscle and the sweat and every hour of the day that the gods have seen fit to grant their indentured labourers. Until, that is, the terms of the indenture (including all subsequent loans in money or in kind) have been earned out. But this rarely happens and the offspring of indentured labourers usually enter the same life of servitude, the impossible terms of the (technically illegal) contract being passed from one generation to the next. With such prospects, no wonder these children appeared indifferent to whether their existence continued or not.

Yet this apparent disregard for life was not their monopoly, not by any means. It afflicted many other users of the road, regardless of caste, creed, or any other social distinction. The businessman-in-a-hurry urging his driver to overtake blind on the hump of a canal bridge; the milkman on his bicycle, aluminium canisters strapped onto every part of the frame, who blithely swings out of a side-road without looking or touching the brake; the old woman running for her bus across four lanes of traffic; the unkempt, red-eyed sadhu, his sense of timing and spacial co-ordinates blurred by the morning's intake of ganja or opium – not one of these appeared familiar with that concept, so fundamental to Western values, of the sanctity of life. Even the pariah dogs foraging among the detritus of the road assume an indifference which their more excitable country cousins cannot approach.

During those first few miles out of Barhi, the road conspired to throw everything at me. And though it was hardly possible, the road surface deteriorated even further, forcing me to follow local practice and push over to the wrong side of the road in search of some way through the minefield of spine-jarring potholes.

It wasn't too bad if the way ahead was clear and you could pick a way through. But when stuck between heavy lorries, half-blinded by the smoke pouring from their exhausts, there wasn't time to take avoiding action before the next pattern of craters appeared just ahead of the front tyre. I had barely ridden through another one of these monsters when there was a loud bang and the front end of the bike started shaking uncontrollably. There was a truck on my tail and I had to struggle with the handlebars to stay upright. I tried braking, but this made things worse. So, using the rear brake only to lose momentum, I gradually edged over to the side of the road.

The bike came to rest under a peepul tree. At first I didn't move. I just stared at the back of the truck which had narrowly avoided me as it disappeared down the road. Its tailgate bore the familiar message *Horn Please-Tata-Okay*. Then I became aware of sunlight filtering through the peepul tree and the dust hanging in the air and the green fields beyond.

'That was close,' a voice exclaimed in English.

I turned round to see Tyrel and Sarah piling out of the Ambassador.

'Are you all right?' she asked. 'What on earth happened back there?'

'Front puncture, I reckon,' said Tyrel, answering for me. I was still too dazed to speak.

Eventually I pulled myself together enough to heave the bike onto its stand. We all knelt down to inspect the damage. At first I thought I had buckled the front wheel. But the rim seemed to have survived intact and, as Tyrel pointed out, none of the wire spokes were broken.

That still left us stranded in the depths of Bihar without a village in sight. 'We'll have to get that front wheel off,' announced Tyrel, who had been through this procedure on any number of bikes. 'But first we have to disconnect all these cables. Have you got the manual?'

I rummaged around in the side panniers until I found it. Misri Lal Ram, meanwhile, was collecting a pile of broken bricks that had been abandoned in the verge. These he wedged underneath the engine block so that they would take the weight of the bike when we removed the wheel. Any bricks left over he placed on the road behind the bike, forming a sort of cordon to warn oncoming traffic. This is standard practice in India, and I remembered speeding past scores of broken-down vehicles with these little piles of bricks or bits of foliage spread out in a protective cordon. Now it was my turn to receive the pitying looks of other drivers as they roared past.

The front wheel detached easily enough and was loaded

aboard the Ambassador. Misri was sure there was a small town with a tyre-shop less than ten miles up the road. I assumed I would be going with him, but Sarah had other ideas.

'Misri and I can deal with this. Why don't you and Tyrel stay with the bike? He can get on with his painting and you look as though you could do with a rest.'

And so they drove off, leaving Tyrel with his paintbrushes, and the Enfield without its front wheel.

'I'll think I'll do a sketch of the bike just as it is,' he said. 'We'll call it Bullet off the Grand Trunk Road.'

Tyrel soon became absorbed in his painting. The Bullet was a sad, almost comical sight with its front wheel missing. Truck-drivers would slow down to take a good look at us, or to ask if we needed help of any kind. 'Tik hai?' they shouted from their garishly decorated cabs. 'Ji, tik hai,' I yelled back, waving and trying to look as though everything was under control, that it was perfectly normal, in fact, for these two Englishmen to be sitting in the dust by the Grand Trunk Road, just passing the time of day, as it were. God knows what they thought we were doing. For we must have been a curious sight – Tyrel with his paintbrushes and me with a book in my lap – rather like a pair of Edwardian gentlemen out on a 'reading holiday' in the Lake District. Except this was not Lake Windermere; it was down-country Bihar, where the very concepts of 'reading' and 'holidays' are alien to most of the population.

The Ambassador returned with a triumphant honking and we unloaded the newly repaired tyre. 'There were lots of little metal shavings stuck into it,' Sarah said, as I was refitting the wheel. 'You must have picked them up when you went off the road in one of those villages.'

Then I remembered the boy who had jumped out in front of me and how all the other children had been laughing, and the glint of sharp metal in the dirt. 'The tyre's all right now,' she continued, 'though it took some time to remove all those bits.'

'It doesn't look like we're going to make it to Bodh Gaya in time for lunch,' commented Tyrel, who still retained a European-sized appetite.

'No time for lunch,' Sarah replied. 'And now,' she turned to me, 'you get back on that bike and put on a little speed, please. We've lost quite enough time already.'

I first noticed the number of pilgrim buses shortly after we turned off the main road at Dobbi. We were now heading towards Bodh Gaya, the place where in the sixth century BC the prince Siddharta Gautama attained enlightenment while meditating under a peepul tree, and so became the Buddha. The original Bodhi tree, was felled soon afterwards by the Emperor Asoka; but before then a cutting had been taken to Sri Lanka, and from the offspring that grew there a sapling was removed and brought back to Bodh Gaya. This tree still flourishes, and the temple complex that has grown around it remains the most sacred shrine of Buddhism, drawing pilgrims from all over the world.

There would be some Indian Buddhists on the buses (today they number around seven millions), though mostly they were crowded with Hindus who nowadays like to include a visit to such holy places as Parasnath or Bodh Gaya along with worshipping at the principal shrines of Hinduism. I don't know whether this is due to the syncretism of their own religion, its ability to draw into its pantheon all the gods and holy men of other faiths, or whether it is just part of a new pre-packaged variety of religio-tourism favoured by the Indian middle class.

In amongst the Hindu majority there was a sprinkling of Buddhists from other lands. On some buses I spotted the occasional arm swathed in maroon and saffron – the colours of the Buddhist monkhood – sticking out from a side window. And there were white faces aboard – the first, I suddenly realised, that I had seen since leaving Calcutta. These European or American pilgrims did not appear especially joyous at being so near their goal. Instead, they stared out at this ancient landscape with a mixture of contempt and that bland piety which sets apart the true Puritan, no matter what country they come from or religion they hold.

Perhaps it was because I hadn't seen other Westerners for a

while that I was shocked by how many there seemed to be at Bodh Gaya. A small minority had adopted the maroon robes and shaven heads of ordained monks or nuns. A few were wearing ordinary Western clothes. But mostly they had affected an incongruous half-way house style – part Eastern, part Gap or Calvin Klein. A technicolour Nepali cap sat uncomfortably atop a mass of carrot-coloured curls; loose-fitted Punjabi trousers ended awkwardly above sturdy hiking boots; and the occasional brave attempt at wearing the sari with some grace usually ran foul of such 'sensible' Western accessories as the mini-rucksack and the bumbag. There was a lot of facial jewellery about. And there was a lot of that self-consciously relaxed gait which passes for 'cool' among subcontinental novitiates.

What were they doing in Bihar of all places? But then, Bodh Gaya isn't really part of Bihar at all. It's become a separate mini-state peopled by a new tribe of international Buddhists – or, at least, waverers who have travelled to the subcontinent in order to 'find themselves' and, having witnessed the austerities of the sadhus at Rishikesh or spent time at the ashram at Pune, are now 'seriously thinking about' Buddhism as 'a way of life'.

As I weaved through the usual chaos outside the bus station I noticed something strange. A number of these 'seekers' had face masks clamped over their features, while others being ferried to and fro in bicycle-rickshaws had scarves wrapped across their faces. At first I thought of the Jains and their fear of inhaling small insects. But these people were clearly not Jains. Then again, the scarves drawn across the face called to mind the traditional modesty of Indian women, both Muslim and Hindu, when travelling in public. Was this some 'New Age' version of purdah? But these Westerners went about with their heads immodestly uncovered, and the fashion seemed as popular among men as women. Finally I spotted a young man holding a handkerchief over his nose and mouth, as if trying to protect himself from some airborne contagion.

I drew up alongside the rickshaw he was travelling in. 'What's with the face masks?' I shouted above the thump of the Enfield. He stared back at me as though I was mad. Maybe he thought I was about to mug him. Or maybe he imagined I belonged to the local chapter of Hell's Apsaras, the All-India Union of Gay Motorcyclists, or some equally crime-ridden and depraved organisation. At any rate, he clearly didn't want to talk to me and motioned his rickshaw driver to move on.

'Why the handkerchief?' I yelled. He stared resolutely ahead. It occurred to me that maybe he didn't speak English. So I tried again, this time pulling out the end of my own neck-scarf and jamming it across my nose and mouth. 'Why this?' I asked. I then removed the makeshift mask and smiled in what I hoped was my most confidence-inspiring manner.

'Ah this,' he finally replied, disconnecting handkerchief from face. He spoke with a German or Scandinavian accent. 'This is to protect against all of the pollution here.'

I nearly fell off the bike I was laughing so hard. What kind of madness was this? Pollution, here in a quiet little place like Bodh Gaya? Of course, there was the usual light cocktail of half-burned diesel coming from the pilgrim buses, and the motorised rickshaws trailed little black plumes of two-stroke mixture as they always do. But there was no heavy industry, no serious through-traffic, nothing that really counts in the scale of things. And the absurdity of all these poor, frightened little bunnies wandering around the backwoods of Bihar, the very spot where the Buddha attained enlightenment, with anti-pollution masks had me laughing uncontrollably.

'What's so bloody hilarious?' Sarah enquired, leaning out of the Ambassador's window.

'All these people wearing face masks,' I spluttered. 'It's because they're worried about the pollution.'

'Ridiculous,' she replied. 'But it's in one of the guidebooks. We should find somewhere to stay. This place is a lot more crowded than the last time we were here.'

The last time had been ten years earlier, when Bodh Gaya resembled an overgrown village rather than a bustling pilgrimage town. We had stayed in the Bihar State rest-house, a spacious but rather rundown place on what was then the outskirts of town, which I remembered with mixed feelings. We'd been woken up in the middle of the night by a rat running across the mosquito netting. Sarah had called in the bearer, whose attitude had been: 'This is a house in rural Bihar, of course there is a rat living here.' I ended up having to chase the creature out onto the roof terrace.

'We could try the Rat Motel,' I suggested, 'though the town's changed so much I'm not sure I can find the way.'

When we found it I hardly recognised the place. A fresh lick of paint, potted dahlias lining the drive and circles of western Buddhists receiving instruction in the garden suggested that the Rat Motel was under new management. It had become a much sought-after residence and there were positively no vacancies. What is more, our arrival was obviously resented by the long-term residents. They glared at the motorbike with ill-concealed loathing, almost as though it was an incarnation of evil, an awful reminder of everything they had fled here to forget. Their testiness reminded me of a huddle of great-aunts at a residential hotel in Eastbourne or Bognor Regis. First glare at the intruder; then studiously ignore. Not much evidence of Buddhist tolerance here, I thought, as I dragged my weary carcase back to the bike and summoned up the energy for another kick-start.

At that moment I noticed their chanting was growing louder. They were trying to chant me out of their collective consciousness, to deny my existence because it didn't fit into their cosy scheme of things. The realisation of what they were up to made me see red. I'd had a rough day, what with the front-end puncture and half a dozen near misses on the road. And now, to be confronted by this bunch of holier-than-thous trying to Om me out of existence – it was enough to bring out the Genghis Khan in anyone. For a full ten seconds after the engine fired I contemplated charging them. Just to see the look on their faces as 400 lb of hot, oil-spewing metal burst into their enclosed little circle. Anything to shock them out of their sanctimonious, self-satisfied, potted-plant ideas of what is real and what is not.

I held still until the moment of anger had passed. Then I

turned the bike round very slowly and left them Omming away in their oasis of self-proclaimed tranquillity. Misri Lal Ram and the others were waiting for me at the gate. 'Did you see that?' I exploded.

'Aren't we a little tired and emotional?' Sarah cut in, trying to calm me down.

'But this place is unreal. First all these miserable geeks going around with face masks, for Christ's sake. And then these self-righteous bastards with their beads and mantras. They should all be loaded onto a truck and taken down to Dhanbad or Asansol.'

'Fine! But that's not going to find us a room, is it? Now you just follow us.'

The first place we went to tried charging ten times as much as we had paid the previous night in Hazaribagh. When Sarah pointed this out the manager shrugged his shoulders. 'Land prices have gone rocket-wise here in Bodh Gaya,' he explained. 'For just one hectare of good land you must be paying one crore of rupees.' A rapid calculation made this about £180,000. It was my turn to give a shrug of the shoulders before walking away. Everything about this town seemed unreal.

Eventually we found rooms in a newly built hotel that was full of Tibetan monks who had turned up for the big prayer session or pöa that was due to commence. Here, at last, were Buddhists of a defined tradition. As I unloaded the bike some of them gathered around, curosity getting the better of their natural reserve. 'Namaste,' one of them said, offering the usual greeting in Hindi. 'Tashi delek,' I responded, using up half of my Tibetan vocabulary in one blast.

'You speak Tibetan?' asked one of the elders.

'No, but I have visited Tibet,' I replied.

This caused something of a sensation. Most of the younger monks had been born in exile. They had lived all their lives in India, where the monasteries they had entered in Karnataka or Himachal Pradesh were often replicas of those left behind in Tibet. But they had never been able to return to their homeland.

They asked me about conditions under Chinese occupation, and for the most part I could only confirm their worst fears – the monasteries destroyed during the Cultural Revolution, the deforestation, the fear inspired by the secret police, the tearing down of old Tibetan houses in Lhasa and the massive influx of Han Chinese settlers into the main cities, part of a deliberate policy to swamp the indigenous population.

One of the older monks drew me aside. 'I was born near Drigung, to the east side of Lhasa. On your travels, did you also visit this place?'

I was happy to confirm that I had been to Drigung, that there were still many monks there, and that I had attended a great pöa in honour of Guru Rinpoche, the miracle-working saint who had brought Buddhism to Tibet, which had drawn thousands of pilgrims to a remote mountain valley.

The old man was deeply moved by this news from his homeland. He asked me detailed questions about the rites I had witnessed, to which I could give only unsatisfactory answers, not being an expert in this field. But he seemed pleased – and somewhat surprised – at the extent to which Buddhism is still a living force in Tibet despite the many attempts at suppression by the Chinese authorities.

The younger monks wanted to know whether pictures of the Dalai Lama were banned. When I told them that it was a punishable offence but that practically all Tibetans would ask foreigners for a Dalai Lama photo regardless of the risks involved, they too seemed satisfied.

For the first time I felt good about being in Bodh Gaya. Sarah called down from an upstairs balcony that I'd better finish unloading the bike.

'We're starving. And do you want to know what we're going to eat?'

'Rice-dal-chapatti,' I answered automatically.

'Momos,' she said triumphantly. 'With all these Tibetans in town we must be able to find a plate of momos somewhere.'

The very idea of a plateful of these plump Tibetan ravioli stirred an appetite that had all but fallen dormant. After the watery food of the plains, a steaming mound of momos seemed to me as substantial as a beef-steak. So we set off towards the centre of town, which in Bodh Gaya means the area just north of the Mahabodhi temple, in search of a Tibetan food stall. But we found the main drag dominated by vendors of jewellery and other knick-knacks. There were fruit-sellers and juice-pressers, garland-threaders and icon-hawkers, but not a momo merchant in sight. We passed the Sudhar Drug De-Addiction and Rehabilitation Centre, which offered 'FREE Treatment in our HOSPITAL For Addicts of any of the following: Smak, Brown Sugar, Heroine, Charris, Ganja, Bhang, Alcohol And all Types of Drugs, Pethedrine Injection'. But they had nothing to ease my craving for momos.

It was growing dark and the Indian day-trippers were forming into groups ready to be bused out to Gaya, a major Hindu pilgrimage centre in its own right where tour operators could put up their clients at less extortionate rates than those prevailing in Bodh Gaya. Abandoning the main drag, we decided to try our luck among the makeshift tents dignified by the title of 'Tibetan Refugee Village'. There was a covered market, where both Tibetan and Hindu traders were selling cheap but practical Western-style clothing, such as anoraks and woollen sweaters and socks. The absence of any specifically Tibetan goods was striking; but then this market wasn't for tourists so much as for the ordinary needs of Tibetans-in-exile.

We found our momos just around the corner in a large tent full of Tibetan ladies drinking butter tea and gossiping nineteen-to-the-dozen. There was a small shrine with a picture of the Dalai Lama beside our table and the lady of the house was busy doing her evening devotions, lighting a butter lamp and burning incense. A hidden stereo was pumping out a medley of early seventies hits – The Eagles and Crosby, Stills, Nash & Young. From previous encounters with Tibetans-in-exile I knew they had a weakness for the gentler kind of 'Old Hippy' music. The ladies in their traditional striped aprons got on with the serious business of discussing marriages still pending and the relative virtues of their daughters-in-law. A young father dandled his baby son on his knees.

Upon the whole, Tibetans-in-exile apper to have achieved a happier marriage of Western and traditional values than their Indian hosts, whose ideas of being 'Western' are still constrained by old-fashioned British snobbery and caste prejudice. There is a refreshing sense of tolerance, of equality in adversity, among these second- or third-generation refugees. They are good traders, readier than most to adapt to new circumstances. And despite the gradual Hinduisation of their culture – most evident in the visual arts and religious iconography, where the soft pastels and sickly-sweet images so prevalent in modern Hinduism are beginning to creep in – they have succeeded in maintaining their Buddhist beliefs and way of life.

The momos arrived and were delicious, both the steamed and the fried varieties. Someone switched the tape to an old Jimmy Cliff number, 'Many Rivers to Cross', and I noticed the young father looking after the baby was softly singing along. It should have appeared incongruous, a Tibetan singing along to a Jamaican spiritual; but the song's sadness, its expression of determination to reach a distant homeland, no matter what the obstacles, seemed to sum up the plight of the Tibetan community-in-exile.

Well-filled with momos, we ventured back onto the main strip. A number of STD-ISD booths had sprung up, catering mainly for the needs of Western and Japanese visitors. Sarah popped into one which advertised a fax service and came back with what looked to me like a menacing grin.

'You know what you're going to do tonight,' she started. I groaned, knowing what was coming next.

'You're going to sit down in our hotel room and write that article you still owe. The fax here works perfectly, so it can reach London before they get into work tomorrow morning.'

'But this is Bodh Gaya,' I protested. 'How do you expect me to write about the goddamn American Stock Exchange from here of all places?'

'Oh for God's sake, just get on with it,' she replied.

And so it came to pass that I despatched an article on the relative merits of listing your company on the New York Stock Exchange, NASDAQ and the American Stock Exchange from within a stone's throw of where the Buddha attained enlightenment. Trying to get my mind around the concepts I was dealing with was the hardest part – a process not helped by an impromptu visit from my monk-friend Thobden Dorje.

He was fascinated by the various bleeps and different graphics that appeared on my computer screen as it was booting up, and called in two other monks to witness this miracle of modern technology. Quite what they expected to happen next I'm not sure – a direct cable link to the BBC World Service, perhaps, or a video show. They sat cross-legged in a semicircle around the screen for a while, chatting among themselves. When they realised there was no more fun and games in store they wandered back to their rooms, leaving me to stare at a blank screen.

The following morning two sheets were fed into a fax machine, the digitalised message bounced off a satellite and the result of my efforts were gratefully received in London. The girl next to me in the queue was using the same technology to send a handwritten scrawl to her parents in Seattle. Judging by the frequency of dollar signs and exclamation marks, this was another example of that timeless classic – the begging letter.

Then I stepped out of the STD booth into the morning sunlight, bought myself a sweet-lime juice from the man opposite with the fruit-press, and prepared to re-enter Bihar.

5

BIHAR (iii):
ENTER SHER SHAH SURI
AND A REFUGEE

It is only 34 miles from Bodh Gaya back to the Grand Trunk Road; but they might as well be sitting on separate planets. The junction town of Dobbi is strictly functional, just another dirt-poor, dirt-coloured, overgrown truck-stop without much in the way of adornment except a roadside bazaar.

I gritted my teeth and rejoined the flow of heavy traffic. Bye-bye, Bodhisattva. Hello, *cloaca maxima*. We were back on the road again.

To begin with it was the same as ever — bunched-up convoys of heavy trucks spewing diesel into the atmosphere. But after a few miles the traffic thinned out and the road took on a pastoral aspect, twisting through villages whose thatched homesteads came right down to the verge. One of these roadside villages had a large artificial tank or reservoir right beside the main road. It was crowded with lotus just coming into flower and on the far side were a number of small temples or shrines newly painted in white and pink. Somehow the proximity of the road didn't impinge upon this peaceful scene.

The great artery seemed to narrow as we moved deeper into Bihar. There were no other private cars whatsoever, and the number of trucks and buses plying this stretch was just a fraction of those back in the coal-and-steel belt. Even the motor-rickshaw became a rarity, the horse-drawn tonga or bicycle-rickshaw taking its place.

Far from any town, I spotted the dhaba of my dreams. It was

a simple, brick-built structure with a thatched roof, surrounded by shade trees. There were half a dozen charpoys out front and wood-smoke emanated from the kitchen area, where there was much slapping of chapattis. We ordered chai, vegetable curry and black dal, all of which were much better prepared than the overpriced and 'Westernised' (deliberately underspiced) meal we had eaten in Bodh Gaya. A small boy kept up a constant supply of freshly baked chapattis. They came straight out of the oven and were so hot that he had to toss them between his palms.

After eating my fill I got up to wash my hands, but the young boy signalled me to remain reclining on my charpoy. I thought he was going to fetch some water but instead he shouted orders at an elderly man who had been squatting beside the kitchen. Somewhat reluctantly the man got up, walked over to the hand-pump, and drew water into an earthenware bowl which he then brought over to the boy. Clearly the man's duties included the drawing and carrying of water. I was nonetheless surprised that this grey-beard should take orders from a boy wrapped in a threadbare shawl, so I asked Misri Lal Ram, who was still savouring his dal and chapattis, to shed light on the matter.

'Ah, this boy is son-of-the-house,' Misri explained between hurried mouthfuls, 'while that old man, he is only some poor relation.'

The son-of-the-house brought the water in metal bowls for us to wash our curry-stained fingers. He also totted up the bill and took a few rupees in payment. There was no doubting who was in command. When I tried to leave a tip after what had been the best roadside meal so far, he resolutely handed back the money.

I could have happily lingered on that charpoy, drinking more of the thickly sweet tea that I had come to appreciate and watching the soft winter sunlight filter through the shade trees. But we still had to reach Sasaram before nightfall. By now the golden rule of travelling in the subcontinent was engrained in my consciousness: no matter how smoothly things seem to be going, somehow your journey will always take you twice as

long as you expected. And, sure enough, we hadn't gone far
before we ran into a line of stationary trucks backed up half a
mile from a railway crossing.

Normally the queue at a rail crossing will clear as soon as the
train has gone past. But this time nothing was moving at all. So I
pulled out into the oncoming lane, with Misri Lal Ram tucked
in behind me, and together we moved slowly past the trucks to
the head of the queue. An assortment of buses and motor-
rickshaws had also attempted this manoeuvre, completely
blocking access to the level crossing on both sides of the track.
To add to the confusion, a team of railway workers were busily
re-laying the hard-core on which the sleepers rest and they had
got to the section right in the middle of the crossing.

There were uniformed policemen at the scene but they
simply looked on with folded arms, as though sorting out this
mess was no concern of theirs. Traffic control had devolved
upon a railway employee armed with a red flag in one hand and
a green one in the other; only he never seemed prepared to raise
the green flag, even when no train was expected. This, I soon
realised, was because he took his orders from a foreman wearing
a tucked-up dhoti below a smart orange shirt across which was
emblazoned the words *Eastern Railway*. And this man's priority
was to get his section of track completed in the short time
between trains. To this end he had arranged for a pile of
aggregate to be dumped in the middle of the crossing. True, he
was rushing around, ordering his work-gang to get on with the
job in between shouting back abuse at irate truck-drivers. But
although he had maybe thirty workers under him, they
appeared to be making no progress at all.

Eventually one lane was cleared of rubble, the flag-man raised
his green flag and the lead vehicle on both sides of the crossing
charged for the gap. They met nose-to-nose half-way across the
tracks and proceeded to blow their horns at each other,
gesticulating in a most threatening manner. But nobody would
give way, so now there was a logjam in the middle of the level
crossing. And within seconds this couldn't be cleared either,
because more buses and trucks had advanced behind the lead

vehicles so that they couldn't reverse out of the mess. In fact, every vehicle within a hundred yards had fired up its engine and crept forward. A hundred stationary exhaust pipes belched in unison, and on my bike I was getting the full benefit.

To get out of there required some off-road work, sliding down an embankment and then bouncing over the railway lines outside the level-crossing area. Unfortunately, a motor-rickshaw driver had the same idea and got there first. I was tucked in behind him, easing the bike over a sharply jutting metal track, when the flag-man started agitating his red flag. At first I thought he was just being officious and tried to ignore him. But when he kept pointing down the track I took a quick look and saw . . . Jesus-shit-fuck. There's a train coming.

I knew there was no going back. Squeezing between the motor-rickshaw and a crazily tilting truck, I bounced over two more metal lines and was through to the other side. Behind me there was utter confusion. Railway workers were suddenly galvanised into action, scooping their mound of rubble anywhere they could find provided it was off the tracks. Engines roared as buses and trucks inched past each other towards safety. I just hoped that Misri hadn't got the Ambassador stuck in the middle of that turmoil. No way could I see how all those vehicles could get off the crossing before the train arrived.

Yet thirty seconds later the crossing was cleared, with Misri driving off last of all. A rust-red goods train rumbled past. It seemed almost miraculous, this sudden victory of order over chaos. But then, I suppose, so much of the chaos in India is wilfully self-inflicted. If there is an urgent need to sort something out, then it will sort itself out. Attempts at imposing order from outside – whether it is Asoka's dharma laws, or the bureaucratic regulations left by the British – tend to be ignored most of the time so that everything slips back into a naturally chaotic state. Rules are there to be avoided, and when something needs to be done it will generally be achieved by methods quite different from those laid down in any rule-book.

I rode a mile down the road to get clear of the exhaust fumes. There, in the shade of a mango tree, I waited for the others to catch up. To my surprise they arrived within minutes and from there on we enjoyed a clear road for about 50 miles – most of the traffic still being stuck at the railway crossing – and I could relax and enjoy riding a motorcycle that was sweetly on song through the calm of rural India.

I should have known it was too good to last. About five miles short of the bridge over the River Son we ran into another line of stationary trucks. Misri Lal Ram got out of the Ambassador and asked a trucker what was going on.

'How far does he say it lasts?' I asked.

'From this place to the Son bridge he is saying no vehicles are moving.'

'And how far is that?'

'Nearly ten kilometres.'

Not for the first time, I looked at the sun going down in the west. There was only an hour or so before it grew dark and Sasaram was maybe another twenty kilometres beyond the bridge. This time there was no way for the Ambassador to weave through the traffic. It was already doubled up in both directions, four lines of trucks occupying a two-lane road.

'Why don't you go ahead and book into the guesthouse,' Sarah suggested. 'On the bike you should be able to get through.'

'What about you?'

'We'll just have to sit it out,' she said resignedly.

That was the beginning of the most serious madness I have ever committed when in charge of a motorcycle. Wedged in between the towering bulk of lorries it was impossible to see whether there was oncoming traffic or not. So I looked for the shadows of moving trucks on the tarmac and dodged out to overtake whenever there was a longish gap.

But to make any real progress I had to go off-road. The Bullet went up and down embankments, through an open sewer or two and around a variety of tree stumps. I narrowly avoided getting tangled up in a chicken coop before riding through the middle of a tyre-shop – much to the amusement of the repairmen who offered their services. I ran the gauntlet of snarling pariah dogs and had a head-on confrontation with an enormous brahminy bull which calmly stood its ground in the middle of a thousand horn-tooting lorries.

When I finally reached the Son Bridge the way ahead was clear. But as I set off across the longest road-bridge in the subcontinent the sun was already going down and on the sand-banks far below fishermen and dhobis were making their way homewards. When it is in full spate the Son is more than two miles wide, a muddy torrent which flows back against itself before it joins the Ganges. The snow-fed Ganges usually rises faster than the Son, and at their confluence the waters of the lesser river cannot escape until they rise to the same level as Mother Ganga. During the monsoon this causes widespread flooding. But now, in the middle of the dry season, the Son was reduced to a meandering trickle.

On the far side I stopped to look back at the sand-banks and lagoons of the river-bed catching the evening light. From here on, for the first time on this journey, I would be travelling up the Royal Road, the ancient trade route which is more than two thousand years older than the British-built Grand Trunk Road.

The old ferry-crossing of the Son was here, near the modern road-bridge. But thereafter the Royal Road curled left, following the south bank of the Ganges to Palatipura (the modern city of Patna) and onwards to northern Bengal. Even under the Mughals the main road went that way, describing a huge semicircle before descending towards the sea. But the British, with their capital at Calcutta and huge tracts of land up-country, needed a more direct line of communication. Their answer was to drive a new road through the Chota Nagpur plateau and southern Bihar. This reduced the distance from Calcutta to Chunnar – a strategic fortress to the west of Sasaram – by some 200 miles. And it is this more direct, southerly route that the GT Road follows today.

For the rest of my journey northwards the modern road would shadow the old route. And the town I was heading for that night, Sasaram, has a special place in the road's history. For it contains the mortal remains of Sher Shah Suri, the Afghan soldier-of-fortune who seized the imperial throne from the Mughals and, during his brief rule, did more to improve the Grand Trunk Road than anyone between Chandragupta Maurya and the coming of the British.

Sher Shah Suri ruled as emperor only from 1539 to 1545, but in that short space of time he laid down an efficient system of administration and revenue-collection which underpinned the later Mughal Empire for another two hundred years. His original power-base was in Bihar, which is why he chose to be buried here rather than – as with practically every other Muslim ruler of India – at the northern citadels of Delhi, Agra or Lahore.

Sher Shah understood the importance of rapid communications in holding his empire together. Even before he usurped the throne he had led his armies and up and down the axis of the Grand Trunk Road. Most of his decisive battles were fought and won within earshot of the main highway. So it was with military considerations uppermost that Sher Shah ordered the construction of a fast paved highway all the way from Bengal to the North-West Frontier.

Along its length he ordained that suitable shade trees – mango, neem, peepul – should be planted to offer the traveller relief from the scorching sun. And he had rest-stations built at regular intervals, with separate quarters for Muslims and Hindus. These caravanserai were maintained at the state's expense and admitted all travellers, for Sher Shah wished to foster trade within his dominions. Foodstuffs and drinking water were provided by servants of the serai – whose wages were also met by the state – with due regard for the different dietary and hygiene requirements of Hindus and Muslims. The Emperor also decreed there should be no tolls levied on the roads or the ferries, nor by any towns or villages along the way. Should any traveller die on the road, his goods were to be restored to his rightful heirs.

It was Sher Shah Suri – and not the Mughals – who was responsible for building the network of roads which drew such fulsome praise from later European travellers to the Mughal Court. He was a great stickler for efficiency; and I suspect that, were he living today, Sher Shah would not tolerate the enormous wastage caused by traffic jams and broken road surfaces – especially not in his native Bihar, where the modern GT Road is at its most chaotic.

Another of Sher Shah's innovations was to place milestones or kos minar along the royal highways. I could have done with a few more of these as I approached Sasaram, since I'd left my road-map with the others and had no idea how many miles I still had to cover.

I asked an elderly Muslim, hoping that he spoke Urdu as well as the local (and, to me, unintelligible) Bhojpuri or Magahi dialects.

'Three more kilometres,' he said most assuredly.

After three kilometres there was no town in sight. I tried again in a petrol station.

'Three kilometres.'

By now it was growing dark and I was worrying that the main road might bypass the town, in which case I would overshoot completely. Again I asked for directions.

'Straight on, three kilometres,' replied a bespectacled gentleman.

At this point I started wondering whether the number three had some special significance locally. Perhaps it was considered lucky. Or perhaps other numbers, such as five or nine, were ill-omened and should therefore never be uttered. I decided the best thing was to keep going until I saw the tell-tale signs of a district headquarters. And sure enough, after another fifteen kilometres I spotted the usual roadside advertisements for licensed tractor dealers and agro-industry distributors, which in rural India are the first indications of a locally important town. Bazaars began to spring up by the side of the road, and behind them I could see the outline of three- or four-storeyed houses against the fading light.

The GT Road runs straight as an arrow through the middle of Sasaram, though the only way of knowing when you have hit the centre of town is by the density of buses dropping off passengers. What finally convinced me I was in the heart of downtown were the lights blinking across the façade of a cinema hall. I pulled over and asked the way to the state-run tourist lodge.

A small crowd congregated and had to have a full debate before offering their considered opinion.

'Three more kilometres,' they chorused.

The Bihar State Tourism Lodge, when I found it, was a monsoon-stained block of concrete. Its entrance hall was cavernous and unattended. The sweeper had to go off to find the assistant manager.

Yes, he had rooms, but neither food nor drink was available. I was beginning to think that travellers fared better back in the days of Sher Shah.

It was too late to see the great man's mausoleum, so I rode back into Sasaram, located the only 'wine shop' in town and loaded up the Enfield's side panniers. There was just one brand of beer available, an evil-looking brew called 'Turbo' that turned out to have few merits other than being highly alcoholic, and I decided that 'Royal Mughal' whisky would be more appropriate.

Sarah and Tyrel had only just arrived when I returned. The entrance hall was now full of travelling businessmen who had also been caught in the snarl-up by the Son. Two of them were busy ordering their driver to pick up a bottle of whisky in town.

'Make sure it's premium quality only, accha?' commanded the more rotund of the two, before turning to us. 'It appears we must all be staying in Sasaram this night. There are no restaurants, only a not-so-bad dhaba that is nearby. We very much look forward to you joining us for dinner.'

Misri also favoured the idea of going to the dhaba, where he would be able to chat to other drivers. 'It is very close by,' he informed us. But the drive there was through complete darkness. The area was subject to a power cut, or 'load-shedding' as it is known across the subcontinent.

In the middle of this blackness we found an isolated pool of light and pulled off the road. This, apparently, was the sought-after dhaba. It had a diesel generator whose metallic staccato was regularly drowned by the roar of trucks as another convoy headed out into the night just a few feet behind us, crashing through their gears.

Within the pool of light there were a number of private cars, Marutis and Ambassadors mostly, their drivers keeping a watchful eye on them, sipping chai on the front steps while the passengers ate inside. Evidently this was an up-market dhaba. We climbed the steps past cauldrons containing the usual rice, dal and vegetable curry, only to find the front table occupied by the two whisky-hunting businessmen from our hotel. 'Good sirs, madam,' roared the stouter of the pair, 'please be seated with us.'

They introduced themselves as K. L. Khurana and Sri Pal Jain. Mr Khurana ran his own ammonia business and he and his companion had been around Dhanbad 'on tour'. They had been heading back to Delhi, hoping to reach Varanasi that night, before they had got caught up in the traffic around the Son Bridge.

'Our driver was not agreeing to proceeding onwards,' Mr Khurana said, 'on account of the danger of dacoits. This GT Road is most dangerous in Bihar State where they are having too much lawlessness. Only twenty kilometres from here, Banaras-side, these dacoit fellows have been stopping goods carriers and private vehicles equally. They are placing barrier across road. Then they are grabbing everything, all cash and valuables, from the passengers. That is why our driver says we must stop here in Sasaram.'

I told them I'd also been worried about dacoits. 'In this bloody Bihar,' growled Khurana, 'the wise man is not venturing forth during nights.'

A bottle of Royal Challenge Premium was produced out of

thin air and our chai glasses filled to overbrimming by Mr Jain, a gaunt individual with a high-pitched laugh and thinning white hair. He was wearing dark glasses even though it was pitch black outside. They both wore Western-style sports shirts and trousers and had put on sweaters of some unidentifiable synthetic weave as protection against the unusual cold.

Our talk turned to road conditions in Bihar. Mr Khurana was at once outraged and fatalistic. 'The road is bad because so much traffic is coming and space is limited. You cannot help it.' A certain fatalism tinged his pronouncements.

'Life in Bihar is particularly the worst,' he declared, expanding on his theme. 'Bihar and also UP,' he added as an afterthought.

At which his companion chipped in: 'Number One Bihar, second number UP,' and started laughing until he nearly choked.

But Khurana ploughed on regardless. 'My feeling is this. In Delhi and Haryana . . .'

'Ah yesss,' Mr Jain exhaled approvingly, 'Haryana Number One.' Obviously he liked ranking all things in life by number.

'. . . you will find lot of facilities, lot of comfort,' continued Mr Khurana. 'Here you can't have even one single comfort.'

I asked whether this sad state of affairs in Bihar was because of lack of development or local politicians, whose corruption is notorious even in India, creaming off funds made available for new projects. Another convoy of trucks passed by, the vibrations making the table wobble.

'Politicians,' muttered Mr Jain, the single word expelled with disgust.

'That indeed is the main reason,' Mr Khurana agreed. 'You have correctly calculated,' he added and then muttered a few words in Hindi to his companion. By now Mr Jain was falling around laughing.

'In Haryana it is much better,' Khurana continued. 'Delhi is also improved well because there is an opposition BJP government and elections are coming up. That is why they are doing a good job.'

'But is that because they are buying votes, maximising their vote bank?'

My question made even Mr Khurana, who in this double act obviously preferred playing the straight man, to break into laughter. 'How are you knowing these things?' he roared. Mr Jain, meanwhile, was laughing so hard he had to wipe up the tears escaping under his sunglasses.

'I am Indian-born man,' I replied, lapsing into the local idiom.

'Fact is there,' Khurana spluttered, recovering his composure. 'Bihar is the richest in minerals, yet no good industry has come so far. All this coal,' he motioned towards the heavily laden trucks on the GT Road, 'is going to Punjab and Haryana. There they are doing very well with new industry. But here in Bihar people are starving for just 100 or 200 rupees a week. In Delhi they are earning 200 rupees per day for just pulling rickshaw.'

'Do you think things will improve here in future?'

'I don't think so. Unless their leaders are all right. If the politicians are making money in crores of rupees, how can you change it?'

Our food arrived and everyone fell silent for a while. Then, as he was wiping up his plate with a fragment of chapatti, I asked Mr Khurana whether his family had always lived in Delhi.

'My family came from West Punjab, which is now Pakistan-side,' he began. I took a renewed interest in this round-faced and slightly drunk businessman. Up to now, nearly all the former refugees I had met had come from East Bengal. The family Khurana had come the other way, from West Punjab, where the impact of Partition had been far more traumatic. Moreover, judging by his age, Mr K. L. Khurana would be able to remember those events. On the other hand, I didn't want to force him to rake over what might well be painful memories. I hesitated, not knowing quite how to ask.

I needn't have worried. Mr Khurana launched into his story without any prompting. 'We were then living in Gujranwala town, near Lahore,' he began. 'In 1947 I lost my parents while coming by train towards Lahore. I was between eight and nine years old. The Pakistan people, they have stopped our train and they cutted so many of the passengers. My father I have lost. My uncle, who before had his job in ICI factory working in soda ash plant, he has got a bullet while he was putting in dead bodies. All night the Pakistan people search everything on the train, taking away everything. Then they started the cutting. This thing I cannot forget.'

Previously I had only known of what happened on these refugee trains third-hand, from histories of Partition based on official reports. Even so they make harrowing reading. Mr Khurana was a survivor of one of those massacres; and it appeared his memory was undimmed by the passing of nearly fifty years, though some of the detail was no doubt hearsay.

'Out of five thousand people on the train,' he affirmed, 'all young ladies they have taken away. My father, I don't know where he was. My uncle, one son and one daughter, all were untraceable. Otherwise, out of five thousand people they have saved only two thousand.

'After this we have gone back to Gujranwala town because our grandfather was residing there. Our guru was also there – that is why we went back. Pakistan people, they have put one bomb where all our people were residing. Our guru helps us to come to India. We are really thankful to him.'

Reliving these memories brought tears to Mr Khurana's eyes. 'This life is terrible. I cannot forget that time. I lost my parents and started service at 20 rupees per month only.' He was weeping openly. 'Life is like this,' he said. 'I can't help it.'

After a pause he began again, on how his shattered family began picking up the pieces after they had escaped to India. 'My grandfather, he used to go to Amritsar and stay since morning to evening to get back his family. From my uncle's children, one son came after two months, one came after six months. This second one is now residing in USA.

'After Partition I stayed in Ludhiana in Punjab, which is one of Asia's main cities. I was unmarried. After that I went to Bangalore, then again I started in Varanasi. Finally I settled in 1964 in Delhi.'

Mr Jain thought this the right moment to top up all our glasses. 'Cheers,' we all chorused, though nobody was feeling that cheerful. The generator tapped out its rhythm remorselessly. A prolonged coughing fit persuaded Mr Jain to lean over towards the balcony, where he discreetly vomited before clearing his nasal passages in the time-honoured way, rejoining the conversation as if nothing had happened.

'Nowadays I am all right,' Mr Khurana declared. 'My grandfather, he died at the age of about one hundred and four years. I cannot forget my grandfather; he used to prepare my khana, give me my food, and he has helped me like anything. Whenever I remember grandfather's name, I always weep. He was such a thorough gentleman, I can't help it.'

Mr Khurana lapsed into tearful silence. His companion tried to comfort him but seemed equally affected by this story. 'I know, I know,' he said quietly, staring straight ahead through his dark glasses.

Their meal finished, they got up to go. A small boy brought them a roughly scrawled chit which I noticed was far too long for their food alone. They were trying to pay for us as well. I protested vociferously. They insisted. 'It is all cared for, all cared for.'

Outside, in the dark, there was much shaking of hands. 'Who knows how it is that we have come together here in Sasaram?' Mr Khurana speculated. To which I had no ready answer.

The tomb of Sher Shah Suri rises majestically from the middle of an artificial lake. In the early morning stillness this ponderous mass of rough-trimmed Chunnar sandstone glowed reddish-gold and seemed to float effortlessly over the surrounding water. There wasn't a breath of wind when we arrived and the still surface of the tank reproduced a perfect mirror image of the central dome and surrounding pavilions. It was hard to tell which was the more substantial, the golden stones or their unmoving reflections – until a light breeze stirred the lake and the inverted image began to dance upon the face of its waters.

I was so overawed by this vision that I left the keys to the bike in the ignition, something I had never done before. Tyrel was moved to get out his paints and brushes. Sarah was pacing around the edge of this perfectly symmetrical, man-made lake, trying to photograph the island-tomb from every possible angle.

Originally Sher Shah's tomb was a true island: the only means of access was by taking a barge from the ghat on the eastern edge of the tank. Then somebody, probably Sher Shah's son Salim, ordered a causeway to be built and a gatehouse to guard this new entrance. These later additions may spoil the symmetry of the overall design, but the causeway was lined with red canna lilies and the shallow waters beside it were clogged with flowering lotuses, offering a bright contrast to the stern architecture of the tomb itself.

There was a sober dignity to this monument which reminded me more of the great mosques of Constantinople than of Mughal architecture. Its architect, the master-builder Aliwal Khan, succeeded in combining a sense of massive strength – symbolising the hoped-for permanence of the Sur dynasty – with an airy lightness. This was achieved by raising the tomb's octagonal walls through three diminishing elevations before they almost merge into the base of the dome. The more decorative elements – the pavilions at each corner of the courtyard, the shaktis or kiosks on both storeys of the tomb chamber, the lotus-shaped finial above the dome – somehow remove all impression of weight from the central mass of masonry. That is the magic which allows Sher Shah's mausoleum to float like a rough-cut jewel in its glassy setting.

This combination of strength and lightness of touch reflect the character of the man himself. He was born plain Farid-ud-Din Sur (the title Sher Khan, 'tiger lord', was granted him after he had killed an enormous tiger with a single stroke of his sword). The son of an Afghan nobleman holding lands in Bihar, he studied both Arabic and Persian and was well-read in religion and philosophy. But he took special delight in the writings of poets and historians, particularly histories of the empires of Hindustan, from which he culled ideas on how to rule effectively.

Disinherited by his father, he served half a dozen warlords, changing sides as it suited his interests, sometimes on the eve of battle. In this he was no different from the multitude of amirs, begs and military adventurers of Afghan descent who were busily carving out private fiefdoms for themselves as the power of the Lodhi sultans in Delhi waned. This internecine warfare allowed a new power to arise in Hindustan; for when the Mughals first arrived from Central Asia they met little resistance.

As an Afghan of the tribe of Sur, Sher Khan resented the intrusion of Mughal 'foreigners'. The Afghans had been in India for more than two hundred years, after all. They were *de facto* rulers of huge swathes of territory, especially in provinces such as Bihar and Bengal, which were far removed from imperial authority in Delhi. Why should they accept the alien Mughals as overlords?

But there was not much Sher Khan could do until he had built up his own power base in eastern India. For a time he even accepted service with the first Mughal emperor, Babur, on an expedition against the Rajputs, which allowed him to observe at first hand the newcomers' military tactics and methods of ruling their domains. This convinced him that the Mughals were no better than the Afghans in either single combat or pitched battles. Only Afghan disunity allowed the foreigner to prevail.

After Babur's death, Sher Khan succeeded in rallying the fractious Afghan warlords to his banner. He chased the new Mughal ruler, Humayun, out of India and in 1539 was himself proclaimed emperor, taking the title Sher Shah Suri. He ruled for less than six years; but in that time he cracked down on corruption at all levels and created a framework of government and revenue collection that was to outlast him by 200 years.

Sher Shah died while besieging a fortress in Rajputana. A rocket stuffed with gunpowder rebounded off the fortress wall and fell into an ammunition dump, causing an immense explosion in which the emperor and his retinue were all terribly burned. Had he not died prematurely, the history of modern India might have been very different. Even so, he had done enough to secure the imperial succession, and his son Islam Shah ruled with a rod of iron for eight more years. But on his death in 1553 the Afghans reverted to their feuding ways, allowing the banished Humayun to return to Hindustan and re-establish the Mughal Empire.

It is for his reforms of public administration and for his road-building, rather than his military exploits, that Sher Shah has been dubbed 'the greatest Afghan in history'. But he would never have got anywhere had he not been, first and foremost, a brilliant strategist and commander of men. The twists and turns of his rise to power make the opportunism of his near-contemporary Machiavelli seem like child's play. Sher Shah switched allegiance countless times; but he made sure he always came out on the winning side.

I crossed the causeway over the waters and approached the great man's tomb. Tyrel was busy with his painting, surrounded by a crowd of curious onlookers, including Sarah. Otherwise the place was deserted. Sher Shah's mausoleum must be the least-visited of all the great Muslim monuments in India.

As I clambered over its empty pavilions I could hear the familiar sound of trucks on the Grand Trunk Road. When it was built the mausoleum would have been visible from the road; and back then its great dome was painted a brilliant white and its lotus-shaped finial was of burnished gold. It is believed that Sher Shah deliberately situated his tomb near the road so that travellers would spread accounts of its splendour from one end of his empire to the other. If so, then he understood the value of propaganda.

At the eastern entrance to the tomb chamber I found an inscription from the days of the British raj. 'This Tomb,' it declared, 'built for himself by Sultan FARID-UD-DIN SHER SHAH, Emperor of India, Wherein he was buried, Anno Domini 1545, Was repaired by the British Government during the Viceroyalty of GEORGE FREDERICK SAMUEL ROBINSON, Marquis of Ripon, under the governorship of the honorable AUGUST RIVERS THOMPSON, Lieut. Governor of Bengal, Anno Domini 1882.'

When this plaque was erected most Englishmen believed their Indian empire would last a thousand years. Sher Shah would probably have been more realistic about the survival of his own dynasty. The monument is his most overt claim on posterity; yet it is for the more mundane achievements of his reign, such as his system of government and revenue collection, that he is best remembered. Even the British adapted the framework he had laid down as the basis for governing their Indian dominions. And then there is the Road. Again, the British built on the achievements of this Afghan usurper, and for much the same reasons: to enable troops to move rapidly through the territories they controlled and to encourage trade. No wonder the British had a sneaking admiration for Sher Shah and felt moved to undertake the restoration of the mausoleum.

The Emperor was a prodigious builder and left other great monuments – the Purana Qila in Delhi and the even larger fortress at Rohtas in Pakistan. Their strategic importance long since gone, they stand empty and forlorn. The Grand Trunk Road is a more enduring legacy: a living thing that still binds together the different provinces of the north Indian plain. Since Independence, the new highway between Agra and Delhi, which now carries all the heavy traffic, has been renamed Sher Shah Suri Marg in recognition of his road-building exploits – an honour that the wily old Afghan would have appreciated.

By now I was accustomed to the rhythm of traffic along the Bihar section of the GT Road. I knew that after ten miles of freewheeling I'd get caught up in a convoy of heavy vehicles. It was like an unchangeable law of nature. There was no point in getting angry or depressed about it. So I was resigned to my fate when, about five kilometres short of the state border, I joined the end of another unnecessary traffic jam.

This time the tail-back was mainly trucks waiting to have their papers inspected. They had all switched off their engines so I knew they'd be there for hours. Without even waiting for the thumbs-up from Misri, I pulled out into the overtaking lane and cruised past the line of trucks. There was almost no oncoming traffic, a sure sign that there was an equally intractable log jam on the other side of the border.

Through the middle of this chaos, peacock feathers in hand and naked as the day they were born, strode two Digambara monks. They appeared not to notice the exhaust fumes or the foul-mouthed truckers, the venal officials and bad-tempered bus passengers. They kept going at an even gait, looking neither left nor right, intent only on reaching the Jain holy places in Bihar.

Everyone else was getting cross. The reason for the hold-up became apparent at the Bihar border post. I could see only two uniformed officials and a handful of octroi men on duty. They were taking their time going through each truck driver's papers and collecting their dues. I was quite prepared to bribe my way out of a long wait at the border – that is the effect Bihar has on you, even if you are only passing through.

It is as though some invisible corrosive agent has been at work. The natural instinct to stick to your guns, to refuse to give in to the wheedling and intimidation, is gradually undermined; until the only thing worth arguing about is how often it's necessary to slip a bribe and how much you have to pay. I saw the same look of resignation on the faces of out-of-state truck drivers as they waited to have their final dealings with Bihar's officialdom.

Surely, I thought, things won't be so bad on the UP side of the border.

6

UP (i):
THE VARANASI SYNDROME

In crossing over into UP we were entering the Hindu heartlands. For UP – Uttar Pradesh or the 'Northern Province', formerly the United Provinces – is the cradle of Hinduism. It contains within its broad sleeve both the source and all the upper reaches of Mother Ganga, the holiest of India's holy rivers. Ayodhya is commonly regarded as the birthplace of Lord Ram; Mathura, on the banks of the Jamuna, of Lord Krishna. And just up the road from this dismal border post was the ultimate pilgrim city.

Call it what you will – Varanasi is the official Sanskrit version, though many locals call it Banaras or even, reverting to English usage, Benares – there is no other city which has been the focus of so much continuous devotion for so long. To the millions of Hindu pilgrims who come every year to bathe in its sacred waters, it is Kashi, the City of Light.

Another hour, I reckoned. The road surface immediately improved on the UP side of the border. Traffic was light. I might even stop at Moghulserai, whose name suggested that at one time it was an important stopping place on the Grand Trunk Road. Perhaps it still contained remains of the caravanserai established by the Mughals at this point. I imagined a ruined brick courtyard with pointed Islamic arches standing amidst fields of flowering mustard.

The reality was somewhat different. Moghulserai, as I rapidly discovered, is still an important transportation hub. It has one of India's busiest railway junctions. But, far worse than that, the area just to the west of town has become the Mother and Father of all truck stops. It continues for mile after mile, a vast swamp littered with abandoned vehicles. The entire strip is lined with repair shops and tyre-fixers and freight forwarders, so truck drivers unable to park near their preferred agent simply abandon their vehicles in the middle of the GT Road.

Having survived Bihar I thought I was up to the worst that the GT Road could throw at me, but Moghulserai was in a league of its own. Sarah and Tyrel in the Ambasssador were completely becalmed, so we decided I should thread my way through and ride on to Varanasi alone, to find a hotel. I did my best, going off-road and slipping between immobilised lines of trucks. At least twice I thought my leg was about to be crushed as, unable to move, I watched a truck remorselessly advance, its offside tyre eventually clearing my boot by less than an inch. It was like watching video recordings of accidents in slow motion – except this was live action and nobody out there knew how to push the stop button.

Even on the bike it took nearly two hours to clear Moghulserai. The traffic remained solid all the way to Dufferin Bridge. Then the road was suddenly clear and I was riding high between massive steel girders, the sacred river Ganges far below. On the far bank I could make out the broad sweep of the bathing ghats and riverside palaces and above them the dome and minarets of Alamagir's mosque. I slowed right down, keeping one eye on the road while catching glimpses of this holy city bathed in golden light.

An ominous rumble came from below and the whole bridge started vibrating. It was a train passing on the rail bridge immediately below; for the Dufferin is a true double-decker, designed to carry both road and rail traffic. Its heavily riveted girders kept blocking the view and I searched around for somewhere to pull over. But the road level is barely two lanes wide, and the honk from a bus which had crept up kept me moving.

The Grand Trunk Road describes a long curve around Varanasi, and together with the main Calcutta–Delhi railway forms a boundary between the old city with its narrow streets and the more spacious cantonment area. I'd been to Varanasi before and knew how difficult it was for vehicles to negotiate the labyrinthine alleyways of the old city, so we'd decided on the Hotel de Paris, a fading colonial pile just off The Mall, in the very heart of the cantonment.

It was like entering another world. I booked two rooms, showered, ordered some pakoras and beer. When the beer arrived it was cold – the first really cold one since Calcutta. I sat out on the lawns to await the others' arrival.

It was nearly dark before the familiar white Ambassador rolled up the drive. Misri looked more exhausted than I'd ever seen him. As for the passengers, their faces were blackened by diesel fumes and they appeared to be trembling. Sarah was reduced to disjointed expletives. 'Christ,' she moaned. 'Moghulserai,' she spat. 'Drink,' she implored.

The next day was declared by general consent a day of rest. It was also a parting of the ways. For this was as far as Misri Lal Ram was coming with us. Sarah and Tyrel, who had been in the car with him, were particularly sad to see him go. But he'd been contracted to drive as far as Varanasi and no further. So he turned the Ambassador round and headed back to Calcutta. I didn't envy him the run back through Bihar – not one single mile of it.

The bike was due its first service. In theory, so far I had been just 'running it in'. I dug out the Enfield owner's manual and read with dismay how I should have been treating the machine. Avoid driving the motorcycle at constant low speeds, it said. Avoid long journeys. Stop the vehicle for five or ten minutes after every hour of run to allow the engine to cool down before restarting. Maximum recommended speed during the running-in period . . . 50 kilometres per hour.

I called the local Enfield dealers, Khurana Automobiles, and was put through to Mr Khurana himself. 'I will send someone to collect you, immediately,' he declared, and half an hour later a Bullet 350 with two mechanics on board turned up at the hotel.

I began to kick-start my own vehicle, but the second mechanic intervened. 'Please permit me,' he said, taking control. Apparrently I was to be chauffeur-driven.

I soon realised the wisdom of this. The route cut through half a dozen different bazaars. Even with a map I would never have found my own way. My chauffeur turned down narrow lanes and sliced through the traffic with habitual ease. There was only one hairy moment, when we clashed wheels with a bicycle-rickshaw. The next thing I knew we pulled up in front of a workshop-cum-showroom. Mr Khurana was standing at the entrance, a garland of marigolds in his hands.

The welcoming ceremony completed, we retired to his office. Mr Khurana's pallid, clean-shaven face fell in loose folds from which there sprouted clusters of wart-like growths. Yet, despite this unfortunate skin disease, he had a commanding presence. His son, sleek, chubby, mustachioed and obviously pampered, scurried around ordering tea and biscuits. A friend, who turned out to be the editor of *Gandiva*, a Hindi-language daily, referred to Mr Khurana as 'being like an uncle to me'. It didn't take long for the conversation to turn to politics.

Although he declared he was not himself a politician, Mr Khurana did most of the talking. He held strong views, most of them influenced by Hindutva or BJP propaganda. Nothing unusual about this in UP, which has long been a stronghold of militant Hindu nationalism. I had expected to fall into this kind of conversation sooner or later. I just hadn't anticipated diving into the deep end quite so soon.

'You will be going to Ayodhya, Mr Gregson?'

I wasn't sure if this was a polite enquiry or a command.

'I think so, Mr Khurana. It's not on the GT Road, of course. But it's played such an important part in Hindu–Muslim relations—'

'Good, good,' Khurana interrupted. 'I am myself a devotee of Lord Ram, whose birthplace this is. And you must be knowing that this place, Ayodhya, was a temple or public place for thousands of years. Then the Muslims came and took possession. This first Mughal emperor, Babur, who made this Babri mosque . . . Mr Gregson: it was a political act. Only the exterior was made to look like a mosque. The interior was still like a temple. And by the grace of Lord Ram, Hindus continued to worship there from the outside, even if they could not go inside. It was always a place where Hindus worshipped.'

'But some reputable authorities say that—'

Mr Khurana held up his hand. 'Mr Gregson, under the Britishers it was not used as a mosque. There was no interference in religious practices, either Hindu or Muslim. Then, after Independence, Hindus wished to reclaim it to build a temple to Lord Ram. It was not being used as a mosque. But the Congress government in Delhi prevented them. "It is in the hands of the courts," they say. And for forty years this Ayodhya case is always in the hands of the courts. Then, by the grace of Lord Ram, in December of 1992, devotees of Ram demolished the mosque. It was not the BJP, though their politicians took credit for it, seeking to profit from it afterwards. All this you must have witnessed on TV.'

'I was in South India at the time. The coverage on Doordashan [India's state-run television] was restricted, they say, though all the newspapers were full of it.'

'Pay no attention to what they were saying. In this country, so much of the media is just toeing the official line. They are saying that India is a secular state and no person must do anything that is against this secularism. But India is not secular as in the West. In India to be secular means this – you must always be giving priorities to the minority populations and most especially to Muslims.

'Come back to Ayodhya, to the facts of the case. In 1992 devotees of Lord Ram demolish the mosque. But then the Congressmen in Delhi send in the army. Now again it is in the hands of the courts. Who knows how long this will continue? Some people are saying that in future it should be half-mosque, half-temple, the two buildings side by side. But this is no solution, Mr Gregson. There should be one temple only, and this temple must be to Lord Ram.'

I doubted that any arguments I came up with could shake Mr

Khurana's convictions. From his viewpoint, there was only one solution. So I asked him about the local situation in Varanasi, where a similar dispute over Aurangzeb's mosque threatened to spark off communal fighting. I knew the Vishwa Hindu Parishad and other militant Hindu organisations had placed it on their 'hit list'. But Varanasi has a large Muslim population who wouldn't accept an Ayodhya-style assault on their mosque without retaliating. The idea of full-scale communal violence in the old city, where Hindu and Muslim mohallas or wards crowd up against each other, was unthinkable. Maybe Mr Khurana would be more sensitive to the dangers when they were that much closer to home.

'There is still a problem,' he declared, 'with the mosque in Banaras. As you must be knowing, it was built on top of a holy temple. This is because the Mughals wanted to dominate, to force their religion on other people, to take their women even. Why should Hindus accept this?

'It was different when the Britishers were rulers. The Britishers built their churches apart. They did not build on top of temples or mosques. Their policy was non-interference in religious affairs. Not so the Muslims. Today there is only a problem with the mosque in Banaras because in history the Muslims have always sought to dominate the Hindus. But history has changed.'

Mr Khurana had a rather different conception of history from my own. In his version, figures from recent history were equated with the heroes of the ancient Hindu epics. Thus, Indira Gandhi was 'a heroic figure' because she intervened in the 1971 Bangladesh War. 'India gave freedom to this country,' Khurana told me, 'and then left it entirely. Never in history is there such an example. It is like in the *Ramayana*, when Lord Ram goes across the sea to Lanka and frees the people from the tyranny of Ravana. He is all-victorious, but he chooses to leave the Lankan people free. This same thing India has done for Bangladesh. I tell you, Mr Gregson, Hindu history has a very special spiritual significance.'

It frightened me, this jumbling up of religion and myth and

historical events, far more than ordinary political rhetoric. For I knew Mr Khurana wasn't just making it up as he went along. For him this was textbook history. Only, the textbooks propagated a version of history unlike anything I had encountered before.

They are written mainly in Hindi and the regional languages such as Marathi and Gujarati, and are probably far more influential than those of the more objective, 'secular' or 'Westernised' Indian historians, who very often publish in the English language. I recognised that this 'Hindu history' was a potent mixture. It helped explain and sanction recent, often complicated events, in terms of epic stories familiar to practically all Indians, regardless of caste or whether or not they were literate. It borrowed from the old myths that simplest but most effective of storylines – the victory of Good over Evil.

It was a glorification of the Hindu present through reference to a mythical Hindu past. In the wrong hands, it could be used to justify just about any course of action. And it worried me that otherwise sensible, middle-class businessmen like Mr Khurana could trot out this stuff as indisputable fact.

'Aren't you at all concerned,' I asked him, 'about there being more communal violence in future?'

'I am not so much concerned with the internal situation,' he said, rubbing his chin, 'as with the external danger. And by this I do not only mean Pakistan – though most assuredly Pakistan will seize any opportunity to do us down. No, I refer to the International Muslim Conspiracy – people from the Middle East with their petro-dollars. These are the ones who are stirring up trouble inside India. Look at those terrible bombings in Bombay [which took place shortly after the Babri mosque was destroyed]. The police have the proof it was all organised and funded by Muslims from outside.'

'But what about here, in Varanasi?'

'Oh, here we had some communal problems in 1947,' he said airily, 'as elsewhere in India. But only rarely since then are there communal tensions in the old city. You see, so many Muslim people left to go and live in Pakistan. But I tell you, they have a very clever idea: whenever one or two Muslims go to Pakistan, they leave four or five others to look after their property in India. That is the reason why, even after Partition, there were nine crores [90 million] in Pakistan, leaving nine crores also in India. Now, only in India, they are 15 crores out of a total of 85 crores. And why is this? Because, I tell you, they do not exercise self-restraint.'

The practical implications of such beliefs were spelt out in the press day after day. The Vishwa Hindu Parishad had drawn up a forty-point agenda, including the banning of cow slaughter, the exemption of Hindu religious activities from income tax, a total ban on religious conversion and the stopping of any foreign funding for such purposes. The Hindutva coalition also wanted a BJP government to scrap the Places of Worship Act (the mainstay of defence for mosques and other minority religions), as well as Article 370 of the Constitution, which gives Jammu & Kashmir a special status within the Union. It demanded the eviction of all those who had 'infiltrated' India since 1970 (thereby including all refugees from the Bangladesh War). And, of course, it required that the derelict site in Ayodhya where the Babri Mosque had been demolished be handed over to the Ram Janam Bhoomi Nyas so that they could build a temple.

The BJP accepted 39 of these 40 points. Only on the question as to whether to include in its election manifesto a Hindu takeover of the disputed sites at Ayodhya, Mathura and Kashi (Varanasi) did the party bosses prefer to 'defer' a decision for the time being. They knew what an explosive issue that could be. Nobody wanted to encourage the more extreme elements into starting another bout of communal violence – not before an election in which the Party might wrest power by legitimate and peaceful means. For now, the Party's respectability must be stressed to win over the floating voter. As for the diehards, they'd vote BJP or Shiv Sena anyway. They could be appeased afterwards.

I decided to find out what local Muslims thought about this, in particular about the inclusion of one of their mosques on the official hit list. What better place to start than Aurangzeb's mosque itself?

Somewhat naively I thought I could just walk in, as into any other of the thousands of mosques in India, provided I first removed my shoes. But then I hadn't yet been to one of these 'disputed sites'.

Mr Banerjee, the assistant hotel manager, was clearly alarmed when I asked how best to get there. 'This Gyanwapi Mosque is a restricted area,' he explained. 'Nobody, or only a few Muslims, is permitted to go in. Security is tight and personal safety cannot be guaranteed.'

Eventually I found a young Muslim named Choudhary who agreed to take us to the disputed mosque. As for getting inside, there was only 'a one-in-ten chance', though he would do his best.

The approach is through the densely populated old city, along narrow streets and galis which twist back on themselves so deceptively that, without a guide, it is only a matter of time before one is completely lost. Choudhary kept up a brisk pace, worried that we might be stopped at any moment.

It was around the Visvanath Temple, where tourist touts tried selling unofficial tickets to view the temple's golden roof from adjacent buildings, that I first noticed the security presence. They weren't ordinary City Police, either. Choudhary said they were PAC (Provincial Armed Constabulary) men drafted in to guard the mosque. Some of them had rifles slung over their shoulders, others were running spot-checks on passers-by with a rather antiquated metal-detector. To proceed further, they said, we had to be frisked. But half-way through the operation they gave up and just waved us on.

The narrow street ran between a number of enclosed temples dedicated to Siva, to the elephant-headed Ganesh and to Hanuman, the monkey-faced god. Between their high walls, perched on ledges and small alcoves, were stalls selling garlands and offerings and sticky sweets. These makeshift shops looked precarious; but they'd probably been held by the same family for generations. Pilgrims shuffled to and fro going about their devotions. The atmosphere was claustrophobic and seemed to me one hundred per cent Hindu. Then the lane broadened out into what appeared to be an open temple courtyard.

'We have arrived,' Choudhary announced. I looked about me. Where was the mosque? All I could see was a covered area, like part of a temple precinct, and behind this a wall of corrugated iron and scaffolding.

'The mosque is beyond the perimeter fence,' Choudhary explained. 'This part is for Hindus to worship. You see this well?' He pointed to a hole protected by a stone screen and canopy. 'The Hindus say that their priests threw the temple jewels and records in the well, being fearful of Muslim soldiers. Also Siva's lingam, you know what this is? Now it is become a sacred well. And this is the nandi bull, always present in Saivite temples.'

I looked at the plump, red-painted figure of a recumbent brahminy bull. Its nose and forehead were heavily garlanded; its rounded back draped with embroidered cloth. A stylised hump stuck out from its spherical torso like the nose section of a Polaris missile. The bull stared out from beneath its shelter at a row of white-painted steel bars that looked as though they were surplus prison stock. It was not a peaceful image.

'You see that the nandi bull is facing towards the mosque,' said Choudhary. 'In Saivite temples the nandi is always facing the lingam. In this way the Hindus are saying that where the mosque is there should be a lingam, and around it a temple.'

We walked around the perimeter fence to get a better view of the mosque. From the front it looked unexceptional and uncared for, its white domes discoloured by the rains. It was completely surrounded by metal fencing topped with overhanging barbed-wire. A troop of monkeys dropped from a nearby tree and went scuttling along this barbed-wire highway. It didn't trouble them. They shrieked and chattered and bared their teeth at each other; for this no-man's-land was theirs and theirs alone. Any human trying to get over that fence was liable to be shot at from the watchtower opposite or from the steel-clad sentry boxes built into the wall itself. They were manned by army personnel, some Sikhs among them.

'Come,' Choudhary beckoned. 'You must see the backside also.'

This was easier said than done. To get round to the back wall of the mosque we had to file through a sort of cattle pen that the security forces had built to facilitate crowd control. We had to do this one at a time, before being frisked and told not to take photographs.

The reason for all this soon became apparent. For the back of the Gyanwapi mosque, with its ornately carved corbels and pillars, is clearly a pre-Islamic structure, part of a sizeable temple which once stood at least as high as the mosque's prayer-hall, whose back wall it now supports. Here was the classic image – so abhorrent to hard-line Hindus – of the mosque literally sitting upon a temple. The two styles of architecture, so distinct from each other, are here fused together in an obscene embrace. At least that's how some people might see it.

Another way of looking at it would be to say that the Muslims who built this only made use of materials at hand, as have followers of most other religions including Hindus, who, in a more distant past, made disused Buddhist shrines their own. The Gyanwapi Mosque has stood here for more than three hundred years and continues to serve the large Muslim community in Varanasi. Why then should this place of worship become such a source of conflict that it needs to be turned into something resembling a concentration camp with the army called in to defend it?

The answer, as usual, is politics. Or rather, the politicisation of religion. There is probably room to build another temple in the open space where the steel pens now stand. But that is not the point. Those who subscribe to the Hindutva story want the mosque pulled down. They want to avenge what they see as humiliating for Hindus. They want to rewrite history, to show the world who's really boss in this New India. And they're not going to let the fact that there are 120 million Muslims in India – more than in Pakistan or Egypt or any country apart from

Indonesia – stand in their way. The real issue has little to do with the local communities or the practicalities of worship. It has to do with the cynical exploitation of communal feeling for political gain. If it's not Ayodhya then it's Varanasi that becomes the flashpoint; and if it's not Varanasi, then it will be somewhere else.

We moved around the perimeter to the mosque's entrance. It was heavily guarded. The PAC men at the gate had machine pistols. Entry was forbidden to non-Muslims, we were informed. Choudhary tried talking his way in, without success, so I asked to speak to their superior officer. After some discussion they agreed and I was escorted into an adjacent building and up many flights of stairs.

I was shown into the office of Ashok Kumar, Deputy Superintendent of the UP Police and, as his name suggests, a Hindu. He had a curt, military manner; and though he listened patiently enough to my request – that we were invited by a Muslim to meet members of the Gyanwapi Mosque management committee – he never even looked like giving in. He was responsible for security, he said, and it was not up to the mosque management committee to decide who comes and goes. He was only carrying out his duty.

'It is such a shame that you cannot meet our imam,' Choudhary said. 'But, you know, these days even the imam is not permitted to live there and can only come at the hour of prayer.' Instead, he suggested we visited another mosque, where he himself went to worship. The head of this mosque, the maulana, knew him well. Perhaps he would agree to talk.

This other mosque was some distance away, in the northern part of town, so we all piled into a Maruti van driven by a friend of Choudhary's. As we honked our way through the downtown traffic and out past the old Sanskrit University, Choudhary pointed to his friend at the wheel. 'You see this man. He is a Hindu. Me, I'm a Muslim, you know. But we are friends always. Some days we are working 18 hours together. How can I fight with him? I help him and he helps me. In this city, Hindu peoples and Muslim peoples are always helping each other. So we live most happily together, side by side.

'This communal violence – it is not because of the people living here in Varanasi. It is the outside people, like the Shiv Sena people, who come here and do some mischief. They throw a bomb at a mosque, or a temple even. And if this happens, then the people will get angry of course. Then there is police intervention; but this only makes things worse.

'This is how it happened most times. There is this place in the old city where we went, Godoulia. From here two roads leave: one to a locality with a very dense population of Hindus, the other to the weavers' quarter, and, you know, in Varanasi almost 95 per cent of the silk-weavers are Muslims. The violence started from this main crossing only. The Hindus and the Muslims come from each side, and they clash. So if you want to start any mischief in Varanasi, you just go to that place and you throw a bomb.'

It sounded so simple. A sort of riot-instigator's ABC. And it made sense, moreover. I'd seen the concentration of PAC men around Godoulia and the Chowk area, with their old Lee Enfields and their lathis and their sandbagged gun emplacements – a deliberately threatening presence intended to overawe trouble-makers and thereby keep the peace. And I knew that this great pilgrimage city was always thronged with visitors from all parts of India, making it impossible to put in place any effective screening. But even if 'outsiders' lit the fuse, that didn't explain why the local communities had to join in. There were hidden tensions – neighbourhood disputes, gangland rivalries, a growing army of young men without real work or any hope of finding it. Maybe the maulana we were going to see would shed some light on this.

We crossed over the Varuna River and passed down back-streets until we reached a place called Ordeley Bazaar. Young Choudhary seemed to be steeling himself for the coming encounter. This was his local community. He had much to lose if the proposed meeting went wrong.

'This mosque we are going to is called Nawab Tok Ki

Masjid,' he said, clearly thinking we needed to be briefed in advance. 'Its name is from a Muslim landowner, a freedom fighter in the great uprising of 1857, who the Britishers kept in the prison nearby. This man built the mosque here so that he could pray.'

As we arrived outside the modest, white-painted mosque, Choudhary jumped out to clear things with the maulana. He came back all smiles. Yes, the maulana would see us; and, if we so wished, in half an hour we could also hear the call to evening prayer.

The maulana was sitting cross-legged, leaning against the back wall of the prayer-hall, surrounded by young religious students who wore embroidered white skull-caps. The maulana himself sported a knitted woollen cap resembling a tea-cosy, the cold weather having set in. His beard was full and orange-coloured from the application of henna. His young daughter played by his side. It was agreed that he should speak in Urdu, with Choudhary acting as interpreter.

His name was Ahmad Nasar and he didn't beat about the bush. 'The main problem for the Muslim community is this fear – that what happened in Ayodhya might also happen here in Banaras. They have no confidence that central government will always defend them and their Gyanwapi mosque. They are confused. They know that they are the minority community in India and that most government officials are not Muslims. They worry that these officials will take the other side, although government should be thinking for the whole community, both Hindus and Muslims. Many Muslims are now fearful about the future, about what will happen to the coming generation.

'But I will confirm this thing,' his voice rang out. 'What happened in Ayodhya will never happen in Banaras.' He paused for a moment. The students around him were nodding their heads in affirmation. They trusted in their maulana's pronouncements.

'In Ayodhya there was no Muslim community to protest when they attacked the Babri Masjid. Here the situation is different. There is an equal distribution of population in the old city, fifty-fifty. The Muslim community here has seen what happened in Ayodhya. Accordingly they have made arrangements to defend their mosque. There is nothing to worry about for Muslim people here. It will not happen.'

The religious students smiled at each other. I couldn't help thinking that if anything did happen here these teenagers would be in the front line.

'And why should there be any problem?' He posed the question rhetorically. 'The Gyanwapi Mosque is not a disputed site. Its history is well known. Ask any educated person – the Governor of UP, Dr Rajendra Prasad, so many Calcutta professors, even the president of India, Dr Shankar Dayal Sharma – they all confirm it is not a disputed site. Why? Because it was never a Hindu temple. It was a Buddhist monument which had become a ruin. The Muslim community bought the land from the Raja of Banaras and made their mosque in this place.'

As with most things to do with the mosque, this version of its history is disputed. But historical accuracy probably counts for less than the symbolism of the place. It is a reminder that for nearly five hundred years this most sacred of Hindu cities was ruled by Muslim emperors and warlords. That is why Hindu fundamentalists want to tear it down, brick by brick.

'The main problem,' Ahmad Nasar continued, 'is that the people of Banaras, both Muslim and Hindu, are confused about what will happen in the future. They are not thinking just about the mosque or the temple; they are thinking about themselves. Because whenever there is trouble in the city their business suffers; and poor people who must work all day for just 30 or 40 rupees, they must go out to buy food for themselves and their families. But when there is an army operation and curfew is imposed, then they cannot feed themselves.'

This I knew was true. Five years earlier I had been in Varanasi while the curfew was still in place nearly a month after an outbreak of communal rioting. The old and the infirm, especially, had been starving to death while the twenty-four-hour curfew was imposed. Even when it was altered to a dawn-to-dusk curfew the impact was frightening. Prices of foodstuffs rocketed and the poor could not get to the bazaar. And just before sunset, the surge of humanity around the Chowk – thousands of people desperately trying to get home with their purchases – lost all semblance of control. The police waded in with their lathis; warning shots were fired in the air.

Apparently this had happened every evening. And while politicians argued about who started the riot (the version I heard was that a procession of Bengali pilgrims carrying a Durga statue clashed with local Muslim boys outside a mosque) and the police filed exaggerated reports on the number of firearms and axe-heads they'd uncovered, the poor of Varanasi suffered.

It took some persuasion, but eventually the maulana agreed to give his personal vision of how communal frictions would work out in future. 'In twenty or thirty years, India will no longer be a secular country. I think that either India will become totally a Hindu country or it will be captured by Muslims, not from Islamic countries, but by Muslims living in India. As things are now standing, first there will be a BJP government; but they won't be able to maintain the unity of the country. Why? Because the Sudras, the downtrodden and low-caste Hindus, will not accept BJP rule, because they see that as rule by the higher-caste people only. They will ask for a separate state, just like the people in Assam or Nagaland have been doing.

'Thus, as time will pass, India will be divided into different parts. And this I must say also. According to the Holy Q'uran and the Prophet Mohammed, after one hundred or two hundred years all countries which do not have the Islamic religion will be divided into different parts, and there will be Muslim religion all over the world.'

He again stressed that these were only his personal views. But my heart sank nevertheless. For I saw his students leaning forward, straining to catch every word, and the fire of belief lighting in their eyes as their maulana spoke of the final victory of Islam. And I was appalled at the fundamental premise: that no way could ever be found for Hindu and Muslim communities to live together in peace, if not in total harmony.

Precisely how India's 120 million Muslims, spread so thinly across the country that they will always be a minority in any existing state outside Kashmir, could ever hope to form separate homelands was not explained. Such details became lost in the grander vision of Islamic history, which in its exclusiveness and its promise of final victory I found as misguided as the Hindutva version I'd got from Mr Khurana. It was less threatening only because it was unrealisable. One was the cry from the ghetto; the other the call of the gauleiter.

Yet the maulana still clung to the idea of a united India, even if he couldn't see where it was going.

'Since 1947 the Muslims of India have always been loyal to their country. In all the cities, Calcutta, Bombay, Kanpur, it is the Muslims who are the businessmen, the industrious trades-men. The Muslims are the backbone of this country. And you must notice this thing: whenever there is a disturbance in the country, the disturbance-creators attack the business ventures of Muslims far more often than they try to kill them. This is because these people are jealous because the Muslims are wealthier and work harder and it hurts them to see the Muslims raise themselves in any way.'

We were back in the wasteland of communal accusation and counter-accusation, and I was quite thankful that the maulana rose at this point to give the call to evening prayer. The sounds of buses honking their horns invaded the calm of the mosque precincts. Some crows were fighting noisily in a nearby tree. Then the maulana's voice issued invisibly from the minaret. Jagged and spiralling, it called the faithful to prayer. As we filed out of the mosque I wondered just how many citizens of India wanted, in the depths of their hearts, to put a stop to that call – never to have to hear it again. Forty per cent? Fifty? Sixty? It didn't bear thinking about. But what I had learned in Varanasi is that Ayodhya wasn't the end of a road. It was just a taste of things to come.

It is scarcely credible that communal tensions exist in Varanasi – not if you're gliding down the Ganges just after dawn, when the bathing ghats begin to fill with pilgrims and the palaces built by rulers of now defunct princely states take on a golden glow. Which is how I saw it the following morning, the wintry sun rising clear of the sandbanks and flatlands beyond to shed its first rays on Mother Ganga's tranquil face. Everything conspires to induce feelings of blissful calm and serenity: the majestic sweep of the river itself, the steep-climbing ghats, the temples and palaces rising above them layer upon layer in such weird and wonderful combinations of style that, in any reasonable world, the overall effect should be discordant – an architectural Tower of Babel. But Kashi does not adhere to reasonable norms; and somehow its motley assemblage of river-facing buildings merge into a harmonious whole.

To begin with the only sound was the creak of bamboo oars as the boatman rowed gently upstream. Then he pulled in closer to the riverbank, where crowds were already forming. For this was a special day, Makar Sankranti, when kite-flying and festivities are in order. There had been crowds out in the streets even before dawn, making their way down to the river for their morning dip. Kite vendors had set up their stalls along the main thoroughfares and were doing a healthy business.

It was a day of celebration and purification. By first light, the more popular bathing ghats were filled to capacity. Hundreds of bathers were moving up and down the steps to the water's edge. They seemed to merge into one rainbow-coloured flow, a slow-moving waterfall of humanity which eased its way through the open channels between the platforms, where brahmins sat underneath their umbrellas waiting to receive offerings, dispense blessings, cast horoscopes.

A low murmuring, like that of somnolent bees, carried across the water. It was the sound of thousands of worshippers, each reciting their separate prayers according to their own ritual, utterly self-absorbed, disregarding of what was going on around them. Despite the crush there was no pushing or jostling. Family groups waited their turn to immerse themselves in Gangaji, while others who had already taken their dip bundled together their wet clothes and the brass pots they'd filled with holy water.

Some splashed enthusiastically, either in high spirits or to clear the surface around them of floating marigolds or less pleasant matter. Some stood stock still, wrapped up in contemplation, while others raised cupped hands and watched intently as their trickle of water caught the rays of Surya, the sun god, before merging again with the mother river.

But mostly the crowd was in a festive mood, laughing and joking about how cold the water was, before taking the plunge and dipping once or thrice in quick succession. Some held their noses, though most took care that the purifying water reached everywhere – nose, ears and mouth. A father and son were soaping themselves so vigorously that, covered from head to toe in white suds, they took on the appearance of painted devils. Then, holding hands, they advanced into the water and dipped together, surfacing moments later transformed back into human form. Nearby, a group of young men had pushed out from the bank and were swimming energetically but inexpertly, splashing water into each other's faces.

The boat slipped past one bathing ghat after another. There wasn't much studied piety or solemnity on display, until, that is, we saw the Hare Krishna Girl. Even with her shaven head and saffron robes, she stuck out from the crowd like a Christmas tree in a rice paddy. And she was going about her puja with elaborate seriousness.

'Do you see that?' Sarah pointed needlessly towards the very pale, very thin, androgynous being who was now advancing to take her dip. 'There is nothing I find more contemptible than parading oneself in that way. She's not born into it.'

'Tut, tut! Bloody white woman gone native!' Tyrel exclaimed in his best Carruthers' voice. Then, serious once more: 'For God's sake, Sarah, stop being such a bloody memsahib.'

'I don't mind what she believes in. That's her affair. But to parade it like that is demeaning, not so much to herself as to all the real Hindus around her.'

Sarah and Tyrel then got into an argument about race and religion and who could belong to what. 'I don't mind if they decide to become Buddhists or Muslims,' Sarah argued, 'because in theory they're universal beliefs. You can belong to them whatever race or colour you are. But Hindus are different. Even if you can recite all their scriptures backwards and meditate until you're blue in the face, you're not one of them. You have no caste. You don't belong. You're a freak, a misfit like that woman. All of our Indian friends despise Westerners who come out here and dress up like sadhus or whatever.'

By now the object of all this scorn was far astern and I was wondering whether the prospect of a mixed marriage, between Hindu and Muslim, would provoke much the same kind of reaction. It's still pretty much a taboo subject. But there are some parallels: the denial of one's original identity or inherited culture, the attempt to belong to another, the likelihood of rejection by other members of that other community . . . But all kind of other things get mixed in: the sense of transgression, of crossing boundaries which should never be crossed, the loss of honour to the family or community left behind.

During Partition the 'dishonouring' of Hindu women, through forced conversion and marriage, was considered one of the worst forms of atrocity possible. It was condemned in far more emotive terms by the Hindu press than plain murder and bloodshed. At the same time, the Muslims stoked up their own fires with stories of rape, of Muslim women being paraded naked in public, their breasts sliced off. Horrible atrocities were committed on both sides; but forced conversion and marriage was one thing the Muslims could do without much fear of retaliation in kind. For most self-respecting Hindus would feel more dishonoured themselves if they married a forced convert.

Even now, fifty years after Partition, marriage between the communities is extremely rare. One hears the occasional stories – highly sensationalised, no doubt – of love matches and elopements. But, as a rule, Hindu and Muslim families consider marriage to a European or American with less abhorrence than one across the communal divide. And since Asians have settled in Britain and the United States, such marriages have become both more common and more acceptable to the families concerned.

Tyrel had brought along his paints and brushes, so we moored up alongside an old covered barge and he got down to some rough sketches. We were downstream from the main burning ghats, where the remains of a night-time cremation were being poked and levered into the river by Doms wielding long sticks. The Doms are non-caste Hindus, 'untouchables', and they alone are entitled to work the funeral pyres. Great mounds of firewood had been carefully graded and stacked in readiness. Another funeral party was waiting its turn. The corpse, wrapped tightly in layers of cloth, had been left on the steps where it seemed in danger of sliding uncombusted into the Ganga.

'No pictures,' the boatman warned. Just ahead of us a boatload of Japanese tourists were trying to snap this scene surreptitiously, when an angry shout went up from the bank. They'd been spotted, and wherever they landed there would be a welcoming committee, all outrage and histrionics until they were paid off. There are self-appointed 'religious officials' who make a living by extorting money from foreigners who foolishly breach the ban on photography at the burning ghats. But then there are also beggars in Varanasi who are rupee millionaires, although they too have to pay serious protection money to keep their prime spots on the main thoroughfares down to the ghats. That has always been the way in Varanasi, where pilgrims have to pay and pay again. The lofty brahmins and temple officials, the quack doctors and garland vendors, the landlords and the goondas who enforce their claims – all must take their slice. If Varanasi is the oldest pilgrimage city in the world, it is also the oldest tourist-trap.

Varanasi is also one of the filthiest of cities. Perhaps this is deliberate, to underline the difference between spiritual purification and physical decay. The sewers beneath the old city date back to the seventeenth century, water supplies are haphazard and harbour an alarming array of microbes, and the river itself is a dumping ground for raw sewage from towns further upstream.

The belief that when bodies are consigned to the Ganga the soul will escape from the cycle of rebirth means that some 50,000 uncremated or partially cremated bodies find their way into the river system every year.

I had been told that certain special categories – young infants, women who die in childbirth, anyone who dies from the smallpox or a snake bite – go straight into the river. We had already seen a child's corpse, bloated and whitened, go bobbing past, a half-dozen scavenger crows perched on its distended stomach. Now another floating object was approaching. It turned out to be a dead monkey, not a human corpse. The pilgrims on the ghats seemed impervious to this and other debris floating on the surface around them, gargling and spitting with what I took to be reckless abandon.

'It says here,' Sarah said, reading from a book, 'that although the Ganga may be one of the world's most polluted rivers it can also cleanse itself. And that's official. Apparently it can reoxygenate very quickly. Scientists discovered the river's exceptional property back in the last century when they found the cholera microbe wouldn't survive three hours in Ganga water, whereas in distilled water it lasted twenty-four hours. So there's some scientific basis to all the claims about purification.'

'I still wouldn't drink it,' Tyrel declared, 'though it's been useful enough for mixing my paints. Adds a touch of authenticity, I think.' He leaned over the side and rinsed out his paintbox in the water before rolling up his work. The boatman came forward to handle the oars. It was time to go back.

Tyrel was oddly silent over lunch. 'Beginning to lose your European appetite?' I enquired.

'I think there's something very wrong with me,' Tyrel replied and promptly left the table.

Sarah and I looked at each other knowingly. We'd both been struck down on our first visit to Varanasi: me when I was a long-haired student; she just five years earlier. We both knew the symptoms. 'I only hope he hasn't got it too bad,' Sarah sighed. 'Otherwise we could be struck here for weeks.'

We were baffled why it had hit Tyrel and not us, since we had all eaten the same food. But with the particularly virulent Varanasi microbe, only the smallest drop of water need get through the defences for all havoc to break loose. In Sarah's case, we'd traced it back to a chai shop in the old town where the proprietor had kindly washed out Sarah's glass before filling it with tea.

As for me, all I know is that I was out on the monsoon-swollen Ganga when I realised my number was up. I remember beseeching the boatmen to turn back, and then we were borne downstream on the flood, seemingly out of control, for the river was dark and angry and full of vicious eddies against which the boatmen had to struggle. I clung to the side of the boat and spat my guts out, knowing that this was only the first wave. As soon as we reached the bank I ran into a dingy hotel and shut myself into a vile-smelling squatter.

Whatever was inside me had a malignant will of its own. It jabbed and twisted my innards like a thousand burning bayonets. And though I fought to retain some self-control, it had me evacuating in stereo, puking and shitting simultaneously, crawling around in my own watery excreta. It wasn't long before it had me praying I could die.

Then the dark walls closed in around me and the flies above and the cockroaches below whispered unto me, saying: 'Behold, what a thing is man! Out of shit you were made, and unto shit you shall return.' And I looked up from the pit and saw pure waters glistening upon the cistern above, and the waters flowed down the cistern pipe just as Ganga descended from heaven down Siva's beard, to cleanse and to purify mankind. But upon the cistern pipe were dark shapes, ascending and descending; and they spake unto me: 'But one drop is within you; yet you spat on Ganga's face. As many drops as make a river, so shall your torments be.'

I was in that black hole for nearly two hours, bent double and wracked by spasms, hallucinating so strongly that, in one of my saner moments, I wondered whether someone had slipped me some bad acid. Since then I've fought with lesser devils all the way from Mexico to Xinjiang. But nowhere have I been brought anywhere near so low as in Varanasi.

When Tyrel didn't return after half an hour I went looking for him. He shouted back through the door that he hadn't finished yet. It was another hour before he finally emerged, his face pallid and filmed with sweat. We made him take some pills and a glass of neat lime juice.

He was still baffled by how he'd been hit so badly when we were both untouched.

'Remember the paintbrushes, Tyrel?' I began. 'The ones you washed in Ganga water.'

'So what? I didn't drink the stuff. I only dipped my brushes in it.'

'No, you didn't. You know while you're painting, really concentrating, you have this habit of sucking . . .'

'On the end of my brushes! But they were hardly even wet. Only an infinitesimal amount can have entered my system.'

'That's all it takes. And don't worry, we've all of us been there before. We all know about Ganga's revenge. Now have a little more fresh lime. It really does help.'

7

UP (ii):
THE ROAD TO AYODHYA

That night I was woken by thunder and lightning. The winter rains had arrived, pushing down from the north where there had been heavy snowfalls in the mountains and unusually low temperatures across the Punjab. I had expected to run into bad weather sooner or later, though not this far down the Gangetic plain. Coming in the middle of the eight-month-long dry season, this unseasonal rain would be welcomed by cultivators. It would benefit the winter wheat, but it would also make the roads extremely slippery. I tossed and turned, dreaming of potholes the size of lakes, where iridescent circles of spent diesel floated like lotus flowers.

It was still raining the next morning. I was relieved Tyrel had decided he was well enough to travel. He'd been sick again during the night but had 'popped enough pills to bung up an elephant'. While he and Sarah organised another Ambassador and driver to take them as far as Kanpur, I put on my waterproofs and wiped down the bike. At least we weren't going far – just a couple of hours down what I'd been told was a good section of the GT Road to Allahabad.

The plan was to spend the day at the Margh Mela, the annual bathing festival held at the confluence of the Ganges and the Jamuna just below Allahabad town. More than a million pilgrims take a dip at the sangam, the point where the rivers meet, on the main bathing day. I knew we'd have to miss that spectacle, for it wasn't due to happen for another week. Even so, large numbers of pilgrims were said to have arrived already. But the rains might still keep the big crowds away.

Just as we were ready to leave the clouds disappeared. I fired up the bike and headed for the GT Road; the Bullet was running much more sweetly now thanks to Mr Khurana's mechanics. I'd hardly spoken to the driver of the replacement Ambassador, but when he nudged my rear wheel on the way out of town I began to have my doubts. He was much younger than Misri Lal Ram and a good deal more reckless. Out on the open road I preferred to keep well ahead of him and took the Bullet up to speeds I wouldn't have dreamed of in Bihar. The road surfaces in UP were much better and the heavy traffic less bunched-up, so I opened up the throttle and soared along.

Unfortunately, the new driver thought it his duty to keep up with me. When I saw him in my rear-view mirror trying to overtake in impossible places, I waved him down and told him to drive more slowly. Sarah and Tyrel had tried this already, but he couldn't speak any English. They both looked seriously rattled and had resorted to frantic use of the hip-flask.

'I've been telling him to go "jaldi",' Sarah moaned, 'but all he does is go faster.'

'Then he's been doing exactly what you told him to. You've got your Hindi all muddled up. Jaldi means faster, you idiot; asti means slow. Now let's all go nice and asti, OK?'

We continued at a more leisurely pace, even though the road was drying out. I didn't mind pottering along at 40, as there were some lovely stretches where the shade trees formed an arch over the road and flocks of green parrots darted through the dappled sunlight. We came across a camel train, the first since we'd arrived in India, and a ruined courtyard which might have been an imperial serai in Mughal times. The fields sparkled after the recent rains. It felt more like a holiday jaunt than a mile-eating journey.

The pilgrim traffic started building up from ten miles out of Allahabad. They mostly travelled on foot or by tonga, though just about every form of transport imaginable had been called in to carry the faithful these last few miles. There were specially chartered buses, which looked antique even by local standards, and those outsized three-wheelers known as tempos which are so popular in rural districts and struggle along with thirty people on board. There were bullock carts and rickshaws; even an official Ambassador carrying a pious government servant and his family. Obviously more pilgrims were expected soon, for the tonga-wallahs were drawn up in lines waiting patiently for fares, their skinny ponies decked out in pom-poms and tinsel to attract custom their way.

I was amazed by the number of professional 'godmen' in the crowds and baffled by the diversity of cults and sects they represented. But then some of them seemed just as baffled by my appearance in their midst, especially a group of saffron-turbaned devotees who were travelling by tractor-trailer. They sat high above me on a load of straw that the tractor was taking to the mela, surounded by their cooking utensils and bed-rolls. Since I couldn't get past because of the crush of pilgrims on every side, I had to endure the unremitting stare of their guru, a white-bearded, fleshy man of ferocious aspect, whose forehead was completely painted over with a bright red triangle on a saffron ground. I suppose he'd never seen a motorcyclist in full-face helmet and leather jacket before. (The leathers – all those slaughtered cows – were making me feel rather uncomfortable.) Besides, this was his home-turf, and I was the one who looked like some extraterrestrial being.

The two of us were still engaged in this staring match when, out of the corner of one eye, I saw something that nearly made me fall off the bike.

There, in full view, was the confluence of the Ganges and Jamuna. But what startled me was the vast encampment on the far bank, the thousands of tents and multicoloured flags fluttering in the breeze. It was like stumbling upon a medieval army; except that even Genghis Khan never assembled as many tents as these.

I pulled off the road and waited for the Ambassador to arrive. Like me, Sarah and Tyrel were struck dumb. Everywhere you looked there were thousands of people. It made Woodstock seem like a village fête. Down below us three floating pontoon bridges had been thrown across the Ganges, probably by army engineers, but there were so many pilgrims crossing them that it was impossible to tell whether they were of wood or steel. The spit of land between the two rivers was covered with tents as far as the eye could see.

'How many do you think?' asked Tyrel. 'How many thousands . . .' his voice trailed off.

'Hundreds of thousands is more like it,' I answered, 'though it looks as if most of them are still arriving.'

There was still plenty of room down on the sand-spit for many more pilgrims, and I knew the Margh Mela could draw them in their millions in a good year. But compared with the Kumbh Mela, the mega-festival which is held at this same site once every twelve years, this is small fry. The last time the Kumbh Mela was held in Allahabad, or to use the ancient name preferred by most Hindus, Prayag, an estimated thirteen million pilgrims bathed during one day.

The Kumbh Mela is unusual because it is not fixed to one place, but is held every third year in one of four sacred places: Prayag, Hardwar, Ujjain and Nasik. The reason for this odd peregrination goes back to the Hindu creation myth of a battle between the gods and demons for possession of the kumbha, or pot, containing the nectar of immortality. The battle lasted twelve days. But since a god's day is the equivalent of a full year to ordinary mortals, it lasted for twelve human years – hence the twelve-year cycle.

In the course of this battle the god Vishnu ran off with the pot, pursued by demons. During his flight four drops of nectar fell to earth. These became the four holy places; but the holiest of them all is Prayag. For here also is the sangam, the confluence of three sacred rivers: the Ganga, which cleanses away all sins; the Jamuna, the river most closely associated with Lord Krishna and divine love; and the third river, which is invisible, though Hindus believe it flows underground to join the other holy rivers at Prayag. This is the Saraswati, the river of wisdom.

For all these reasons it is especially efficacious to bathe at the sangam during the Maha Kumbh Mela. This is why some 26 million people came to Allahabad in 1989; and even more are expected in the year 2001.

The Margh Mela had nearly two weeks to run and only the advance guard had arrived. This accounted for the high proportion of godmen and stall-keepers, who needed to set up shop ahead of the main crowds.

The path down to the pontoon bridges was lined with vendors of religious mementoes and bathing accessories: coloured powders and pastes for marking the forehead; postcards of the gods; pocket mirrors to assist in rearranging hairstyles and caste-marks after that special dip; marigolds in various guises – crushed, loose or ready-strung. Already they were doing brisk business.

Across the bridge there were stricter controls on where such salesmen could operate. It was all very organised, with broad access roads separating different zones. The authorities had laid on standpipes and cess-pits, electrical wiring and public-address speakers. All this has to be rebuilt every year, because during the monsoon the entire area is flooded.

The speakers were broadcasting a mix of 'lost-and-found' announcements and political messages. The BJP seemed to be getting the most air-time, though all the main parties – the Congress, BJP, Janata Dal – were represented. This was an election year, after all.

Their tented enclosures, along with those of such umbrella organisations as the Vishwa Hindu Parishad, were up towards the city end of the encampment. Most pilgrims arriving in Allahabad by train or bus would approach the mela that way.

The godmen set up camp closer to the shoreline. Closest to the bathing spots were the ghatias, small-time operators who assist the bathers and murmur hurried prayers for a few rupees. Far grander in appearance were the single-thread Brahmins, whose encampments flew their personal standards, brightly coloured flags with strange devices, to announce their presence to devotees.

Then there was 'Sadhu Street', a long avenue where various orders of sadhus had planted their tridents in the sand before their tents. A sharp wind was blowing and there were no naked sadhus abroad. With so little custom about, they remained huddled around the smoking embers of last night's fires, wrapped up in blankets and oddments of army surplus clothing. Some of these ascetics are said to have mastered control of the body's temperature through yogic exercises, but today was not a day of major processions when such attainments might be displayed to maximum effect.

And it was unusually cold. A north wind whipped up the surface sand and stretched the particoloured flags on their bamboo poles. A steady trickle of pilgrims were nonetheless making their way down to the tip of the sand-spit to take their ritual dip. The better-off among them were taking boats out to wooden bathing platforms in mid-stream, where the three holy rivers are supposed to merge.

We had to ward off a small army of touts before finding a boatman who would take us out for a half reasonable fee. The recent rains had swollen the river and the boatman had to labour hard to stay clear of larger craft as they swept downstream to the sangam. He tied up alongside one of the line of boats which stretched half-way across the Jamuna and waited for us to prepare for our dip.

It took some time to explain that, not being Hindus, we weren't that interested in bathing. What was interesting us were all the elaborate preparations going on in the other boats. Our immediate neighbour, an elderly gentleman who said he was the headman of a village near Bhopal in Central India, seemed unwilling to get started. 'Five years now am I coming to Margh Mela, but this year – arrcch! the cold is terrible.' He was wrapped in a new woollen blanket and had tied a yellow cloth around his chin and ears. For all that, his great walrus moustache was quivering, either from the cold or in anticipation of the shock to come.

Eventually he stripped down to his lungi and took the plunge, assisted by a couple of ghatias. He was in and out within a minute, finishing off his ablutions on a wooden bathing platform. I searched for any signs of fulfilment, but all I saw was an old man hunched up with cold. In fact, he looked considerably less serene than the pensioners who insist on swimming in the English Channel on Boxing Day. He clambered back aboard his boat, shivering and mumbling about how cold it was. 'Good bathe?' I asked. 'Very good – sangam is Number One,' he replied.

He seemed content. He'd fulfilled his dharma, his moral obligations, according to his own lights. The sacred waters would do the rest, no matter what state of mind he was in. Having a spiritual experience isn't what all this bathing is about. It's about doing one's duty as a Hindu.

For those in search of spiritual pyrotechnics there's plenty to choose from away from the river: babas reputed to be hundreds of years old; fierce-looking sadhus; shrivelled-up ascetics or sanyasi whose austerities beggar belief – all of them competing for the crowd's attention with more straightforward charlatans, contortionists, illusionists, herbalists and fortune-tellers. At times it reminded me of a supermarket with different brands of godmen on display. Little packets of gifts and rupee notes were constantly changing hands, usually through the medium of disciples rather than the revered personage himself. There was no attempt to disguise the venality of it all.

It was at just such a religious fair that one of the nastiest, and most mysterious, of all Partition massacres took place. The killing was so horrific that a total news blackout was imposed in an attempt to prevent massive retaliation. For once, official censorship was effective; and in so leak-prone a country that is part of the mystery. It's equally mysterious that although an official enquiry into the Garhmukteswar Massacre was ordered it was never carried out. But then the provincial government was Hindu-controlled and all the victims were Muslims.

All reports agree that a motorcyclist was involved. The

incident occurred in November 1946 at another bathing site on
the Ganges, further upstream and far less popular than the
Allahabad sangam. As with most religious melas there was a
fairground section and it was here that the trouble started.

The motorcyclist was a Muslim, part of a side-show called
'The Wall of Death'. The crowd was mainly Hindu, a small
fraction of the million or so pilgrims who had made their way to
Garhmukteswar to bathe in the Ganges. Among them was a
large contingent of Jats, peasant-farmers from the Punjab and
western UP. When the Muslim performer threw a jest to a Jatni
woman all hell broke loose. The shout went up that a Muslim
had insulted a Hindu woman. Immediately, groups of Jats set
about massacring all the Muslim stallholders at the mela. They
did their gruesome work swiftly and with unnatural cruelty.
Neither women nor children were spared. Even pregnant
women were ripped open, their unborn children torn out and
their brains dashed against walls or on the ground. The
motorcycle side-show was burned down and the bodies of both
dead and dying thrown into the flames.

The killing went on all night until there were no more
victims left at the fairground. Their blood-lust still unsated, the
Jats then moved on to the Muslim quarter of Garhmukteswar
town. The mob rushed through the narrow streets howling for
blood. There followed an orgy of murder, rape and arson
which, even by the harrowing standards of those times, is
reported to have been carried out with 'disgusting brutality'.
The town's police force, commanded by Hindus, failed to
intervene. Estimated casualties were between one and two
thousand men, women and children, though no official figures
were ever released.

All it had taken, in the charged atmosphere of a mela, was an
idle remark from a motorcycle stunt man. And although
communal tensions were running high in late 1946, there had
been no Muslim-inflicted atrocities immediately prior to the
massacre at Garhmukteswar. In fact, the most recent riots had
been in Bihar, where practically all the victims were Muslims. It
was not so much tit-for-tat retaliation as the knowledge that

murder could be committed with impunity that explains this horrific episode.

The same thing happened in the Punjab on a far larger scale in the spring of 1947. In the months after Partition, when the authorities on either side of the new border either turned a blind eye to the massacres, or in some cases actively participated in them, the awful truth of what Nehru and Jinnah and Mountbatten had brought about became plain for all to see. It was not the transfer of power so much as its complete breakdown. The killing multiplied because there was no one to protect the minorities, and the perpetrators knew that they would never be brought to book. There was no risk involved. That, as much as the barbarity of the acts committed, is what makes the Partition massacres so morally repugnant.

The Garhmukteswar Massacre has a peculiar horror because it grew out of a religious festival. There is a bitter irony that pilgrims who travelled many miles to the Ganges to wash away their sins should end up committing the most revolting crimes. But there is also the mass hysteria of large crowds and the dreadful inevitability of what follows when the first stone is cast.

It doesn't take much in a crowded mela to set off a chain reaction. Every year hundreds of Hindus are crushed, drowned and trampled to death by other Hindus in the stampede to reach some holy spot or see some holy image. If that same mass hysteria were directed outwards, the consequences are too awful to contemplate. Yet these great religious festivals would not be complete without the godmen and their political retainers broadcasting their hymns of hatred. 'Kick out the Muslims'; 'Make Hindustan a Hindu State'; 'Recover our Temples'; 'Prepare to sacrifice yourselves for Lord Ram'. I have even heard demands that Partition should be undone so Mother India can be one country again. All this, and much besides, goes on at melas up and down the country, year after year. Sophisticated Hindus try to distance themselves from such extremist or atavistic pronouncements. But the question is this: how far are they prepared to go if the genie really looks like getting out of the bottle?

*

If there was one man who managed to keep that genie in the bottle, it was Jawaharlal Nehru. Whatever his responsibility for allowing India to be divided in 1947, during the seventeen years that he was Prime Minister he did his utmost to build a secular state in which the minorities could participate and feel relatively secure. He had no truck with the Hindu Mahasabha and others who wanted to create a Hindu raj. Instead, he reinforced the position of Muslims and other minorities through laws which safeguarded their religion, their places of worship and their cultural indentity. He built up the system of reservations – for government jobs, education and access to loans – so that the minorities would not be shut out by the Hindu majority. He brought the Muslim community in India back into the Congress fold and they have voted fairly consistently for Congressmen ever since. For all these reasons his memory is detested by Hindu nationalists today.

Allahabad was the Nehru family's home. I had my own reasons for wanting to visit the old house where Jawaharlal grew up and, later on, retreated to from Delhi. I was born into Nehru's India and it was his voice on the radio that I remember best, his silver image flickering on the screen during the newsreels that always preceded the feature film. It was because he stumbled into war with China in 1962 that my mother was so busy knitting woollen socks and mittens for the soldiers, many of whom died of cold before they even reached the battle at 18,000 feet. The other world leaders of that era were strange and remote, and with the passage of time have become mere historical figures. Nehru remains a living memory.

Security was tight at Anand Bhavan, the Nehru family mansion: armed soldiers at the gate, grey-uniformed officers with machine-pistols inside. Family groups were wandering around the tastefully landscaped gardens. Most of them looked middle class, Westernised, progressive – the kind of people who supported Nehru's drive for modernity and progress while he was still alive.

The house itself was late raj in style, freshly painted a

restrained white and grey livery. Most of the rooms were sealed off behind plate glass, so the public can stare into Jawaharlal's study or Indira's bedroom without actually being able to enter them. The place had been turned into a museum, or rather a shrine, to the Nehru-Gandhi dynasty. Here was the veranda where Mahatma Gandhi sat; there the bookcases lined with the heavy tomes on Soviet history and economic planning that had such a disastrous impact on India's post-war development. There were many medals and tokens of esteem from other heads of state; the Soviet Union was clear leader in the medals table.

Anand Bhavan has a distinctly Anglo-Indian atmosphere. The books and furnishings are more Bloomsbury than Bombay. It is the kind of place that an enlightened, Cambridge-educated ICS (Indian Civil Service) officer might have set up for himself in the 1930s. Which is pretty much what Nehru was, except that he went into nationalist politics rather than the ICS. His first language was English, even at home. And the manner in which he governed India drew much on the old ICS approach: central control; even-handedness; incorruptibility. His detractors have labelled him 'a brown sahib' and criticise the Nehru–Gandhi dynasty for being 'insufficiently Indian'.

Though born a Hindu, Jawaharlal Nehru was throughout his adult life a champion of secularism. Long before his death in 1964 he worried that he might be reclaimed by the Hindus or that they would try to make political capital out of him after his death. All this is clear from his Will and Testament, dated 21 June 1954, whose full text is reproduced in Hindi and English on notice-boards just outside the house. It states he wished to be cremated and a small handful of his ashes be thrown into the Ganga. 'No part of these ashes,' he insisted, 'should be retained or preserved.' If he fostered the cult of personality during his lifetime, he didn't want to prolong it after he was gone.

But it is the next clause which I found most moving and, in the light of recent developments in India, most significant: 'My desire to have a handful of my ashes thrown in the Ganga has no religioius significance, so far as I am concerned. I have no religious sentiment in the matter. I have been attached to the

Ganga and the Jamuna rivers in Allahabad ever since my childhood and, as I have grown older, this attachment has grown. I have watched their varying moods as the seasons changed, and have often thought of the history and myth and tradition and song and story that have become part of their flowing waters.'

There follows a lyrical description of the Ganga and her importance to Indian civilisation. 'The Ganga', he wrote, 'has been to me a symbol and memory of the past of India, running into the present and flowing on to the great ocean of the future. And though I have discarded much of past tradition and custom, and am anxious that India should rid herself of all shackles that bind and constrain her and divide her people, and suppress vast numbers of them and prevent the free development of the body and spirit; though I seek all this, yet I do not wish to cut myself off from the past completely.'

The handful of ashes to be thrown into the Ganga were Nehru's 'last homage to India's cultural inheritance'. For the major portion of his ashes, however, he required a different kind of symbolism. 'I want these to be carried high up in the air in an aeroplane and scattered from that height over the fields where the peasants of India toil, so that they might mingle with the dust and soil of India and become an indistinguishable part of India.'

And so it was done. Indira Gandhi went aloft in a Dakota of the Indian Air Force and scattered some of her father's ashes over his beloved motherland in Kashmir, while other IAF planes dropped the remainder from high above the toiling peasants in different regions of the country.

As we left Anand Bhavan I asked the others what they thought of it. 'It's a political shrine, like Lenin's mausoleum,' said Sarah, 'except that here it's not just to one man but the whole Nehru dynasty.'

'Or the Congress Party,' said Tyrel. India was making him cynical.

As for me, Anand Bhavan represents more than that. It is a temple to secularism, to the ideal of India as a secular state.

Which is why the godmen down the road would have this place closed down, given half a chance. 'Think what would happen if you tried to distribute copies of that document,' I pointed to Nehru's will, 'down by the sangam. Try reading all that stuff about shackles holding back and dividing the people. That's anti-priest and anti-caste as far as they're concerned. They'd have a lynch mob on you before you could explain you were reciting the words of their first and greatest Prime Minister.'

Allahabad was once renowned for its Urdu writers and poets. As its name suggests, it was an important city during the Mughal period; the Emperor Akbar built one of his strongest fortresses on the banks of Jamuna, a little upstream from the sangam. And in a quiet garden, just off the Grand Trunk Road, are a group of beautiful though half-forgotten Mughal tombs. They are not in a good state of repair, which adds to the garden's sense of melancholy. The day I visited, an impromptu cricket match was being played in the paved space between the tomb of Prince Khusrau and that of his mother, Shah Begum.

Neither of them came to a happy end. Khusrau made the mistake, common among Mughal princes, of rebelling against his father, the Emperor Jahangir. The upstart prince was locked in chains for a year and forced to ride an elephant down a street lined with the heads of his supporters. Such punishments were not unusual in the rough world of dynastic politics; but neither was it odd that a wayward royal son should be set free soon afterwards.

But when Khusrau encouraged another assassination attempt against the Emperor he was blinded, and the rest of his life he spent in captivity. Finally, in 1615, he was murdered by his own brother, who went on to become the Emperor Shah Jahan, that great lover of beauty and creator of the Taj Mahal. On hearing of her son's death, Khusrau's mother, a Rajput princess by birth, committed suicide. A third tomb is believed to be that of his sister.

These tombs of disgraced royalty are small when compared with the imperial mausoleums; but they are still finely wrought and beautifully proportioned examples of Mughal architecture at its zenith. Their interiors are now dark and musty, and have been partially colonised by bats. Water has seeped in and dissolved the intricate plasterwork; but here and there some of the original painting remains intact. Stylised fruits and gardens with poplars and running water serve as reminders of the Mughals' distant homeland in Central Asia. They are fitting symbols for a clan which claimed descent from both Genghis Khan and Tamerlaine, whose idea of paradise was a mountain valley far to the north and whose methods of settling dynastic quarrels were as bloody as those of their infamous ancestors. The evidence is all there, in this tranquil garden.

It was time for some hard decisions. The 'Gang of Three' was soon to split up. Sarah needed to get back to her work in London. Tyrel was also going back, to his wife and child and to his painting. They needed to be in Delhi in three days; from then on I'd be on my own.

We had a choice of continuing gently down the Grand Trunk Road to Kanpur, from where they could take the train to Delhi, or we could divert northwards to Ayodhya, returning via Lucknow to Kanpur. The timing of the second alternative would be tight. It would also mean skipping a short section of the GT Road. But I'd heard so much about Ayodhya, it had cropped up in so many conversations, with Hindus and Muslims alike, that I decided it must be the linchpin.

It took some persuading. 'But the mosque is already demolished,' Sarah protested. 'There's nothing left to see but a bloody great hole in the ground.'

'If that's all there is, then it's a bloody important hole.'

The 'Gang of Three' being a true democracy, Tyrel had the deciding vote. 'Our policy shall be,' he declared with mock solemnity, 'Ayodhya or bust.' Then, as an afterthought, 'I mean, who needs sleep?'

'That's it,' I said.

We were on the road in half an hour. As they packed up the Ambassador, Sarah and Tyrel were singing some ghastly 1960s pop tune. I recognised it as Tom Jones's 'Delilah'; but instead of the usual chorus they'd inserted nonsense rhymes:

Ay, Ay, Ay, Ayodhya!
Ay, Ay, Ay, Ayodhya!
New brakes and new gears and a whole new refit
Through the hole in the bloody thing's bottom . . .

'Oh, for God's sake,' I shouted. 'We're not marching off to war, you know. And you two are not the Poor Bloody Infantry.'

'Look,' said Tyrel, 'I don't mind busting my balls to go and see this non-existent Sri Ram temple. But you can't expect us to be all solemn about it.'

He kept on singing that idiot song for a day and half – right up until we reached the site of the Babri Mosque. Then he fell silent.

The road to Ayodhya was very different from the overflowing highway we had grown used to. It was a back-route and, once clear of Allahabad, there was hardly any motor traffic. There were handcarts and bullock carts; tongas and bicycles. But when we stopped for tea at the main junction with the Jaunpur Road there wasn't another motorised vehicle in the entire village. The countryside grew poorer, the crops thinner, until attempts at cultivation petered out altogether and we were moving through eroded pastures and brushwood. This eastern part of UP seemed not much better off than Bihar.

It had rained again the previous night and the road was badly flooded in places. Approaching large expanses of muddy water, not knowing where the potholes lay or where the road gave out, was unnerving. I soon discovered that the best way to negotiate these water hazards was to follow a local kid on his bicycle. They always knew where the ridges were and how best to avoid the deep water. This combination of floods and badly rutted roads slowed down our progress, so it was evening before we reached Ayodhya.

I cruised up and down the brightly lit strip looking for

somewhere to stay. Behind the bazaar section, down unlit side-roads, I caught glimpses of substantial buildings, some of them palatial in scale. They loomed out of the darkness, apparently uninhabited, definitely eerie.

The main strip was lined with shops and bazaars and at first looked like that in any provincial town. Then I noticed that most of the shops were selling devotional accessories, Lord Ram postcards and calendars. The cloth merchants had a strong line in red and orange prints covered with praises to Lord Ram or scenes from the *Ramayana*, while next door you could choose between images of the Baby Ram, Ram and Sita, or Ram and Hanuman. The music shop had a huge selection of Lord Ram cassettes by various artistes. No need to guess what was the mainstay of the local economy.

When I enquired about hotels I was told the looming palaces were all pilgrim hostels, but that they took in Hindus only. Foreigners should apply to the UP State Tourism Bungalow near the railway station. This turned out to be another modernist block, with another cavernous entrance hall. The cell-like rooms grouped around stairwells reminded me of a prison. When I opened a window, I heard the chant of 'Ram, Ram' being relayed by loudspeakers across town. The cafeteria was vegetarian only, in deference to the religious sensibilities of pilgrims, who accounted for most of the guests. We were the only non-pilgrims staying that night.

Over dinner the man at the next table told me about his own remarkable pilgrimage. Mr Desai had settled in San Francisco, where he had worked as an engineer at the city's water board for many years. But then he had felt the call to visit twelve holy Siva temples in India and to gaze upon Lord Siva's lingam in each place. To do this he had borrowed his brother's car and driver in Bombay, and he and his wife had been on the road for two solid weeks. He proudly recited a list of the holy places they'd already visited.

'And you did all this by car?' I said in amazement. They'd been up and down the country – Gujarat, Maharashtra, Bihar, as well as way down south – in a remarkably short space of time.

'Already we have completed more than seven thousand kilometres. Before we are finished we will have driven ten thousand in total.'

'Every day, five hundred kilometres,' his wife added. She looked exhausted.

Although Ayodhya wasn't on his main list of Siva temples, they had decided to come 'because Siva visited the birthplace of Lord Rama too'. They said they were pleased that the mosque had been torn down but that they now wanted a temple in its place.

Mr Desai had no doubts whatsoever that a temple had been there before the mosque: 'Why, so many people have seen the imprint and the images of Lord Ram and Krishna in this place.'

His wife waggled her head in agreement. Between them they'd spent nearly half a century in the United States, but it hadn't dented their belief in miraculous apparitions.

'We have seen where Sri Ramji went into the forest,' he went on. 'Also the place where he became king. But the holy place he was born is under lock and key. Even we Hindus cannot go in.'

'Isn't that to prevent more communal bloodshed?' I suggested hopefully. 'Besides, some experts say there is no evidence that a temple existed before the mosque.'

'Only pro-Muslim people, Congressmen and so on, are saying this. For Hindus there is no question that this is truly the birthplace of Lord Ram! All Hindus want to build a temple on this same place to honour Lord Ram.'

'And Sita also,' piped in Mrs Desai. 'You must be knowing of this Sita. She is the same to Rama as Parvati is to Lord Siva.'

'Like the perfect wife is to her husband,' explained Mr Desai. And he looked with melting eyes at the hunched-up, ageing woman opposite him.

I had just gained an insight into why Lord Ram and his wife Sita are two of the most popular deities in modern Hinduism. They are divinely sanctioned role models. Rama is revered as an incarnation of the god Vishnu and comes as close as anything in the Hindu pantheon to the idea of God Incarnate. Yet his qualities are essentially human – honesty, charity, selflessness, the willingness to do whatever is necessary to spread harmony and concord. His bride, Sita, is well-born, meek, self-sacrificing, always obedient to her husband. In this divine couple are embodied most of the 'family values' so important to Hindu society.

Ram's other attributes are also held up as ideals to be followed by ordinary Hindus. The overweening affection most Indians feel for young children, and especially for male infants, is crystallised in the image of Baby Ram – always plump, always smiling, and as sweetly cloying as Bengali sweetmeats. Apart from his blue-tinted skin – the sign of his divine origin – the Baby Ram is portrayed as every mother's ideal son, and is probably adored in much the same spirit. Of course other religions have played on the same emotions, most obviously in the Baby Jesus. But not even Murillo's sugared confections can compete for sheer gooiness with the popular images of Baby Ram that can be found in so many Hindu households.

Then again, Lord Ram was a mighty warrior, endowed with superhuman strength. He alone could bend the mighty bow and thereby win Sita as his bride. As such, Ram is an inspiration to Hindus who think they must fight for their religion. His martial feats are an inspiration to soldier and goonda alike. When excitable young men start shouting 'Ram! Ram!' trouble is usually not far away.

Lord Ram has long been a popular divinty. His legendary deeds, as recounted in the *Ramayana*, are familiar to nine out of ten Indians. Every year his victory over the demon-king Ravana of Lanka is celebrated in the Ram Lila festivities. Then there was the televised version of the *Ramayana*, a low-budget production with laughably unconvincing 'special effects' which nonetheless held hundreds of millions of viewers in thrall through all seventy-eight weekly episodes. The whole nation ground to a halt while the *Ramayana* was being broadcast. The popularity of Lord Ram had never been higher.

By then the politicians were on the bandwagon. They recognised the potency of the Lord Ram cult. Here was a specifically Hindu hero whose legendary doings made most Indians feel good about being Hindus. From here it was just a short step to the demand for a Hindu state governed by Hindu principles in the interests of the Hindu majority. No more Westernised secularism! No more appeasing the minorities! The champions of Hindutva claimed Lord Ram was on their side, at once an inspiration to act and the justification for their actions. No matter what Congressmen did to prove their devotion to Ram and Sita and traditional Hindu values, the BJP and Shiv Sena could always go several steps further.

Ayodhya became the flashpoint of Hindu–Muslim tensions because it suited the right-wing Hindu politicians. It fulfilled all the necessary criteria and pressed all the right emotive buttons – from sentimentalism through to a heroic call-to-arms. What right-thinking Hindu could not feel ashamed that a mosque stood on the very place where the Baby Ram was born? How sad Lord Ram must feel that he was being treated so poorly. And this in an independent country, where Hindus were in a huge majority.

It was time to avenge the injustices of the past. Not just by replacing the mosque at Ayodhya with a vast new temple to Lord Ram, but by doing away with all the other special privileges enjoyed by Muslims, including the government jobs reserved for them, which prevented 'better qualified' caste Hindus from gaining such desirable, semi-permanent employment, and the allowance that they could conduct their own affairs according to Muslim personal law, taking up to four wives so that 'they' could outbreed 'us'.

All these grievances crystallised around that most glaring symbol of injustice, the Babri Mosque at Ayodhya. No wonder the Muslim community sees the Ayodhya dispute as the thin end of the wedge. It doesn't matter that there is no real scientific evidence that a temple stood on this site before Babur, the first Mughal Emperor, or one of his generals, ordained the building of a mosque in 1528. If historical facts had any bearing on this case they would suggest the contrary.

The original version of the *Ramayana* is believed to have been composed in the fourth century BC by the poet and sage Valmiki. But the popular cult of Lord Ram did not gather momentum until much later, with the missionary work of Guru Swami Ramanand in the fourteenth century. If there ever was such a temple, it can have dated back only to this period, by which time Muslim rule was already established in northern India.

It is also odd that Tulsi Das, the author of the most popular Hindi-language version of the *Ramayana*, who lived around Ayodhya at the same time as the Babri Mosque was going up, never mentions the destruction of an earlier temple to Lord Ram. Nor does he in any of his writings identify this as the spot where Ram was born. In fact, the first such claims were put forward by local Hindus in 1855, when the area was under British administration. The result was a Hindu–Muslim riot which cost seventy-five lives.

The issue of who has the right to worship on this precise spot has been running ever since. While British rule lasted, a compromise was adhered to whereby Hindus could worship in one half of the outer yard and Muslims in the other; and to prevent any further violence the British built a wall down the middle. That compromise lasted until 1949, two years after Partition, when a statue of Lord Ram was surreptitiously installed inside the mosque. The word went out through the bazaars that the god himself had appeared. In the immediate aftermath of Partition the Muslim community was not in a mood to insist on their rights and possibly provoke a Hindu backlash. There were only a few Muslims left in Ayodhya anyway. Better to allow the mosque to be locked up and hand the matter over to the courts to decide, which is how things remained for another thirty-five years.

Then, during the 1980s, militant Hindu organisations started agitating for the demolition of the Babri Mosque. In its place they called for a grand new temple to Lord Ram. After all, as the BJP leader L. K. Advani pointed out, the mosque hadn't been used for prayers since 1949, so it had ceased to be a mosque.

When the politicians entered the arena, Ayodhya became a testing ground for much broader issues. Would the Congress Party stand by the rule of law and its commitments to the Muslim community? Or could the BJP and other militant Hindus force the issue in some way? The Vishwa Hindu Parishad commissioned stonemasons to prepare ready-made sections for their new temple, a scale model of which was installed in their recruiting centre right next door to the mosque. The kar sewaks, the shock troops of militant Hinduism, were told to prepare to sacrifice their blood for Lord Ram.

The communal violence which flared up across India in 1989 claimed some six hundred lives, most of them Muslim. And while Ayodhya occupied the political centre stage, no less than three duly-elected governments had to resign. It had become a trial of strength. The disputed mosque was turned into a fortress, the entire area fenced off with razor wire. The first time that the kar sewaks tried to storm the mosque the army beat them back. But media images of soldiers beating their co-religionists with lathis ignited another bout of communal rioting across the country. The Hindu militants were blooded in Ayodhya. But now they had their own 'martyrs'; and besides, they had taken vengeance on Muslims elsewhere.

If the command had been given the army could have held the perimeter fence. But on 6 December 1992 no such command was given. The police refused to control the mob and the army stood aside as thousands of kar sewaks stormed the perimeter and proceeded to tear down the hated Babri Mosque stone by stone.

The rubble was cleared from the site overnight. By morning a platform was built and the statue of Lord Ram installed where twenty-four hours earlier the mosque had stood. A few thousand religious zealots had defied with impunity the Government of India and the rule of law. Terrible rioting broke out in Bombay and Ahmedabad and thousands, again mainly Muslims, were killed or had their houses burned down.

The dust may have settled at Ayodhya for the time being. But the fall-out from December 1992 is still there, contaminating

Hindu–Muslim relations and invisibly eating into the body politic. The Government has sealed off the area again and promised to rebuild a mosque. Nothing has been done to fulfil that promise and the whole matter is back in the hands of the courts. There it is likely to remain as long as India is run by minority or coalition governments. Nobody, not even the BJP, wants to grasp that nettle.

It isn't easy to ask for directions to a place that doesn't exist any more. I discovered this as I wandered through Ayodhya's bazaars the next morning, trying to find out how to get to the site of the former Babri Mosque. When I asked for the 'Babri Masjid', all I got was incredulous looks.

'All finished,' said the tea-seller outside the Hanuman Temple. 'No mosque, no Muslims, nothing.' He appeared to be pleased about this. Music blared from the cassette vendor's stall across the street, the chorus of Ram, Ram, Sita Ram just audible above a thumping disco beat and anguished string section.

'Good, good,' gloated another customer. 'All Muslims finished now. When BJP government is coming, all Muslims must go to Pakistan!'

'You want to see beautiful temple, mister?' asked a prospective guide. 'I show you Sri Hanuman Garhi. Very beautiful.'

'Already been,' I replied cheerfully. In present company I thought it best not to add that, as temples go, it was gaudy rather than 'beautiful', that the temple priests had been unfriendly and the temple monkeys out of control.

'Where you want to go?' the tout persisted. 'I show you Kanak Bhavan, very beautiful.'

'I want to go to the Ramjanam Bhoomi,' I said, trying out the name of the temple the Hindu militants would like to build on the site of the mosque.

The tout avoided my suggestion. 'I show you Kala Rama temple. I show Bara Palace. I show Sri Ved Mandir, very beautiful temple. All tourists are coming to these places.'

'Hindu tourists?'

'Only Hindu tourists are coming to Ayodhya.'

'You don't know where the Babri Masjid used to be?'

He shrugged his shoulders and walked away.

Eventually I got directions from a picture-postcard seller. He thrust a booklet of cheaply reproduced photos of Ayodhya into my hand. There, on the first page, was a picture of the triple-domed mosque with human figures clambering over it. The caption below read *Victory of Kar Sewaks*.

As I showed interest in this particular scene he dug out another booklet for inspection. This one was entitled *Sri Ayodhya Bathed in Blood*. It was a pictorial record of the 'sufferings' of the kar sewaks during their unsuccessful attack on the Babri Mosque between 30 October and 2 November 1990.

A picture of government security forces wielding lathis was captioned *Torture by Police*. A snapshot of a burly police officer with a beard – the implied suggestion being that he was a Muslim – was simply labelled *Killer of Kar Sewak*. There was a grisly sequence of dead or wounded Hindu rioters, martyrs to the cause, interspersed with smiling pictures of BJP leaders. A picture of a monkey sitting on top of a portion of the mosque showed how, on this historic occasion, Hanuman had again come to the assistance of Lord Ram, just as he had done in the battle against King Ravana in the *Ramayana*. I was amazed that this visually disturbing and propagandist material was being peddled as souvenirs.

For the postcard seller this was business as normal. Such pictures, he said, were very popular with pilgrims. And he was only too happy to give me directions to the scene of the historic victory.

We set off in the right direction but still got lost among the temples and pilgrim hostels – the back-streets of Ayodhya are as confusing as those of any temple city. Then a squad of armed police, ancient Lee Enfields slung over their shoulders, confirmed we were nearing our goal.

'Hurry, hurry,' shouted a youngish police officer. 'You are just in time.'

'Just in time for what?' I asked. But without elaborating further, he informed us that we were most fortunate. 'Now, please give me full passport details for all three persons.'

Our details were taken down in triplicate, each time by a different official. The youngish officer kept on saying 'You are from the UK? That is very good, very good.' I suspected that our visit was helping to fill some quota and that the authorities wanted to chalk up as many foreign visitors as possible.

We then proceeded to Security Check, where we were required to hand over cameras, shoulder bags, pens, notepads, and anything metal, including spare change. On top of this we had to leave our passports as 'surety of good behaviour'. I still didn't know what we were being let into, but events had acquired a momentum of their own.

The second time I was frisked the guard felt something in the lining of my biking jacket. It was the spark plug cap I'd replaced on the first day of my journey, back in West Bengal. 'Explosive?' the guard suggested. I couldn't work it loose from the lining, so I had to leave the jacket behind as well.

Two women officers had been giving Sarah a thorough going-over. Her initial reluctance to be parted from her cameras had marked her out as unco-operative. 'I hope it's bloody well worth it,' she whispered. Already we were made to feel guilty, though about what I couldn't say.

'Please proceed now, only one at a time.' I went first, through a barred gate and into a sort of cattle chute. There were steel bars on either side and above me, and all I could see were more cattle pens and, in the distance, a wall covered in razor wire. There was no one else about apart from the occasional soldier armed with a sten gun. I looked back. They hadn't allowed the others into the pen yet. Ahead of me was a metal gate manned by an armed policeman. As he let me through, I heard another gate clanging behind me; Sarah had now been allowed into the first section. It was like being in a high-security prison.

I wondered what all these elaborate precautions were for. Outside the cage there was nothing; an open space covered in pale rubble. I guessed we were being funnelled across the area where the Babri Mosque had once stood. I picked out a glint of reflected sunlight from a watchtower on the perimeter. Binoculars? Our progress was being monitored. But what for? What lay at the end of this cage that snaked its way across nothingness?

I eventually arrived in front of a tented pavilion, where I was told to wait. The pavilion stood on a raised platform. It was the Sri Ram Janam Bhoomi, the temporary shrine built on the very spot where Hindus believe God became incarnate. A couple of army officers were lounging in camp chairs, chatting to a civilian with a full beard and dark glasses who I guessed was either an intelligence officer or some form of temple official. Or, most likely, a combination of the two.

A few minutes later Sarah was let through the last gate to join me. When Tyrel arrived, we three were told to stand in a row. A plain-clothes man approached and asked through the bars whether we had anything unlawful in our pockets. Satisfied by our denials, he told us that we were about to witness a special puja and that we should always behave in a respectful manner. Just to make sure, he stationed two soldiers in front of us.

One of the officers began to get ready for the ceremony. To judge from the brass on his epaulettes he was quite high-ranking; but he was unfamiliar with the religious protocol and had to be called back to remove his Sam Browne before approaching the pavilion: it was leather. The soldiers in front of us found this highly amusing. The bearded man removed his dark glasses and disappeared into the tent. We all waited in silence, thankful that this section of cage had a tin roof to shield us from the sun.

With a tinkling of bells and cymbals the cloth covering the front of the pavilion was drawn back and we gazed upon the image of Lord Ram. At least I supposed it was he. It was hard to tell whether the revered idol was in there behind all the rich draperies and garlands and subsidiary statuettes. All this sacred paraphernalia mounted up, layer upon layer, to form a sort of pyramid. But from somewhere in the middle a small dark face peered out, the statue of Ram which 'miraculously' appeared in the mosque.

I recognised this part of the ceremony as darshan, the gazing on a sacred image which is so important a part of Hinduism. An assistant to the priest came down from the pavilion, carrying a flaming vessel. We were told to extend our hands through the bars and the purifying flame circled above and below them. Then a handful of sugary white stuff, like solid popcorn, was doled out to each of us. This was prasad, the ritual gift which we were to take away with us. No sooner had this been done than we heard a screeching nearby and the corrugated iron above us reverberated to the impact of running feet. A troop of monkeys had spotted the prasad and had charged up to see if they could steal any. Perhaps as soldiers in Hanuman's army they expected a share of the spoils; but for the rest of the ceremony the two human soldiers with us were fully occupied in keeping them at bay.

We knew we should feel highly honoured to be present at this private puja. Any number of pilgrims would have given their eye teeth – or paid out handsome bribes – to be there. The senior officer for whom this ceremony was being conducted had bowed his head respectfully. But the event seemed to me to be happening in a vacuum.

I wondered what the effect would be on a crowd charged with religious fervour. It was to control such excitement that the army had installed this maze of steel bars and security gates. Most ordinary pilgrims would have only a few moments' darshan before being prodded on towards the exit. And what if some fanatic smuggled in a weapon or just threw a stone at the sacred image? There would be riots right across India. Hundreds, possibly thousands, would be murdered in a matter of hours.

The ceremony over, we proceeded down more steel-clad tunnels towards the exit, still pursued by monkeys. Now that we had passed the 'danger spot' we were allowed to walk together.

'I thought the army was supposed to be neutral,' Sarah whispered. We still felt under observation.

'It is. But that doesn't stop them from being practising Hindus or Sikhs or whatever.'

'Well, that ceremony didn't look like neutrality to me.'

'It's not so much the army's presence. They're here to protect the site. It's the fact there's a temple there, even a makeshift temple, that gives the game away. It shows that the boys who took the law into their own hands could get away with it.'

'I don't suppose there are any Muslim soldiers guarding Ayodhya,' Sarah replied.

We stopped and looked around. Apart from that raised platform and pavilion there was nothing but waste ground. Whatever existed before had been completely flattened. It conjured up images of Ground Zero after a nuclear explosion.

The more militant might even be pleased at the desolation. For them it symbolises the victory of Hindu over Muslim. It was a first step towards the building of their grand temple and a Hindu raj. But there was still unfinished business at Ayodhya.

I very much doubt whether any Muslim would venture, or even be allowed, into this fortress today. But if they did, what would they feel? A sense of shame? Betrayal? Or fear that the same thing might happen elsewhere? As for me, I felt like a UN observer surveying the no-man's-land between two warring tribes. I saw the legacy of hatred and the seeds of future destruction.

We marched past neatly parked lines of police buses and army trucks, the rows of tents where the defensive garrison lived, and out through the main perimeter gate into the normal world beyond. A street vendor tried to interest me in bootleg videos of the *Ramayana*. Just above his head a juvenile monkey was swinging playfully from the barbed wire.

The faithful might see in this an auspicious sign, or pray for the final victory of Hanuman's army over the poor disgruntled infantry on the other side of the fence. What I saw was just a young ape on a piece of wire that protected a hole in the ground.

Sadly for India, its internal peace, the rule of law, the authority and very nature of government, all depend to an unreasonable extent on that wire perimeter never being broken down again.

8

UP (iii): VIEWS FROM
THE HINDU HEARTLAND

It was time to get back to the GT Road. To cut off a corner we had decided to go via Lucknow, and the first few miles of the road to Faizabad seemed normal enough. The town itself was bustling with traffic and shops spilled onto the pavement. Unaware of what lay ahead, we stopped to look around the tomb of Bahu Begum, widow of one of the fabulously wealthy Nawabs of Oudh. It was a massive pile of white marble in the slightly fanciful late Mughal style. Predictably, it was locked up and the caretaker couldn't find the key.

Only when we were clear of Faizabad did I notice something wrong. There was no traffic on the road apart from the occasional bicycle or bullock cart, and no sign of the buses and trucks which should be plying this busy route. When I saw some village children playing cricket in the middle of the road, I became convinced that normal traffic must be banned for some reason.

I flagged down the Ambassador to see if the others had any explanation. Sarah dug out a scrunched-up and unread copy of a day-old newspaper. There it was, right across the front page. Trouble was expected in Lucknow, where the Samajwadi Party, one of the political groups campaigning for the interests of the backward castes, was planning a mass demonstration. Their aim was to surround Government House with a human wall, effectively locking state government servants out of their offices, or, if they were already there, locking them in.

This tactic is known as gherao and is commonly used in

industrial disputes. Though technically a non-violent form of
protest, the slightest push can lead to bloody clashes – especially
if the police then wade in with their lathis.

The Samajwadi Party had called on a million of its supporters
to turn up and protest against the dilution of reservations of
government jobs and education for the backward castes. To
prevent this gherao happening the state government had
brought in extra security forces and water cannon. And to stop
Samajwadi supporters from even reaching Lucknow it had set
up road-blocks on all routes into the city. Local bus operators
had protested, but to no avail.

'We appear to be missing a rather interesting riot,' observed
Tyrel. 'Are these Samajwadi a revolutionary party?'

I was in no mood to discuss theoretical anarchism, in which
Tyrel had taken a youthful interest. We had decided to go via
Lucknow to save time and to avoid retracing our steps by
returning to Allahabad. Our plan appeared to be up the spout.

'Here we are heading for Lucknow and according to these
reports all roads are closed. What the hell do we do next?' I
asked rather pathetically.

'Oh, we'll sneak through,' Sarah replied. 'Whatever trouble
there's been, it will probably all be over by now. And besides,
we're obviously not Samajwadi supporters.'

'That's not the point. You know how it is with rules and
regulations and government bureaucracy. Even you can see that
this particular load of red tape,' I prodded the newspaper, 'is
pretty damn fresh. We'll never get through.'

'At least we could try. I mean, what's there to lose?'

I thought of hours of fruitless explanations by the roadside.
And then Sarah came up with what, to her at least, was the
clinching argument.

'I've heard of this delicious hotel in Lucknow . . .'

We held our last roadside executive meeting. The lure of
comfort won over reason. It was decided to push on and hope
for the best. I was instructed to 'talk my way through' whatever
police checkpoints we encountered. I dug out the crumpled

letter of recommendation from Electoral Commissioner Dutt. I had this feeling we'd be needing all the 'clout' we could muster.

It was eerie to be motoring down such a broad, well-paved and yet totally deserted road. The bike was flying along at speeds undreamt of in Bihar, and the afternoon sun sent golden shafts between the dense mango topes. Cattle were being led home and villagers wandered down the middle of the road. For a moment I had a vision of what the great highways of India were like before they were clogged by motor traffic. Then I saw ahead of me a roughly built wooden barricade. It was road-block number one.

I drew up and dismounted with elaborate formality. When the officer in charge saluted, I saluted back. When he told me it was impossible to proceed to Lucknow, I looked astonished. When he insisted we turn back, I insisted on seeing his superior officer. Reluctantly he led me into a roadside police post where I went through the same rigmarole. It was a game of bluff, but you had to play by the rules. I twice let him turn down my request that he make a 'special exception' before throwing on the table my dubious trump card – the letter from Mr Dutt.

This he read through slowly several times, weighing up the possible consequences of his next move. If he let us through and anything untoward happened, he'd face an official reprimand. On the other hand, if these persons had friends in high places and lodged a complaint of 'police obstruction' it might prove even more tiresome.

'You will now give me,' he declared, 'all passports and vehicle documents.' It took twenty minutes for all the details to be copied into an official record. But from the moment he uttered those words I knew we were through.

I returned to find the bike surrounded by armed policemen. They were eyeing it up, pointing at the engine and the brakes with informed interest. 'Is this the 500 cc machine?' asked the officer who had first stopped me. 'It is very fine, very fine indeed. We only get the 350 model.'

The Enfield Bullet is standard equipment for the army, the

police and most other government services. Now we were friends, the officer wanted to discuss the relative merits of the two models. From here on, I decided, I'd play the Enfield card as well as the Dutt letter. We would become the 'official Enfield touring party'. This worked so well at the next road-block that I didn't have to drag out any other papers. At the third I simply argued that if we'd got this far we must be OK. We were waved through.

Then, five miles short of Lucknow, we ran into a policeman who would not be moved.

To every argument he simply replied, 'I have no authorisation.' Sarah attempted to become tearful. I threw around all the clout I could muster, most of it imaginary. I even invoked the names of a couple of state ministers which I remembered from a newspaper column. Still no effect.

'But we can't stay here,' I exploded. 'If it's so dangerous to enter the city, why can't we go in convoy with a police vehicle?' His eyes flickered interest so I pressed on, though I knew I was entering dubious territory. 'Of course, we would be willing to make good the additional expense.'

Now this could easily be interpreted as an attempt to bribe a police officer. He thought about it for a while, before saying, 'This will not be necessary.' Then, with a dismissive flick of the wrist, he announced 'You are free to go now.'

'To Lucknow?'

'Yes, to Lucknow. We have now received authorisation.'

No telephone had rung; no peon had entered with a sheaf of papers. Does the UP police receive orders by telepathy? Whatever the reason for his change of mind, I wasn't going to query it. I almost ran back to the bike.

The streets of Lucknow were lined with security forces. Small groups of protesters were making their way home. Only a few thousand of them had made it to the demonstration. Access roads to Government House were blocked by triple barricades. We skirted the no-go zone and headed for our hotel, which turned out be a very large, very raj sort of establishment with hunting trophies in the entrance hall and Indo-Saracenic turrets sprouting from the roof. Sarah ran up and hugged me. 'We made it,' she cried. 'I think this calls for a celebration.'

A wedding feast was being held on the hotel lawns that evening, and the scent of biryani and tandoori meats made me realise I was half-starved. But this delicious food was for the wedding guests only. The main restaurant was shut and all that was on offer was sandwiches. 'Let me deal with this,' Sarah announced. 'In the meanwhile, why don't you wait in the bar?'

The bar was crowded with non-residents, mainly groups of young men who had come to get drunk without their families finding out. I was invited to join a table that was well on its way, which included a couple of English boys who turned out to be interested in motorcycles.

They were brothers, Con and Jules, and this was their first trip to India. They were art students, free spirits, going where the mood took them. And they were totally out of their depth in this vast and unscrupulous subcontinent.

So far they had commissioned a load of silver jewellery of their own design, intending to sell it to tourists outside the Taj Mahal and so fund their onward journey. They were surprised that the local stall-holders and street-vendors took exception to this enterprising initiative. I explained that setting out your wares in Covent Garden is one thing; doing the same in Agra is quite another. The shopkeepers and vendors have to pay high rents and protection money to keep their prime sites. Naturally they object to interlopers – especially to Westerners, who in their eyes are all stinking rich anyway.

This did not go down well with Con and Jules, so we switched to talking about motorbikes. They had already 'checked out' the Enfield and felt that they had gone one better. In Agra they'd found an old BSA 350 – a real antique – and were having it rebuilt from scratch. A snapshot of the machine in its original condition suggested that there was a lot of work to be done. But it was when Jules started explaining how they were going to bolt on a sidecar and install a stereo system and how he was going to have the whole damn thing painted in psychedelic colours – again to his own design – and how, after they'd finished riding it all over South East Asia, they were going to ship the bike back to England and make it the centrepiece of an art exhibition – it was then that I started seriously worrying about them.

They had already paid out more than the price of a brand-new Enfield and the bills were still coming in – but that wasn't my main concern. Neither of them had ever ridden a motorcycle in England, let alone India. They hadn't got a valid licence between them, and couldn't understand why on Indian roads a sidecar combination is far more lethal than an ordinary bike. They were two innocents abroad. I tried to caution them without completely puncturing their dream.

The younger brother, Con, was slightly built and wore his long hair free, while Jules kept his in a woolly Rasta bonnet. 'What's up with that bloke?' asked Con, pointing to one of the local boozers who'd had rather more than he could handle. 'Is he gay or something? He keeps on trying to put his arm round me.'

The man next to me, Rajesh, was still pretty sober, so I asked him about his friend. 'Oh, he's just drunk,' he laughed, 'and is deeply enamoured with this young madam here.'

'So what's up?' asked Con again, by now looking hassled.

'He thinks you're a lady, Con, and says he's deeply smitten.'

'You must be joking.'

'Sadly not. But don't worry, the same thing used to happen to me in Asia when I had long hair. Don't pay any attention to him. His friends know he's drunk too much and they'll look after him.'

I looked up to find Sarah smiling triumphantly. 'I've swung it,' she announced. 'We are to have a choice selection of dishes from the wedding feast.'

'How the hell did you manage that?' asked Con.

'Natural charm,' Sarah said airily, 'and just a little baksheesh.'

I didn't need any further bidding and immediately left the bar. After exposure to Con and Jules's innocence I felt old as well as hungry.

'They reminded me of how I used to be,' I said, 'when I first came out to India on the Hippy Trail.'

'Nonsense,' Sarah snorted. 'Even you weren't that gullible. Now for God's sake let's eat.'

'There is no city – except Bombay, the queen of all – more beautiful in her garish style than Lucknow.' Thus wrote Kipling a hundred years ago; but if he were to return today he would find her garish charms sadly faded.

The grandiose buildings, most of them erected by the Nawabs of Oudh in bizarre combinations of debased Mughal and European styles, are still there, from the Bara Imambara, with its great vaulted hall and labyrinth, to Constantia, once the palace of a French mercenary and now home to La Martinière School. But of the handsome town houses, the haveli, which once crowded upon each other around the Chowk, only a handful remain. What was once an elegant city, the 'Paris of the East', is now just another regional administrative centre. Its broad avenues are kept cleaner than most of its peers, but they are just as choked with fuming trucks and motor-rickshaws.

And there have been other changes. Lucknow was once famed for its refinement and culture. The purity of its Urdu was said to be matched only by that of Delhi. The extravagance of its poets, the delicacy of its calligraphers, the grace of its courtesans, were a source of great pride, as were the skills of its artisans in concocting sumptuous perfumes and shadow-work embroidery. Lucknowis developed their own distinctive cuisine and school of music, which on special occasions can still be appreciated – we had enjoyed it at the wedding the night before. But there is always the feeling that these are just remnants of a far more splendid past, and that even in its heyday Lucknowi culture was backward-looking.

The natural patrons of this culture, the landowning classes or zamindars, were mostly Muslims. It was among these land-owners that many of the ideas which finally led to the creation of Pakistan were first mooted. They were equally proud of their heritage and fearful of what would happen to their culture and their landed estates under a Hindu raj. Many of them joined the Muslim League and campaigned for a separate Muslim homeland. In 1947 most of this class opted to move to Pakistan, leaving the mass of their co-religionists who stayed behind without the leadership and local influence that might have afforded them some protection.

Since then, some of their worst fears have been realised. Their cherished Urdu, adopted by Pakistan as its national language, has gone into near terminal decline in its traditional strongholds around Delhi and western UP. Their vast estates were broken up by the land reforms of the 1950s. And now, half a century on, the spectre of Hindutva has risen again.

Whether things would have been different had they stayed put, defending the culture and interests of fellow Muslims, is hard to say. For all their refinement, as a class they were backward-looking. Not all who left for Pakistan have prospered there. Their snobbery is proverbial, as when a refugee landowner just arrived in Karachi was asked what were his qualifications. 'I am a Rajput,' he declared, affirming his noble ancestry went back even beyond conversion to Islam. Such airs and graces were hardly likely to help these exiled zamindars fit into the new and struggling Muslim state they had chosen to join.

Kanpur, where we were to rejoin the GT Road, has no such pretensions. Its inhabitants like to think of it as the 'Manchester of the East', a down-to-earth, industrious city, whose cloth mills and tanneries are as worthy of respect as Lucknow's flights of architectural fancy.

As I approached it I saw a dark industrial smog ahead. Crossing over to the south bank of the Ganges, I searched around for directions to the city centre. Our departure from Lucknow had been delayed by another garlanding ceremony at the local Enfield dealer (roses had replaced marigolds – a sure sign we were entering Upper India), and although we had covered the fifty miles which separate the two cities at record speed, not even slowing down when an elephant crossed the road, it was lamp-lighting time before we entered Kanpur.

I crossed and recrossed the railway line, hopelessly lost, dodging between the heavy traffic and an endless stream of handcarts piled high with cotton bales or foul-smelling hides. My headlight picked out the shadowy figures of these carters, bent double as they heaved and pushed their loads up the incline of a railway bridge.

Then I was over the bridge and in amongst the main bazaar, clashing wheels with bicycle-rickshaws and snaking my way between pedestrians who always thought they had the right of way. I was more confident now about riding in such conditions; but I was still mightily relieved when we reached our goal at last.

This was The Attic, a sprawling colonial bungalow that takes paying guests in one wing; the family live in the main part of the house, which also serves as headquarters for a charity helping children with cerebral palsy. As soon as I arrived I knew it was an unusual set-up. A pre-war Riley drophead coupé sat in the drive and a Yorkshire Terrier snapped at my heels as I dismounted.

This was the last night we'd all be together. Sarah and Tyrel were taking the morning train to Delhi and then flying back to London. From here on I would be on my own; but there was no time to feel maudlin.

I had to repack the bike several times, stripping out non-essentials, since now I'd have to carry everything I needed. The others had their own packing to do. Then we went in search of a suitable place for our last meal together, ending up in a Muslim-style restaurant which was mainly occupied by two private parties. One was a group of Army and Air Force officers; the other looked like the local mafia. A soldier stood guard on one side of the door, a goonda with an ill-concealed pistol on the other. When one of the mafia bosses left by car he drove straight into a cyclist and just kept on going. The man was bleeding, his front wheel bent in two, but he didn't wish to lodge a complaint. He knew better than to tangle with that particular class of citizen.

The next morning we had to rush to the station to catch the

Gomti Express. Jostled by all the frantic passengers and hucksters crowding onto the platform, we tried to exchange our farewells. Tyrel was fascinated by all the bustle of a main-line railway station – the cries of chaieee! chaieee! as the tea-vendors passed down the platform – and seemed to be the only cheerful soul among us. 'Stay cool, be well and all that stuff,' he said, and then gave me a hug.

Sarah was close to tears. 'Just don't go and get yourself killed,' she murmured. But as the train shuddered in anticipation of departure, she yelled through the window grille: 'You know, you're really the lucky one; staying out here – you bastard.'

The train started moving; a final wave, and they were gone.

I walked back over the tracks and through the now empty booking hall to where I'd left the bike. It was going to be a fine day, and the morning sun was just catching the Gothic towers of Kanpur Central Station. I was alone. From here on, I'd have just one constant companion on the GT Road – the inanimate metal lump I still referred to impersonally as 'The Enfield' or 'The Bullet'. I hadn't even bestowed a gender on it, as so many motorists do with their vehicles; it was neither 'he' nor 'she'. But I'd grown to like the way it performed on Indian roads. Most modern breeds of bike would have cracked up under that pounding. But that was no reason to get attached to a machine.

The engine started first time. I slid the bike off its stand and was just about to engage first gear when the damn thing coughed a couple of times and died on me.

'YOU BITCH!!!' I screamed, and my voice echoed round the empty station forecourt. Then, feeling ashamed of myself, I started her up again and headed off for the day's engagements.

It helped with shaking off my new-found loneliness that I had a busy time of it in Kanpur – starting off with a visit to Sunil Rashtogi, the local Enfield dealer. He'd called a press conference of sorts, so that local journalists could ask me about my trip. I wasn't too keen on the idea, being more accustomed to asking questions than answering them. And when the Press Corps arrived, it was soon apparent they were more interested in my views on the British Royal Family and divorce than my journey through their country.

I was amazed at the articles which appeared the following day. 'Even today,' screamed the headline in the Hindu-language *Amar Ujala*, 'English people prefer marriages settled by their parents.' When I pointed out to Sunil Rashtogi this was the precise opposite of what I had said, he shook his head resignedly. 'But this is what their readers want to see.'

The most probing questions came from Radkhika Sachdev, a woman journalist from the *Pioneer*, the paper Kipling once worked for. 'What is your opinion of this account, Hell's Angel?' she asked.

Thinking the question had something to do with motorcycling, I gave my enthusiastic response to Hunter S. Thompson's account of California's motorcycle gangs, *Hell's Angels*. 'A great story about sex'n'drugs and living dangerously,' I burbled '. . . difficult to research . . . dangerous people to deal with . . . morally reprehensible, of course, but great fun.' As she scribbled this down I noticed her frown of incredulity.

'But do you think what Mother Teresa is doing in Calcutta is given full justice?' she demanded.

I realised I was barking up the wrong tree. She was asking about *Hell's Angel*, Christopher Hitchen's documentary on Calcutta's most famous Albanian nun, and not about a saga of bikes, booze and other dangerous substances. She had the decency to strike out all my previous comments, though if she'd printed some of the things I'd said about the San Bernadino Chapter as my views on Mother Teresa it could have made a sensational story.

Among the guests who stayed on for a snack-lunch of pakoras and samosas was an elderly man, Mr B. L. Bhatia, who had worked for the big LMC Scooter factory in Kanpur until he retired. He was knowledgeable about the Grand Trunk Road and its history, particularly the section now in Pakistan.

'You see, my family used to live in Bannu, in the North-West Frontier Province, where they had a business in dried fruits. We left everything behind in 1948 and came to Kanpur.

It was a tragedy, because before Partition the Muslims and Hindus in NWFP were living like brothers together. You know, it was the politicians who stirred up all the tensions between the communities. But by 1948 nearly all the Hindu community in Bannu had left or were leaving for India.

'I joined the Indian Air Force in a civilian capacity and was posted all over – Kanpur, Bangalore, Shillong. You know that this Enfield motorcycle you are riding is named after a gun? Very fitting, don't you think? If you are interested in our past conflicts with Pakistan, while you are in Kanpur you should see the battle tanks we captured from them in Gujarat. Three wars we have fought with them since Partition.'

Such casual encounters with former refugees were becoming a daily occurrence now that I was in Upper India. The previous day I had run into a man whose family had fled from Multan in fear of their lives. 'Many generations we had been shopkeepers in Multan,' he said, 'and never was there any trouble. But in 1947 this fear grew among the Hindu community; now that the Muslims were ruling us, they could come and kill us as they pleased. It was a most difficult decision. Everything we had we left behind.'

His family escaped by train to Delhi, where they joined thousands of other refugees in the temporary camps being set up. They were put into the Purana Qila, the old fort built by Sher Shah Suri, along with six or seven hundred other families. And there they stayed for the next seven years, trying to piece together a new life. 'Grandfather opened a shop; my father stayed in the army; I got my diploma in mechanical engineering and worked for a company making harvester machines. Eventually we moved to a new colony in south Delhi. Most of our relatives went there.'

Compared with many they had been lucky. Their train got through safely; the family remained intact; there was always at least one wage-earner; and now, fifty years on, they had worked their way back to prosperity and middle-class respectability. I knew there were hundreds of thousands who had fared much worse than this; yet these tales of uprooting and starting out afresh in a new country affected me nonetheless. There was a hidden nation of these people in India and their shared trauma still moulded the way they thought about family loyalties, the need to make money and, inevitably, about Pakistan and the Muslim community in India.

My landlady at The Attic, Mrs Santosh Mahendrajit Singh, had her own memories of Partition. She had been brought up in Lahore, where her grandfather had been 'a very prominent lawyer' (her father had studied law in London together with Jawarharlal Nehru). Though always a Hindu, she had attended one of Lahore's Catholic schools, the Convent of Jesus and Mary, up to her Senior Cambridge.

Everything about the cool, high-ceilinged room in which we sipped our English-style tea spoke of 'old money' – the marble vase containing a single rose, the watercolour landscapes, the collection of antique Hindu and Buddhist bronzes in the corner cabinet. 'You see those old sofas?' She pointed. 'They were in my father's house in Lahore, but before it was ransacked he managed to get them out.

'Ah, my memories of that house! So many years ago! As a girl, my passion was for Shakespeare. I wanted to become a teacher but,' she spread her palms, 'there was an arranged marriage, and by the time of Partition we were already here in Kanpur. Now all my children have grown up I can devote more of my time to our organisation for looking after children – both polio cases and cerebral palsy.

'We began with polio children. Did you know that today is Pulse Polio Day? We are aiming to inoculate eight million children across the country. Here, of course, we began in a small way. We are purely NGO [non-governmental organisation] and have received not one penny from state funding. An orthopaedic surgeon volunteered to operate free of charge. The children come from such very poor families, you understand, that they cannot afford to be treated otherwise.

'Then some mothers brought in their children with cerebral palsy, so we started on that too. We have to explain to the mothers that there isn't a medical solution, that it needs rehabilitation and physiotherapy. You see, there is this shame in the family if there is a spastic child. So often they are just locked away, spending all their life between four walls. We must educate the mothers; but even then they find it so hard to find time to do all the exercises. They are so poor, these families, usually the woman has to go out and work and then do the cooking. They cannot afford even the rickshaw fare to bring their child for treatment. Now at least we have a bus to bring in the children for their sessions.

'I'm not in favour of just dispensing bounty,' she declared. 'On one level it's humanitarianism, pure and simple. And as we are mostly talking to mothers, we are seeking to create awareness of women's rights, to make them more equal partners. We are also closely linked with the All-India Women's Conference.'

A private secretary entered the room and whispered in her ear. 'A poor woman is here,' she announced. 'She has brought her infant child who has polio. Please excuse me a few minutes. These people I cannot refuse.'

I was left to reflect on Mrs Santosh Singh's charitable work. Most of it seemed to be filling in the gaping holes in government-run healthcare and social services. There are thousands of small charities in India doing similar good works. Her approach seemed sensible and enlightened.

My surprise was all the greater when, on her return, she launched into a tirade against reserving posts for Muslims and other minorities. 'In medical colleges such people are given many chances to resit their exams, and at the end of the day perhaps the examiners will say, "Let's give him twenty extra marks to get him through." So an unqualified person becomes a doctor. That is butchery, for you are playing with human life – and this just for the sake of the reservation system. In professional and technical fields they shouldn't be promoting unqualified people. Equally, these reservations should not apply to the academic sector.'

I mentioned the recent demonstrations in Lucknow by lower-caste Hindus trying to protect reservations in their favour.

'That is just politicians muscle-flexing,' she snorted. 'But I agree some kind of reservations are necessary – up to a point, mind you – in a country where the very poor and the backward castes have always been downtrodden. This caste business is so complicated: for over time each caste bifurcates and the number of castes multiplies to the nth degree, and between each subgroup there are these frictions. Things have improved in some respects; some people of the lowest caste are now government ministers and suchlike, whereas at one time it was unthinkable for anyone to touch leather. And in helping the backward castes become forward castes, yes, reservations can be useful. But it all becomes so political and communal. In a very caste-conscious society this communalism exists even within one religion.'

'What about with Muslims? I have recently been to Ayodhya.'

'As a totally non-fundamentalist person, as I consider myself, I would never say one religion is better than another. Nor do I believe that religion should be a justification for any kind of destruction.' I nodded eagerly. 'The only thing,' she continued 'is that people aren't applying their minds to the fact that this particular Babri Mosque wasn't really in use. It was a ruin. I regret that in Ayodhya the mob became hysterical. But we have been asking to worship in this place again and again. And you must know that this Ayodhya is as sacred to us Hindus as Jerusalem is to Christians, Mecca to Muslims, the Golden Temple at Amritsar to Sikhs. If the Muslims want a new mosque, let them build it nearby, in Faizabad.

'But the same problem is there in Benares, with Aurangzeb's mosque.'

'Ah, that mosque is all surrounded by temples. Why don't the Muslims just give in gracefully?'

'So you agree with the aims of Hindutva?'

'Look all over the world,' she said. 'People say they live in a Christian or an Islamic country. Is there anything wrong in that? Or in calling India a Hindu country? It is only pointing out that the majority follow a certain creed. And up to now the Hindus have been very subdued. This Hindu ethos, Hindutva, has been concentrated in the Hindu heartland, here in UP. But now it is growing up everywhere. Why? Because the Hindus, who are basically not aggressive people, have been badgered into it by the way that Central Government has been pampering the Muslims. The Congress has been playing that game for a long time, and just to win the Muslim vote bank.

'You must be careful,' she warned, 'not to draw hard-and-fast lines. There are Muslims who are selling "Ram Ram" scarves to pilgrims, wooden sandals, even the puja materials. Again, the threat to the Benares mosque is exaggerated. If a handful of so-called Hindu fanatics issue some threats, it's only to prove to themselves that they're not cowardy-custards. Be sure, their bark is worse than their bite. Besides, all this going on about buildings – this isn't the essence of Hinduism. You know what Aldous Huxley once said about Benares: "It's the Army & Navy Stores of the Hindu Religion". No, with Hinduism you can worship in a field just a little black figure of Durga. That is Hinduism. The rest is so much politics.'

That night I heard the klaxon call of the GT Road. It was time to be moving again; and this time I would be on my own.

I felt apprehensive as I loaded up the bike and slipped out of Kanpur as dawn was breaking. But once out on the open road, I experienced a sense of freedom and clarity which comes only when ties have been cut and you are travelling unencumbered.

The northern plains are best seen at this early hour. The night-time mists begin to disperse and are transfused with pink and saffron light. Great flocks of rose-ringed parakeets arise from trees in which they've passed the night. Even the ungainly vultures dropping from their perches with a great beating of wings seem less horrible than in the midday sun.

This section of the Grand Trunk Road is less used by heavy traffic, which these days mostly cuts west to Agra along the more modern Sher Shah Suri Road. My route via Aligarh was more direct; but the road is narrower and has not been upgraded much since the British left. It squeezes its way through villages and curls around their water tanks, while the new road bludgeons its way through.

About forty miles out of Kanpur I bumped my way over an open railway crossing. Strangely, the barrier was down on the other side. A bus had got there before me, so I stopped behind it and tried to see what was going on.

To my horror, the bus started reversing straight towards me. There wasn't much I could do about it. Motorbikes don't have a reverse gear. The railway lines were directly behind me. I honked my horn for all I was worth and tried to roll the bike off the road. Some passengers in the back seat shouted and pointed at me – but still the bus came on.

Everything seemed to be happening in slow motion.

The impact knocked the bike flat and sent me sprawling. When I looked up I was half underneath the bus, its rear wheel inches from my head. Thank God the driver had felt the crash and stopped. His ticket collector jumped down and was peering at me. Satisfied that I was still alive, he told the driver to roll forward again.

I straightened out and patted myself gingerly to see if anything was broken. Nothing serious. But the bike was another matter. The front fork had taken the impact and was badly bent. There were bits of glass around. I picked up the wounded Bullet and wheeled her off the road.

Damage assessment could come later. First I was going to confront that stupid son-of-a-bitch who'd run me over. By now he'd reversed across the railway lines. I walked up to the first bus I saw and indicated to the driver to step down. He was unwilling to leave the safety of his cab, so I stuck my head round the open door.

'He is not your man,' said one of the passengers. 'It was that other bus, further down the road. We all saw him do it. He didn't even care to look. Shall we come with you now to deal with him?'

I wanted witnesses, not a lynch-mob, so I marched off alone to the second bus, the one that had run me down. The driver's seat was empty. I was told he'd jumped out and disappeared into the fields. What the hell was I going to do now?

I took down the bus's licence plate and permit numbers. By now the train had passed and the barriers were being raised. As I trudged back across the rails the bus that had hit me bounced past, the driver making good his escape. There was nothing I could do to stop him. I shook my fist in the air.

A couple of railwaymen were staring at the bike. It looked a mess. Broken glass from the headlamp and rear-view mirrors and oddments of clothing lay scattered by the roadside. The right front fork had a nasty dent in it, though I couldn't find any traces of oil. The suspension cylinder inside it must have been an unusual shape but it looked like the seals had somehow survived. I then checked the front wheel spokes and rim, which again seemed undamaged.

Now the moment of truth. I switched on the power and tested the controls. Everything working, even the bulb inside the smashed front indicator. I built up cylinder compression and tried the kick-start. When the engine fired on the second attempt I could have hugged that gunmetal machine. The steering felt a bit loose but it would get me to the nearest village with a repair shop. Then I'd have to get that front fork straightened out.

I found the kind of place I was looking for – a lock-up shack with half a dozen battered Vespas and Rajdoots out front – just two miles up the road. The sole mechanic looked over the bike and disappeared into his shop.

He returned with an assortment of wooden and steel hammers and some greasy rags. These he wrapped around his hammer heads before setting to work. As he bashed away, I held the bike steady, worried that the cylinder inside the bent fork might break, checking for any sign of oil leaking. He beat the metal patiently, never exerting too much force, as though he was happy to spend all week on this task.

The village policeman looked in. I told him about the accident and read out the licence numbers. He didn't want to get involved. The mechanic warned me that if I lodged a complaint I'd have to remain in the district for weeks. The bus company would call witnesses who then wouldn't turn up, and those who did would be bribed. I decided to let it pass. I was lucky not to be stuck in some rural hospital.

Eventually the fork returned to a tube-like shape. There was still an indentation where the bus's bumper had struck and the paintwork was a mess. But as roadside repairs go, it was a pretty good job. At least it should get me to the next town, Kannauj.

The lower section of Kannauj, where it meets the GT Road, was a huge and bustling bazaar, amongst which were a fair number of repair shops. Several mechanics volunteered to take the bike to pieces for me, but none seemed any better qualified than the village man who'd already worked on it. By now I was fairly sure that the front suspension was still working. The steering felt wobbly at low speeds; but that was soon sorted out by tightening the steering nut. Rather than risk creating further problems I decided to continue – all the way to Delhi, if necessary – with things as they were.

I still felt shaken up. What I needed was a quiet chai-house where I could recover from the shock and humiliation of it all. This was my first day on the road alone and I'd managed just forty miles before running into trouble.

The tea was thick and sweet and helped revive my spirits. I'd lost several hours, but I still wanted to look around Kannauj. A camel caravan loped past – a reminder that I was in Upper India. To hell with my plans of reaching Aligarh that night. I was a free agent. Surely I'd find somewhere to stay along the way.

Kannauj is no longer the great city it was in ancient times. During the seventh century it was the capital of Harsha, who held sway from Kashmir to the borders of Assam. It was sacked by Mahmud of Ghazni in 1018 and from the end of the twelfth century was permanently controlled by Muslim overlords.

One of these dynasties, the Sharqui kings of Jaunpur, built a mosque here using the remains of a Hindu temple. It could therefore qualify as a 'disputed site', as at Varanasi or Ayodhya; but the Jama Masjid at Kannauj has so far escaped controversy, and Hindus and Muslims worship side by side. This mosque is a rare survivor of the many known to have been built by the Sharqui dynasty, the rest having been destroyed by the Lodhi kings of Delhi. They were also Muslims; but medieval rulers were as likely to destroy the palaces and mosques of their rivals for dynastic reasons as to pull down Hindu temples on religious grounds.

The town is also famous for its perfumes, especially Attar of Roses; but as this was a Sunday all the factories were shut. I wove my way through the narrow streets and up a steep hill to the old citadel, where I found a line of solid, unadorned mausoleums built for Muslim rulers of the town. They were deserted apart from a herd of buffaloes and the young boy in charge of them.

The modern Hindu temple at the base of the hill was much busier. I tried asking directions to the battlefield of Kannauj, where Sher Shah Suri won a decisive victory over the Mughal Emperor Humayun, but nobody I asked had ever heard of it.

This may be because the course of the Ganges has shifted south since then, and the battle took place beside that holy river. Humayun's army had built a bridge of boats to cross over and force the issue. They had the larger army and better artillery; but they'd suffered defeat at the hands of the wily Afghan before, morale was low and desertions a problem. The Afghans were in higher spirits, especially after Sher Shah's melodramatic address in which he reminded them it was only because they had been disunited that Humayun's father, Babur, had been able to conquer Hindustan.

Battle was joined on 17 May 1540, the Mughal right wing gaining the initial advantage. But the Afghans pushed them back on their own centre until they completely surrounded the Mughal army. Panic broke out among the camp followers, who burst the chains between the heavy gun carriages. As the Mughal army tried to flee across their bridge it collapsed under the weight of numbers. The battle became a rout in which thousands were slaughtered. Humayun was forced to flee into exile in Persia. Only after Sher Shah was dead did he venture back to reclaim his Indian domains.

I may well have crossed the battlefield down side-roads, working my way back to the GT Road around Kannauj. Once on the main road I didn't waste time. The bike was handling well enough, my own morale restored, so I pressed on northwards.

By sunset I had reached Etah, a large market town where I knew there would be an Enfield dealer who could check the damaged front fork. The centre of town was crowded with country people who had come to a fun-fair. There was a big wheel and hundreds of sideshows, among them a motorcycle stunt team. It made me think of Garhmukteswar, which was now only a hundred miles to the north.

I spotted the Enfield dealership on the way out of town. The shop was shut up, but a boy ran over and beckoned me to follow him. We ended up at the office of a tractor company which I knew was part of the same industrial group. The local manager, Mr A. K. Singh, asked me to come in. Thankfully there was no garlanding ceremony. Instead, he ordered his servant to go and buy a bottle of whisky. Then he phoned up a hotel and booked me in. I was warming to Mr Singh.

We sat there in his office, drinking Indian whisky by the mugful, while he explained about his business and his plans for the future. His wife was upstairs cooking, but his twelve-year-old daughter had the run of the place. 'She is a very intelligent girl,' he said proudly, 'and will be doing an MBA and afterwards look after the family business. I have also one son who is to become qualified in medicine.' His future, and that of his family for the next twenty years, was mapped out and spoken of as certainty. 'It is God's gift,' he smiled.

I wanted to go and wash and change in whichever hotel I'd been booked into, but Mr Singh would have none of it. 'You must eat with us,' he beamed. 'My wife is making a most excellent khari. You see, our caste is Jat, our forefathers all farmers, our food homely but,' and here he smacked his lips, 'I assure you, most tasty.'

The whisky bottle did the rounds again. 'In our constituency,' Mr A. K. Singh announced, 'there are not less than
80,000 Jats.'

'Constituency?' I queried. What was all this about?

'Oh, did I not tell you? I am BJP candidate for Jalasar, a rural
constituency 42 kilometres towards Agra. I have been much
involved in BJP politics these past years. When BJP leadership
like Mr R. J. Singh came to Etah, he took breakfast in our own
place.'

The tractor dealer-turned-politician rummaged in a steel
filing cabinet. 'There are approximately ten lakhs [one million]
in our constituency,' he recited. 'Rural areas are Jat or other
caste Hindus. But in the town there are many castes. Thakur, 15
per cent; Yadav, 10 per cent; Brahmins, 5 per cent; Muslims,
4–6 per cent; backward castes, 20 per cent . . .'

The list went on. Campaigning on the local level seemed to
be caste-driven – a numbers game.

'What about BJP policies?' I asked.

Mr Singh was well-drilled on this. 'Number one,' he
bellowed, 'is honesty. We are anti-corruption. Number two: we
are a strong party, a united party. Number three: we want a
strong India. We are anti-foreign investment.' It sounded like a
set-piece to be delivered from the hustings.

'Other policies,' he continued. 'If BJP forms government, we
shall do away with reservations [for Muslims and backward
castes]. On terrorism in Punjab and Jammu-Kashmir, we will
crack down. The BJP is a totally Hindu party. We will be tough
on Muslims. This Aurangzeb mosque in Varanasi: it should be
changed to be a temple. India should be a Hindu state. If
Muslim people do not like this, they should leave to Pakistan.'

I looked at my host, with his strong nose and full moustache,
so certain of the righteousness of his views. A BJP candidate and
a hardliner at that. I hadn't expected this when I rolled into
Etah.

'Don't you think all this will cause problems with Muslims?' I
ventured.

'Who is to cause problems?' he retorted. 'Pakistan? Military conflict with Pakistan is finished now, because India is too strong. Pakistan is a very poor country.'

It was the politics of the school bully. India's 120 million Muslims could stay put and shut up, sinking yet further into their communal ghetto, an under-class in a Hindu raj. Or they could 'leave to Pakistan'.

I tried another tack. 'Looking back on it, do you think Partition was justified?'

'Gandhiji, the great father of Indian thought, did not agree with this dividing of India. Prime Minister Nehru was very different, an Indian European, a socialist. He allowed this Partition while knowing it was not good for India. Sardar Patel was the better man, a strong man, very honest.

'India was hijacked by this Gandhi dynasty. They behaved just like a royal family. But now the BJP is winning votes from Congress. This Sonia Gandhi, she is nothing.' He spat out some red betel juice. 'She is not even Indian; but Congress people say she is. Congress is finished.'

He swilled his mouth out with whisky and refilled the cups. He raised his own and declared: 'I love the English, you know. My father, who is a landlord, he says to me: "With the English there was always very good justice." Now, for any kind of justice you have to pay. The BJP is anti all this corruption.'

His daughter whispered something in his ear. 'Now we will take khana,' he announced. The meal was as good as he'd promised – especially the creamy yellow khari prepared by his wife.

The hotel was outside Etah town, opposite a big dairy products factory. Most of the other guests were seconded as visiting managers or trainees from other parts of India. I drank tea while my room was being cleaned. Here I was in a different culture, that of the box-wallah, the aspiring corporate man. It seemed light years away from the world of small businessmen like Mr Singh and their home-grown politics.

'Do you mind if we have a chat?' asked a young, round-faced Bengali who introduced himself as Raja Roy. He was a management trainee, Calcutta-educated, a graduate in engineering. He expected to end up working in the fish products division but had been sent here, hundreds of miles from the sea, on a six-week rural training course 'to find out what the real India is like'. He'd just returned from a week living in a village: 'A real eye-opener, I assure you, because like most management trainees I'm from an urban background. To begin with it was difficult, getting up in the morning and crapping in the fields. But that's what 90 per cent of Indians do. Now I know how they live,' he added with quiet pride.

'And after staying in a village I don't believe much of what the government says about rural development and self-sufficiency in foodstuffs. Development? These last fifty years there's been no real development.'

'Why does your company send you on these courses?' I asked.

'Oh, for good business reasons. With our products, actually 40 per cent of revenues are coming from rural areas. But this sector is growing at up to 20 per cent a year, compared to maybe two or three per cent in urban markets. More rural people are buying more manufactured products. To understand them better – that is good business sense.'

The hotel manager, who had been staring at a television, decided to join us. He was a very fair-skinned Brahmin and his pale, blue-green eyes and reddish-brown hair made me think of Ireland rather than India. The Bengali management trainee didn't like this turn of events. 'I must be up very early in the morning,' he said, and promptly fled.

'All this economic liberalism,' said the Brahmin with heavy sarcasm. 'It is good for these multinationals, for people like this Bengali babu.' His tone was condescending, contemptuous even. 'But it will not last. Not after the BJP gets in.'

I wasn't up for another dose of politics, so I asked whether my room was ready.

'Yess, yess. All is seen to. But are you not interested in what is truly India? Just twenty kilometres from here, Ganj-Dundwara way, there is this holy man. He has very great spiritual power;

he can cure any problems. Special powers, he has, what we are knowing as the Third Eye. He is part of the God. He has had this since birth.'

He paused, to let this take effect. 'This Pandit, he is a relative of mine. Nobody can say his age. He lives in his own house, very strictly, with no alcohols. It is his private house, not an ashram. If you wish to see him . . .'

'No, thank you.' He acted as though he was doing me a favour; but in reality he was touting for business on behalf of his guru relative. And I didn't like his insinuating ways.

'The Pandit,' he persisted in a thin, wheedling voice, 'he has man's human form. He looks very old now. But he is part of the God Power. He can make the polio-afflicted man walk! He has given sight to the blind man! My own father, he is under this Pandit.'

Right then I didn't care if he could conjure elephants out of thin air. What I needed was sleep. 'You are the acting hotel manager?' I queried. 'Then please may I have the key to my room?'

His pale eyes glowered at me. He didn't like being reminded of his not-so-elevated professional status. 'Here,' he hissed, flinging down the keys before turning his back on me. As I walked out he was switching up the volume on the TV set.

A thick mist blanketed the country next morning. It was cold – even for midwinter in North India – and for the first time I was thankful for the warmth of my leather jacket.

The temperature wasn't the only thing to change as I rode on through the Doab, the fertile flatlands between the Ganga and the Jamuna. The road broadened out and I encountered such novelties as flyovers and diversions round towns.

The closer I got to Delhi, the more private vehicles appeared. The Hindustan Ambassador was no longer king, its place usurped by the Maruti, a small, Japanese-designed runabout whose owners generally prefer to drive themselves rather than employ a chauffeur. The towns I passed through had more modern buildings, more telephone wires, more up-to-date infrastructure. People in the street seemed more businesslike and purposeful.

Somewhere in western UP I had crossed an invisible boundary between two different Indias. Behind me were the backward-looking heartlands of eastern UP and Bihar; ahead, the fast-developing region around Delhi. The contrast is far greater than between, say, Naples and Milan.

Not that everything changed all of a sudden. As I rode over the flyover into Aligarh the opposite lane was filled with a brightly caparisoned elephant and its escort of naked sadhus.

Aligarh is a busy metal-working town. But what I wanted to see was the Aligarh Muslim University. It is still famous throughout India as an élite institution. But during the run-up to Independence and Partition it acquired a special notoriety; for it was here, among Muslim intellectuals, that the Pakistan movement gathered strength and impetus; and it was from here that young students fanned out into the villages to carry the Muslim League's propaganda to farmers and small landowners, who, though their families had been Muslim for generations, had previously lived in harmony with their Hindu and Sikh neighbours.

I rode the Enfield slowly around the pleasant, tree-shaded campus, past old Victorian buildings in the Indo-Saracenic style and more recent additions, such as the Medical College, which attempt to blend Islamic features into basic modern architecture. I stopped in front of Strachey Hall, where the Quaid-i-Azam, Mohammad Ali Jinnah, delivered some of his most famous speeches. I could almost hear the packed rows of students, the élite of Muslim India, roaring their approbation and shouting, '*Pakistan Zindabad!*' – Long Live Pakistan!

It is hard to see how in the 1940s Aligarh could have stayed out of communal politics. Many of its graduates were prominent Muslim Leaguers and its student body was a fertile recruiting ground for young activists. Jinnah called it 'the arsenal of Muslim India'. Others have described how the very idea of Pakistan sent its students into a 'mystic frenzy'.

Yet it should have been obvious that any division of the country would leave Aligarh on the Hindu-majority side. To back Pakistan was tantamount to institutional suicide. Some wise heads held out against the headlong rush for Pakistan, among them the senior Muslim Congressman, Maulana Abul Kalam Azad. The university library is named after him.

Since then, the university has tried to distance itself from the actions of some of its students and staff during Partition. It stresses that ever since Sir Syed Ahmad Khan founded the first nucleus of the university, the MAO (Muhammadan Anglo Oriental) College, in 1875 it has been a secular institution, open to students of all races and creeds.

Sir Syed stood out against communalism and obscurantism in all its forms. He wanted to provide a modern, scientific education instead of the traditional Koranic learning of the madrasas. His college would be primarily for Muslims, but not exclusively so. That secular ethos continued after the MAO College became a university in 1920. During the last twenty years of British rule, Hindu students accounted for between 8 and 12 per cent of examination passes.

The Aligarh Muslim University still clings to that secular ethos today. However, as a primarily Muslim institution it faces peculiar problems and potential hostility. It is in much the same position as a Catholic college when the Protestant Ascendancy was still a live issue in Britain.

I talked with the librarian and several other learned professors gathered in his office; but they were wary of offering opinions, especially when they understood my interest in the events surrounding Partition. Instead they referred me to experts or books I should read.

Outside the Maulana Azad Library groups of students were lying on the grass. The university canteen was closed. It was the first day of Ramadan.

About two hours down the Delhi Road I had the worst 'near miss' to date. The road ahead was clear and I was moving fast when an oncoming bus pulled out to overtake a lorry. The GT

Road was now a good three lanes wide, so I just kept going. Plenty of room to spare. Then the lorry pulled out to overtake a tractor and suddenly I had three vehicles coming at me in line abreast.

I flashed my headlight – the standard warning in India for 'I'm here and coming through'. Surely the bus driver would back down. Not a bit of it. He just kept on coming. Bus and lorry were locked in combat like something out of *Ben-Hur*, edging each other further over until the bus was close to coming off the tarmac on *my* side of the road. There were people squatting by the dusty verge, probably waiting for a bus, so I couldn't go completely off-road. I had no choice but to go for the gap flat out because it was shrinking every second. By now I was riding on the very edge of the tarmac.

As the bus rushed past, missing me by inches, my back wheel slid down onto the loose surface. I hauled the bike back onto the tarmac but now I was fish-tailing, the back end swinging violently from side to side. Somehow I kept the bike from spilling over and slowed to a halt. I looked back at the fast-disappearing bus which had nearly wiped me out. It was only then I noticed all the passengers on the roof. They were waving at me.

I now knew why the bus had kept on coming. With that load on the roof he didn't dare slam on the brakes. Once committed he had to keep going or he'd have lost half his passengers. Running down a lone motorcyclist was by far the lesser evil.

Understanding this didn't make me feel any calmer. I crawled along to the next dhaba and gulped down some tea. After the second glass I stopped shaking. The problem with these northern roads was that everything – buses, trucks, the whole damn lot – was moving much faster. But the insanity quotient didn't seem to have diminished one iota.

I still had to get to Delhi that night. A friend of Sarah's, an Englishman who now lived and worked there, was expecting me. The sun was sinking behind a grey pall to the west, the end result of all the exhaust fumes sent heavenwards by Delhi's two million vehicles. I reckoned I was just beyond Bulandshahr, in among the big factory belt. Another hour, maybe two, on the road, provided I didn't get lost. Then I'd have to find his place in the dark.

From Ghaziabad onwards the traffic was intense. Most of the road was dual carriageway now, and little Marutis buzzed in and out of the heavy traffic. I saw the first foreign cars since Calcutta, Mercedes and BMWs mostly. They announced that a great metropolis lay ahead as surely as floating trees inform the seafarer that landfall is near. The roadside dhabas now had white plastic chairs instead of charpoys and little umbrellas advertising soft drinks – the visible signs of economic liberalism and consumerism.

The road ran between uniform lines of shoddy modern housing blocks which sprouted up in the middle of arid scrubland. In some places bustees had grown up; but unlike Calcutta, where they meld in with the city, these looked more like refugee camps deliberately isolated from mainstream society. Although Delhi has as chronic a housing shortage as any Indian city, it also has more space in which to disperse its unsightly poor.

I crossed the River Jamuna and turned south down the six-lane Ring Road. I needed to get to the smart residential district of Sunder Nagar, but when I asked for directions nobody had heard of it. I knew it was somewhere near Humayun's tomb, so when I saw the bulbous domes of Mughal mausoleums outlined against the fading light I turned right and crossed over the main railway lines. The road petered out and I found myself crawling along through the middle of a bazaar. I'd imagined my entry to Delhi more in terms of cruising down its broad boulevards. Instead I was slipping in through the back door.

An evening shopper told me I was in Nizamuddin East. When I reached a main road I turned north into the rush-hour traffic and realised I had overshot my target only when I saw the high walls of Sher Shah's fortress, the Purana Qila. I turned about and again missed the exit lane to Sunder Nagar. Modern traffic systems are all very well if you know your way or there are road signs; but Delhi's seemed designed to prevent me from going where I needed to. Despairing of riding up and down this stretch of dual carriageway all night, I adopted local practice and eased the bike through a gap in the concrete barrier. It worked and within minutes I was outside the house.

I rang the bell and waited. A Tibetan opened the door. 'Ah, Mr Jonathan,' he smiled. 'We were expecting you. Mr Bond is still at the office, but he has left instructions. Now first, may I pour you a cold beer?'

9

DELHI: UNREAL CITY –
THE MARTYRED AND THE DEAD

I felt like some awkward, down-country hick as I trudged up
the marble staircase in my dirty boots. Jigme, the Tibetan
bearer, showed me the spare bedroom and bathroom. I took the
hint and wallowed in hot water – a rediscovered sensation, this
– before dressing in clean clothes. It was like going through a
decompression chamber.

The flat was tastefully furnished with Kashmiri carpets and a
couple of eighteenth-century Indian landscapes by one of the
Daniells brothers. I thumbed through back-copies of the
Spectator before turning to a book of Cartier-Bresson photographs of India. Some of the pictures had been taken in refugee
camps just after Partition.

I'd known Jonathon Bond for more than a decade. No matter
whether he was in London or Paris or New Delhi, he always
lived in tasteful surroundings. He rang to apologise for being
late; he was near to closing a multi-million-dollar venture capital
fund designed to allow foreign investment in smaller Indian
companies.

'Help yourself to anything you want,' said Bond. 'Jigme
makes an excellent Bloody Mary, so do ask him to mix you
one.'

'He already has,' I replied, sipping at the pale red and highly
nutritional cocktail. This was just the first instance of the
Tibetan's Jeeves-like ability to divine whatever would be
required of him in advance.

When Bond arrived he had his arm in plaster. He was

obviously tired and announced he had to catch the first flight out to Bombay the following morning. He worked to tight schedules, yet even under pressure he was charm personified.

He insisted that I meet his circle of friends, including a Kashmiri gentleman – 'a real sweetie who provides food for the poor every day at Nizamuddin Aulia' – and the 'truly charming' Mr Kaikers, an art dealer who lived downstairs (I'd already noticed the garden was filled with intricately carved doorposts from Rajasthan).

I was introduced to 'Tipu Sultan', a diminutive pi-dog Jonathan had adopted when on holiday in Goa. 'We thought it was a male,' he explained, 'but when we got it to the vet it turned out to be a bitch. Perhaps we should change the name to Tipu Sultana.' Tipu scampered onto one of the sofas, was severely scolded, but nonetheless stayed put. Tipu was clearly the most spoilt pi-dog in all India.

I didn't argue when Jonathon declared that he needed an early night. I was myself exhausted and still felt like a fish out of water. Back in my bedroom I spent half an hour trying to work out how to switch off the lights. I didn't want to wake up Bond and eventually I fell asleep with the lights on.

The next morning Jigme explained that the light switches were concealed behind a picture – a convincing copy of a Mughal miniature. My poor rusticated brain was still unable to cope with such artful devices. I definitely needed time to adjust.

There are said to have been twelve cities in Delhi. The flat in Sunder Nagar lies close to the ruins of an earlier city founded by Sher Shah Suri. Recent excavations have shown that this stood on top of the oldest settlement, Indraprastha, which goes back to the ninth century BC. But the world in which I moved had nothing to do with these earlier cities.

My first priority was to sort out visas and vehicle documents for entering Pakistan and this meant sticking to the city of embassies and office blocks, the twelfth city called New Delhi. And as far as I'm concerned, this side of New Delhi isn't really part of India. Its broad and well-shaded avenues are almost

Bullet on the Grand Trunk Road: escaping from another traffic jam.

'Hell on Earth': Durgapur, one of Nehru's 'temples of modern India'.

Weaponry
for sale
beside the
GT Road,
Bihar (p. 67).

(*Below*) Grim
determination,
Bihar.

(*Above*)
Tyre-mender
at work on
the front-end
puncture,
near Bodh
Gaya.

Truckers'
Rest: a
dhaba in UP.

A pilgrim takes the easy way up Mount Parasnath in a dhooli (p. 76).

(*Below*) Sher Shah Suri's tomb at Sasaram, with Tyrel painting surrounded by onlookers (p. 123).

The bathing ghats at Varanasi, with Alamgir's Mosque against the skyline.

(*Above*) Godmen afloat on the Ganges, Varanasi.

A guru and his followers arriving at the Margh Mela, Allahabad (p. 155).

A devotee of Lord Ram near the former site of the Babri Mosque, Ayodhya.

Memories of Partition: Mirza Nazim Changrezi at the Jama Masjid, Delhi (p. 237).

To be a Sikh ... the Golden Temple, Amritsar (p. 279).

(*Left*) A Pakistani minibus driver appreciating Sarah's attention, Rawalpindi.(*Right*) Cricket as war by proxy: an impromptu match in the Mughal water gardens beside Jahangir's tomb, near Lahore. That night, after the Pakistan cricket team was defeated by India, a young man shot himself in despair.

The Bullet as a 'buffalo', on the riverbed road to Rohtas Fort, near Jhelum (p. 328).

Sher Shah Suri's caravanserai beneath Attock Fort,
looking towards the North-West Frontier (p. 345).

ATTENTION
ENTRY OF FOREIGNERS
IS PROHIBITED
BEYOND THIS POINT

BY ORDER OF
GOVERNMENT

On the Khyber Pass with bodyguards Momin Khan and Zar Khan.
We ignored the instruction (p. 368).

devoid of human life — apart from armed sentries outside the nicely graded residences of high officials. The only clue that India cannot be far away is the put-put of auto-rickshaws. That and the vultures circling high overhead.

I rode over to Shantipath, the hugely empty avenue along which most of the larger embassies can be found. The Pakistan High Commission would issue a standard visa but were unable to advise on what documents I'd need for the bike. 'Ask the Indian authorities,' they said, and that was the end of the matter.

I knew I was an unusual case: a foreigner on an Indian-owned and -registered vehicle. While I wanted to take it out of the country I didn't strictly speaking want to export it. After riding to the end of the Grand Trunk Road in Pakistan both I and the Bullet would be returning to India. What papers would I need? I sought advice from the Customs Office and the British Consul. Nobody had ever heard of a foreigner bothering to take a vehicle into Pakistan and then returning with it. There were no precedents. Perhaps the Automobile Association of Upper India might be able to assist?

Trying to sort out papers for the bike was one problem. Another was fixing the damaged front fork. I'd ridden the bike for three hundred miles since that bus had reversed into me. The roadside repairs had held up so far, but now I wanted someone who knew about Enfields to check it out. The company's representatives in Delhi suggested I take it to a licensed dealer in Karolbagh, near where the GT Road skirts round the north of the Old City.

The ride across town became interesting once I got north of Connaught Circus and its merry-go-round of snarling traffic. Here at last the unnatural calm of New Delhi's government and diplomatic enclaves gave way to the honking and lurching and fist-waving I knew so well. In a strange way it felt good to be back in the mêlée, though in my excitement I took the wrong exit and found myself heading towards the Old City.

I wasn't in any particular hurry, though just what possessed me to turn right at Ajmeri Gate and enter the labyrinth of alleyways and crowded bazaars beyond I still do not know.

Once inside Old Delhi I was soon well and truly lost; but the sights and sounds and smells of the place led me ever onwards.

As often as not the way ahead was blocked by handcarts being unloaded or by a funeral procession or a string of overladen donkeys, so I had plenty of time to admire the occasional old town-house or haveli that had survived. A truck ahead of me carrying chickens dropped part of its load and I had to sit there, the bike surrounded by hobbled and loudly squawking poultry, until they had been retrieved.

The smells of newly butchered meat and stale fish drifted across a bazaar. I must have been passing through a mainly Muslim quarter. Though the bazaar was crowded, life on the street was almost exclusively a male affair. Occasionally a veiled and shapeless female form flitted past. Most of the houses turned their back on the street, but through open doorways I glimpsed once-stately courtyards, now crumbling or given over to cloth-dyeing or metal-beating.

Much of Old Dehli retains a strongly Muslim flavour. Nowadays its population is far more evenly mixed than at the time of Independence and it has even become fashionable for 'outsiders' to buy up and restore haveli abandoned by the old Muslim gentry. For all that, Hindus and Muslims still tend to live, as they have always done, in separate mohallas or wards.

These can be so jumbled together that for an outsider it is impossible to tell where one mohalla ends and the next begins. But the inhabitants of the Old City know precisely where these invisible boundaries exist. In times of trouble they can easily be fortified and barricaded off from each other – as happened in the run-up to Partition. And once the storm broke in the capital, thousands of Muslims from other parts of the city sought refuge in Old Delhi, particularly in the area around the Jama Masjid.

Just when I thought I was irretrievably lost I saw what looked like a main road ahead. I exited the Old City by the Lahori Gate and, crossing the railway lines, made my way through Sadar Bazar to Karolbagh. These areas of mixed Hindu–Muslim population had seen some of the worst killings in 1947. Now they are crammed with bazaars and wholesalers' godowns and cheap hotels.

By the time I found the Enfield workshop down a side lane it was growing dark. The chief mechanic looked over the damaged front fork, clicking his tongue in a critical way. It would hold out, he said, though some skilled metal-bashing was in order. I agreed to come back in three days' time and handed over the keys.

Back on the main drag I stopped an auto-rickshaw and bundled myself into the back. It seemed strange to be transported like this, hunched up and hardly able to look out, as the rickshaw driver piloted his way across New Delhi's sepulchral gloom.

Half the roads were closed off for the big Republic Day parade that was coming up and we were turned back by military police before we could cross the Rajpath's main axis. The ponderous state buildings designed by Lutyens and Baker, the former Viceroy's House, the Government Secretariat, the Lok Sabha, were all cordoned off. I had a brief glimpse of their red sandstone façades and fake-Mughal embellishments lit up in the dark. They seemed to frown at anyone presumptuous enough to approach more closely.

This is the city the British intended as the capital of their Indian Empire – grandiose, well-ordered, hugely impersonal; an artificial city, far removed from the chaotic vitality of Bombay or Calcutta or lesser provincial towns. It is as though the handful of élite civil servants who governed India deliberately cocooned themselves from all that seething humanity and its petty day-to-day problems. It was in this unreal environment that the Partition of India was decided upon.

On 22 March 1947 a converted Lancaster bomber landed at Delhi airport. On board was British India's last Viceroy, Lord Louis Mountbatten. He had been sent out with instructions from the Labour Prime Minister, Clement Attlee, to negotiate the transfer of power as quickly and in as orderly a fashion as possible. A final date for Britain's withdrawal from India was set for 1 June 1948. Mountbatten was a man in a hurry. He didn't really want the job and accepted only when he was granted near plenipotentiary powers. It took him less than five months to push through a settlement. That he managed to do so says much about his personal charm and powers of persuasion. Whether the final outcome was to the benefit of the peoples of the subcontinent is another matter entirely.

The previous Viceroy, Lord Wavell, had hoped to oversee an 'orderly withdrawal'. A military man who knew India well, Wavell estimated that it would take more than a decade of British rule before a peaceful transfer of power could be achieved. In the meantime an additional three or four British Army divisions would be needed to maintain law and order in India.

This did not go down well in London, where Attlee's government had other priorities – rapid demobilisation and the setting up of a welfare state. Wavell's alternative was simply to 'scuttle and run', leaving a country in the throes of civil war. His name for this plan was 'Operation Madhouse'.

Like many British officers in the Indian Army, Wavell was personally well-disposed towards Muslims from the North-West, whose fighting qualities he admired. He distrusted Gandhi and the Congress leadership. On the other hand, he earnestly sought to preserve the unity of India – a sentiment shared by most British officers and civilians in India. But he lacked the negotiating skills to get the Congress and Jinnah's Muslim League to agree on anything.

The 'federal solution' proposed by the Cabinet Mission through mid-1946 – probably the last real hope of a peaceful outcome – was allowed to sink into oblivion. After the Calcutta Killings and the spread of communal violence to other provinces, Wavell despaired of either unity or a peaceful transfer of power. His final effort was to persuade Nehru and Jinnah to form a coalition government, but the two sides started falling apart immediately. By then Wavell was more worried about the Indian Army – the only real guarantee of law and order – disintegrating along communal lines.

Nehru and Jinnah were called to London for a summit at which nothing was agreed. What did emerge was that the old Field-Marshal was being sidelined by Attlee's Labour government. He was scuttled ignominiously before his own 'scuttle and run' plans became known to the public. Some semblance of honour or decency had to be preserved.

By the time Lord and Lady Mountbatten installed themselves in the Viceroy's House events had taken on a momentum of their own. The situation in the Punjab was deteriorating. Calcutta had just gone through another bad period of rioting. Something had to be done to prevent the slide towards internecine war. The comings and goings at the Viceroy's House grew more and more frantic.

On the surface all seemed calm. The Mountbattens extended invitations to far more Indian politicians and community leaders than any previous viceregal couple. There was a constant stream of Congressmen and senior Muslim Leaguers, Sikhs, nawabs and emissaries from Princely States. The hundreds of staff at the Viceroy's House had a busy time of it. Lord Louis and Lady Edwina were charming. Now that a deadline for British withdrawal had been set their sincerity could not be doubted.

But to achieve this rapid solution, Mountbatten abandoned any attempt to come up with a settlement acceptable to all parties, preferring to deal with just the key players who could deliver some form of political agreement. This would mean Nehru and Jinnah.

Gandhi was courted early on. But when he asked Mountbatten to have the courage to stand by India's unity, and proposed that Jinnah be invited to head an Interim Government as soon as possible, the Viceroy and his advisers started backpeddling. Although Gandhi claimed he could deliver Congress support for this last-ditch attempt to prevent Partition, it was an unorthodox solution which might well prevent Independence being delivered on schedule.

That same afternoon Nehru arrived at the Viceroy's House and dismissed Gandhi's plan as impracticable. Mountbatten did put Gandhi's idea to Maulana Abul Kalan Azad, the senior

Muslim member of Congress, who thought it was feasible. But that was as far as it went. By the time Mountbatten first met Jinnah it had already been decided to drop Gandhi's suggestion. The offer was not even mentioned. Instead Mountbatten assured Jinnah that no solution 'patently unacceptable' to himself would be put forward. The last possibility of preserving a united India was allowed to wither in silence. As for Gandhi, it was decided to keep him in good humour, but in reality he was sidelined.

So India's progress towards Independence began to resemble a three-handed game of poker. The stakes were incalculably high; and, what is more, the game was being played against the clock.

It has often been suggested that Mountbatten and Nehru were in cahoots. Jinnah first accused the Viceroy of 'favouritism' towards Nehru; and the cry was later taken up by some Congressmen who thought the two contrived to push through Independence as quickly as possible, with Nehru accepting Partition as the price to be paid for himself becoming Prime Minister. Did such a conspiracy exist?

Certainly, the Mountbatten–Nehru relationship was unusually close. Just how 'special' this 'special relationship' was has been skirted around by official biographers for half a century. What is clear is that they charmed the pants off each other. The elegant English aristocrat and the Cambridge-educated Pandit felt they belonged to the same world. It may even have been on Nehru's suggestion that the British Prime Minister appointed Mountbatten as the new Viceroy. And then there was the romantic attachment between Nehru and Edwina Mountbatten. Their mutual attraction began early on, though it would appear to have come to fruition only towards the end of the Mountbattens' stay in India, well after Independence and Partition.

Yet this curious, three-sided relationship didn't always work in Nehru's favour. In early May the Mountbattens escaped from Delhi's ferocious heat to the 'summer capital' of Simla, where Nehru joined them as a private guest at the Viceregal Lodge.

Over an after-dinner glass of port, Mountbatten, acting on 'a hunch', decided to show Nehru his still secret plan for an independent India. Since the British Cabinet had approved the plan only that same day, Nehru was being given access to highly privileged information.

When Nehru started reading through the file he was appalled. And no wonder: it was called 'Plan Balkan' and recommended the transfer of power not to a centralised state but to individual provinces and princely states. In essence, it was a reworking of the previous year's Cabinet Mission Plan. The central government in Delhi would exercise only limited powers. Nehru was horrified with this 'Balkanisation' of India, which he saw as far worse than partitioning it into two nation states. It might lead to a dozen fractious nations arising and hold the seeds of civil wars.

According to Mountbatten's timetable this plan was to be published a week later. So was his decision to leak it to Nehru, in the name of friendship, as spontaneous as he claimed? Or was it a deliberate bluff, to frighten Nehru into accepting the more straightforward surgery of Partition? Whatever the motive, the result was that the very next day Mountbatten and Nehru had a private talk during which Nehru agreed to Partition and the creation of Pakistan, provided that the Punjab and Bengal were also divided along religious lines.

The Viceroy was delighted that grounds for a rapid settlement had been reached. 'Plan Balkan' was jettisoned with alacrity and a new plan built around Partition drawn up. If these were the fruits of a special relationship, they were bitter fruits indeed.

Nehru sipping port in the Viceregal Lodge at Simla. Gandhi strolling across the lawns of the Viceroy's palace in Delhi. Nehru, again, taking a cooling dip in the viceregal swimming pool – with or without Lady Mountbatten. All those rounds of private interviews held in the cavernous interior of that great red palace at the top of Rajpath. The conversations which decided the fate of India were mostly taken amidst such splendour, far removed from reality. The Viceroy's advisers spoke in terms of a clean, surgical operation. In India? They should have known better than that.

The Mountbattens also tried to charm Mohammad Ali Jinnah, though with rather less success. He was coldly adversarial, and once he had been assured that no agreement would be reached over his head he could sit back and wait. The Viceroy's initial appeal that partitioning India would be suicidal left Jinnah unmoved. His demand was always the same – Pakistan, Pakistan, Pakistan. All he needed to do was to hold his cards close to his chest and keep upping the ante.

But just what Jinnah meant by Pakistan is often hard to tell. At times it sounded more like guarantees of autonomy for Muslims within an Indian Union; at others a fully-fledged nation state. This made his demand for an undefined Pakistan a highly flexible bargaining counter. Yet, skilful player that he was, Jinnah had his weaknesses. He was a dying man, desperate to see his dream of Pakistan realised during his own lifetime. His medical condition was kept secret; but he was every bit as much a man in a hurry as either Mountbatten or Nehru. And the very flexibility of his conception of Pakistan meant that he did not foresee all the practical difficulties of bringing it into existence.

The 'two nation' theory demanded the separation of mainly Muslim provinces from the rest of India. Yet Jinnah couldn't – or preferred not to – see what that might imply for Muslims who had to 'stay behind'. Nor would he accept that the logic of Partition might also require the division of the two largest provinces, Punjab and Bengal, into Muslim- and Hindu-majority zones. Only late in the game did he realise that while he'd won Pakistan, it was what he called the 'moth-eaten' variety, without much in the way of industry or infrastructure. Some of his later demands, for a thousand-mile-long land corridor across India, reveal a desperation born of the knowledge that it would be very difficult to make this new Pakistan work in practice.

As for Mountbatten, he got his agreement and handed over India in less than half the allotted time. Given the mutual suspicion existing between Congress and the Muslim League, this was no mean achievement. He had to force the pace, setting down impossible deadlines in order to win concessions from all sides, throwing out one set of proposals and then coming up with a completely different set.

The Viceroy was not the only one throwing up novel solutions. From Bengal, a chastened H. S. Suhrawardy (the man who had made possible the Calcutta Killings) now called for a united Bengal separate from both India and any future Pakistan. Other Muslim-majority provinces, the Punjab and the North-West Frontier Province, had elected governments opposed to the Muslim League and wanted neither Partition nor to be forced into joining any future Pakistan. The Sikh leadership wavered between opposing Partition, demanding a separate Sikh state of Khalistan, and requiring that the Punjab be split in two so that their people might have some safe haven.

As the countdown to Independence gathered pace, increasingly desperate last-minute 'solutions' were raised. The comings and goings at the Viceroy's House began to resemble a high-speed game of musical chairs.

External events helped force the pace. Outside Delhi the death toll was mounting. The Punjab was ablaze and the horror of what was happening forced the most intransigent spirits to seek compromise: Gandhi's heartfelt opposition to Partition was muted; Nehru accepted it as a temporary failure which could, he imagined, be made good later; Jinnah welcomed a truncated Pakistan as better than no Pakistan at all. And everyone thought that by reaching a settlement quickly they would avert further bloodshed. In the light of what happened later, this is perhaps the bitterest irony of all.

The area around Sunder Nagar is littered with Mughal monuments, and after a day of battling with red tape and unhelpful officials I would retire to one of these islands of calm. Immediately to the south was Humayun's tomb, the most gracious of Delhi's many Muslim mausoleums, where I would sit and take stock in its formal gardens. Or just the other side of Delhi Zoo was the Purana Qila, the 'Old Fort' built by

Humayun's rival Sher Shah Suri as the centrepiece of his own new city of Shergarh.

I had already run into these two imperial rivals at Sasaram and Kannauj. They did not deal kindly with one another, each in turn destroying the handiwork of his predecessor. So when Sher Shah assumed the imperial title after his victory at Kannuaj, he set about laying waste the new capital of Dinpanah that Humayun had started building just six years earlier.

Sher Shah did not destroy all of his predecessor's work. It is now thought that the Purana Qila's massive gateways and walls were begun by Humayun. But then Sher Shah was a practical man, readier than most to adapt solid fortifications to his own ends. What he did instead was complete the great fortress and construct an elegant palace complex inside its walls. The imperial mosque still stands, a richly ornamented, perfectly balanced example of the Indo-Afghan style that even today breathes a spirit of calm. But practically all the other buildings inside the Purana Qila were in turn razed to the ground. And who could have undertaken this demolition job with greater pleasure than Humayun himself?

He may have been defeated and forced into exile by Sher Shah, but he outlived both the wily Afghan and his son, Salim. And when the Afghans fell to fighting among themselves, Humayun returned to Delhi in triumph and destroyed the palaces and the surrounding city of Shergarh built by his arch-rival. But the Grand Mughal did not have long to savour his revenge. The following year he died after falling down the steps of his library. By a strange irony, this library was housed in a converted pleasure pavilion known as the Sher Mandal – one of the few buildings erected by Sher Shah Suri inside the Purana Qila to have survived.

Humayun's body was interred in the elegant, Persian-influenced mausoleum erected by Hamida Begum, his senior wife and the mother of the Emperor Akbar. On previous visits I had admired its lofty dome and pleasing symmetry, my thoughts escaping to the distant age when it was built. Now I looked on it and the nearby Purana Qila in a different light; for in 1947 both of these ancient monuments had been turned into holding centres for refugees.

At first they were used as assembly points for Muslim refugees awaiting transport to Pakistan. Among them was the writer Masud Hasan Shahaab Dehlvi, who has described in *Delhi ki Bipta* how he moved with his family from the Old City to the greater safety of the Purana Qila. Here he found complete confusion: everyone looked out for themselves and water carriers charged extortionate rates for a single leather bag. Special refugee trains were leaving from the nearby Nizamuddin railway station; but then word came back that these trains were being attacked and the passengers butchered before they reached Pakistan. With great difficulty he managed instead to get his family on a plane to Rawalpindi, where he found equally distressing scenes of devastation, though here it was the Hindus and Sikhs who had suffered.

Later on, when the outflow of Muslims from Delhi had slowed, these same camps were turned over to Hindu and Sikh refugees from the West Punjab. For many of them, the camps became semi-permanent homes. Back in Lucknow I had met a Hindu refugee from Multan whose family had spent seven years in the Purana Qila. Seeking further information, I applied at the fort's museum and the Archaeological Survey of India. Here I was told about the discovery of 3,000-year-old painted Grey Ware pottery, which confirms this was the site of the fabled city of Indraprastha. But nobody knew about its more recent history, apart from the fact that it had once been used as a refugee camp.

In a corner of the Purana Qila, near where the legendary city of Indraprashta once stood, a Hindu temple was erected earlier this century. According to a notice the site is linked to Maharani Kunli, 'Mother of the Pandavas', the royal house whose heroic deeds are celebrated in the *Mahabharata*. All this refers to what many Hindus still see as their 'golden age', long before verifiable history and its tiresome succession of foreign rulers. I noticed as many visitors made their way to this modern temple as bothered to traipse round the older Muslim monuments. As always in

India, current preoccupations colour perceptions of the past. Everyone knows about the *Mahabharata*, especially since its serialisation on television. But who the hell was this Sher Shah character?

The terrible consequences of Partition are another episode of history which most modern Indians prefer to forget about. I looked around at the other visitors to the Purana Qila who were simply enjoying the gardens, scarcely bothering with the monuments at all. In front of me a young soldier, still wearing his full uniform from a dress rehearsal for the Republic Day Parade, had his eye out for some attractive girl. Why should he care that this fortress was once a refugee camp? I was probably the only person in the entire place seeking out that particular set of ghosts.

Yet, strangely enough, the arrival of those refugee convoys from the Punjab has probably changed the character of Delhi more than anything else in the last thousand years. Before 1947 it remained a mainly Muslim, Urdu-speaking city, with a distinct culture and traditions of craftmanship going back to Mughal times. Now it is overwhelmingly a city of immigrants, and Punjabi culture and values have gradually risen to the top of the pile.

That process really began with Partition and the massive inflow of Punjabi refugees into the Purana Qila and other camps. And in the fifty years since then these immigrants have created the thirteenth city of Delhi, as distinct from its predecessor as the artificial capital of the Raj was from Mughal Delhi. Of course it doesn't get a mention in the guidebooks, for it is not a city of historic monuments. But it's out there among all the new colonies and housing projects that have sprung up, a new culture and work ethic based on immigrant values, the determination of the dispossessed to make their way in the world.

Half a century on, and the children and grandchildren of those Punjabi refugees have joined the capital's new plutocracy. I ran into a few of them at a big wedding in Sunder Nagar, at which the principal topic of conversation was how many crores of rupees had been lavished on the huge marquee and the extravagance of the catering.

I tagged along with Mr Kaikers, the antiques dealer and property developer who lived downstairs from Jonathan Bond. The bridegroom's wedding procession had already formed up in the street. Two rows of lantern carriers (both electric-powered and gas), some forty men in all, formed a cordon around the wedding party. The bridegroom himself was dressed up like a Hindu raja in a white silk tunic topped by a turban of red and gold. He looked self-conscious and rather uncomfortable on his milk-white steed – a well-fed and distinctly upmarket animal, richly caparisoned in turquoise and red cloth into which a hundred mirrors had been sewn.

I asked why the procession was hardly moving. 'Oh, they must take at least two hours to progress just around the block,' explained old Mr Kaikers, his eyes twinkling mischievously. 'The father is a Bania,' he continued, 'and we have this saying that there are only two things a Bania will spend his money on. One is when he is building his house. The other is for a marriage such as this.'

A uniformed brass band was blasting out a medley of favourite wedding anthems. Soon they were joined by a more rustic troupe of drummers, whose efforts redoubled when the bridegroom's younger brother joined in the dancing, tempting the drummers into even faster rhythms and more sustained drum-rolls by waving great wads of rupees in his fist. A third band, the pipes and drums of some mountain regiment, awaited the guests inside the marquee. 'You see,' smiled Mr Kaikers, 'this is a three-band wedding.'

The front of the marquee was covered with plywood towers and battlements to make it look like a ruler's palace. Inside was room for several thousand guests. The perimeter was lined with buffets groaning with the costliest wedding food. A tray of something rather special wrapped in silver leaf and stuffed with pistachios was doing the rounds. 'Oh, you should take two of these,' I was advised. 'They must be costing at least five thousand rupees per kilo.'

The bride and bridegroom sat on their thrones in a corner, ignored by the vast majority of guests, who were bent on just two things – sampling as many of the delicacies as time and decency permitted and networking furiously. Little knots of businessmen nodded sagaciously as they discussed how much a certain plot of land had sold for. Gawky but eligible sons in shiny mohair suits were pushed forward. Mothers and daughters in iridescent saris patrolled invisible borders.

This being an orthodox Hindu wedding there was no alcohol, and not many people seemed to be enjoying themselves. They came to see and be seen, to get on with the serious business of financial self-advancement. And while this lavish display probably counts as a society wedding in New Delhi, very few of those present could claim to be more than first or second generation Delhi-wallahs. They had no time for the Anglophile airs and graces of the senior civil servant or military man. Here, it's what you're worth that counts. Conversations were studded with casual mentions of crores and tens of crores. The benefits of the new economic liberalism were on parade. And I must confess, the food really was delicious.

New Delhi puts on a big show to celebrate Republic Day. Or rather, the military do. For the Republic Day Parade has become an opportunity to display before the grateful masses the full panoply of the Republic's armed might. It is when the latest additions to India's arsenal are revealed in public, just as the Soviets used to do with their May Day march pasts. The same thing goes on in all major Indian cities. Back in Calcutta, at the very outset of my journey, I'd got mixed up in the dress-rehearsal for Republic Day by the Victoria Memorial. But nowhere, I was assured, puts on anything to compare with Delhi.

I made my way towards India Gate to see the show, only to find that a large crowd had already gathered there. Access to Rajpath's ceremonial avenue was restricted to official guests and ticket-holders. Security-men were swarming all over the place, so I decided to stay put where I was. The Prime Minister's cavalcade arrived and there was a brief ceremony paying homage to India's soldiers, before the élite presidential guards clattered up on their horses and the diminutive figure of President Shankar Dayal Sharma hoisted the tricolour as the national anthemn was played and the artillery fired off a salute.

The infantry regiments marched smartly past, a blur of brightly coloured pugrees and cummerbunds. The camel corps was splendidly anachronistic. But it was the fly-pasts and the rumbling of heavy weaponry that had the crowds oohing and aahing. A MiG fighter soared vertically into the sky; helicopters showered rose petals along the length of Rajpath. Three examples of India's new main battle tank, the Arjun, rolled past with gun barrels depressed. And then there was the really serious hardware, including India's home-made surface-to-surface missile, the Prithvi. In any 'worst-case scenario' this missile or the 'discontinued' longer-range Agni would probably be used to deliver India's home-made nuclear bomb.

It was all very impressive, but I couldn't help wondering against whom all this military firepower might be directed. The obvious answer is Pakistan. After all, India and Pakistan have fought three wars since they gained Independence, and differences over Kashmir have resulted in a more or less constant state of unofficial hostilities along the cease-fire line. Given the two countries' long record of failing to agree on anything there's certainly the potential for future conflict. But even after receiving large dollops of US military and economic assistance, Pakistan is in no position to challenge India's eminence as the predominant regional power. To put it simply, Pakistan could start a war, but it couldn't win one.

Then there is China, a long-time friend of Pakistan and a nuclear power bent on modernising its armed forces. India shares more than 2,000 miles of border with the People's Republic. Again, the two countries have gone to war. That was back in 1962, when the People's Liberation Army came piling over the passes from Tibet and inflicted a psychologically damaging defeat on the Indian Army.

If India ever tried to take on China unassisted, it would have about as much chance of success as Pakistan v. India. But what if Pakistan and China combined? Unlikely as it is, that is the nightmare scenario which has fuelled India's determination to be a self-sufficient nuclear power. All the sanctimonious stuff about the right to self-determination and self-defence which Indian diplomats trot out whenever their country is criticised for not signing up to nuclear non-proliferation treaties is just a smokescreen. If China wasn't part of the nuclear club, India would feel a lot happier about promising not to turn its peaceful nuclear capacity into weaponry.

Three wars with Pakistan, one against China ... By international standards that's a fairly belligerent record. Certainly it doesn't fit with India's 'Gandhian' image as a peace-loving democracy. And the tally doesn't include more limited use of military resources in what India considers its own back yard. Such as sending the army in to 'liberate' Goa from Portugal's imperialistic rule in 1961; or 'integrating' the Kingdom of Sikkim into India in 1973. And then there was the Indian Army's intervention in Sri Lanka, an episode that earned little thanks from either Tamils or Sinhalese but which is commemorated on war memorials in military cantonments all over India.

What is most remarkable about the Indian Army is that it has resolutely stayed in its barracks. Not one military *coup* in fifty years – that's a record which puts the Pakistani military's predilection for intervening in politics into perspective. In fact, it's hard to think of any post-colonial country, except some of the smaller city or island states, where there hasn't been a military *coup* of some kind.

Some observers trace this restraint on the part of India's generals to a professional military ethos inherited from the British. But then that's equally true in Pakistan and professionalism never stopped *their* generals from seizing power or hanging the Prime Minister. Or maybe it's that India's military have accepted the view that India is too vast and diverse to be effectively ruled by force. For decades their troops have been called in by the civil authorities to restore peace or put down insurrections – in Kashmir, the Punjab, Assam, Nagaland. But after the army operations are completed the political problems remain.

Dealing with communal tensions is particularly worrying for an army which still recruits from among the minorities and sees this diversity as one of its strengths. So while it is one thing for the Indian military to stay out of politics as long as there is an avowedly secular government in power, it might be altogether trickier should a right-wing government whose ideology equates nationalism with Hinduism ever be in command of India's armed forces.

The marching infantry and bands disappeared off towards Connaught Circus and the Old City. Behind them came a series of floats representing the different States and Union Territories: near-naked and fuzzy-haired fishermen for the Andaman and Nicobar Islands; dancing maidens picking apples for Himachal Pradesh. The succession of *tableaux mouvants* was a reminder of the great diversity of peoples belonging to the Indian Union, and the crowd enjoyed trying to guess what each float represented in advance. As often as not, the people next to me got it wrong.

Delhi is a city of pundits, crammed to bursting with politicians and political observers, newspapermen and lobbyists, retired generals and administrators, all of them ready to give their views on matters of state – present, past and future. I met them at private houses and at the Delhi Gymkhana Club, where I had moved to make way for other house-guests at Jonathon Bond's place.

I liked the Gymkhana. Once the bastion of British generals and ICS officers and now the preserve of India's top civil servants and staff officers, it retains old-fashioned standards. The Club Secretary was a retired brigadier who kept various mementoes from his military career on the wall behind his desk. There was the badge of a parachute regiment with its motto

'Men Apart. Every Man an Emperor', and photographs of the military operations on the Siachen Glacier in Kashmir, where Indian and Pakistani élite troops have been conducting an undeclared war at 21,000 feet for decades. I also appreciated the fact that I could turn up at the Gymkhana in biking leathers and the staff didn't bat an eyelid, whereas in Delhi's more upmarket hotels I was regarded with suspicion if not hostility.

In the evenings I would sit in front of one of the four log fires around the vast expanse of the old ballroom – whose wooden floor, I was told, was fully sprung – and it was never long before some club member, a retired naval commander or an electoral commissioner, started up a conversation. And maybe because I was interested in something other than Delhi's tourist sights, these conversations took some fascinating turns. I heard about different methods of electoral corruption and why India needed to be a nuclear power. Then I went into the dining-room, where I faced a choice between Brown Windsor and tomato soup before studying the mutton cutlets in their silver chafing dishes.

My days were spent unprofitably shuttling between offices, trying to assemble the paperwork that would allow me to take the bike across the Pakistan border and back. But in between I looked up old friends and acquaintances, who recommended I should talk to this minister or that politician. Along the way I ran into yet more pundits – some of them eminently qualified to discuss Partition and its enduring legacy.

Take Natwar Singh, for instance: a career diplomat, former ambassador to Pakistan, Minister of State for External Affairs and Member of Parliament. 'The tragedy of Indo-Pak relations,' he told me, 'is that so much is determined by the past. It's fifty years now, but the two countries continue in a state of permanent and not-so-happy mutual misunderstanding. People talk about globalisation of trade and information sharing. Yet between these neighbouring countries there's virtually no trade or travel or any other forms of exchange. Why, it's impossible to buy one country's newspaper in the other.

'It's become almost an automatic response when anything goes wrong to blame the other side. That is less true of India, where we face issues that have nothing to do with Pakistan. You'll find the further you go from Delhi, the less you'll hear about Pakistan. It's not such an issue in Tamil Nadu, for instance. But over in Pakistan you're always hearing about the latest awful thing that India's supposed to be planning.'

'Why do you think that should be?'

'It's partly because they're a small country, just a tenth of our size, and because they haven't resolved their own identity crisis. They're all Muslims: but they're also Punjabis, Sindhis, Baluchis, Pathans . . . Of course, before 1972 there were also the Bengalis. The people in Islamabad think India's an aggressive power, that we want to break up Pakistan – just as they say we did when Bangladesh was created. But that was first and foremost an internal problem of their own making. And as for nowadays, India has no intention of undoing Pakistan. We've got quite enough problems as it is. We don't want to add to them.

'I'd like to hold out some hopes for the future. After all, this endless antagonism is so fruitless, a drain on the resources of both countries. Why should there be an arms race between peoples who speak the same language, eat the same food and wear the same dress? What does hold up any progress is that there's a very strong military-bureaucratic complex in Pakistan. If Indo-Pak relations improved they'd go out of business. Calls for cutting military expenditure don't go down well with these people when they're having a damn good time of it.'

'The sad thing about Partition,' said Pran Chopra, 'is that until it was too late to stop it nobody really wanted it.' Chopra's family came from Lahore, where his father had practised Ayurvedic medicine. He himself started out as a journalist in 1941 on the *Civil and Military Gazette* – 'the same paper that Kipling and Churchill worked for'. By 1944 he had joined All-India Radio in Delhi. 'I particularly remember doing a recording with Mahatma Gandhi in the sweepers' colony. He was explaining to the sweepers in his broken Hindi all the complex negotiations between himself and Nehru and Mountbatten. I cannot convey how beautifully he did that through the screen of an inadequate vocabulary.'

Chopra laughed when I repeated the dictum that Independence was brought about by two Gujaratis – Gandhi, who could hardly speak Hindi, and Jinnah, who struggled with Urdu. 'It's true, it's true. And, you know, to begin with even Jinnah didn't particularly want Partition. He was using it to drive the best possible bargain.

'I really do believe that Partition could have been avoided if a firm decision had been taken against it by early 1946. If the full horror of it had been put sufficiently strongly to leaders on both sides, perhaps they would have tried harder to work towards a more satisfactory solution. As it was, both sides jostled themselves into Partition. After their experience of not being able to work together in the Interim Government they just said "To hell with this, it won't work", and took the line of least resistance.

'Nobody could believe this thing was happening to them. My own family were typical of the non-Muslim people living in Lahore. Until three or four days before Partition they hadn't woken up to the realisation that they might have to leave. They listened to assurances from their leaders that if necessary India would give up Calcutta so that she could retain Lahore. I myself was in Lahore just three days before Partition, trying to persuade my parents to come away. "No, no," they said, "nothing is going to happen here." I had to persuade them by saying that they normally went to a hill-station further east at that time of year. Why not leave a little early? If everything was fine after Independence then they could always come back to Lahore.

'Of course I knew there was no question of that. I only put up this argument to get them out in time.'

Independence Day, 15 August, was celebrated peacefully in Delhi to joyous shouts of 'Jai Hind!' Hundreds of thousands crowded the Rajpath to witness the arrival of Jawaharlal Nehru at the Durbar Hall where he was sworn in as India's first Prime

Minister by Mountbatten — now no longer Viceroy but Governor-General of the independent Dominion of India. Mountbatten recalled it as 'the most remarkable and inspiring day of my life'. The chief architect of India's division was touched that the crowd shouted 'Pandit Mountbatten ki jai' as well as 'Pandit Nehru ki jai'. The Indian tricolour was run up the flagpole at India Gate. So great was the throng that a large part of the elaborate ceremony had to be curtailed. As the flag unfurled a rainbow appeared in the monsoon-laden skies.

Only the absence of Mahatma Gandhi dampened the universal jubilation. He was in Calcutta, at Hydari Mansion, trying to avert yet another bout of massacres. He refused to take food or to give any message to an expectant nation. The bitterness of Partition weighed heavy upon him. From here on he saw his role more in terms of disaster control.

Delhi remained quiet for another two weeks. But more and more refugee trains arrived from Pakistan, each of them bearing yet more horrible accounts of murders and atrocities. By the end of August communal tensions in the capital reached breaking point.

At first there were isolated stabbings and incidents of arson in the suburbs. A fierce curfew was imposed allowing only two to four hours to buy rations. Then on Sunday 7 September, while Gandhi was *en route* to Delhi by train, the bloodletting began in earnest.

Connaught Place, the commercial hub of New Delhi, was pillaged by Hindu and Sikh mobs bent on looting and arson. They targeted Muslim shops only, and they knew there was nothing to stop them. The author and broadcaster Nirad C. Chaudhuri was bicycling past and immediately twigged what was happening. 'It was not that the hearts of the most cowardly class in India had become stouter,' he observed, 'but only there was no need for cowards to become heroes to commit overt acts of robbery and violence.'

The army and police turned up eventually. But what struck Chaudhuri was 'the extraordinary coolness and self-possession shown by the looters. They just slunk round the corners when the police or soldiers approached and then, like incompressible water, spilled out again.' Even when Prime Minister Nehru put in a personal appearance it didn't stop the looting for long. Within three weeks of the 'transfer of power' the rule of law had collapsed at the very centre of India's capital.

By the second week in September there was uncontrolled rioting and massacres. Worst hit were suburbs just outside the Old City – Karolbagh, Paharganj, Sabzi Mandhi – where there were large but not easily defended Muslim populations.

All over the city signs went up on buildings proclaiming they were Hindu shops, this being the surest defence against looting. Christians took to displaying crosses prominently to avoid being mistaken for Muslims. Rumours circulated that Muslims had assembled arms caches and were conspiring to take over the city. This provided an excuse for Hindu and Sikh mobs to commit yet more massacres. Politicians scarcely dared call for restraint without mentioning that parallel atrocities were happening in the West Punjab.

Nehru was so rattled he asked Mountbatten to deploy those British army units still in Delhi. The Governor-General declined, pointing out what an adverse effect calling in British troops would have on the new government's credibility. Instead he agreed to head an Emergency Committee armed with exceptional powers to restore order to the capital.

One of the government servants brought in was John Lall, an ICS officer of nine years' standing, whose job at that time was vice-principal of the Indian Administrative Service Training School in Delhi. Rather than prepare for the challenges of governing a new country, he and his pupils were drafted in to help restore order and keep vital public services functioning.

Now in his eighties, Lall lives quietly in a secluded colony in Nizamuddin East. But his memories of those first months of Independence remain undimmed. Lall believes that given the scale of the upheavals in the Punjab, where ten million people were on the move and refugees were being massacred in their thousands, the authorities in Delhi 'put a stop to the local violence quickly. Once the worst was over it was largely a matter of arranging further evacuation and resettling thousands of people.'

He made it sound so matter-of-fact. All-in-the-line-of-duty, and so on. But when I asked him who was responsible for Partition his eyes grew angry. 'I think it absolutely scandalous that the British should have cut and run,' he declared, 'dividing up the very country they had actively created.

'India is not — and never has been — two nations. The Muslims had been absorbed into the country centuries ago. They made a very significant contribution to its culture. The creation of Pakistan amounted to a political failure on the part of leading politicians on both sides who stuck out for their own entirely selfish ends. There were alternative plans on the table which took in Muslim concerns but would have allowed the unity of the country to be preserved. And just look at the end result fifty years on. There's still a deep-seated mistrust of Pakistan, and to some extent this rubs off on the Muslim population in India — despite their having made highly creditable and even heroic adjustments to the new situation.

'The Muslim minority remains an integral and valued element in the Indian body politic; but at times of communal tension the old suspicions surface on both sides. That was evident during the crisis over the Babri Mosque and its aftermath. And today there is a surge of confidence amongst some parties that are — how shall I put it? — tinged with a communal colour.'

Gandhi arrived in Delhi as the first wave of massacres broke. He was unable to stay in the sweepers' colony as usual because it had been taken over by refugees. Instead he went to Birla House, the home of one of the wealthiest Marwari business dynasties. His days were spent touring the refugee camps that had sprung up all over the capital, trying to organise relief and, by his personal example, to stem the bloodshed.

For a while it seemed to be working. But each trainload of refugees from Pakistan brought news of further massacres, and the impetus towards revenge was constantly reinforced. The stabbings and arson continued. By January 1948 Gandhi felt that the situation in Delhi had deteriorated so far that he resorted once more to his ultimate weapon: he announced he would fast unto death.

The politicians flocked to his bedside to dissuade him. They failed, and when Gandhi demanded that state assets which had been witheld from Pakistan be handed over, they were in no position to refuse. But this time the hatred among the Punjabi refugees would not be assuaged. Even when he was so feeble that he could barely speak, there was a small group outside Birla House chanting, 'Let Gandhi die.'

The politicians signed up to all Gandhi's demands – that Muslims be able to go about freely; that their mosques be returned to them; that the economic boycott against them be ended. Two hundred thousand citizens of Delhi took an oath to do all they could to protect their Muslim neighbours. For the first time in five months, peace descended upon India's capital.

But Gandhi's defence of India's Muslims angered not only the refugees but also the more extreme wing of the Hindu Mahasabha, the R. S. S. Sangh. Far to the South, in Pune, a secret R. S. S. Sangh cell decided to assassinate Gandhi.

Their first attempt, just two days after he had broken his fast, was bungled. The police caught one of the conspirators and had him under interrogation; but they failed to follow up on his information rapidly enough. Gandhi continued to hold his daily prayer meetings. On Friday 30 January a young fanatic called Nathuram Godse called out, 'Father, Father,' to Gandhi before emptying three rounds into 'The Father of India' at point-blank range. Of all the tragedies surrounding Partition, Gandhi's murder at the hands of a Hindu extremist is the most twisted.

That night Jawaharlal Nehru broadcast to a grieving nation. 'Friends and comrades,' he began. 'The light has gone out of our lives and there is darkness everywhere . . .'

During the worst of the communal rioting some 30,000 Muslims took refuge inside the Jama Masjid, the greatest of

Delhi's mosques, which stands between the Old City and the Red Fort. I had been to this mosque many times before, to admire its graciously swelling triple-domes, its slender minarets and its imposing gateways. This time I came with a different purpose – to see if I could find old Delhi-wallahs and other Muslims with memories of 1947.

In the north-east corner of the mosque, beside the shrine where a hair of the Prophet's beard and a footprint made by his camel shoe are preserved, I spent the afternoon chatting with three old men, each with his own very distinct memories of Partition days.

The first was Mirza Nazim Changrezi, a slight, refined old gentleman with pale eyes and a wispy white beard, who told me he had first come to pray at the Jama Masjid in 1911. He wore an ancient Kashmiri shawl over a white kurta and pyjama.

He was now eighty-four years old; but in his scale of things that was nothing. What mattered to him was that his family had been in Delhi for more than 400 years. 'My ancestor was a general in the armies of the Emperor Akbar,' he told me. 'First he was in Sind before coming to Agra and then to Delhi. Since those times my family have always been living in Delhi.'

When discussing the wrongs suffered by Muslims it was sometimes difficult to tell whether he was referring to 1857 and the aftermath of the Indian Mutiny or 1947 and Partition. 'Thousands of Muslims were slaughtered and the old Muslim culture uprooted,' he declared; and it was only when he continued about the British and the Sikhs occupying the Jama Masjid that I realised he was referring to events of nearly a hundred years earlier.

His attitude towards the British was ambivalent. He blamed them for ending the rule of the last Mughal emperors in Delhi and for then turning against the Muslims. Yet he recounted with pride how some of the most renowned nineteenth-century British soldiers in India, including Sir David Ochterlony, had married into his clan. His grandfather had served in military campaigns from Afghanistan to Burma, and his father had held a senior post at the Post and Telegraph Office under the British.

'At that time,' he said, his amber ringed finger pointing skywards to emphasise the point, 'candidates were appointed on education and ability, not on whether they were Muslim or Hindu. Now all appointment is by corruption only.'

I asked him what happened in Delhi after Partition. 'In September 1947, at the time of the troubles,' he specified, 'I made one false identity card in the name of a Hindu. With this I went out of the Old City into Sadar Bazaar: and there, as I was walking the streets, I saw many Muslims being killed by Hindus, and many rich houses being sacked. I saw dead bodies of Muslims everywhere – in Paharganj, in Chandi Chowk, around the Purana Qila, at the Railway Station. All these things I saw with my own eyes.'

'Many people came here to the Jama Masjid for safety. Some decided to go to Pakistan. For them it was arranged that they went to a refugee camp. They were worried for their religion and culture; they were fearful of being forced to convert to Hinduism. They were told by the authorities it was better for them to leave to Pakistan, where they could have their own country.

'But many people, including Muslim leaders like Maulana Azad, didn't want there to be this division and a separate Pakistan. Of the Old Delhi families, those living in Mughal houses, maybe half decided to stay put. But the Delhi culture has changed so very much since Independence. In the old times we Muslims had our own language, our own culture. Most of the music and poetry in Delhi was performed by Muslim artists. Now there is a change in that atmosphere. Young people are not so interested in these things. Now they are wanting Western culture. Now they are saying more and more India is a Hindu society, and there is this new generation which does not want any separate Muslim culture.'

From behind thick heavy-rimmed glasses his pale eyes stared up into the winter sky. Throughout our conversation a persistent fly had buzzed around his nose, but not once had he deigned to brush it away.

*

Next I talked with Mohamed Tahit, a dirwan or nightwatch-man by trade. Although born in Bihar, he'd been in Delhi early in 1947 before moving to Panipat — an important town some two hours up the Grand Trunk Road — where he had been engaged in Koranic studies at the local madrasa.

'While I was in Panipat,' he told me, 'I saw so many Muslim people being killed in the road. That was about the time that Gandhi was shot at the Birla House. Then there was a curfew and nobody could leave their house. I was trying to come to Delhi, but could not. Then some people were leaving for Pakistan and I went with them. From Panipat we left in a convoy of fourteen trucks, all filled with refugees. We went by the Canal Road to Ambala and then to Jullundur, where we stayed overnight. Then we went by way of Amritsar in the early morning, and crossing over the border at Wagha proceeded to Lahore.'

I asked him why he had chosen Pakistan. He looked at me as though I was mad. 'What choice did I have? In Panipat there was a curfew, but still so many Sikhs were coming from house to house with swords and everything. If you ran away they were waiting to shoot you. It was the Sikh people doing the killing, not the British. In Amritsar so many thousands of Muslim women were being raped and then killed by these Sikhs.

'When we were going by truck to Lahore there were also 70,000 people on the road going through the forest, with oxen and cattle. Sikhs and Hindus coming east while we were going west.'

I thought of the potential for conflict as the two columns of embittered refugees passed each other. 'Did you have a police escort?' I asked.

'The Indian Army accompanied our fourteen trucks with a green flag to the Pakistan border. The people from the other side, they had no escort.

'In Pakistan I went first to a refugee camp in Lahore and then to Jhelum, which is on the road to Rawalpindi. For one year more I stayed in the camp for refugees at the Shalimar Garden

near Lahore. There were 80,000 refugees from different parts –
Amritsar, Delhi, Ambala.

'I came back to Delhi in 1950 and completed my reading of
the Holy Qu'ran. Since then I have been a dirwan. I have been
to the holy places in Quetta but am too poor to go on the Haj
to Mecca. But this one thing I will tell you. Since 1947, all the
Muslims of India have been silent.'

'I used to own a bicycle-repair shop in Karolbagh,' said Aziz
Uddin, at seventy years of age a comparative youngster.
'Originally my family came from UP, but eight years before I
came to Delhi to start this business. Then, just after Independence, all this criminal fighting started. Old Delhi side was safe,
but in Karolbagh, Sidipura, Paharganj . . . there Muslims were
cut by Hindus and Hindus by Muslims. Many, many Muslims
were killed. Almost all their houses and shops, including my
own bicycle shop, were looted or burned down by Hindus and
Sikhs. If I'd stayed in Karolbagh I would most certainly have
been killed.

'Some other Muslims had a house and we took refuge with
them. Going there I saw in one place two dead, in another four
dead. I tell you, blood was flowing like a river in the road.
There were children who had hidden in corners of the house
while their parents were killed. Then two army batallions came,
some Gurkhas, some Indians, and they asked us where did we
want to go. They said there were only two safe places in Delhi
for Muslims, the Jama Masjid and the Red Fort. So we came to
the Jama Masjid, where already there were thousands of people
like us, many of them wounded.

'There were many houses left empty in the city, either by
people who had left for Pakistan or because their owners had
been killed. I moved into one such house in Mattia Mahal. I had
lost my own house and nobody knew what had happened to the
owner. But the Indian Government appointed custodians of
properties left by people who went to Pakistan, and always I am
having to pay rent to these custodians.

'After 1947, I started a paan business. We were three brothers, and it was not easy to make money. But slowly and slowly the business grew, and so we started in ready-made garments. I always remember it was here in the Jama Masjid that I found safety. I have been coming to this Jama Masjid ever since.'

The loudspeakers hidden around the mosque courtyard came alive with static. A moment later the call to evening prayer, amplified almost to the point of distortion, boomed out from every corner. Aziz Uddin got up, adjusted his embroidered skullcap and joined the growing throng of men and boys who were aleady lining up in rows. It was Friday and so many were coming to pray that I could hardly push my way through them to the north gate.

I decided it was time to leave Delhi. The weekend was looming and I wouldn't be able to get anywhere with the bike's paperwork until Monday. All the advice I'd received was that since Enfield technically owned the bike it was up to them to procure the right papers. Besides, I needed to get some more miles under my belt. Sarah had called me the previous evening from London to say that she was coming out for the final leg of the journey through Pakistan. The plan was to meet at Amritsar in about ten days' time and to cross the border together.

The next morning I packed up the bike. But before leaving town there was one more thing I wanted to see. Curiously enough, it was just across the road from where I'd been staying at the Gymkhana Club, at No. 1 Safdarjang Road – the modest, white-painted bungalow where Indira Gandhi had lived when she was Prime Minister and where she had died in a hail of bullets fired by her own Sikh security guards.

I had already seen the Nehru family house in Allahabad where she had grown up. Next I would be heading into Sikh country and eventually to Amritsar. It was because Indira Gandhi had ordered the Indian Army into the Golden Temple complex at Amritsar, and in so doing desecrated the Sikhs' most holy shrine, that her security officers Beant Singh and Satwant Singh felt it their duty to assassinate her.

I crossed over the road and went through the security check

at the gate. The official visit winds through the PM's former office and family rooms, the walls lined with informal photographs of Indira with her family: Sanjay, whom she hoped would be her political heir but who died in an air crash; and the elder son, Rajiv, who tried at first to avoid politics but who took over after his mother's death. He too was assassinated, in Tamil Nadu, while he was campaigning for re-election. After both assassinations the Congress Party swept the board at the next general election. India may tire of being ruled by a dynasty, but it seems it will always vote for martyrs.

The house had been turned into a shrine to these later generations of the Nehru-Gandhi dynasty. There were blown-up press clippings of Indira's greatest victories and defeats – her expulsion from the Congress Party in 1969, the defeat of Pakistan and the creation of the new state of Bangladesh in 1971. I stared into a cabinet of medals and decorations from foreign governments, the Lenin Prize occupying centre stage, and at the wedding sari made from yarn woven by her father, Jawaharlal Nehru, when he was imprisoned by the British. All of this was leading up to the bloodstained saffron sari she had worn on that fateful morning of 31 October 1984. Then it was out into the leafy garden, to the spot where she had been gunned down.

Two soldiers were standing guard over the simple memorial, across which were strewn two clumps of rose petals. A family group stood in silence, their heads bowed. When a busload of infantry on a day's outing turned up, they stopped joking and spoke to each other in whispers. Whatever one thinks of Indira Gandhi, it was hard not to be moved.

The night after his mother's assassination Rajiv Gandhi made a radio broadcast to the nation. 'This is a moment of profound grief,' he began. 'The foremost need now is to maintain our balance. We should remain calm and exercise maximum restraint. We should not let our emotions get the better of us.'

His appeal for calm was not heeded. The cry for revenge went up among Congress-workers and other Hindus. In Delhi's suburbs, hundreds of Sikhs were dragged from their homes, bludgeoned to death and set on fire. Once more mob instinct had won, allowing the cycle of violence and hatred to continue.

10

HARYANA: BIKER'S DHARMA, THEN COMMUNICATIONS BREAKDOWN

It felt good to be back on the road. The Enfield was running sweetly, all traces of low-speed steering wobble eradicated by the hammering-out of the dented front fork. The engine felt more flexible now it was run-in, accelerating smoothly from low revs. I'd even given her a wash and polish before setting out for the Punjab. Now all I had to do was rejoin the GT Road.

When I stopped to ask the way at a bus stop a kindly-looking gentleman carrying a furled umbrella said he was going in the same direction. If I gave him a lift he would see me on to the right road. Somehow he squeezed his portly frame in between my rucksack, the side-panniers and my back, and off we went. I suspected we should be heading more north but he was emphatic that this was the right road, stabbing at the air with his umbrella to point the way or to indicate a change of direction to other traffic.

It was when I saw a road sign for Rohtak that I knew he was deliberately taking me the wrong way. 'Yes, this is Rohtak Road,' he said, 'and you will drop me after just two more kilometres.'

'But I don't want to go to bloody Rohtak,' I shouted.

'This thing I am understanding,' he beamed, 'and from where you will drop me there is a most excellent short cut to GT Road.'

I bowed to the inevitable. The only alternative was to double back through city traffic. And he was right: the cross-road he showed me ran directly north through sparkling wheatfields to the main highway.

The countryside looked prosperous, with modern, purpose-built granaries and storage depots. Power lines stalked across the plain; sections of concrete pipeline were being laid beside the road. Here in Haryana, signs of new investment in infrastructure were everywhere to be seen. After going through Bihar and Eastern UP it was like entering a different country.

Near Panipat I turned left off the main road, following signs towards the historic battlefield. Not once, but three times, has the fate of northern India been decided on this featureless plain. The first Battle of Panipat confirmed the rise of Mughal power, for it was here, in 1526, that Babur's army defeated the massed troops and war elephants of Ibrahim Lodi, the last Sultan of Delhi.

Thirty years later it saw the final showdown for control of northern India between Mughals and Afghans. Humayun had but recently fallen down the library steps at the Purana Qila, and his thirteen-year-old successor, Akbar, was being challenged by Sher Shah's old general, Hemu. Things were going badly for Akbar and his own general, Bairam Khan, when an arrow struck Hemu in the eye. Seeing that their leader on top of his war elephant had been badly wounded, panic set in amongst the Afghans. The victorious Mughals beheaded Hemu, slaughtered their prisoners and built a victory pillar from their skulls.

The third battle occurred when Mughal power was in terminal decline. Delhi had recently been sacked by an expedition from Afghanistan and the enfeebled Mughals had to call on the Marathas, Hindu warlords from Central India, to defend what remained of their empire. So when the Afghans under Ahmad Shah Durrani again advanced on Delhi it was a Maratha army that went out to meet him at Panipat in January 1761. The Afghans won the day, but almost immediately the victorious soldiers mutinied over arrears of pay. So neither army enjoyed the prize of Delhi.

I watched the sun sink over this plain where six great armies had met. Directly overhead a mixed patrol of vultures and kites spiralled downwards, either to investigate something that looked like supper or simply to return to their roosts for the night.

Right beside the GT Road I found the Blue Jay Motel, a modern establishment run by Haryana State Tourism. Someone had left the heating on in my room, so I opened the window; fast traffic roared down the four-lane highway just outside. If it wasn't for the distinctive two-tone note of Indian truck horns I might have been anywhere in the world.

Just down the road was a dhaba where through-buses stopped. Their passengers sat on metal chairs at long tables under neon lights, munching their way through a bewildering variety of dishes and side plates. For someone who was used to smaller places with charpoys out front where you ate whatever was cooking, the choice in this mega-dhaba was overwhelming. I sat at a row of smaller tables, alongside the truck drivers. Inevitably I ordered too much food.

'You are liking this food?' a gruff voice enquired. I was being addressed by a Sikh trucker, a huge bear of a man. His central features poked out from between a dense black beard and he had hands the size of pudding plates. A steel bangle slid up and down his bulging forearm as he pushed aside the pile of aluminium food-bowls he'd just emptied.

'Yes, it's very good,' I replied. 'The best food I have eaten in a dhaba.'

'Arrachh! This is like water beside real Punjabi food from the North. That is where I am coming from, from Pathankot. There you may eat a hearty khana, enough to make you a strong man. Are you going Delhi-side or to the North?'

'To Amritsar,' I said, deciding it best not to mention Pakistan.

'Why do you not come with us to Kashmir? There is room in the cab. We are taking a consignment to Srinagar. No payment is necessary.'

It was a tempting offer: to ride over the snow-filled Himalayan passes with this burly Sikh and his equally burly co-driver. Srinagar wasn't exactly on the Grand Trunk Road; but the whole question of Kashmir had bedevilled Indo-Pak relations since 1947. Maybe I'd learn something useful along the way.

But I needed to get the bike to Amritsar, where I would meet up with Sarah. I needed to obtain the right papers to take it into Pakistan. I remembered that foreign hostages were still being held in Kashmir and the dire warnings against going there from the British High Commission in Delhi. From the newspapers I knew that Srinagar was usually under curfew. They'd never let me in. And half the time the mountain passes were blocked by snow. Still, if I'd been a free agent . . .

'How many days?' I asked non-committally.

'Two to three. Maybe more if there is snow or problems at army check-points.'

'And isn't the road dangerous?'

'We are Sikhs,' he roared. 'We Sikhs do not fear anything. We will go on any road, anywhere, even if there are terrorists or dacoits waiting there. From Jammu onwards to Srinagar, you will see that one hundred per cent of transport have Sikh drivers. Travelling with us your safety is assured.'

I didn't doubt him. 'Thank you for your offer, but I have a motorbike . . .'

'Here is no problem,' he interrupted. 'It can be loaded on my lorry. Free of charge.'

'And I must stay in Jullundur and other places before Amritsar,' I continued.

'Ah, then we cannot stop for you. Three days with this consignment to Srinagar . . .' He got up and thumped me on the back. 'We must go now. The road is good all the way to Amritsar.'

He strode out of the dhaba like a warlord, a silver dagger tucked into his belt. I saw his truck's headlights pull out onto the road and turn northwards. Three days non-stop to Srinagar . . . What had I missed?

It was around midday that I caught up with the tail of a military convoy heading north. I'd just clearned Karnal, a busy market town whose origins go back to the epic deeds recounted in the

Mahabharata. The long line of drab green vehicles were travelling in groups of ten or twelve, each with a lead jeep. Most of the trucks were filled with infantrymen who waved as I accelerated past. Others were supply vehicles or towing heavy artillery. It looked to me as though an entire division was on the move.

When I took the turning off to Kurukshetra I noticed the army vehicles were doing the same thing. There were military police on hand diverting the traffic. The convoy was turning into some kind of transit camp.

It was then that I remembered there had been a big refugee camp here in 1947. I'd seen Cartier-Bresson's photographs of it back in Delhi. Probably the same piece of government land was now being used by the army. I pulled up beside a line of stationary trucks. The soldiers were friendly but had never heard of there being a refugee camp here. They were in transit.

'Where to?' I asked, before realising I might be arrested for soliciting military secrets. But the subedar in charge only laughed out, 'Why do you ask?'

'For so many soldiers there can be only two places,' I ventured, 'J&K [Jammu and Kashmir] or the Pakistan Border.'

This he found tremendously amusing. 'What difference,' he spluttered, 'J&K or Pakistan? Always we must be fighting mischief-making Muslims.'

Kurukshetra is the scene of the epic battle which forms the centrepiece of the *Mahabharata*. It is the culmination of a long rivalry between the Pandavas – whose capital of Indrapastha probably lies under the Purana Qila in Delhi – and their cousins, the Kauravas of Hastinapur. Modern archaeology suggests that the events described took place around 900 BC, when the Aryan invaders were restricted to India's northern plains. According to the legend, this battle endured for eighteen days and ended with the total defeat of the Kauravas. The Pandava brothers then ruled over the kingdom in peace until they renounced all worldly dominion and went to the city of the gods in the Himalayas.

Over the centuries this legend was elaborated, so that a local feud over land rights was transformed into an epic worthy of a cast of thousands. From being a mainly secular tale of warlike deeds, later episodes – most notably the *Bhagavad-Gita* – introduced high religious and moral concerns which remain central to Hindu beliefs. The concept of Dharma, the divinely sanctioned moral law, is explained through a dialogue between the god Krishna and Arjuna, one of the Pandava brothers, who is unwilling to kill his own kinsmen in battle. Krishna is Arjuna's charioteer on the battlefield and persuades the reluctant warrior that in fighting a just war he is acting in conformity with his Dharma. Even in killing, his actions are necessary and therefore not sinful; for every man must do his lawful duty without questioning the end result of his actions.

So the *Mahabharata* is much more than an assemblage of ancient legends. It is about duty and morality and religion. For centuries it has been at the centre of the traditional canon of Hindu scriptures; so it is hardly surprising that Kurukshetra should have become an important centre of Hindu pilgrimage.

The most propitious time to visit and take a dip in the holy tank is when there is a solar eclipse, for it is commonly believed that then the waters of all the sacred tanks in India miraculously come together at Kurukshetra. An almost complete solar eclipse had occurred just three months before and pilgrims had arrived in their millions. As I rode towards the main bathing tank I noticed modern and well-maintained railway and bus stations and carefully laid-out camping grounds, where the millions could stay during the mela.

Traditional and modern are combined around the Brahmasar or main bathing tank. With its overhead walkways and regimented steps leading down to the water's edge, it reminded me of a 1950s Lido at a now unfashionable seaside resort. But the scale of this man-made lake dwarfed any bathing complex I had ever seen. It is more than half a mile in length. At peak times hundreds of thousands could find some space on the bathing ghats, though now only a trickle of pilgrims was going down to bathe.

The sadhus and other godmen had staked out prime positions on the lawns that run between the tank and the main access road. They sat in little groups, looking out of place in such neat surroundings, wild-haired ascetics against a municipal background. One group called me over and, as the chillum went round, explained to me that although the tank is called Brahmasar, and despite the fact that this area is associated with Brahma, there is only one temple to God the Creator in all of India, and that is at Pushkar in distant Rajasthan.

When I passed on the chillum without partaking, one of the sadhus – a devotee of Vishnu whose eyes were shielded by what looked suspiciously like a pair of Ray-Bans – asked me what was wrong. 'All foreigners smoke ganja,' he declared, as if he'd discovered some universal law.

'But I have to ride a motorcycle,' I said. 'Ganja and motorcycles don't mix.'

'Where is your motorcycle?' he demanded. 'We will go now, you and me. You motorcycle; me ganja.'

For a moment the idea of taking this wild-haired sadhu for a spin on the Bullet had a madcap appeal. That was until he removed his shades and I saw his eyes. He was very far gone indeed, and I wouldn't have put it past him to try out some high-speed yogic exercises while riding pillion, which would have resulted in both of us being splattered across the tarmac.

'Maybe,' I said, fearful of causing offence. 'But first I want to look round this temple.'

'OK, no problem,' he chuckled, taking another hit off the chillum. 'You come back later.'

I didn't spend long at the modern temple, which was a pink and white confection trying to imitate classical Hindu architecture and manifestly failing to do so. Nor did I go back to find Mr Joy-Ride. The afternoon light had taken on that golden glow that told me I'd best hit the road in earnest. Otherwise I wouldn't arrive in Ambala until after dark.

If I was half-way superstitious I might be persuaded that the sadhu had put a curse on me. For just half an hour down the GT Road I came very close to wiping out in terminal style.

It was on a four-lane stretch, traffic was light and I was going flat out. A tractor started pulling out from behind a parked truck to cross the road. No trouble, I thought. It has plenty of time to cross my two lanes and wait behind the central barricade. I shifted into the inside lane and didn't even bother to reduce speed.

Only when it was too late to brake did I see it was towing a long trailer and that this was full of passengers. Tractor and trailer stretched right across both lanes ahead of me. There was no way round that barrier on the inside.

'Christ-all-bloody-mighty!' I yelled, and went for maximum throttle, aiming for the narrowing space between the tractor's nose and the gap in the central reservation. I made it with inches to spare, already leaning the bike over in the hope that I could curl left quickly. Straight ahead was a high concrete kerb and a lamp-post, the beginning of the next section of central barrier on this four-lane highway, and it was coming up fast. Again I missed it by inches.

Just how I managed to pirouette around that tractor's blunt nose I still don't understand. For those few seconds I saw everything with crystal clarity – the lumbering tractor advancing, the look of horror on the driver's face, the oncoming truck which ruled out using the opposite lane as an emergency escape route. I'd been compelled to action, forced to take an absolutely final decision, putting my trust in speed and manoeuvrability to get me out of trouble.

A couple of months earlier I couldn't have done it. Back then I'd have gone for the brakes. Maybe I'd have lived. But there wasn't the slightest possibility of coming out of that situation without being in traction for months. Instead I'd done what was necessary without questioning the rightness of my action. That's biker's dharma for you – even if it's driven by raw adrenalin and nothing nobler than wanting to live to ride another mile.

Ambala has been an important road and rail junction for 150

years. The British established a large military cantonment there even before the Indian Mutiny. It was here that Rudyard Kipling set the scene where Kim delivers a secret message from the Pathan horse dealer Mahbub Ali, concerning the pedigree of a white stallion, to Colonel Creighton, the ringmaster of those who played at 'The Great Game'. Ambala was then an important enough garrison town for the Commander-in-Chief to be there also; and when he and Creighton Sahib read the message it unleashed a punitive war on the North-West Frontier.

There is still a strong military presence in Ambala, including an Indian Air Force base. The Grand Trunk Road runs between the cantonment area and the commercial town with its factories and textile mills. Right beside the road, just before the junction of the main route up to Amritsar and the road to Chandigarh and Simla, I saw another of the Haryana state-run motels, this one called The Kingfisher. After my near escape I was in no mood to hunt out cheaper lodgings down by the bazaar or the railway station.

No, I wanted to get drunk, if only to cut out the flashbacks of those terrifying three seconds when I thought I was going to plough into that tractor. So after unloading the bike I went straight to the bar, ordered some high-octane beer with cheese and vegetable pakoras on the side and settled in for the evening.

Before long the place was buzzing – mostly with non-residents who'd come with exactly the same game-plan as I had. The bartender was cracking open bottles with the speed of automatic weapons' fire. When I'd finished eating, a group of local boys on a birthday outing asked me over to their table. Another order of beers went in. The birthday boy was a Jain and I was surprised to discover he had just turned twenty-four.

Both he and his friends looked a lot younger than that; or at least they acted much younger. Although they had degrees in commerce or electro-engineering, they behaved like a bunch of High School kids on an illicit boozing spree. That probably comes from still living at home with strict parents. They asked me about how easy it was to meet up with girls in Western countries. For them, Delhi was the pot of gold at the end of the rainbow and they detailed various escapades they'd had in the Big City. At the same time they were defensive about living in Ambala. Rich kids with small-town hang-ups, they downed their beers and all shook my hand before going home. It was 9.30 p.m.

As soon as they left somebody shouted at me across the room. 'Hey, Eenglishmarn! D'yu varnt t' treenk beer vith urs?'

Neither the etiquette nor the accent were typical of Indians. I turned to find a pair of middle-aged Russians in check shirts, one of them waving a can of imported beer in my direction.

They introduced themselves as mechanical engineer Sergeyev, Alexei, and electrical engineer Yuralev, Alexander. They both came from Nizhniy Novgorod and had been three months in India, installing diesel engines in textile mills. Another round of beers was ordered.

Their contract was with a Moscow-based export company and they'd leapt at the opportunity to earn three times their normal pay back in Russia. 'But zis India vairy expenzif country,' complained Alexei; 'people alvays taking money-money.'

I guessed the exchange rate between rouble and rupee couldn't be too healthy. I offered to pay for the beers. '*Nyet, nyet,*' protested Alexander, who lapsed into Russian while slapping me on the back.

Alexei explained, 'My colleague speak only leetle Engliz. He is saying for hotel room, for all food, for all beers, factory pays. You want anything,' he waved expansively towards the bar, 'is all right – my factory pay.' So that was it. I was drinking on the Russians' expense account.

'Zis India,' he continued, 'I, my friend, not liking. Zis country, always I am working. Sunday, every day, always working twelve–fourteen hours. No extra-money! In Russia, working Sunday, extra-money is good. Here, factory owner want only I work more time. No extra-money.'

The absence of overtime was obviously a sore point. This was their first trip abroad and they found working conditions in

Indian factories even worse than in Mother Russia. 'First we go to factory in Ahmadabad,' explained Alexei. 'Zis vairy dirty city. And in factory is no light, no air-conditioning. Every day I am working with diesel engine, vairy hot, exhaust temperature 400 degree centigrade.'

He mopped his brow and took another swig from the can. The label read *Stroh's Super Strong. The Great American Beer since 1775.*

'Here, in Ambala, is better. Hotel is good. Beer is good. Chandigarh City, only fifty kilometre, vairy good – like Russia. But here no wodka. In zis country, Ahmadabad, Ambala, all places – no wodka.'

The absence of vodka made my gloomy companions even more maudlin. I decided not to add to their misery by telling them that the stuff can be bought in Delhi and other cities. Alexei couldn't wait for his contract to finish so that he could get back to Nizhniy Novgorod and see his six-year-old son again. Alexander started humming some Russian tune.

They were like fish out of water, these two Russians, in India's cut-throat capitalist society. They were being treated more like *Gästarbeiten* than technical experts. It was pretty clear they felt they were being exploited. 'Vair do zese rich people make money?' asked Alexei, pointing to the sharp suits and glittering saris all around us. 'In Russia, zey say to me: "India is a poor country." From vair is all zis money coming?'

I woke up with a thick head and the horrible realisation that it was Monday morning. That meant I'd have to get on the telephone to Enfield, the Customs Office, the Automobile Association of Upper India, and anybody else I could think of who might help me to get the papers I needed to take the bike into Pakistan.

I found an STD telephone booth and spent two hours trying to get through to either Madras or Delhi. All trunk lines were permanently engaged. I must have redialled those numbers a hundred times before I got through to Madras, only to be told that the person dealing with my case was out. Was there a number he could call me back on?

The frustration of long-distance telephone communication in India was getting to me. I had to sort this thing out, even if it meant spending less time on the Grand Trunk Road. The best thing, I decided, was to find some reasonable but efficient businessman's hotel where there would be a phone in my room so I could take incoming calls. That and a fax machine. I'd hole up for a couple of days and bash the telephone lines until I had the answers I needed.

Chandigarh looked like providing the best base. Besides having plenty of business hotels, it was the state capital of the Punjab. And since the border post by which I would be leaving India was in the Punjab, maybe I could get clearance through the state customs office in Chandigarh. At least they should be able to advise me.

So instead of turning west up the GT Road, I took the road north towards the Siwalik Hills and beyond them the Himalayas. It had been snowing recently up there and I caught the occasional, tempting gleam of whiteness. A cool wind blowing down from the hills cleared the remnants of my hangover. I convinced myself all would be well.

It took less than an hour to reach the outskirts of Chandigarh. I knew I was getting close when for no apparent reason the two-lane road turned into a four-lane boulevard with roundabouts every five hundred yards that had neatly mown grass and flower beds in the middle of them. There wasn't much traffic about, but that's beside the point. For Chandigarh is a prestige project rather than a working city.

Created out of nothing during the 1950s, its purpose was to provide a new capital for the half of Punjab that came to India during Partition. Before that the provincial capital had been Lahore, but that had gone to Pakistan. To begin with, the Indian half of the province was administered from Simla; but Nehru wanted a gleaming new monument to the future of

independent India. So the most prestigious international architects were called in to realise this vision. Le Corbusier got to
design the really big structures, the government buildings and
the museums. Maxwell Fry and Jane Drew dealt with the
residential and commercial blocks. Together they created a
thoroughly modernist city, a model of post-war urban planning,
an Indian Brasilia.

I'll give those architects one thing: with their passion for
rigorous grid-plans, their insistence on dual carriageways and
roundabouts, even when they aren't really needed, they've
designed one hell of a biker-friendly city. The Enfield swung
through the roundabouts and roared up the wide, tree-lined
boulevards at speeds I wouldn't have dreamt of in any other
Indian town.

But as I entered Chandigarh I had the impression of being
somewhere other than India. The road system made me think of
Harlow New Town or Milton Keynes. The drab concrete
boxes of the residential and commercial districts looked like
they'd been uprooted from the old Soviet Union and dropped
into a sunnier clime. There were no industrial fumes because a
blanket ban on industry had been imposed, and there is not
much street life because the town is so spread out that it rules
out moving around on foot. Instead there are parking lots full of
little Rajdoot motorcycles and scooters. Chandigarh must have
the highest ratio of two-wheelers to total population in the
entire subcontinent.

I checked into a characterless business hotel and started my
telephonic blitzkrieg. I had three hours before most offices
would close for the day. I arranged to see the Punjab customs
authorities the following morning. But on long-distance calls I
got nowhere. Lines to Delhi and beyond were constantly
engaged. I resorted to faxes, hoping that somehow they might
get through. I was very probably driving the telephone operator
insane. But for all this manic, late-twentieth-century behaviour,
I'd made no progress whatsoever come close of play.

The following morning I was handed back a sheaf of faxes
with slips confirming they'd been transmitted overnight. I was

also given a telephone bill that made my heart stop. The hotel was charging three times the standard tariff. At this rate it would be cheaper to fly down to Madras and back. But there wasn't time for that. And now that I'd sent out the hotel's phone and fax number I couldn't move elsewhere unless I wanted to miss incoming calls. Christ, what a mess I'd got myself into. I should have fixed the documents back in Delhi, or in Calcutta, or right at the very beginning when I was in Madras.

I decided to revise my plan of attack. From now on I'd make outgoing calls from one of the STD booths around the bus station. Then I'd dash back to base and await incoming communications. It didn't work. While I sat waiting in my room, willing the telephone to ring, it remained silent. But when I went out the calls would come flooding in and on my return a smiling receptionist would hand me a packet of messages with the numbers I should call back. And by the time I started dialling all trunk lines were engaged. Time was slipping by. I stared out of my bedroom window at the Siwalik Hills to the north, pumping out telephone numbers and cursing the vagaries of not-quite-modern telecommunications.

When not waiting for calls that never came, I spent a good deal of time at the Punjab State Customs Office in Sector 17. This was located in another modernist block, better maintained than most. But once inside, the shuffling of clerks and peons was the same as in any other bastion of Indian bureaucracy. I was offered tea – always a sure sign that there's plenty of waiting to come. Eventually I was shown into the office of Additional Commissioner Ishwar Singh, who was at least kind enough to recognise I had a major problem on my hands.

'You are telling me that you wish to take this motorcycle into Pakistan, correct?'

'Correct.'

'Then you will be needing to complete export clearance procedure.'

'But I'm not exporting it,' I protested. 'I've got to return it to India. You see, I don't actually own the bike myself.'

I handed him photocopies of the Bullet's licence and registration details, which was all that I had.

The Additional Commissioner looked at me curiously. 'Never have I known a precedent for this, Mr Gregson. Now let me see . . .' and he started thumbing through a blue paperback copy of *The Practical Guide to Customs Law and Procedures.* From outside came the sound of political chants and shouting. A protest rally was being held in the square opposite. Riot-police armed with sub-machine-guns and lathis stood by, ready to intervene if necessary. 'Pay no attention,' remarked Ishwar Singh: 'this is just some political agitation.'

After due consideration, he dictated a list of documents I should procure. It began with a letter of guarantee from the Pakistan Embassy in Delhi (I'd already knocked on that door) and ended with the requirement that Enfield issue a formal letter authorising me to take the bike out of the country.

I also had to go through the 'triptych procedure' in order to acquire an international carnet from the Automobile Association of India. I dutifully copied all this down, even though I'd already been to the offices of the AA of Upper India in Delhi, pleaded with the top man himself and been turned down because they could only issue a carnet to an Indian national. If these things were possible – and it was a very big if – I reckoned it would take at least a month to assemble all these documents. My entry visa to Pakistan expired in ten day's time.

I fought to control the rising panic inside me. Maybe I could persuade Enfield to issue a letter of guarantee. It was my last hope.

Ishwar Singh consulted his watch. 'Now it is lunch hour,' he announced. 'Perhaps if you come back after taking something to eat, we may bring your case before my boss, Commissioner S. S. Khosla.'

I spent the lunch hour in the basement of a cloth merchants which had been turned into a telephone-cum-fax centre. Trunk lines to Madras were all engaged, so I composed a begging letter to Enfield asking them to stand guarantee. An hour later the lines were still busy so I asked the fax operator to send it and paid in advance.

I kicked myself for not dealing with these problems earlier.

Back in the Customs House I was ushered into Commissioner Khosla's presence. Tea was brought and I waited for half an hour while he talked down the telephone. How come he could always get a line?

A well-built man, tending to plumpness, the Commissioner had the easy manner of a politician rather than the dutifulness of a public servant. A stream of peons entered and left the room, carrying bundles of paper which he signed off as he continued talking down the line. On the wall behind his desk was a map of the world. It announced: 'The whole world is within your reach with MCI International'. I wondered whether getting into Pakistan would ever be within my reach.

Eventually he put down the hated instrument and turned to me. 'Now, how may we be of assistance?'

I explained my sad predicament. 'Let me see,' he interrupted, 'don't we have some fellow here in this office who was posted to the Attari Road land crossing? He should know what the correct procedure is.'

A peon was despatched to bring up this subordinate, who explained at great length how the rule-book was interpreted down at the Indo-Pak border. At the end of this interview Commissioner Khosla dictated yet another letter of guarantee I needed, which should be on stamped paper, that someone at Enfield would have to sign. I had a suspicion that Madras wouldn't like issuing all these legal guarantees.

In this I was correct. That evening a call finally came through from Madras. The rather ineffectual individual who was 'dealing with my case' had received and circulated my faxes. He sounded distinctly rattled. Their lawyers had advised them that as a limited company there was no way they could provide such guarantees. Instead he suggested a technical transfer of ownership.

'You mean you're handing over the bike?'

'Technically speaking, yes. By these means you will be

responsible for procuring the necessary permits. And, ahem, Mr Gregson . . .?'

'Yes?'

'You will be bringing the vehicle back to India, won't you?'

'Of course, of course,' I assured him, my mind racing to work out all the implications. This put things into an entirely new perspective. It basically ruled out getting any travel documents from the Indian authorities; for that to happen the bike had to remain under Indian ownership. But if I technically owned the bike then I might just be able to get an international carnet issued back in England. There were three days before Sarah was due to fly out to India and meet up with me.

I decided it was time to call in the airborne cavalry.

'You want me to do what?' Sarah's voice, 5,000 miles away, combined outrage and disbelief.

'Just phone the AA in Basingstoke and see whether they can issue an international carnet.'

'Oh great! So I just phone the AA and say: "Excuse me. My husband wants to take his motorbike from India to Pakistan and then back again. And by the way, he's already out there and he's got to get across the border in ten days or his visa runs out. Can you help?'

'Er, something like that . . .'

'You must be mad. Today is Tuesday; I fly out Friday evening. What do you expect? Fucking miracles?'

'I bloody need them. This is India. The customs want a bank guarantee and God knows what else. Enfield turned me down on that. There's no other way!'

'That's because you fucked up! Don't you realise I've got two projects to finish before getting on the plane?'

She was screaming now. I tried to explain that if I jumped through the hoops to please the Indian authorities it wouldn't work for Pakistan and vice versa. 'Just give it a try,' I begged.

'OK. One call and that's it. Just wait by that phone until I call you back.'

The line went dead.

Sarah called back three hours later. 'You are a lucky bastard,' she began. 'I phoned the AA and they said it normally takes a month to issue a carnet. They do it all the time for hippies who buy motorcycles in India. Standard procedure, they say. Why the hell didn't you organise this in the first place?'

'Because I didn't own the bleeding bike,' I shouted. 'How the hell was I to . . .'

'Anyway,' she interrupted, 'they put me through to this marvellous woman in Basingstoke named Margaret. She said it was most unusual but that she liked a challenge. She's just rung back to say she thinks she can swing it. But there is a snag.'

'What's that?'

'Ownership of the bike has to be transferred to my name. Somebody has to sign all these forms she's sending over to me by motorcycle courier. And it's no good faxing over a copy of your signature. That's not legally valid.'

'But you can't ride the bike,' I protested. 'You haven't got a licence.'

'That doesn't matter, apparently, provided I'm on it when we go over the border. In effect you'll be the chauffeur and I'll be the vehicle's owner sitting on the back.'

It sounded insane. 'I don't know how the Enfield people are going to react to this,' I warned her. 'I'll need to give them your passport number and all that stuff.'

'Nothing compared to what you've got to fax over to me. Got a pen ready? OK, engine number, chassis number, colour, registration number . . .'

Over the next forty-eight hours things got pretty weird. Faxes went off, incoming and outgoing, like artillery salvoes. Mostly they had to be followed through by telephone. The three of us – Sarah in London, me in Chandigarh, and St Margaret (as I came to regard her) in Basingstoke – were applying global telecommunications to slay the dragon of bureaucracy. It helped that it was far easier to make an international call to England than it was to get an internal line in India. But what tilted the balance was the gung-ho, can-do, rapid-fire approach which was brought to bear on the problem.

It didn't matter that we were stitching together a total fabrication. Sarah was taking out an international carnet and putting up guarantees for a motorcycle in another country which she didn't own and couldn't ride. It didn't make sense; but it was what was required.

I had to clear this with Enfield and provide additional information about the bike. When I noticed I hadn't included the licence number along with all the other details I immediately put a call through to St Margaret of Basingstoke.

'Ah yes, we did notice that was missing,' she said in a calm, matronly tone. 'So I talked to Sarah and asked her to look out any photographs of the motorbike she'd taken. It was simple, really. She read back the licence number from a photo. So it was good of you to call me from India but rest assured – it's all been taken care of.'

And there had been some startlingly rapid advances on the Madras front; the Enfield people were doing their stuff. The bike's original papers had been sent off to the Tamil Nadu authorities; the registration was being switched to Sarah's name; and the new documents were to be air-couriered to Delhi the evening after her flight arrived.

After two solid weeks of slogging it out in the bureaucratic swamplands I scented victory. I'd tried playing by the rules and got nowhere. Now we were bending the facts to fit the rule-book. I even checked with an ex-diplomat who'd served in Pakistan what was the approved technique of bribing border officials – should that prove necessary.

Everything had to be ready by Friday evening. I waited anxiously for the call from Sarah confirming the carnet had arrived safely. At that moment a motorcycle courier was riding up the M3 from Basingstoke to London in freezing conditions to deliver a piece of paper that would free another motorcycle half-way across the globe to cross over from one country to another. It was absurd.

The call came through very late. 'Christ, that was cutting it fine,' Sarah told me. 'The courier's only just arrived and my plane leaves in two-and-a-half hours' time.'

'So you've got the carnet?' I asked in disbelief.

'Yes, I've got the bloody carnet. And don't ever ask me to do this kind of thing again. Because next time it's divorce.'

It poured with rain those last two days in Chandigarh, turning the carefully planned open spaces into lakes of muddy water. Some of the rain seeped into the Bullet's carburettor – the problem eventually being traced by a mechanic at the local Enfield dealer.

The old Sikh who had started this business – and the dealership in Ambala as well – was Sirdar Manohan Singh. He began repairing imported British bikes in 1949, and he still spoke the names of ancient marques with pride – BSA, Ariel, Matchless, Norton, AJS, Triumph and, of course, Royal Enfield.

'In those days it was mostly army and air force people who bought motorcycles,' he remembered. 'I learned to be a mechanic through on-the-job training. The English engineers always trusted me to do a good job.' Since then motorcycles had been his life and he had kept on riding Enfields even after he'd retired. But now he was sixty-five he had decided to call it a day.

The family originally came from Lyallpur in the West Punjab, where his father had been a wine and spirits contractor. After Pakistan was created the family got out, his father and mother by aeroplane, the rest by train to Lahore and then across the new frontier to Amritsar.

'We were fortunate there was no trouble on the train,' he said. 'And the old family house in Lyallpur is still there. Of course a Muslim family is living there now. I met them and took tea with them when I went back four years ago. Each year a small number of Sikh people are permitted to go to Pakistan to visit their gurdwaras and holy places.'

Though I didn't know it when I arranged to meet him, Jargtar Singh Grewal also once lived near Lyallpur. I knew of him as one of the foremost modern Sikh historians; yet it was his

personal memories which intrigued me most as we sat in a
friend's house drinking tea.

He too had recently been back to Pakistan. 'In Lahore I
looked for the Christian College where I was studying in 1947,
but it is not there any more. Now there is a government college
in its place.'

With a historian's memory, he retraced the gathering sense of
unease among non-Muslim students in Lahore: the first riots in
the city; the Muslim students leaving the mixed hostel at their
college; the worsening news on the radio . . . Towards the end
of March all students were asked to leave the hostel. Grewal
went back to his family's village among the canal colonies near
Lyallpur.

He explained that the Sikhs had moved from East Punjab to
the canal colonies in the 1890s, when new irrigation schemes
allowed previously waste land to be cultivated. They were good
agriculturalists, willing to adopt the latest improvements in
ploughing or selective seeding. As a result they prospered; but
they lived among Muslim villages and by 1947 ancient
resentments came up to the surface.

'Because of the riots in the cities and rising communal
tensions, it was decided in my village to prepare a local defence
force against attacks. Since I was the best-educated young
person I was put in charge of organising this. We had around
forty volunteers and these were provided with uniforms and
whatever weapons we could procure – if not a revolver or gun
then at least a sword.'

I was reminded of the martial traditions of the Sikhs. The
carrying of the kirpan or sword is one of the rights and
requirements of all adult male Sikhs. It was not their tradition to
accept intimidation of any sort without vigorous self-defence.
Yet once Partition was agreed, the position of Sikhs in the
western part of the Punjab became untenable. They were too
thinly spread out among a mainly Muslim and increasingly
hostile population. Although more than 2.5 million Sikhs left for
India, there were only small pockets of West Punjab where they
had ever formed a majority.

'By the beginning of August,' Grewal continued, 'we had patrols out and had put petrol around the village. Nothing serious happened until after Partition. Then we began to hear angry slogans about the Muslims who had been obliged to leave India. This added to the pressure.

'Around the twentieth of August our village defence force started experimenting in making crude home-made guns. It was suggested I go to Lyallpur town to fetch the chemicals needed for this. As we passed through a village on the way I noticed a crowd of some one or two hundred people carrying javelins and other weapons. All these people were Muslims.

'I decided to put up a brave front. Immediately we stopped, I came out of the tonga we were travelling in and walked over to the hand-pump beside the road. I wanted to give the impression we had stopped of our own accord so that I could take a drink of water. One man in the crowd threw down his javelin and began talking to me as though nothing had happened – "Not seen you for a long time," and other such pleasantries. Then he said to me: "Don't come back from the city by this same road."

'It was a narrow escape. Later I learned that three or four persons had been killed by this same crowd.'

'How much longer did you stay in Pakistan?'

'Not long. At first the message from the Sikh leadership was that we should stay put. Then we received the message to move. From then it was only a matter of time.

'A friend in a neighbouring village told me about an emergency airlift being organised to take people out from Lyallpur to Delhi. I was hesitant; I was supposed to be leader of the village defence force and didn't want to abandon them. But my father insisted. We travelled to Lyallpur down unmade roads through Sikh villages only. On the main road we would have been killed.

'When we drew near the airfield we saw thousands of refugees on one side. Thank goodness the army was there, because on the other side there were crowds of Muslims waiting for some opportunity. To reach the airfield we had to pass through Muslim crowds on both sides. There were just the two of us, unarmed, but no one thought to attack us. We were really very fortunate to get through.'

'Was there resentment about having to leave?'

'Many people felt this, of course. But the advice from the Sikh leadership, that we should all leave to India, was realistic. Otherwise far more people would have been killed.'

'Was there ever any real hope that the Sikhs might get their own homeland?'

'You mean Khalistan?' he retorted, arching his thick black eyebrows. 'No, the demand for an independent Sikh state never really became a mass movement. Some of the more radical leaders and intellectuals thought this idea could be pressed in 1946, when the Cabinet Mission arrived, but that lasted only for about two months. You see, if there was going to be a division, it was impossible to create a large enough area with a Sikh majority to be viable. This is why Partition had such tragic consequences for the Sikhs.'

The Punjab used to be an enormous province stretching from the River Indus almost to the gates of Delhi. In 1947 it was sliced right down the middle. Then in 1966 its mountain region was separated off into the new state of Himachal Pradesh, while the plains on the Indian side of the border were again divided between the predominantly Hindu and Hindi-speaking state of Haryana in the south-east, leaving a Punjabi-speaking and Sikh majority state of Punjab to the north-west.

A compromise was reached over the sparkling new city of Chandigarh. It was to serve as state capital for both Haryana and the Punjab. This dual status may well add to the sense of unreality. For as often as not there is some dispute between these neighbouring states, over territory or water rights or the continuing status of Chandigarh itself. When these come to the boil it is like having two feuding brothers living under the same roof.

I was happy to leave this soulless and contradictory city behind and head on into the Punjab's heartland. I stuck to the main road, which in these parts is mostly a four-lane highway with broad drainage ditches on either side and a line of eucalyptus trees screening off the rich countryside beyond.

Soon I was over the Sutlej, one of the five rivers after which the Punjab (literally 'land of the five rivers') is named, and moving rapidly into the Jullundur Doab. All the market towns and villages along the road seemed to have tractor dealers and agro-stores with the latest in ploughing and harvesting machinery. The Sikhs take their farming seriously. Herds of sleek water buffaloes were being taken in for milking. The distant fields were under intense cultivation and when the sun finally came out they became a dazzling patchwork of emerald-green wheat, brilliant yellow mustard and paler squares of high-growing sugar cane.

I was aware that most of the Sikh population of Britain originally came from this corner of the Punjab. At a bus stop before Jullundur I met one of them. His accent was straight West Midlands; and, sure enough, one of the first things he told me was 'Ah cum frum Woolvur'ampton.'

He was back for 'anoother bludy fahm'ly weddin' – the third either he or his wife had attended over the winter. This time his wife had stayed in England to look after their Post Office shop, while he'd come out with his three-year-old son. Over a glass of milky tea he complained about being hassled by immigration officials every time he went through Heathrow and the state of land prices around Jullundur.

'Ah've bin thinkin' uv bahyin' an 'ouse back 'ere, boot land's so bludy expensive,' he moaned. And while it used to be 'UK-returned' buyers who pushed up the price of land, nowadays it was people from Canada and the United States. So now he was thinking about looking for something down in South India, more of a holiday place by the sea. 'But if ah do thut ah'll be 'avin' a right earful frum all me relayshuns.'

Back on the bike I found myself racing the sun again, hoping to reach Jullundur before nightfall. On the way into town I asked a group of bystanders for directions and one of them leapt on his scooter and led me down backstreets to a hotel. I was beginning to suspect he might be a tout when he turned into a quiet place with a garden out front run by Punjab State Tourism. He hopped off his scooter, dug into his breast pocket and pulled out his ID card.

'As you will see,' he smiled, 'I am a police officer.'

For a moment I thought he was going to arrest me on some trumped-up drugs charge. I was becoming paranoid.

'Actually I am off-duty,' he continued, 'but it's my pleasure to be of assistance. You will be finding this hotel has every comfort. Also, it is most reasonable.'

With a crisp salute he jumped back onto his scooter and disappeared into the night. The hotel was all that he claimed.

'Oh, but you must come and join us,' exclaimed the jovial and tubby gentleman who was waiting, like me, in the hotel's lobby. 'We are taking some drinks and snacks outside in the garden. Now come along,' and he shepherded me out into the cool night.

It soon became clear why Bhitu wanted me to join his party. Apart from himself, there was his business partner, a whisky-soaked, lovelorn individual with a drooping moustache, and the girl who was the object of his partner's affections. She was petite and wore her hair in a short bob, rather like a 1920s 'flapper'. It was apparent that these two had had some lovers' tiff, and I was there to jolly things along.

'We are both in the construction business,' said Bhitu, waving airily at his partner, whose response was to down another slug of whisky. 'Residential, commercial,' he continued, 'anything that makes money. The main problem is that land values are so high nowadays and it's hard to find a plot with building permissions. But today we have won a new contract. So, cheers.' He raised his whisky glass to the assembled company.

'But I love her,' moaned his partner, staring doggy-fashion at his beloved across the table. She hissed back at him in Punjabi and wrapped her shawl more tightly about her. I was seated between these two. Bhitu tried to cover up what was potentially an embarrassing situation by laughing a lot and bragging about his visits overseas. He'd been to Tucson, Arizona, and down to the Mexican border town 'for the girls'.

'The girls' featured large in his trans-global wanderings. He'd been particularly impressed by Amsterdam's red-light district. 'All the girls sitting in the windows, open onto the street,' he enthused, 'and then you go through a screen and it's all fixed prices. The girls have certificates for AIDS. Compare that to the prostitution centres here in India, in Delhi and Bombay. You see, we Indians must be more modern-minded.'

'But I love her,' the partner announced.

The girl was looking uncomfortable. Neither the turn of conversation nor these romantic outbursts were to her liking. She became happier when our talk turned to astrology. Bhitu claimed to be able to read palms and seized the girl's hand in his meaty paws. 'Look here, this is the love line. How very deep it is!' The girl snuggled up to him, eyes dancing in her head. I suspected she wanted to make her paramour jealous.

'I LOVE HER,' he bellowed like a buffalo under the axe.

'I say, why don't we all drive down to Delhi?' suggested Bhitu, mainly to the girl. 'Have a really good time there. You know, there's this girl at one of the big international hotels who looks just like you.'

'Oh, don't be joking so,' the girl tittered.

'I swear it's true. She's 101 per cent same as you.'

'And I swear I am in love with this girl,' the partner muttered into his whisky.

'Do you have any issue?' Bhitu asked me, changing the conversation again. 'No? That might be OK in the UK; but here, in India, family values must come first.'

I was beginning to lose track of Bhitu. First prostitutes and modern-mindedness. Now family values. He was a bundle of contradictions. I told him as much.

'Ah, so you are thinking I do not believe in God?' Quite where he'd got that idea from I'll never know, but he was already off on another tack and there was no stopping him. 'Of course I believe in God,' he declared. 'But is it not by the grace of God,' he added, looking intently at the girl, 'that we are meant to enjoy all these pleasurable things?'

'I love her, I love her . . .' The drooping moustache was whisky-soaked and quivering with emotion.

This was too much for the girl. 'It's too cold to keep sitting out here,' she announced. Picking up her dainty handbag she fled to their car.

'Good idea,' said Bhitu, standing unsteadily now, throwing rupee notes down on the table. 'Let's all go to Delhi.'

I could imagine nothing worse than being stuck in a car with those three as the whisky slowly wore off. All this modern-mindedness was causing a great deal of confusion. I thanked Bhitu for the drinks and made good my escape. The partner was leaning against a car, shouting 'I love her, I love her,' at a waning moon.

EAST PUNJAB: A BLOODY DIVIDE

Beyond Jullundur the GT Road narrows again to a two-lane highway. Thin sunlight and a rain-washed sky held the promise of first-spring, but the trees lining the road still wore their wintry brown uniform. The recent rains had flooded some of the fields and every few miles the road narrowed further to pass over a canal. Some carried a muddy torrent southwards to Rajasthan. Others had been closed off since the last monsoons and their dried-out beds had become a jungle of weeds where goats were taken to graze.

An hour later I rolled into Amritsar and checked into a hotel not far from the Golden Temple. A wedding was in progress, a modest affair compared with what I'd witnessed in Delhi. Most of the guests had arrived on scooters. I unpacked the Bullet and looked about for an STD booth. There were more beggars and stray cows in the street than I'd seen elsewhere in the Punjab; but then Amritsar is a pilgrimage town.

When I finally got a line through to Sarah in Delhi the news was bad. The bike's documents hadn't arrived from Madras. She'd tried phoning Enfield to find out what was happening, without success. Now she was mutinous. 'Look, I've brought you the bloody carnet from England. I don't see why I should hang around in Delhi waiting for yet more documents that won't turn up.'

'Just hang on one more night,' I pleaded. Not that I wanted her to be in Delhi with me up in Amritsar. But the courier might be on his way at that very moment. 'I'll contact Madras and find out what's happened.'

I spent the next four hours cooped up in a glass telephone booth trying to get a clear line. A couple of times I got through to the Enfield switchboard, but before the call could be transferred the trunk line to Madras was cut. 'It is usually like this for cities beyond Delhi,' explained the grizzled Sikh owner of the STD booth. 'For national calls, the Punjab is not receiving priority.'

I could have murdered whatever official decided who should get priority lines. My life was being ruled by the inefficiencies of India's telephone network. By now the Enfield office would be closing down for the day.

The booth-owner, Mr Harbans Singh, kindly agreed to try sending a fax overnight. As I composed a series of questions which added up to 'What the hell's going on?' Harbans Singh started chatting about this and that. It turned out that he too was a refugee from Pakistan.

'I was sixteen years old,' he remembered. 'Our family was living in Lyallpur. Two weeks after Partition we came out by bullock cart. In one place there was firing from Pakistan people during the night. We hid underneath the bullock cart – myself, two younger brothers, my father, mother and one sister. We all came out safely to Amritsar, but some of my relatives were killed.'

It seemed that half the population of the Punjab were former refugees. I didn't need to go looking for them. Harrowing tales were to be heard at every turn. Only nobody appeared to be interested any more.

Harbans Singh explained how his education had been interrupted for lack of funds. 'For five years we were without land,' he said – a terrible plight for a family of Sikh farmers. He himself tried his hand at various jobs – selling weighing machines, dental goods, family-planning appliances. He joined the Communist Party, worked in Bombay and Chandigarh, and was now back in Amritsar running a tyre retreading shop. His life had been uprooted by Partition.

To my immense surprise the fax went through first time. 'When offices shut, lines are freed up,' explained Harbans Singh.

I tried phoning Madras and got through, but there was nobody left at the office. I also got through to Delhi, only to be told that Sarah had just gone out.

I arose well before dawn, started the bike and rode through Amritsar's empty streets down to the Golden Temple. The night air was chill and a mist hung over the hollows where rainwater had collected.

There were more people moving about around the temple precincts. Like me, they had come to witness the daily procession when the Sikh holy book, the Guru Granth Sahib, is carried across the causeway to the Golden Temple.

Everything was highly organised. I was told to park the Enfield in a shed set aside specially for two-wheelers. My shoes and socks I handed over at what looked like a railway ticket office. There was no charge and I was given a numbered slip. Next, a Sikh helped me wind my long cotton scarf around my head to form an improvised turban. I then washed my hands and feet before entering the temple precinct. The white marble underfoot was almost too cold to walk on.

I followed an orderly line of pilgrims through the Clock Tower gate. Rising up in the middle of the great tank known as the Amrit Sarovar – the Pool of the Nectar of Immortality – was the Golden Temple itself, its jewel-like brilliance caught in a crossfire of floodlights so that the shrine and its unwavering reflection seemed to leap out of the surrounding darkness.

I walked briskly around the marble-clad parikrama that surrounds the tank – partly because of the cold but also because I didn't want to miss the procession. Temple guards in their black turbans and saffron cloaks watched me hurry past, leaning on the shafts of their spears. From the Akal Takht, where the holy book is kept overnight, there came a fervent cry and the sound of brass instruments. I tried not to break into a run.

The palanquin containing the Granth Sahib was already crossing the open space between the Akal Takht and the beginning of the causeway. The crush of pilgrims straining to touch the jewel-encrusted casket slowed its progress and I was able to reach the causeway just in time. I squeezed back against the polished railings to let the head of the procession come past. The next thing I knew somebody was pushing me forward, urging me to join the male pilgrims who were carrying the silver poles that supported the Granth Sahib. I put my shoulder to the pole and, surrounded by the Sikh brotherhood, found myself helping to carry the Holy of Holies across the causeway.

I didn't know what to think. A sense of honour that I was included in so holy a ceremony. Trepidation, lest I slipped on the wet marble and brought the sacred canopy crashing down. It lasted for only a few seconds before another pilgrim took my place. As many pilgrims as possible try to help in carrying the Granth Sahib. For a Sikh it is both an honour and a sign of devotion.

Back in the crowd I was being slapped on the back and congratulated. An overseas-returned Sikh – American or Canadian by his accent – told me I'd 'done just fine'.

'But you know I'm not Sikh,' I protested.

'So what?' he grinned. 'Coming here at this hour of the morning makes you an honorary Sikh.'

We followed the procession into the Harmandir, the Golden Temple itself. The crush of pilgrims would have been intolerable if there had been any pushing and shoving, for the interior is surprisingly small: so small that the marble inlay and gilt mirrors on its walls were filmed with moisture, the condensation of pilgrims' breath. But within this temple order and restraint prevailed. Bearded elders made way for young boys and women. There was a rare sense of equality and community.

The Granth Sahib had been placed on a dais. Layer after layer of precious cloth was being unfolded so that the faithful could gaze upon the holy book. For the Sikhs are now very much a 'people of the book'. From the time of Guru Nanak in the fifteenth century until their tenth and last Guru, Gobind Singh, they had followed charismatic and often warlike religious leaders. But since the early eighteenth century the hymns and sayings of previous Gurus contained in the Granth Sahib have superseded the tradition of living Gurus. The book itself, and the continuous reading and singing of its hymns, are the centre of Sikh worship.

The professional singers began on a new text, to the rhythmic accompaniment of tablas and a simple harmonium. Their singing had verve, but it never went too far beyond the bounds of harmony. I couldn't understand the words, but the impact on the pilgrims around me was almost tangible. They stood unmoving, abstracted, some of them leaning against pillars, their eyes glistening with contained emotion.

I slipped out quietly and walked back over the causeway. Somewhere back there I too had been touched by the feeling of brotherhood among Sikhs, and understood something of what they mean by the Khalsa.

The dawn was breaking, casting dull beams on all the white wedding-cake structures that enclose the sacred tank. For a few moments they turned a flamingo pink, as though suffused with blood; the Golden Temple glowed like the embers of a fire about to reignite. Then the sun rose clear of the buildings to the east, and the temple roof sent golden darts of light in all directions.

I skirted around the parikrama, stopping occasionally to read the memorials to soldiers fallen on the field of battle and other martyrs to the Sikh cause.

It was this tradition of martyrdom, combined with a sense of outrage that this holy place had been defiled, that led to Indira Gandhi's assassination in Delhi. Even now it was hard to believe that this tranquil place had reverberated to the sound of artillery and machine-gun fire, that Indira Gandhi could have ordered the army and its heavy tanks into this sacred compound, that the marble pavement I was now crossing had become a killing ground.

That was Operation Blue Star, in June 1984. The Indian Army had been under strict instructions not to fire on the Golden Temple. But other buildings, including the Akal Takht, which Sant Jamail Singh Brindranwale's followers had turned into a fortress, received a real hammering. Twelve years later and there was still scaffolding around the Akal Takht; and, I guessed, resentment still in the hearts of many Sikhs.

I rode the Enfield back to my hotel as most of Amritsar was waking up. As for me, I already knew what I'd be doing the rest of that day. At eight o'clock I started telephoning. By mid-morning I had twice got through to Madras only to have the line cut before any meaningful conversation.

The inside of that stuffy telephone booth became a second home to me. Whenever another customer came in to make a local call I'd let them take over the booth. There was no problem with local calls. Then I'd go back to the 'hot seat'. To keep myself going, I'd lay odds against getting a connection within the next twenty or thirty times I dialled and kept a tally of how my imaginary bets were doing. At the end of the morning I was 1,260 rupees down.

I'd have rather been at the Golden Temple, riding the bike, talking to people – anything but this mindless dialling of numbers that wouldn't even ring. But I had no option. I had to find out where the bike's papers were. And I knew it was a numbers' game I was playing. Sooner or later the trunk line to Madras would come free and I needed to be first in the queue. All over the Punjab there were other invisible players with their own urgent messages trying to access that line. So I increased the odds to thirty-to-one against and set to redialling.

They had lengthened to 120–1 by the time I got through to Enfield. I was so elated that at first I didn't fully understand what was being said to me. The news was not good. The bike's ownership papers had been sent off to be transferred to Sarah's name, as agreed. But now there was a strike at the Tamil Nadu transport department and nobody knew how long it would continue. Nothing could be done until the strike was over. 'Another two or three days, maybe,' said the hopelessly optimistic individual down the other end. I had five days to enter Pakistan before my entry visa would be invalid.

I tried calling Sarah; the lines to Delhi were engaged. Hysteria was bubbling up inside me. When I finally got through Sarah's voice was almost as hysterical as mine.

'Where the hell have you been?' she shouted. 'I've been trying to phone you at your hotel all morning.'

'And I've been stuck in an STD cabin trying to raise Madras,' I shouted back. Then I told her the news.

'I knew something like this would happen,' she groaned. 'And I've had it with Delhi. Whatever happens, I'm coming to meet you tonight. So get out of that flea-bitten hotel you're staying in and book us into Mrs Bhandari's. It's a private guesthouse. Jonathan Bond says it's the only place to stay in Amritsar.'

Once again Mr Bond had been well-informed. Time stood still at Mrs Bhandari's. The kitchen and buttery were piled high with 1930s sauceboats and soup tureens. The bedrooms had fading prints of English landscapes. The bathroom plumbing was so magnificently obsolete that it belonged in a museum. There was every sign that this household was ruled over by a real mcmsahib.

I collected Sarah from the railway station. 'Just for tonight,' she said, 'we're going to forget about all these hassles.' A wood fire was lit in our bedroom and we dined on butter chicken and roast potatoes. The embers were still glowing in the grate when I last closed my eyes.

Breakfast at Mrs Bhandari's is a leisurely affair. We sat in the sunlit garden, watching a flock of electric-green parakeets assemble on their favourite branch, while plates of papaya and toast with home-made jams and perfectly poached eggs followed each other in slow succession. Then Mrs Bhandari put in an appearance herself. After issuing various commands to her staff, she settled down in the sunshine to have hcr head massaged with coconut oil.

'Why don't you come over and have a chat,' she said imperiously. 'It's so rarely one gets to talk to sensible people in this day and age. I'm ninety-four, you know. And don't pretend to look surprised. Good manners are one thing; but I can't abide flattery when it's so obviously insincere.'

'It's a lovely old house,' Sarah replied, 'and the gardens are beautiful.' Mrs Bhandari's eyes glowed with pleasure. This kind of flattery was acceptable, because she knew it was true.

'Yes, I've been here in this house since 1930. Used to be my uncle's, who was a mill-owner. I always say that without a garden a house is nothing.

'It needs a bit of tidying up here and there,' she added, scowling at some unruly hedges. 'I do try to keep up standards, but it's so difficult to get decent staff these days. We used to have Muslim servants, but they had to go after Partition. Then we had servants from UP. At least they could speak Urdu or English. I've never really taken to talking in Punjabi.'

'So you were here during Partition?' I interrupted.

'Oh, and long before that,' she countered. 'My father was born here in Amritsar. My mother was from Bombay. We're Parsis, you know, and a lot of Parsis come from Bombay.

'In the old days, before they invented this Pakistan, my uncle and I used to go over to Lahore all the time. It was the capital of the Punjab in those days. We'd jump in the car and be over there in forty minutes. Go for the afternoon, do some shopping, tea and meringues in The Mall, then to the pictures or dancing at Faletti's Hotel.

'Or people from Lahore would drop in here all the time. There used to be a biggish Parsi community in Amritsar. But after 1948 they mostly left – some to Bombay, some to Lahore. Now there are only two or three families left.

'Oh Lahore used to be such a beautiful city,' she sighed. 'But those days are gone. I haven't been back since 1947. Faletti's and The Mall . . . It's like a dream now . . .'

'Did things get difficult here in Amritsar during 1947?' I asked.

'Oh, there were some problems down in the town and around the railway station. But it wasn't so bad as all that. The Muslims went; the Hindus came. People just went and came. They left their houses to someone from over there.'

'There's one thing I've been longing to ask you,' Sarah said as we got up. 'Why is there that inscription on the balcony above the kitchen door?'

'You mean "Commando Bridge"? That's because I sit up there and give orders. We had some German guests here and they named it Commando Bridge. I liked the name and it's stuck up there now. And there it will remain until long after I'm dead and the house falls down.'

Sarah and I went down to the Golden Temple that day. The busy market area just north of the temple complex was crammed with shops catering specifically for pilgrims' needs. There were plenty of milk and ghee sellers – the Sikhs being big consumers of dairy products and sticklers over quality. I noticed the banks offered up-to-date exchange rates against Sterling and both Canadian and US Dollars, while travel agents advertised cheap flights to New York and Toronto – all for the benefit of Sikh emigrés who had come back to the land of their fathers.

We deposited our shoes and cigarettes outside the temple – tobacco is strictly banned in Sikh holy places – and after washing our hands and feet descended through the Clock Tower entrance. The Harmandir glittered in the sharp light of noon, its golden refections broken now by the ripples on the holy pool caused by pilgrims taking their dip. And while the Golden Temple remained the central focus, in the bright sunshine the surrounding buildings seemed much larger, their elaborate rows of cupolas and minarets more fantastic, than when I'd seen them at dawn.

Sarah was entranced by the gentle singing that came floating across the still waters of the tank. I left her there, listening to the music, while I went off in search of the Secretary of the Shiromani Gurdwara Parbandhak Committee, an elected body responsible for all historical Sikh shrines in the Punjab. I found their offices just beyond the eastern gate to the temple.

I passed half a dozen Sikh guards before reaching the secretariat building. I was told that SGPC Secretary Manjit Singh Calcutta would see me in thirty minutes. Rather than sit around waiting, I went round the corner to Jallianwalla Bagh. It was here, on 13 April 1919, that Brigadier-General Dyer commanded his troops to open fire on a crowd of unarmed civilians and to continue firing as they fled, desperately seeking escape from the relentless hail of bullets. When the firing ceased there were 379 dead and some 1,200 wounded in and around Jallianwalla Bagh.

The reason for this massacre was that General Dyer resented the assembly in defiance of an order banning more than four people coming together in a public place. He thought it his duty to teach them a lesson, as is apparent from his own official statement: 'I fired and continued to fire until the crowd dispersed,' he said – this despite the fact that his own troops had blocked the only exit from an enclosed place so there was no way the crowd could disperse. 'I consider this is the least amount of firing,' he testified, 'which would produce the necessary moral and widespread effect . . . It was no longer a question of merely dispersing the crowd but one of producing a sufficient moral effect from a military point of view, not only on those who were present, but more especially throughout the Punjab. There could be no question of undue severity.'

What happened at Jallianwalla Bagh is one of the most repulsive episodes of British rule; but equally appalling is how Dyer was championed by the British press as the 'Saviour of India'. And even though nearly eighty years had passed, I felt the weight of collective guilt on my shoulders as I walked through the memorial garden that now fills Jallianwalla Bagh. The bullet holes are still visible on the walls and around the well down which innocent people threw themselves to escape the fusillades. I felt shame at being born an Englishman, in that terrible place.

Back at the SGPC headquarters Secretary Manjit Singh Calcutta was ready for me. 'The Sikhs were the worst sufferers of this Partition,' he declared. 'There was a total migration of our people from the West Punjab. We Sikhs had to leave behind hearth and home, our most cherished and historical gurdwaras.'

He spoke with the assurance of a politician and the authority of a priest. Which is hardly surprising, since politics and religion are closely interwoven within the SGPC. He wore an immaculately folded blue turban and his silvery beard was groomed to a single point – unlike all the other men in the room, whose beards were forked. Never had I been in a room with so many full-bearded men.

'Many of the Sikh leaders at that time, Master Tara Singh and others,' he continued, 'were in the forefront of opposition to the Muslim League and their demand for Pakistan. The general populace was against this division. But the Congress leaders, in their eagerness to assume political power, agreed to Partition. The result: hundreds of thousands of innocent people were killed. It was a complete holocaust.

'At the time when most of India was rejoicing on Independence Day, the Punjab was echoing to the cries and wailing of the people. Family after family was killed in cold blood. Many times they seized on the male members of a family, leaving behind orphans and widows. Terrible atrocities were committed against women. It was a very dark chapter in our history.

'But it wasn't only the Sikhs who suffered,' I interrupted, and immediately his eyes flashed beneath heavy brows.

'It is true,' he said, weighing every word carefully, 'this communal madness was on both sides. It started with the Muslim League, and then there was retribution on the East Punjab side also. It became a complete communal frenzy in which humanity was lost sight of.'

'How do these memories affect the Sikh community today?'

'The Sikhs are a very hardy people – extroverts, go-getters, always ready to pick themselves up. But the loss of their sacred places in Pakistan remains a painful sore. The one thing which keeps on kindling our enmity is that we are not free to visit and make obeisance at the gurdwaras and sacred places of Guru Nanak and other gurus, martyrs and heroes of Sikh history which are now in Pakistan. These links have been severed by cruel destiny and even now it is part of our prayer, twice every day, no matter whether this prayer is made in North America or

India, that we be granted free access and management of these gurdwaras.'

'Aren't some Sikhs allowed to visit their shrines in Pakistan?'

'There is an allowance for only a very limited number from India, and only four times a year.'

'What about Operation Blue Star?' I asked. Again the eyes flashed, and the background hum of conversation in the room suddenly ceased.

'You refer to the most brutal attack on the Golden Temple by the Indian Army?' he queried. 'Such an act is unparalleled. Even during wars between nations, the invading army does not attack the church, the mosque, the temple . . . But here, the government led by Indira Gandhi ordered an attack by our country's army on the *sanctum sanctorum* of the Sikhs. This thing the Sikhs cannot forget.

'And not only was it an attack on the Golden Temple. It was meant to be an attack on the self-respect of the Sikh people. They were made to feel that they were on a lower plane in their own country. And then, in the aftermath of Mrs Gandhi's assassination, there was a countrywide attack on the Sikhs during which thousands were butchered. These attacks were organised through hooligans and antisocial elements by Congress leaders. It was a heinous crime against humanity, but not even a single word of solace or apology has been uttered by the Indian Government up to now. The culprits and political leaders responsible are known and have been identified. More than ten years have passed, but still not one has been brought to book.'

The turbanned heads around the room nodded in assent. I had the sense that the sufferings endured during Partition were now part of Sikh history. This, on the other hand, was unfinished business.

'Before the time of Independence, the Congress leaders gave the Sikhs solemn assurances of their political rights and separate identity. But they backed out of their promises; and since then there has only been unending struggle to achieve what was promised to us. We of the Akali Party did this through non-violent struggle and democratic process. But, you know, whenever we Akalis were elected to form a state government in the Punjab, not once were we allowed to complete the full term before President's Rule was clamped down.'

Manjit Singh Calcutta proceeded to detail the many times that Sikh-majority governments had been dismissed. There was no doubting the sense of grievance felt; and not much hope of seeing any real redress in the futue. So I was feeling downcast by the time I crossed back over to the Golden Temple to meet up with Sarah.

I found her sitting near the ancient jubi tree where women – Hindus as well as Sikhs – tie strings to the branches in the hope of being blessed with a son.

'Sorry for being so long,' I muttered.

'Oh, that's all right. I love it here. There's a real feeling of peace . . .'

I dreaded ever having to walk into a telephone booth again. The near impossibility of getting an open line to Delhi and beyond had worn me down to the point that I broke into a sweat even before I entered the loathsome booth. I must have developed a new strain of telecoms-phobia. But I still needed further documentation to get the bike into Pakistan.

My next communication with Madras was depressing. There was no sign of an end to the strike at the Tamil Nadu transport department. The bike's ownership and registration papers were stuck inside some office and there was no way to get them out.

I decided to give up on this line of attack. The bike would have to stay under Indian ownership. I laid out what few documents I had. The carnet Sarah had brought out from England was fine. But apart from that all I had were photocopies of the bike's registration, tax and insurance. I added a loosely worded letter of recommendation from the British High Commission in Delhi. Hardly an impressive dossier.

The problem was that there was nothing to link the bike and the persons who would be taking it out of the country. On paper it would look like a stolen vehicle. What I needed was some kind of letter of authorisation from Enfield. There were now just two days left before my Pakistan visa expired. I steeled myself for another day of telephoning.

Four times I got through to Madras only to have the line cut after ten or fifteen seconds. I must have sounded hysterical by the time I finally spoke to the managing director at Enfield, Praveen Purang. He understood the gravity of the situation and acted immediately. An hour later a faxed letter authorising Sarah and me to have use of the bike – even if we didn't own it – came off the printer at Mrs Bandhari's. I added this precious sheet of paper to my dubious collection. It was a fax only, which might cause problems if the border officials chose to make our lives difficult. But there might just be enough to get us into Pakistan.

Early next morning a heavily laden motorcycle eased its way through the empty streets of the Amritsar's cantonment area. We'd left some surplus luggage at Mrs Bandhari's and made sure we weren't carrying alcohol, Indian maps showing *their* version of the international boundary in Kashmir, or anything else that might upset Pakistani officials. But with Sarah riding pillion and luggage for two, the Bullet felt sluggish at low speeds.

The road to the border ran straight as an arrow, crossing a network of canals that I guessed would figure prominently on military maps. This was still the GT Road, but it was strangely empty apart from local traffic and the occasional army truck. Water buffaloes wandered unattended down the middle of the road. Clearly there wasn't much through-traffic between the two countries.

We rode past military depots and what looked like quarters for married men. The sun was burning off the morning mist. Green parakeets flitted between the eucalyptus trees lining the road. It was going to be a beautiful day.

When we arrived at the Indian border post at Attari Road the immigration and customs officials hadn't turned up yet. Eventually a red and white government bus disgorged its prim-faced occupants and we were allowed to proceed to the concrete-and-glass bunkhouse where we would be processed. The officials settled down in the sunshine for a glass of tea and a chat before reporting for duty. I pulled out my sheaf of documents, feeling nervous as hell.

The customs building hadn't been there the last time I came through this land-border. That had been early in the 1970s, just after the Bangladesh war. Then there had been a deep swathe of no-man's-land between the two border posts. Indo-Pak tensions were still running high, so nationals from either side weren't allowed into this zone. Foreigners-in-transit had had to proceed unassisted. The temperature had hovered around 100 degrees and the humidity was tremendous. It was just two days before the monsoon finally broke.

I remember dragging my ill-arranged baggage along that blistering stretch of tarmac, past camouflaged gun emplacements and occasional local farmers exempted from the blanket prohibition. Upon reaching the Indian check-post I had collapsed in a patch of shade. A couple of young men wearing sports shirts had come over and offered me a cold drink. I was eternally grateful.

We began chatting. It was when they discovered I was born in India that one of them started taking down notes. 'Do you love your country?' he asked. I replied that I was a British citizen but, yes, I was very fond of India. Another round of Thumbs-Up was ordered, even though I had no Indian currency to pay for them. Then one of them asked me about the anti-Hindu riots I had witnessed when I was in Lahore.

Communal riots? Something peculiar was going on here. So I protested, quite truthfully, that I had seen no such riots; that all I'd seen in Lahore was Jahangir's tomb, the Shalimar Gardens and other famous monuments. The man with the notebook persisted with this line of questioning; and though I might have been a raw, long-haired teenager, I knew I was being set up. What these two wanted was independent confirmation of some propaganda story about attacks on Hindus inside Pakistan. Their smiles were interspersed with veiled threats about how I might have problems with immigration if I didn't co-operate.

By now I was pretty sure they were intelligence officers of some sort. I had no desire to be stranded in no-man's-land, but neither was I prepared to prop up some half-baked story intended to stir up yet more bad blood between India and Pakistan. There was enough of that already. So every time the conversation came back to anti-Hindu riots I simply told them I hadn't seen a thing. Eventually they gave up on me and I was allowed to proceed through immigration. But the incident had left a sour taste in the mouth.

Now I was back at Attari Road, wondering what expedients might be required this time. The immigration officials were still drinking tea. Half a dozen vultures had colonised a tree behind the vehicle pound. The tree was half-dead as a result of their toxic droppings, its bare arms stretched out against the pale blue sky.

Another biker rolled up on an old BSA 350. A Swede, he was planning to ride it all the way home through Iran and Turkey. He too was worried about getting his machine through Indian customs and had armed himself with false receipts. But at least he owned the bike and was going in one direction. Our own situation was more complicated. I was still arguing with customs officials when he waved farewell and headed across the border.

There were times when I thought I'd never escape from that customs building. I produced my documents one by one. It was like playing poker, hoping that the other side will fold before you have to show your full hand. Four separate officials were called in to deal with my case.

'Most clearly you are exporting this vehicle,' announced the bespectacled man, who I took to be in charge. 'Therefore you must be paying all the fixed duties as per schedule.'

'But we're only taking it to Pakistan for two or three weeks,' Sarah explained. 'How can we be exporting it if we are returning with the bike to India?'

'Never before have I known such a case,' the official countered. 'There are no precedents.'

So case books of customs law and procedure were produced

and consulted. Another hour slid by. 'You must be paying export taxes,' the official repeated. 'This is the law.'

I felt like telling him that in this case the law was an ass. Instead I went outside to check what some other customs men were doing to the bike. I'd already had to unload and repack it once. Fortunately they were otherwise occupied. A bus from Iran had just crossed over from Pakistan and they were methodically taking it to pieces.

I returned to the fray, sick to death with all these inflexible bureaucratic procedures. It looked as though we had reached deadlock, when one of the officials got excited about my letter of recommendation from the British High Commission in Delhi. With this, he said, it might be possible. He wanted to keep the original, but I was worried we might need it on the Pakistan side and suggested they take a copy of it.

Here another intractable problem arose. There were all kinds of X-ray machines in that customs hall, but not one photocopier.

'You must go back to Attari Town,' said one official. 'There you will find one copying machine.'

'But he is already half-way processed,' argued another. 'How can we be letting him out of the customs area?'

A compromise was reached whereby I was allowed to go back to Attari Town with an armed Border Security Guard riding pillion. I made two photocopies – just to be on the safe side – and returned to find a furious argument in progress between Sarah and a woman official.

'She's torn out a page from the carnet,' Sarah shouted. 'That's completely the wrong thing to do. According to the bloody rule-book that means we've left the country permanently.'

In this we were supported by a young Sikh official wearing an apricot-coloured turban. Our complaint was taken to their supervisor, an older woman who agreed that procedures had been incorrectly carried out. 'But now it is done, it is done,' she concluded philosophically. 'We cannot replace this torn page.'

After much argument we reached another compromise. The page was returned minus one section which they insisted on keeping. 'I am sorry for this trouble,' said the young Sikh, 'but here it is the women who rule.'

Sarah was not best pleased when I handed back her mutilated carnet. 'I'm the one who's legally responsible,' she complained. 'They've done it all wrong.' I pointed out that if we fought it out any longer the Pakistani border post would close. Then we'd be stuck between the two sides.

We'd spent five hours there already. Half a dozen officials had been called in to deal with our case. It was a stunning waste of government employees' time. But then they hadn't got much else to do. In all that time just seven vehicles had come through, none of them Indian or Pakistani. The barrier between these two countries made the old Iron Curtain look feeble by comparison.

I was called up to sign yet more documents. 'What next?' I asked.

'That is all,' replied the official, handing over my dossier of papers, now in considerable disarray.

'That's all?' I queried in disbelief.

'Yes,' he said distractedly, twisting a rubber band around his fingertips. 'Now you are free.'

12

LAHORE:
BIRTHPLACE OF A NATION?

The Pakistani soldier who stopped us to inspect our passports looked positively raffish in his dark grey kurta and voluminous pyjamas – more like a member of some irregular force than the Indian guard in his khaki fatigues who stood across the way. And there was another difference: the way he looked Sarah up and down, smiling profusely all the while. His inspection of our documents was cursory, but in those few seconds he managed to convey a combination of male self-esteem and unabashed sexual curiosity that rarely comes to the surface in India.

We were waved on to immigration and customs. As I pulled the bike onto its stand a customs official sidled up. 'You have whisky?' he enquired.

'No, I don't have bloody whisky,' I shouted back, thinking of the unfinished bottle left behind at Mrs Bhandari's.

'No problem,' he said, still smiling. 'You want change money?'

In this country the free-market ethos appeared to take precedence over bureaucratic niceties. Nonetheless, I wanted to clear whatever hurdles were ahead.

'Immigration first,' I replied. 'Then change money.'

'OK, OK. Change money, ten minutes.' I stared at him. Ten minutes? He must be joking.

In practice it took a full quarter of an hour to log the bike's details. The Pakistani authorities were concerned only about the carnet. 'These Indian people have done it wrong. Why are they removing this piece? These Indians never understand and I am positive you will be having more problems when you are returning to India.' A rubber stamp crashed down and entry procedure was completed. 'Now,' the official turned to me, 'you will be wanting to change money?'

At customs I was asked again about whisky, but that was all. No need even to unlock the side panniers. It was like entering another world.

When I returned from changing money I found Sarah taking tea with a group of border officials. 'Come join us,' said the most senior; 'we are discussing the absence of flowers. I was just telling your lady wife that it is too early in the season. But in one month's time all here,' he waved expansively, 'we will be having most lovely blooms.'

We talked of Pakistan's cricket team and their prospects. The senior official recalled an eccentric English colonel and his wife who used to patronise the local village sport of ram-fighting. 'That was when I was still a young boy. My family was living in Gurdaspur District, which is now on the Indian side.'

'From Gurdaspur?' I repeated incredulously. I hadn't cleared the border post and already I was talking to a former refugee.

'Oh yes, you must have been hearing of this place. Before 1947 Gurdaspur was a Muslim-majority district. But your Lord Mountbatten gave it to Pandit Nehru. And why? Because in this Gurdaspur district there is the road going to Kashmir. Already the Indian Congress was plotting to snatch Kashmir. That is why so many Muslim families from Gurdaspur had to leave their houses and the lands of their forefathers.'

Not only had I met a former refugee, I'd run headlong into two of the most enduring grievances felt by Pakistanis about Partition and its aftermath. One is the Radcliffe Award's assignment of the mainly Muslim Gurdaspur district to India. The other is the continuing wrangle over Kashmir, whose initial letter provides the K in the acronym PAKISTAN.

P is for Punjab, where I now was. A is for Afghana, the land of the Pathans, which extends on both sides of the Afghan border. K is for Kashmir, most of it 'stolen' by India. S is for

Sind; while Baluchistan provides the last three letters. There is nothing here about Bengal, which accounted for more than half of Pakistan's population until it split off to become Bangladesh. But then Bengal didn't really figure in the equation when the idea was dreamt up by Choudri Rahmat Ali while he was an undergraduate at Cambridge in 1933.

The name for this imaginary country also had another meaning. For Pakistan is 'the land of the pure', denoting the followers of Islam as opposed to the 'impure' idolaters. An effective rallying cry for the Muslim minority during the 1940s, the name still conveys a sense of in-built superiority over their larger neighbour to the east.

'As you are proceeding to Lahore,' the official suggested, 'it will be better for you to take the Canal Road. There is not so much traffic as on the main road, so you will be arriving in Lahore in less than thirty minutes.'

He was probably right but I stuck to the main route, wanting to enter Lahore by the Grand Trunk Road. To begin with there was no appreciable difference in the landscape. The fertile flatlands of the Punjab stretched away to the horizon, a patchwork of brilliant greens and yellows, just as they had on the Indian side of the border. There is no natural boundary separating the two nations. The artificiality of red lines drawn across the map in 1947 by Radcliffe's Boundary Commission is striking. Villagers on both sides speak the same Punjabi language; they raise the same crops and consume the same basic foodstuffs. It was ridiculous.

Any thoughts about the ancient indivisibility of this country were shattered when we hit the first roadside town. I had grown so accustomed to the rotting vegetable smells of Indian bazaars that I had ceased to notice them. But here in Pakistan the bazaars stank of dead meat. I looked around and saw piles of offal and sheep's heads, skinned and unskinned, proudly displayed by the roadside. There were entire carcasses and rear quarters hanging on hooks, and rising above it all an unaccustomed swarm of flies.

Nowhere since Calcutta had I encountered so many flies. I pulled down my visor but then they splatted against the clear plastic. Of course there were vegetable and fruit stalls, hardware shops and general provisioners. But the flies and the stench of dead meat – these were unusual in India. Here was a signal of how Pakistan has gone its own way in the fifty years since Partition.

Once clear of the bazaar area I stopped to clean my visor. Sarah asked to borrow my scarf. She had an open-face helmet and I assumed it was for protection against the flies. 'No, it's not that,' she said, tying it over the bridge of her nose to form a mask. 'It's just that when we're going slowly I'm getting a lot of stares from the men. After all, I'm in jeans and astride the bike – that's provocative enough. If it's all the same to you, I'd rather cover my face.'

By the time we rode through the Nawankot Gate into central Lahore I was getting used to the smells. I'd also realised why there was such a rush on the meat markets. Ramadan had just ended and with the new moon came the feast of Eid-ul-Fitr. At such times it is customary to slaughter a kid and to indulge in a meat-eating spree. The butchers were being kept busy.

What I hadn't yet got used to was Pakistani road manners. These are completely different from the snake-like driving technique that prevails in India. Given that motorised transport in both countries dates almost exclusively from after Partition, this is hardly surprising. Apart from the fact that they both still drive on the left they have few traditions in common.

The Pakistani approach is generally more aggressive. They drive faster, overtake more suddenly and cut in more ferociously than their Indian counterparts. This is partly because they have completely different equipment: Toyotas and Nissans instead of underpowered Ambassadors and Marutis; Yamahas and Suzukis rather than Enfields and Rajdoots. All this imported Japanese technology means that, on a like-for-like basis, the Pakistani can travel faster and live more dangerously. They use the horn more as a challenge than as a warning. But when it comes to blind fatalism, the two sides are pretty evenly matched. Here it is the will of Allah; back in India it's one's karma and the efficacy of any number of protective deities. The result, in terms of accidents and life-threatening behaviour, is much the same.

To celebrate our successful border crossing we went straight to Faletti's – the same Faletti's that Mrs Bhandari used to pop into of an evening back in the old days, when Lahore was just a forty-minute drive from Amritsar. By the time we pulled up in front of the old hotel's low, white-pillared façade, the amplified voices of muezzins were summoning the faithful to evening prayer. It had taken us nine hours to cover the 27 miles from Amritsar.

As it grew dark the city's skyline was lit up by the occasional burst of fireworks. All over Lahore families were preparing to celebrate the feast of Eid. 'It's a pity we didn't get here a day or two earlier,' Sarah commented. 'If we'd had time to meet people we might have been invited out to some feast.'

'They're mostly family affairs,' I answered. 'And it's too late to start ringing around the few people I know in Lahore, fishing for invitations. I'm not going anywhere near a telephone.'

'We ought to celebrate somehow. It's pretty inappropriate, but I don't suppose you can get a drink in this place?'

'Is sir wanting whisky?' enquired the bearer who was making up our beds.

'Whisky, gin, beer – anything,' I said in desperation. It all came out in a hurry, so surprised was I at the prospect of finding anything stronger than a fresh lime juice.

'Government Liquor Store is now closed,' said the bearer, 'but I will search in Special Reserve.'

The 'Special Reserve' turned out to be a broom cupboard that had been well-stocked for precisely such emergencies. The bearer returned with two bottles, one whisky, the other gin, both products of the Murree Brewery. I snapped them up. 'Sorry no beer,' he said, pocketing the wad of rupees I'd handed him. 'Maybe beer tomorrow,' he added optimistically as he left us to our ill-gotten hoard.

I felt guilty because I knew that there's a general prohibition on alcohol in Pakistan. But I also knew that foreigners and 'local Christians' could obtain liquor licences, that there was a factory making the stuff, and that it was sold through government-controlled shops attached to certain hotels. Apparently Faletti's was one of them. But I still felt rather desperate, like a junkie making sure there was enough for the next fix.

I shouldn't have bothered, for I soon discovered that double standards apply when it comes to the sale of alcohol in this Islamic state. The Government Liquor Store was just across from our room, so I was able to observe how this market operates in practice. The official shop was unable to open because of 'supply problems' – something to do with there being a strike at the Murree Brewery. This interruption of supplies coincided with the launch of a new brewery in Karachi, fronted by a Parsi businessman but whispered to be backed by none other than Benazir Bhutto's husband.

Although the official outlet was shut, this didn't prevent there being a lively market on the premises. Each morning the auto-rickshaws arrived with cases of black-market hooch filling the space normally reserved for passengers. A frenetic, free-for-all market developed, with buyers and sellers haggling furiously over the prices. Some of them claimed to be 'local Christians', though few would have been seen dead inside a church. If beer or whisky stocks had sold out, you put in an order and the same rickshaw driver appeared with a case of it the following day, procured from another hotel or what was described as 'a private collection'. So much for my worries about not having a drink in Pakistan.

In India I hadn't worried too much about the bike being stolen. The Bullet has the reputation of being a 'hard man's' bike – the kind of person who wouldn't just report its theft to the police, but would use his underworld connections to trace the culprit and carry out a little private retribution. But in Pakistan the position was rather different. A Royal Enfield Bullet was a rarity on this side of the border and apparently a highly collectable one at that.

I was advised to keep it locked up on the veranda outside our room and on no account to park it down by the Old City. 'When you return,' I was warned, 'it will be gone.' So we left the Bullet at Faletti's and squeezed into the back of a gaily decorated auto-rickshaw which, after stopping to fill up with petrol, delivered us to the Delhi Gate.

Beyond what remains of the city walls lay a maze of narrow streets lined with bazaars. Within ten minutes we were completely lost, so cunningly did the alleyways turn back on themselves. The Old City wraps itself around you like a cloak. In many places the houses, some with their lattice screens intact, are built so closely together that the sun never penetrates to the lower levels. Shopkeepers who pass their lives in this perpetual gloom keep bare light bulbs and neon tubes burning even at midday.

We wandered through different sections of bazaar given over to different trades. There wasn't much distinction between the older, artisanal crafts and modern, factory-produced goods. In the metal-beaters' lane, ancient samovars and carefully crafted brass-work were mixed up with aluminium cooking pots; while in the shoemakers' section traditional chappals and ladies' slippers of velvet embroidered with gold thread were displayed between plastic sandals and Adidas or Nike sports shoes – fakes, probably, made in China and then carried down the Karakoram Highway by Pakistani traders.

The Punjabi menfolk wore the loose cotton shalwar kameez, their faces mustachioed or bearded, though not extravagantly so. The women kept their hair beneath a shawl, which also served as a veil when required, a fairly informal arrangement and one that Sarah was happy to imitate because, as she put it, 'it saves so much hassle'. When we reached the spice market she was in her element, haggling over a packet of Kashmiri saffron in between enquiring what went into all the different ochre and reddish spice mixtures that were piled high in perfect cones. Precisely what we were going to do with saffron I wasn't sure, but Sarah was convinced she'd got a better price because she was wearing a veil.

At times the narrow lanes were blocked by bicycles and donkeys, handcarts and scooters, which somehow threaded their way through Old City. We passed shops selling fancy gowns covered in sequins or with hundreds of tiny mirrors sewn into them. Voluminous bras in lime green or purple satin looked like they'd been designed for a Las Vegas floor show based on Ali Babar.

Through a gap between the surrounding houses I glimpsed a pair of intricately tiled minarets. In our wanderings we must have described an enormous figure-of-eight, taking us back to the eastern part of the city. For there is only one Lahori mosque with such fine minarets and that is Wazir Khan's. He was Governor of Lahore during the reign of Shah Jehan and although he built on a much more modest scale than his imperial overlord, this brick-built mosque is a true gem. The plain-fronted prayer-hall and the octagonal minarets are typical of Mughal architecture at its best, but it is the glorious tile-work depicting trees of paradise and fields of flowers that sets this building apart. The forms may be Mughal, but the lavish decoration harks back to their Timurid ancestors from Central Asia and the polychrome masterpieces they had erected in Bukhara and Samarkand.

After the bazaar bustle I was happy to linger in this quiet courtyard, watching the pigeons flying to and fro between minarets that glowed golden in the pale sunlight. There had been too few moments of such calm and I let the feeling wash over me. Now that we'd made it across the border I felt that a huge weight had been removed from my shoulders. Whatever happened from now on, out on the road, would be my responsibility. That I could cope with. It was the impenetrable workings of the subcontinent's bureaucracy I couldn't hack. Inshallah, that was all behind me now.

Back in Chandigarh, when I had been desperate for information on what I needed for the Pakistani border, I'd put in a call to the British Honorary Consul in Lahore. His name was Fakir Syed

Aijazuddin and he had given me some useful advice. Now I was in Lahore I wanted to thank him in person.

I knew he was an international banker and it was at his bank's head office that I met him. What I didn't know was that he was also an art historian and political essayist, as well as a bibliophile whose collection included some early gazetteers relating to the Punjab section of the Grand Trunk Road. His opinions he expressed in the most concise, almost epigrammatic form.

Discussing the mass exodus caused by Partition, he said that 'in terms of what had to be left behind, there was no real equivalence. The exchange was heavily loaded in favour of the Muslims.'

Astonished to hear such views on this side of the border, I asked him to elaborate.

'The Sikhs were agriculturalists, farmers. They didn't lose just their houses; they lost their livelihood. Which is why the Sikhs keep harking back to the West Punjab, the land they left behind.

'The Muslims were either urban-dwellers or zamindars – landowners as opposed to real farmers. So in effect the exchange was land for houses. Who do you think got the worst of that bargain?'

He was deeply sceptical about the original Pakistan with its two wings, East and West, separated by a thousand miles of India. 'Few countries have been welded together so artificially,' he declared. 'It should never have happened. To me, the break-up of 1971 was the logical resolution of an impractical settlement too hastily agreed upon in 1947.'

As for the Muslims who stayed behind in India, they were fooling themselves if they now thought they'd be welcome in Pakistan. 'They can go to another Muslim country; but they cannot keep on looking at Pakistan as an alternative option.'

But it is not so much for the unorthodoxy of his judgements that I will remember him. It was a story he told about his duties as Honorary Consul. 'It's not exactly the sinecure you might imagine,' he said, 'though it does lead to some interesting situations. Take the visit to Lahore by Princess Diana. It was a private visit, of course, to see Imran and Jemima Khan. But do you know how Her Majesty's representatives in Pakistan found out about it? This may surprise you, but it was through my plumber.'

He explained that this plumber had been working on his bathroom. 'Then he calls up one day and announces he cannot come in. There's a very urgent job at the Khans' residence, installing an indoor gym. I put two-and-two together, made some discreet enquiries. The High Commission in Islamabad hadn't been informed. An unusual route, don't you think, to hear of a royal visit – via your plumber?'

Although Lahore has never been the capital of Pakistan, it feels as though it should be. Its broad, tree-lined avenues, the massively over-the-top Indo-Saracenic buildings put up by the British, the sophisticated ease of its ruling élite – all suggest that here is a capital city.

It has the right credentials. For nearly a thousand years it was capital of the Punjab, which even since Partition remains by far the most populous province in Pakistan. It has the history, the depth of culture; yet it was passed over in favour of Karachi in the early years, then Rawalpindi, and finally the new, purpose-built capital of Islamabad.

The main reason for this lies just down the road: the border with India. Lacking any natural defences against invasion from the east, Lahore was judged too vulnerable to be the seat of national government. So instead, this most gracious of Pakistan's cities remains a provincial capital.

Several of the Mughal emperors established their court at Lahore, and in the early nineteenth century it was the capital of the expansionist Sikh state presided over by Ranjit Singh. Most of the monuments to those glory days lie just to the north of the Old City. The mainly Mughal fort, with its exquisite Pearl Mosque and Palace of Mirrors, rivals the 'Red Forts' of Agra and Delhi in terms both of scale and former magnificence. The Badshahi Mosque may fall short of the near-perfect balance achieved with the Jama Masjid in Delhi, but it is an impressive ensemble, far better than the third great imperial mosque, at Agra. It is an unfortunate by-product of continuing tensions between India and Pakistan that relatively few visitors to the subcontinent get to compare all three centres of Mughal architecture.

When the Sikhs stepped into the power vacuum left by the declining Mughal Empire, their wily, one-eyed leader Ranjit Singh captured Lahore and made it his seat of government. For a time the old fortress was home to a glittering Sikh court, whose splendour is captured by European-style portraits and paintings of visiting embassies, now in the Lahore Museum. But within the fort itself there are few reminders of this period of Sikh rule.

The main concentration of Sikh monuments are opposite the Shah Burj Gate, immediately to the north of the Badshahi Mosque. They are hidden behind the ochre walls that enclose the Sikh gurdwara, and as I made enquiries at the gates I had the distinct impression of entering a beleagured fortress – almost a state-within-a-state like the Vatican in Rome. To the left, beyond the bare flagpole from which the Sikh standard would normally fly, stood the main gurdwara that Ranjit Singh built, a tall, heavily ornamented confection in ochre and white. To the right is the smaller gurdwara of Arjan Singh, fifth in the line of Sikh Gurus. It is this shrine, with its fluted and gilded dome, which is the goal of those Sikh pilgrims who are allowed over the border.

A blue-turbanned Sikh named Gurcharan Singh Khalsa told me there were three pilgrimages a year and that in all some six thousand pilgrims came. He himself had been in Lahore for eight years, part of the small, self-contained community of between seventy and eighty Sikhs. 'Before Partition there were very many Sikh people in Lahore,' he told me, 'but almost one hundred per cent had to go to India.'

His own origins were more exotic. He belonged to the Sikh community in Afghanistan. For many years he had lived in Kabul, where the Sikhs had been engaged in trade and money-changing. 'At one time,' he told me, 'there were 150,000 Sikhs in Afghanistan. But after the wars and government pressure, many of them have now left for India.'

I asked him why he hadn't done so as well. 'I have been to Delhi and did not like it. My family is there, but in April they will come to Lahore. I like it in Pakistan. My temple is here.'

He complained about problems with the border, something I could sympathise with: he wanted to go to Amritsar but was unable to; when he had been in Kashmir he had wanted to cross over from the Muslim-controlled area to the Indian side, but that had proved impossible. A remnant of the wide-ranging community of Sikh traders who had once operated all over the North-West, he found all these closed borders irksome. For rich people it was easy: there were four flights a week from Lahore to Delhi. But to all intents and purposes the land borders were still closed.

I wanted to find out about any Hindus still living in Lahore. 'I think they have one mandir [temple] still,' he told me, 'but I have not been there. You should ask of the Christians, who have their big temples in the cantonment. They perhaps know more of the Hindus.'

So that was the form around here. To find out about one minority, enquire at another. Not that there are many Hindus or Sikhs left in Lahore. The 'population transfer' in 1947 was much more complete in Muslim-majority areas – something closer to 'ethnic cleansing', though it would be another forty years before that term became common currency. The handful of Sikhs remaining in Pakistan are there only to look after their gurdwaras.

As I was shown out of the gurdwara the armed policeman at the gate saluted me. He, of course, was a Muslim.

I walked back up the hill and across the open space between the main entrance to Lahore Fort and the Badshahi Mosque. In the far corner was a low, oblong building, faced with the same red sandstone as the mosque. A group of visitors – Baluchi tribesmen, to judge by their dress – strode past the smartly turned-out sentries. Before entering the building they halted briefly and muttered a prayer or two; for this is the tomb of the poet and philosopher Allama Muhammad Iqbal, whose vision of a separate Islamic nation eventually gave birth to Pakistan.

Iqbal was opposed to British rule and racial discrimination, as is apparent from his verses inscribed on the marble headstone of his grave. His teaching was a fusion of modern and distinctly Islamic ideas and inspired the younger generation of Muslims in the 1920s to seek out a separate destiny. Today, he is venerated alongside Jinnah as one of the 'fathers of the nation'.

But whether Iqbal, the visionary and poet, would have approved of the Pakistan that the more pragmatic Jinnah negotiated for so skilfully in 1947 nobody can be certain, for he died in 1938, two years before the Muslim League formally adopted the concept of Pakistan as its goal. What he had proposed was more a federation of Muslim provinces than a separate nation-state. He was concerned for the integrity of the provinces, and especially for his native Punjab – so much so that he resigned as Secretary of the Muslim League because his colleagues wouldn't press for full provincial autonomy in the Punjab.

And what would Iqbal think of the current condition of Pakistan? His words – and the mantle of authority they bestow – are pressed into service by practically all of the political parties and religious groups, usually to suit their own ends. But the persistence of feudalism, corruption, internal divisions? I stared hard at the white marble cenotaph, with its restrained lapis inlay and simple pattern of grapes carved in bas-relief, and wondered whether the great man was turning in his grave.

Muhammad Iqbal's name has been given to the park which stretches north of the old fort's walls. Beyond it runs the Grand Trunk Road and the main railway line to Rawalpindi. And in the middle of Iqbal Park, rising nearly two hundred feet in the air, is a strange modern tower, the Minar-e-Pakistan.

It marks the spot where, on 23 March 1940, the Muslim League passed a resolution calling for the creation of a separate homeland. This became known as the 'Lahore Resolution' and it is usually taken as the beginning of the struggle for Pakistan.

At the base of the tower a party of schoolboys and maybe a dozen family groups were waiting to ascend to the viewing platform. Their behaviour reminded me of the middle-class Indian families' outside Nehru's house in Allahabad. There was the same self-conscious seriousness. These Pakistanis knew they were visiting something significant – a monument to the birth of their nation.

I felt very much the outsider – as I always do when confronted with such official celebrations of modern nationalism. And the physical appearance of the tower didn't help. It is said to be a bold combination of Mughal and modern architecture. To me, it resembled a stunted version of the Eiffel Tower, executed in stressed concrete; and the manner in which the central tower rises from its curvilinear, almost floral base to its round-domed tip, it might be mistaken for a phallic symbol. If the design was approved by men who wanted above all to demonstrate the virility of their new nation then the Minar-e-Pakistan succeeds admirably.

Muhammad Khan Akter is an academic publisher whose family belonged to the old Muslim aristocracy. But he is also a former refugee, and an unusual one at that. His family came from Hyderabad, by far the largest of the quasi-independent Princely States.

Until 1947 the Nizams of Hyderabad ruled over a territory nearly the size of France, with a population of seventeen millions. Their wealth was stupendous. They owned vast estates and controlled the diamond mines at Golcoonda. The ruling family and most of the aristocracy were Muslims; but more than three-quarters of the population was Hindu. And since Hyderabad stretched across central India, it was surrounded on all sides by Hindu-majority provinces.

Muhammad Khan Akter was twenty-one when the British left India. His uncle was a minister of state, a confidant of the Nizam. He had grown up in a refined, courtly environment. 'Our hobbies were collecting jewels and fine carpets, or attending poetry recitals,' he told me. 'That was our culture. But do not misunderstand me: our moral values were very high; our respect for humanity, for social equality, was very deep.'

He claimed that the Hindu majority were perfectly happy under Muslim rule. 'There was complete amity and understanding between us. I had many Hindu and Sikh friends. I used to play with them. My family did business with them.'

But as Independence Day loomed, the future of the 362 Princely States in India – some of them covering only a few square miles – was increasingly precarious. Various proposals were put forward for a confederation of Princely States. That these came to nothing was due as much to disunity and jealousy among the nawabs and maharajas as to Congress hostility or British disinterest. Both the Labour Government and public opinion in Britain considered them anachronistic. In the end, the princes were given no option: they had to accede to a neighbouring successor state – either to India or Pakistan. Because of its size and the military forces at its disposal, Hyderabad held out longest; but in the summer of 1948 Indian forces were finally sent in under the pretext of a need for 'police action' against extremists.

Muhammad Khan Akter had no problems in leaving for Pakistan. He was educated and had a new job in Pakistan working for Columbia Pictures. Later he called his mother and two sisters to join him. 'I felt great sadness,' he said, 'in leaving my Hindu and Sikh friends. They asked me why was I leaving. "You belong to a rich family," they said. "You have so much land." But I knew I had no choice.'

'Why did you think that?' I asked. 'Not all Muslims felt that way.'

'Because after 1947 Pakistan represented Muslim sovereignty in the subcontinent. The British had stirred things up between Muslims and Hindus through their policy of Divide and Rule. Now they were leaving they decided to Divide and Quit. They imposed their own ideas of democracy, which in practice meant rule by a Hindu majority. They forced Muslim rulers to join this India because most of their people were Hindus, but the Muslim people of Kashmir had no say when their Hindu Raja also chose to join India rather than Pakistan. They left this legacy of Kashmir so the two countries would keep fighting. My father said to me this was their final policy – Divide and Destroy.'

I was beginning to feel uncomfortable. The British, it seemed, were responsible for everything. But Muhammad Khan Akter was only just getting into his stride.

'So many of you British,' he continued, pointing his finger, 'were bitter at leaving India. You still thought you should be ruling India. You used your talk of democracy to undermine Muslim sovereignty. For more than five hundred years there had been Muslim rulers in India. They became Indians themselves, no matter whether they came from Iran or Turkey. They developed a mixed culture and unlike the British never considered themselves as foreigners. If there had been two more capable rulers after Aurangzeb, India would have emerged as a very strong power under Muslim rule. But they were tolerant of other religions. If they had wanted to they could have converted the entire population – there was no Amnesty International in those days. But they did not. Instead it was you British who made the Hindus feel like slaves and told them they had been captives to the Muslims for so many generations. It was your ideas of democracy that made it necessary to forge a Muslim state, that made Partition inevitable.

'I do not think democracy is best suited to all people,' he declared, digging his hands into the pockets of his old tweed jacket. 'For thousands of years there was no democracy, only monarchies, and yet there was good rule. Democracy is only the governance of men through other men. Islam stands for the governance of God through man.'

'So do you think Pakistan should be an Islamic polity?'

'I think so, but I doubt it could come into being because the influence of the West, through television and so on, is so great. It has changed the texture of the world. But I believe the role of religion, everywhere in the world, is very important. No religion teaches hate, or injustice, or tyranny. They all speak of love and peace among peoples. An Islamic polity should keep these precepts before the eyes of men. It should ensure that some form of social justice is introduced. Equality, fraternity, liberty – these I believe are more likely to be realised within an Islamic polity than through some degenerate species of democracy.'

Our conversation was interrupted by a burst of gunfire from the street. 'Oh, that is just the rickshaw-wallahs,' explained the exiled aristocrat-turned-publisher. 'They have put up a television in the street to watch the cricket. The Pakistan side must be doing well.'

That evening I returned with Sarah to the Old City. She wanted to find a place where we could eat nihari and other Lahori specialities. As dusk fell we made our way through the narrow streets. Usually this is a busy time of day, when shoppers come out in force and the mosques have just emptied. But tonight the city seemed deserted. The reason was simple. Everyone was watching the big cricket match on TV.

Even the shops that stayed open had ceased trading, their attention focused on the portable television sets which had been rigged up on shop counters or perched precariously on top of rolls of cloth. The atmosphere was tense. Pakistan had lost another wicket.

Most of the restaurants in the Old City hadn't bothered to open, including the one we were looking for. With the cricket on they couldn't expect much custom. I bought some cashew nuts to stave off my hunger and headed back towards Mochi Gate. On the way, hurrying down a dimly lit street, I almost walked into a strange-looking beggar.

The fact that he was wandering the streets for alms rather than sitting outside one of the mosques was odd enough, and by his dress he was clearly not a Punjabi. His greasy jacket of quilted down marked him out as a hillman, as did the flat-topped felt hat on his head. But underneath he wore a saffron-coloured lungi and sleeveless maroon vest.

At first I thought he was a Hindu. But when I asked him

about this he seemed not to understand. 'Where do you come from?' I persisted. 'Hindustan? Kashmir?'

'It is no use,' intervened one of the shopkeepers across the street. 'He speaks no Urdu or English, not even Punjabi. Many days he has been coming here asking for alms. He is an unbeliever, a kafir; but he is not Hindu. They say he comes from the north, beyond Kashmir. Always at this time he is passing by here, asking for food or money.'

So he was a Buddhist, a Ladakhi or from up Baltistan way. Judging by his orange and maroon robes he was a monk of some kind. What he was doing in Lahore, of all places, I had no idea. I gave him a few rupees and he mumbled some kind of blessing. The Muslim shopkeeper looked on with an expression of mild amusement. I suppose it's not every day that an Englishman is to be found in the Old City giving alms to a kafir priest.

As for me, it put me in mind of the meeting between Kim and the Tibetan Lama at the very beginning of Rudyard Kipling's novel. That too was supposed to have happened in Lahore; not in the narrow lanes of the Old City, but on the steps of the 'Wonder House', as the Lahore Museum is usually referred to in *Kim*.

The setting that Kipling described is still easily recognisable. The Museum moved to grander premises in 1894, but its rather fanciful Indo-Saracenic façade still looks across to Zamzama, the mighty cannon upon which Kim and his playmates were sitting, 'in defiance of municipal orders', when Kim first spied the strange-looking lama. Nowadays the cannon is in the middle of a traffic island, but the occasional street-boy can still be found rubbing his palm along the barrel or clambering over the gun carriage.

A more recent adornment to this stretch of The Mall is the fuselage of an Indian jet fighter downed over Lahore in one of the Indo-Pak wars. As for the legend attached to Zamzama, that too had been undone, or at least partly so. It was once believed that whoever held Zamzama held Lahore, and whoever held Lahore held the Punjab. This was true, albeit briefly, of the gun's original owner, the Afghan ruler Ahmad Shah Durrani, who put it into service at the third battle of Panipat. It was certainly true of Ranjit Singh, whose Sikh armies ranged far beyond the Punjab; and it remained true during the century of British rule. But since 1947 Lahore has governed only the western half of a divided Punjab. I wondered whether the positioning of the downed MiG fighter opposite was intended to divert attention away from this.

Pakistan is often accused of being a militaristic state. Since Independence, the Army has ruled through martial law for as many years as there have been democratically elected governments. Even today, after years of so-called democratic rule, around half of all public expenditure (after paying interest on the national debt) goes on the defence budget. It is unlikely that any government could survive for long without the tacit support of the Pakistan military.

I'd met several Indian Army officers before, and marvelled at how in so many ways – their demeanour, their turn of phrase, their professional approach to soldiering – they can seem more British than the British. I hadn't encountered anything quite like them anywhere else in the world; until, that is, I ran into Colonel Dotani.

Lieut-Colonel Muhammad Kamran Khan Dotani (retd.) is an unusual character. The first time I met him he was wearing kurta pyjama; but even in this informal attire his trim moustache and military bearing suggested that here was a seriously gung-ho infantry officer.

His personal record backs this up. He had been through the Bangladesh War, a company commander on the Jessore front – 'the only decent tank country in East Pakistan', as he still usually refers to what is now Bangladesh. When the Indian armour advanced his troops were outnumbered and outgunned. Dotani took three bullets – 'one of them's still in the hip; the bone's grown over it' – and shrapnel wounds. (I later learned that two of his fingers had been grafted and that five of his vertebrae were fused.)

He made it back to his Army HQ in a wooden canoe, more

dead than alive, the only survivor along with seven corpses. When the Pakistani armed forces in Bangladesh surrendered, Dotani was in hospital. Rather than be taken as a PoW, he and four of his colleagues escaped and walked across India, fifteen hundred miles of hostile territory, to West Pakistan. 'It took us four months and twenty-seven days,' he remembered with precision. 'We had to play hide-and-seek with all the Indian people there. Three died *en route*; two of us made it.'

Dotani later commanded the 59th Punjab Irregular Frontier Force Regiment on the Siachen Glacier in Kashmir. 'We were operating at 21,800 feet,' he told me, 'which I think makes this the highest theatre of war in all military history.'

Since retiring from the Army, Dotani has run the Punjab Club with military efficiency. He deplores the absence of true professionalism in Pakistan's armed forces today. 'Officers became too involved in politics and running martial law courts,' he told me. But 'the old British Indian Army – that was the finest fighting machine ever. Imagine what it would be like if it had survived intact. The Americans – they don't like to suffer casualties. They haven't won a real war since World War II. They didn't even beat Saddam. Why? Because they need him there. He is the necessary enemy.'

The Colonel is not fond of Americans. 'In the 1980s they poured money and arms into Pakistan because it was the front-line against Communism. When the Communist threat in Afghanistan went away they just abandoned us. Now all they are concerned about is to stop us from having nuclear capability. There are now seventeen countries, I think, which have it. If India has attained nuclear capability, why not Pakistan? I assure you that if Pakistan had nuclear weapons in 1971, Bangladesh would never have come into existence. And if we didn't have that capability now there would be no Pakistan.'

The vision of nuclear Armaggeddon in the subcontinent arose before my eyes. It was too horrible to contemplate. I tried to shift the conversation back to catastrophes on a more human scale, like Partition.

'It was the Britishers who did it,' Colonel Dotani began in his matter-of-fact way. 'India was never a country before 1947. Neither was Pakistan. It was just a piece of land. But the difference is this. Throughout history, the Hindus had never ruled a country called India. You must go back to Asoka and Chandragupta Maurya for that, but even then the Hindus were not a nation. They became a nation only in 1947, and that because the outside rulers, the British, helped them to put it together.

'The Muslims did form a nation. For a thousand years they ruled over most of India. But since the first Muslim ruler, Muhammad bin Qasim, there has been an ongoing battle between Muslims and Hindus in the subcontinent. Sometimes the Hindus won, sometimes the Muslims. And it's not over yet. Why? Because of what the Britishers did in 1947. First they divided the country; and then, to ensure we don't live in peace, they left this conflict over Kashmir.

'There was deep thinking behind it. Otherwise the two countries, India and Pakistan, would have been more equally divided. If they were able to live in peace, not using up so much of their resources on defence, then these countries would have become super-powers. Together they hold a quarter of the world's population. But we have fought three wars with India, and with defence spending so high it means that in both countries people are still dying through hunger.'

Colonel Dotani was not afraid to criticise the competence of Pakistan's armed forces. When I asked him about corruption in politics, and particularly allegations against Benazir Bhutto's husband, he replied: 'We have a proverb in this country, that the fish rots from the top, especially the head.'

Dotani was a straight-talking infantry officer, with a penchant for shooting from the hip. But some of his views, about the historical inevitability of conflict between Muslims and Hindus, for instance, or the necessity of nuclear weapons, left me feeling uneasy. They reminded me of something, not a person I'd actually met, but a composite character in a film or a book. It was only later that I realised Colonel Dotani reminded me of Dr Strangelove.

*

The next morning I walked purposefully down The Mall, past
the GPO and the High Court and other extravagant examples
of colonial architecture. Nowhere, apart from Bombay, and,
possibly, Madras, did the Victorians go quite so far in their
doomed attempts to combine Mughal and Gothic styles.
Outside the Vanguard Bookshop I asked for directions to the
Cathedral.

Ever since visiting the Sikh gurdwara I had been enquiring
about representatives of the other minorities. I'd got nowhere
with what's left of the Hindu community in Lahore; but with
the Christians I'd come up trumps. I now had an appointment
to see John Alexander Malik, the Bishop of Lahore.

Arriving early, I continued past the bishop's residence to the
cathedral – a fairly restrained, straightforward Gothic ensemble
in reddish stone. Inside, preparations were under way for a
wedding. The ends of pews had been decorated with yellow
bows and in a corner a guitarist was tuning his instrument. As I
wandered down one of the side-aisles, looking at memorials to
English subalterns who'd never made it home or tireless servants
of the North-West Railway, the entire cathedral suddenly
reverberated to a reggae rhythm. The guitarist had been joined
by a drummer and bass player and together they were blasting
out a competent cover version of a Bob Marley song. A sacristan
by the altar was tapping his foot to the music as he unfolded a
freshly pressed altar cloth. This was not something I had
expected to encounter in Pakistan.

'Ah yes, the wedding,' Bishop Malik exhaled, the gold chain
and crucifix sinking slightly lower down his chest. A purple shirt
beneath his clerical collar signified his episcopal status, but
otherwise he was dressed in a plain dark suit. 'We have a lot of
those, particularly at this season. It may surprise you, but we
have a thriving Christian community here in Lahore.

'If you were to put together all the churches, you'd probably
find there are above four million of us in Pakistan, of which 80
per cent live here in the Punjab. There are two or three dozen
villages which are completely Christian. You won't find that in

other provinces like Sind or the North-West Frontier Province, where the Christian communities exist in the towns only. That's because the early missionary movement was concentrated in the Punjab,' he smiled, 'the bread-basket of India, as it was then known.'

'Did many leave at the time of Partition?'

'There was no mass exodus in 1947,' the bishop replied. 'Most of us simply stayed put. Of course, some Christians have been divided from members of their family on the other side. It's very difficult to get visas, even for family weddings and funerals. And we church leaders don't make contact with Indian Christians. Otherwise such contacts might be misrepresented.'

I asked him what it was like being a leader of the Christian minority in a Muslim state. 'I'm a religious leader, not a politician,' he warned me, obviously worried that we were entering treacherous waters. 'I always try to express solidarity with what is right. Take the case of Kashmir, for example. On this, we Christians stand in solidarity with our Muslim brothers. But from time to time it is incumbent upon us to allay suspicions, to stress that we Christians are not traitors or Fifth Columnists, that we are part of the nation. Similarly, I try to keep good relations with the mullahs, so that they see me more as a Christian mullah.

'You see, there is always this danger of spill-over. If something happens against Islam, anywhere in the world, there is a danger that the strong feelings this creates among Muslims might spill over against the Christians in their midst. This happened when there were anti-Hindu feelings after the mosque was destroyed at Ayodhya. Then they burned down one or two churches in Karachi. And during Desert Storm, a war against another Islamic country, I tell you we were on pins and needles. But, by the Grace of God, nothing happened.'

Yet it isn't all damage limitation. 'If something affects my community,' proclaimed the bishop, 'then I wage my own wars.'

Top of the list is the threat posed by the Sharia Courts and particularly their interpretation of Islamic laws against blasphemy. 'In recent years the number of cases has increased manyfold,' he said, and 'today the list of cases goes beyond 4,000, though only a minority of these involve Christians. All the same, the blasphemy law is like a sword hanging over us. Not because it is there, but because so many people have misused it. They bring charges of blasphemy to settle their own scores. Often they arise from trivial arguments, like taking water from a common tap.

'Because of the abuse of the blasphemy law, people have been attacked and put to death – some even when they were in prison. And since I am chairman of the Peace, Justice and Human Rights Commission of the Church of Pakistan, I speak out whenever there are human rights violations – not only for Christians but for others as well.'

The Bishop of Lahore is concerned about the 'ghettoisation' of Christians in Pakistan.

His other fear is of syncretism, that the similarities between Islam and Christianity will gradually erode the distinct values and beliefs of Pakistani Christians, which is precisely what some Indian Muslims fear will happen to them in a predominantly Hindu culture. I left the bishop to get on with organising a diocesan meeting – a busy man trying to look after an isolated and sometimes fearful community.

The Bullet had remained locked up since our arrival in Lahore. I felt it was time to take her on an outing. An excuse was readily at hand: two of the finest Mughal monuments, the Shalimar Garden and Jahangir's tomb, are to be found just outside Lahore, both of them beside the Grand Trunk Road. What's more, the dirwan I'd met at the Jama Masjid in Delhi had spent some time in 1947 living within the walls of the Shalimar Garden, which then served as a transit camp for Muslim refugees coming from India.

To reach the gardens I had to backtrack down the GT Road towards Wagha and the Indian border. It being a holiday, hundreds of Lahoris had decided to spend the day there, sitting in family groups on the squares of lawn that are dissected by symmetrically arranged water channels and fountains. When I asked the ticket vendor about it being a refugee camp he looked blank. 'This is pleasure garden,' he said. 'For history, please apply at Lahore Museum.'

I decided not to press my case. The gardens, built by the Emperor Shah Jahan for the pleasure of his household, were too beguiling and for an hour I left behind the problems of modern-day Pakistan and the horrors of Partition to slip into an idealised world where bejewelled courtiers walked these same pathways reciting Persian couplets. I wandered through the empress's sleeping quarters where Shah Jahan's beloved wife, Mumtaz Mahal, had once stayed. That was before she died in childbirth, causing her grief-stricken husband to create in memory of her perfection the most perfect of all Mughal tombs, the Taj Mahal.

It is all too easy to slip into such reveries. The Shalimar Garden was intended to be an enclosed world, a retreat from the suffocating heat of the nearby city, a temporary escape from the bloody realities of dynastic politics. Back in the present, a gardener was feeding a troop of orange-crested hoopoe birds, winter residents who fly back over the Himalayas to the Tibetan plateau come spring. A lawnmower pulled by a couple of bullocks was being wheeled into action. It took a real effort to drag myself away.

Rather than go back through the town centre I decided to cut across to the Bund Road that runs between the outskirts and River Ravi. While this was instructive, it was definitely not a short cut. The road twisted its way around factory estates and working-class suburbs. The tarmac soon gave out, then a herd of water buffalo blocked the way and before long I was completely lost. When I asked the way I was told to proceed across a lumpy maidan whose possession was disputed between the local cricket team and a herd of goats. By now I could see the Bund Road ahead of me on its raised embankment, but there was no way of getting to it apart from charging up a bank of loose earth. Sarah dismounted and clambered up on foot. I opened the throttle, slipped the clutch and charged the embankment, arriving at the top in a self-generated dust storm.

Not that there was anything to celebrate. The Bund Road was being rebuilt from scratch, its surface reduced to a mixture of rutted earth and loose sand. There was nothing for it but to crawl along in second gear, the back end slithering from side to side, until we rejoined the Grand Trunk Road. I crossed over the Ravi by the Old Bridge – another mistaken route, since it was clogged with livestock and handcarts and horse-drawn ekkas. The horses commonly used in Pakistan to pull ekkas were in terrible condition, mostly skin and bone and sometimes lame. A half-starved horse now collapsed in its traces right in front of us, whinnying in terror as the ekka-wallah beat it repeatedly in an attempt to get the poor beast to stand up again rather than make his passengers alight.

Behind me, Sarah was screaming. 'Oh God! I can't look!'

'There's nothing we can do,' I shouted back, and accelerated past the mêlée. I stopped fifty yards up the road and looked back. The horse was still down.

There wasn't much I could do when just half a mile up the road a child ran in front of the bike. It was another game of street-cricket, and he was fielding, chasing after the ball, not looking as he ran across the road. Though I slammed on the brakes I knew I was going to hit him. He was not more than five years old, his shaven head covered in light brown stubble, infinitely fragile as he bent to pick up the ball.

I was waiting for the sickening crunch when he leapt backwards – a real acrobat's leap – and the Bullet slid past him. There was nothing in it, but he was unscathed.

Meanwhile I'd skidded and stalled the engine. I was hugely relieved, but all that I could do was yell at him about what a stupid little fool he'd been. His response was to smile and pick up the tattered tennis ball he'd been chasing. He'd reacted fast enough; but I don't think he realised how close to death he had been.

He ran off, leaving Sarah and me in the middle of a growing

crowd, Sarah shouting that she'd had e-bloody-nough of all this
and me trying to restart the bike. We were still tense when we
arrived at Jahangir's tomb. I slumped on the grass, cursing the
national mania for cricket. (That morning I'd read how a fan
had shot himself because Pakistan lost the big match.) Sarah
stomped off into the second courtyard. Maybe bringing the bike
on this little outing hadn't been such a good idea. Those last few
miles had left our nerves in tatters and we both needed time to
calm down.

Eventually I regained a more-or-less even keel and started to
take in what was around me. This first courtyard had been built
as a serai, a rest place for travellers going up and down the
Grand Trunk Road. There were rooms built into the walls on
all four sides and I guessed that in those days the courtyard
would have been an open space for their pack-animals, whereas
now it had been turned into a pleasant garden planted with
chinar and peepul trees.

I let the calm of the place take over from the explosive
cocktail of fear and outrage that I'd arrived with. Then I walked
through to the second courtyard, where I found Sarah sitting by
a dried-up fountain, staring intently at Jahangir's tomb.

Neither of us mentioned the incidents down the road. 'I've
already been inside,' she informed me coldly. 'The tomb and
the screens around it are all in marble, with very fine carving. As
for the building, I think the minarets are too high for the main
body. You go and look around if you like. I'm staying here.' So
I inspected Jahangir's tomb on my own.

As we retraced our steps to the main gateway, where the
Bullet was parked, she turned to me. 'There're only three things
I have to say. Poor bloody animal. Stupid bloody kid. And for
Christ's sake, Jonathan, let's go carefully on the way back into
town. Because nobody else seems to give a shit.'

Safely back at Faletti's, I unfolded a map and began planning the
final stages of our journey. From Lahore, the Grand Trunk
Road runs almost due north across the flatlands of the Punjab,
then over the Salt Range to Rawalpindi, before striking out

west to the Indus and the North-West Frontier Province. The British made the garrison town of Peshawar the western terminus of the GT Road; but in the time of the Great Mughals the imperial highway continued all the way to Kabul. If I could muster the necessary permits I wanted to follow that road through the Khyber Pass and right up to the Afghan border.

On a previous visit to Lahore I'd met an Afghan trader who had offered to take me across the border and on to Kabul in the back of his truck. 'It will be quite safe,' he had assured me. 'You will go disguised as an Armenian merchant.' But I'd heard that the mujahiddin were battling it out around Jalalabad at the time, so I declined his offer.

Since I was back in Lahore I decided to look up my Afghan friend. With his flowing beard and immaculately folded turban, Haji Abdul Zahir is a solemnly patriarchal figure who could have stepped straight out of the world of Rudyard Kipling. But whereas Kipling's famous Afghan, Mahmud Ali, was a horse trader who dyed his beard with henna, the Haji's beard is silver and black and his trade is in carpets. The walls of his home off Empress Road are piled from floor to ceiling with carpets: ruby-red Turcomans, wine-dark Baloch rugs, elegant Isfahanis and Tabrizis, and Afghanis of every shade and variety from Kabul, from Herat, from Mazar-i-Sharif, of such quality and authenticity that professional buyers from America and Europe and Saudi Arabia beat a path to his door.

The Haji speaks Persian and Pashtu but no English, so his son acted as interpreter. 'My father says you bestow a great honour on his house once more. When last you took tea with my father you promised to return again and this promise you have kept, which brings great joy to my father's heart.'

'Please tell the Haji,' I replied, 'that the honour is done to us.' I wasn't sure whether it was because his words were translated directly from Farsi, but the intricate formality of his speech was definitely contagious. As we continued to exchange greetings for a full ten minutes, I uttered such phrases as 'It is a source of profound happiness to us both that we find the Haji in good health.' Meanwhile green tea and rock sugar was produced, along with little bowls of plump raisins and unsalted almonds. The tea was poured with elaborate ceremony into clear glasses. The Haji asked me what was my 'mission' this time and I explained how I was journeying by motorcycle up the Grand Trunk Road.

'My father asks whether on this occasion you will be going to Kabul. He says that on a motorcycle this would not be advisable. He says he has a lorry coming from Afghanistan soon with 3,000 carpets.'

I replied that I was continuing only as far as Peshawar or, the authorities permitting, up to the Afghan border. The Haji grunted disapproval, as though he had little time for the authorities.

Changing the subject, he asked after my father's health, which led, through tortuous exchanges, to the fact that he had served in the Indian Army.

'The Haji asks was your father also in Afghanistan,' the boy translated. This I sensed was dangerous ground, for the British had kept on fighting the border Afghans and bombing their villages right up to Partition. 'Please tell the Haji that my father was never on the North-West Frontier, but that he fought alongside Pathan soldiers in other wars. Please tell him that the British officers admired the Afghan,' I continued, becoming carried away, 'both as a true friend and as a courageous enemy.'

I don't know how this was translated, but the Haji sat up and stared at me most coldly. His son tried to cover up the embarrassment but was immediately silenced. Obviously my remark had not been well received. I remembered the Afghans' reputation, how swiftly they take offence. Finally, Abdul Zahir muttered a complicated formula in Farsi, staring at me all the while. 'My father says,' the son translated falteringly, 'that if you wish to be his enemy, then this is also to his honour, and he will make a good enemy. But if you come to his house in friendship, then he will be a true friend, and this is his pleasure.'

The awkward moment had passed and we got down to discussing the situation inside Afghanistan. But before this could begin Sarah, who had thus far been treated as an 'honorary man', was invited to go upstairs to the women's quarters so that she could spend some time with his wife and younger children. She was to rejoin the men when the evening meal was served.

The Haji was not optimistic about peace returning to Afghanistan. He himself had left in 1984 because of the Russians, but his brother looked after the family home near the western city of Herat, and either the Haji or his agents were always going to and fro across the border to bring back more carpets. On the basis of this intelligence, all he could foresee was more internecine fighting for years to come. And while the newspapers had made much of the rapid advance of the Pakistan-backed Taliban, he doubted whether any one militia would be able to unite Afghanistan.

That left between one and two million Afghan refugees living in Pakistan on a more-or-less permanent basis. The Haji had managed to found a flourishing export business; but most of his compatriots languished in refugee camps along the border. He admitted that many so-called Afghan carpets were now made in the refugee camps, but he disapproved of their turning out non-traditional patterns such as Kalashnikovs and helicopter gunships. 'We should not be doing this,' he declared, 'otherwise what will the young children be thinking? Already this Kalashnikov culture is too powerful.'

We broke off our conversation as preparations were made for the meal. An appliqué cloth was laid out across the floor carpets. A younger son was sent to fetch Sarah from upstairs. We leaned back on cushions as plates of fat lamb cutlets, finely ground meatballs, salted cucumbers and yoghurt were produced. The centrepiece was a massive pulao sprinkled with dried fruits. (The quantity of grated squash in it reminded me of the heavily northern version of this dish known as plov, which is more typical of Tajik or Uzbek cooking.)

Sarah entered into the spirit of things, praising the food with long floral sentences. 'There is one thing I wish to ask your father,' she said to the son who sat beside her. 'I thought that most Afghan people prefer to live in Peshawar or close to the border. Why did he choose to live in Lahore?'

The Haji pondered this for a while, as was his custom, before replying. 'My father says that when he left Afghanistan he went first to Quetta, where he stayed for a few days. Next he went to Peshawar for a few days. Then he came to Lahore. He looked and he saw everything, and he said, "This is a good city." Since then he has been in this city twelve years. This is what my father says.'

13

WEST PUNJAB AND ISLAMABAD: UNREAL CITY – ABIDING GRIEVANCES

Lahore is a city of hidden depths; and while most Lahoris are proud of their city's past, some episodes they feel are best forgotten. What happened in the summer of 1947 is a notable example of this.

Then the city was aflame, and it was mainly the Hindu and Sikh population that was being burned out. Many of the areas around the Old City – Bhati Gate, Mochi Bazaar and other places off the Circular Road – suffered arson attacks. Sikhs had been butchered around Lahore Railway Station, in the Railway Workshops Area just to the north and in Baghbanpura – all of which I had passed through on my way to the Shalimar Garden. Hindu shops had been attacked and looted throughout the city, even along The Mall.

Today there is virtually no trace of the large and prosperous non-Muslim population that the city once harboured. Apart from the gurdwara I had visited, practically all the other main Sikh and Hindu temples have been torn down or converted to other purposes. Their houses, left empty in the mass exodus of 1947, have been lived in by Muslim families – many of them refugees from the east – for two generations. It is not a subject people like to talk about.

On the other hand, I could have amassed an enormous dossier of stories from Muslims who had fled from India, most of whom resettled in the cities. According to the 1951 census, nearly half of Pakistan's urban population were former refugees.

Since then, there has been further immigration from rural districts; but in Lahore practically every other person has some family connection with refugees from India. It was hard to know where to begin.

Besides, the same upheavals affected the entire area where I was headed next. All the towns along the Grand Trunk Road – Gujranwala, Wazirabad, Jhelum – had been forcibly 'cleansed' of their non-Muslim populations in 1947. Refugees from the east had come to take their place. The scale of this 'transfer of populations' is mind-numbing. Around seven millions left for India; perhaps eight millions came the other way. The next stretch of the GT Road, and the main railway line that runs beside it, was one of the principal conduits of this mass migration. During that monsoon season, millions of bedraggled refugees were moving up and down this corridor.

Unseasonal rain-clouds were gathering as I loaded up the bike with our luggage. This would be the first long day's journey with Sarah riding pillion. The Bullet was heavily laden and the steering felt distinctly wobbly at low speeds. I tried tightening the steering nut, but there was no real improvement.

The rain started just as we approached the new road bridge over the Ravi – the third of the five rivers of the Punjab I had to cross. I hoped the rain would blow over and didn't bother to put on my waterproof leggings. Sarah had only a felt pahari jacket to protect her from the elements.

At least the road was good – an evenly surfaced four-lane highway running straight as an arrow. The inside lane was occupied by fancifully decorated trucks, most of them equipped with chain-mail mudguards which jangled menacingly but didn't stop their wheels from throwing up a blinding spray. I had to pull over every ten miles or so to clear my visor.

The rain showed no sign of letting up, and the dull light had robbed the Punjab's fields of all their vibrant colours. As the mud built up in front of my eyes I felt as though I was entering into some hellish landscape – 'Flanders, 1916', as interpreted by the *pointilliste* school of painters.

I imagined the columns of refugees moving down the old two-lane road, their families and the few possessions they could take piled high on bullock carts, through the interminable monsoon which swept away bridges, breached the embankments and carried off the weak and the unlucky on a muddy flood. There are no statistics on how many refugees died in transit through drowning, waterborne diseases or malnutrition, though it is likely that as many lost their lives through indirect causes as were killed during attacks on convoys and trains.

A sheet of water across the road brought me back with a jolt to the Here and Now. For a moment we'd been aquaplaning. There was nothing for it but to reduce speed and concentrate on the road surface. Even if it was smooth it was no less treacherous.

Just short of the turn-off to Gujranwalla I stopped at a petrol station, where for a few minutes we would be sheltered from the rain.

I'd intended to spend some time in Gujranwalla, which had once been an important centre for both Sikhs and Hindus. Ranjit Singh was born here, and there are still rare remains (for Pakistan) of Hindu art to be seen. Before Partition nearly half the population of the town were non-Muslims, and it was they who owned most of the businesses and other property. But from July 1947 the number of stabbing attacks on Hindus and Sikhs increased, as did cases of arson. The minority communities were well organised and fought back; but when a Muslim took over as Deputy Commissioner their leaders took fright and prepared for a mass exodus. During the week around Independence Day most of the Sikh and Hindu quarters of town were burned out. The exodus began in earnest.

Nowadays the area is famed for its metal-working, a tradition that goes back to pre-Independence days when the cutlery workshops in nearby Nizamabad turned out thousands of knives to arm the Muslim National Guards. Most of the communal killings were done with the most basic of weapons – knives, lathis, farm implements. What happened during Partition was probably the greatest low-tech massacre since the Middle Ages, if not in all of history. It was completely different from shelling civilians or machine-gun executions. It was fuelled by different passions and engendered different fears.

I stamped out the cigarette I'd been smoking. Sarah was drenched through and shivering. 'Shall we stay here until the weather blows over?' I asked.

'Bugger that,' she said quietly. 'We've only come forty miles. Now get that bike back on the road and take me to Jhelum.'

By the time we reached Jhelum the sound of Sarah's teeth chattering could be heard above the roar of the engine. I wasn't feeling much better. The front of my jeans were stiff with wet mud and my boots squelched loudly from the water that had collected inside them.

We'd stopped once, at a dhaba outside Wazirabad, to stock up on sweet tea and had ended up eating chapattis and dal as well, sitting under a canvas tent surrounded by a muddy wasteland. The food helped raise the body temperature, and the crowd of teenagers and young boys who surrounded us at least acted as a wind-break. All they wanted to talk about was cricket; except for one of the teenagers, who offered me drugs – hashish, heroin, cocaine, anything I cared to name.

Beyond Wazirabad we crossed the Chenab River, and kept on motoring, the rain coming down all the way, to the Jhelum, the fifth and last of the Punjab's five rivers we had to cross. It looked angry, its waters swollen by the unseasonal rains and snow-melt up in the hills. The town of Jhelum lay on the far bank. As we crossed the toll-bridge I started singing some old ditty about it being 'jolly boating weather'. Sarah rapped the top of my helmet and told me to shut up.

I took a wrong turn off the GT Road and was immediately stopped by a military policeman. Apparently I was entering the Military Cantonment, which was off-limits to civilians. I turned about and rode through the Civil Lines, past the bedraggled outline of the old Anglican church, and down into the market area, where we stopped outside the Zelaf Hotel.

It was, as Sarah had predicted, a dump. The manager

produced an electric-bar fire so that we could dry our clothes, which would have been kind if either of the bars had functioned and if he hadn't demanded a hundred rupees for this 'extra service'. In fact nothing seemed to work in this hotel: the hot water, the light switch, the window shutters. Each time I went downstairs to complain I found the manager staring at the hotel's new colour television, which was permanently turned to MTV. The manager would doze off whenever a music video was shown, but his eyes reopened with reptilian alacrity when the show's female 'video jock' – an archetypal Californian babe, all long blonde hair and plunging neckline – came back on screen.

In the clear, rain-washed light of morning, Jhelum didn't seem such a bad place after all; it was a solidly provincial market town, home to a sizeable army base but not much else. Around the central bus stop was a bazaar area filled for the most part with country people, farmers and herdsmen and landless labourers, who came and went by horse-drawn transport. The long line of ekkas and tongas waiting to collect bus passengers vastly outnumbered the auto-rickshaws and light trucks. Beyond the main Lahore–Rawalpindi railway line was a more modern commercial district, some timber yards and light industry.

I rode down to the Old Bridge across the River Jhelum, which carries not only the railway tracks but a narrow and much decayed roadway. This was once the GT Road, but is used today mainly by horse-drawn traffic and two-wheelers. The river didn't look so angry but there was still a hefty volume of water flowing between its tree-lined banks. I realised that the recent rains might scupper our plans to visit Rohtas, the fortress built by Sher Shah Suri to guard his northern frontier. It has the most extensive walls of any fort in the subcontinent; and since I had visited the Afghan's tomb at Sasaram and the Purana Qila in Delhi, I wanted to see Rohtas as well. The only problem was that to reach the fort involved crossing a ford in the Kahan River. For 90 per cent of the year the river bed is dry, but given the recent rains . . .

Back at the Zelaf Hotel I told Sarah about my worries. Maybe it would be better to stay in Jhelum another night. 'No way am I staying here tonight,' was her response. 'We'll just find somewhere along the road.' So she packed up the bike while I studied the road map, trying to work out what to do if the river was unfordable.

The map showed that although we'd ridden more than a hundred miles through Pakistan we'd been running parallel with the Indian border. Just six miles up the road from Jhelum you leave Pakistan proper and enter Azad Kashmir. This 'Free Kashmir', as it is known throughout Pakistan, is a thin strip of territory that was 'liberated' by Muslims in 1948. Ten miles further on you run into the Ceasefire Line, beyond which lies what is marked on Pakistani maps as 'Disputed Territory' and on Indian ones as the State of Jammu and Kashmir. No wonder there was a large army base at Jhelum.

The landscape changed almost immediately we left town. We had left the flatlands of the Punjab behind us and the road began climbing through the eastern outcrops of the Salt Range. The land became drier and cultivation was restricted to irregular terraced plots that had been carved out of heavily eroded hillsides. I noticed several trees had knotted lengths of cotton attached to their branches – prayers or supplications to some local Sufi saint or pir who had once made the spot his hermitage. The GT Road came down to two lanes for a while, though works were in progress to upgrade it all the way to Rawalpindi.

At Dina I turned off the main road and asked whether we could get through to Rohtas Fort. The news was not good. A local bus had been unable to cross the river ford that morning. The waters were receding, however, and it was suggested that we 'try our luck' later. So, to pass the time, instead of continuing towards Rawalpindi we took another side road out of town, up towards the Mangla Dam and Azad Kashmir.

How far up this road we'd be allowed to go I wasn't certain. It soon became obvious that we were entering a militarily sensitive area, for the road went past one army base after another. Some had trophies of war on display, mostly Indian battle tanks or artillery pieces captured in the 1965 war. All had armed sentries manning the front gate, but nobody tried to stop us and we motored on at a leisurely pace up to the Mangla Dam. Practically every other vehicle on the road had Azad Kashmir licence plates, so when we did run into a road-block on the approach to the dam I was pretty certain we'd be turned back.

But the guard didn't even ask to see our papers. Visiting the dam was fine, provided we didn't try to continue into Azad Kashmir. I was not expecting so casual an approach. In India we'd have spent hours going through our papers and unpacking the bike to prove that it wasn't full of explosives. The guard insisted only on shaking hands before waving me through the check-point and out onto the roadway that runs along the top of the barrage.

The Mangla Dam is an impressive monument, one of the largest of its kind in the world. The Bullet accelerated over the smooth surface of the roadway and for a brief moment I felt as though I was cruising up some US Interstate, with the artificial lake on one side and on the other a sheer drop down to the valley bottom.

Roughly half-way across is a rocky outcrop on which perches an old fort that had been used by the unruly Ghakkar tribes to defend their lands in the foothills. The modern dam had been built into this hill and the area around the fort was laid out as a picnic area. A souvenir shop and information centre was run by Azad Kashmir Tourism – apparently we had already crossed what is technically the border between Pakistan and Kashmir.

We tramped over the old fort's battlements, looked out across the Potwar Plateau and wandered around a museum filled with old photos of the dam's construction and cut-out models of its turbines. The fact that the dam exists is thanks to one of the few examples of Indo-Pak co-operation over the previous fifty years, the Indus Waters Treaty of 1960. Practically all of the main rivers flow through Indian territory before reaching

Pakistan and arguments over water rights soured Indo-Pak relations in the immediate aftermath of Partition. Only when agreement was reached over how these water resources should be shared could major projects such as the Mangla Dam or the Tarbela Dam on the Indus go ahead. It remains the case, however, that Pakistan is dependent on India's goodwill for much of the water it needs for irrigation.

I noticed that not a great flow of water was being released into the Jhelum. This meant that most of the rise in its level further downstream was due to run-off from the land. Presumably the same applied to the Kahan River.

So I wasn't feeling optimistic about reaching Rohtas Fort when I turned the bike round and headed back to Dina.

This time the news was not so bad.

A bus had left for Rohtas and not returned. This, I was told, meant that it had either got through or was stuck at the ford. By all means I should drive down the road and investigate. If the waters were still too high I could always turn back. What had I to lose?

Well, my peace of mind, for one thing. I soon discovered that the 'road' to Rohtas petered out after a couple of miles. From there on the only road was the river bed, which may provide a good enough surface most of the time but is treacherous in the extreme after a flood. Still, from the assortment of tyre tracks heading out into the sand it was obvious that other traffic had come this way recently, including a few motorbikes or scooters. So I followed the tracks thrugh the higher sandbanks that hadn't been touched by the floods, trying to keep in as high a gear as possible and avoiding the soft patches which made the back wheel slew around in a disconcerting manner. The Bullet wasn't designed for off-road trailblazing and with Sarah and all our luggage on board I had my work cut out keeping the bike upright.

The midday sun was turning the sandy waste into a furnace, the engine was overheating and I was cursing the day I'd ever heard of Rohtas Fort. A shallow side stream blocked the way ahead. I took it at speed, but when I slowed down on the far bank the rear tyre got stuck in wet sand. The same happened when I crossed a small lagoon left behind by the receding flood. The bike was simply too bloody heavy for this kind of work. I remembered a comment made by one of the people who'd helped me haul the Bullet onto our veranda at Faletti's. 'Good sir,' he'd said, 'this motorcycle is heavy like a buffalo.' But unlike the native water buffalo it was not amphibious, which is what appeared to me to be necessary to cross the final and deepest channel that separated us from Rohtas Fort.

Sarah rolled up her trousers and started wading across. When the waters reached her knees I began to think it was useless. Just then a local kid on a little 100 cc machine came whizzing past and without hesitating for a second went straight through the water. He'd even taken care to tuck up his legs so that his baggy trousers didn't get splashed. 'Why don't you try it where he went,' Sarah shouted, pointing to the spot. 'It must be shallower there.'

It was, by a few crucial inches, but the surrounding sand was much softer too. When I put the Bullet up on its stand, in order to survey the scene, it immediately sank into the loose sediment and the whole bike started toppling over.

Sarah was standing in the stream urging me to give it a try. 'Come on,' she shouted, 'don't be such a sissy. If that kid managed it, so can you.'

'I saw him,' I shouted back. 'But his bike weighs about a third of what this buffalo does.'

'Come on in,' she yelled as though we were at the seaside. 'The water's lovely.'

'Not if I bog down and it gets sucked into the motor, it isn't,' I shouted back.

I knew that if water got into the cylinder or the electrics we'd be stuck for good. And trying to repair the bike on these sandbanks would be a nightmare. So instead I began wheeling the bike away from the river, looking for a patch of firmer ground where I could leave it. We'd just have to walk the rest of the way.

Coming over the crest of a hill the ramparts of Rohtas Fort stretched right across the horizon. From this distance, seen across the low scrubland, they appeared to be laid out in a flat line; but as we approached it became apparent that they jutted out in some places and receded in others, making the best use of the natural contours. The arch-shaped crenellations glowered down upon us, giving the distinct impression that we were being watched by unseen eyes. The sheer scale of this undertaking took what was left of my breath away.

At the height of his power, Sher Shah Suri ordered its construction to defend his north-west frontier against the depredations of Ghakkar tribesmen. The fortress also served as a deterrent against any attempt at invasion by his old rival, the exiled Mughal emperor Humayun, or anyone else for that matter. It was built for a garrison of twelve thousand men and guarded Sher Shah's new road, which he ensured marched right past the East Gate of his fort. A few surviving paving stones below the Gatali Gate show where the imperial highway once ran.

Before entering the fortress I paused. So far my entire journey from Bengal onwards had been through lands which had been part of Sher Shah's empire. Even more remarkable is that he started out with nothing, the disinherited son of a minor landowner in Bihar, and yet he conquered all this territory and welded it into a coherent and well-administered empire in less than a decade. And although he was of Pathan stock, Sher Shah's power base had been in eastern India. His strategy was to gobble up Hindustan from the base upwards – just as the British were to do two centuries later.

All previous invaders for a thousand years had come from the north-west. Sher Shah knew this well enough, which is why he built his principal fortress on this frontier. But he hadn't forgotten where he came from. The very name of this fortress, Rohtas, is borrowed from another fort in the hill country of south Bihar which Sher Shah seized right at the beginning of his victorious campaigns.

If he thought the name brought good luck, however, he was mistaken. He himself died in an accidental explosion before the new fort was completed. And when the exiled Mughals finally returned to Hindustan in 1545 the garrison at Rohtas surrendered without a fight. Its massive defences have never been tested, for the Mughal Empire extended right up to the North-West Frontier and beyond. So Rohtas Fort became a white elephant. Rather like the mighty English fortress at Berwick-upon-Tweed, built at huge expense by Queen Elizabeth I to keep out the Scots, it was left guarding a frontier that no longer existed.

Nowadays Rohtas's massive walls enclose a sleepy village in which fat-tailed sheep and goats outnumber the human population by about ten-to-one. Most of the low dwellings appeared to have been built from stone taken from older and much grander structures. A few houses still had intricately carved doors. We were the only visitors that day and it was not long before we were being followed by a group of curious schoolboys, one of whom insisted that we meet his elder brother, who was training to be a lawyer and wanted to practise his English.

This was Adil Hamid Khan, a shy young man who didn't seem cut out for the law. His pale, thoughtful face was topped by a shock of hennaed hair, and while he wore the usual kurta pyjama, his was made of a fine grey-striped cloth. His father had served in the army and was a man of some consequence in the village. Adil felt it his duty to escort us around his home turf and requested that his younger brother and a visiting cousin also accompany us. To begin with I suspected they would claim payment as guides, but nothing could have been further from the truth. Theirs was an old-fashioned courtesy and the only argument that arose was when I tried to pay for a round of soft drinks.

It soon became apparent that Rohtas village occupies only a small part of the area enclosed by the walls. With our escort we wandered across open country covered in thorn bushes, where villagers keep their livestock, out towards the Sohal Gate. Adil was telling me about the big celebrations held at the Feast of Eid-ul-Fitr and how, like so many educated but poor Pakistanis, he was hoping to enter government service. The afternoon light was softening, lending an air of mystery to the age-blackened piles of masonry all around us. In front of the ruined imperial mosque a young shepherd unrolled a threadbare cloth which would serve as his prayer mat.

The sandstone of the monumental Sohal Gate glowed blood red as the sun began to set. As the most ornate of the fort's ten gateways it was probably intended for triumphal entries, though few can have passed this way before Rohtas fell into disuse. From the gate tower I looked out over an empty plain defended by more than three miles of curtain wall. It was an object lesson in the futility of fixed defences. Compared with Sher Shah's other great undertaking, the Imperial Road, it served no useful purpose. Yet its immense grandeur rises above such practical considerations.

The light was fading fast and I needed to get back to the bike. Adil's father insisted on escorting us down to the river – just in case there were any bandits about. He now worked as a security guard in Jhelum, but during his time in the army he'd served on the Khyber Pass. With him there, he assured us, we would be perfectly safe.

The Bullet had toppled over in the soft sand and was lying on its side, which made me worry about petrol leaking or sand getting into the carburettor. However, when we'd righted it everything seemed to function perfectly. Sarah decided to hitch a ride back to town aboard a lorry carrying coriander and vegetables to market in Dina. 'That way you'll be carrying less weight,' she said cheerfully as she climbed in amongst the crush of male passengers. 'I'll be waiting for you in the chai-house by the main road.'

Night fell just as I set off up the river bed. In the dark it was hard to tell which set of tracks to follow. A couple of times I followed some old tracks which eventually disappeared into the river. There was not a single light to be seen and I began to wonder whether I'd ever find my way back. Things improved slightly when the moon rose; but there was no way that I could gauge where the sand was firm or where it would give way under the Bullet's weight. I dropped the bike twice and got bogged down innumerable times. If I hadn't been able to follow the tail lights of a passing Jeep I might have spent all night looking for the spot where the river-bed joined the tarmac road. As it was, it took me two hours to cover less than ten miles.

I arrived in Dina exhausted. Sarah had been worrying about what had happened to me. But her relief gave way to anger when she discovered there was nowhere in Dina to stay the night. She was all for pressing on to Rawalpindi. I wasn't feeling up to riding the bike for another two or three hours through the night. We had a flaming public row, to the immense amusement of half the population of Dina. If I'd been a Muslim I would have divorced her thrice, there and then. Instead, I jumped on the bike and announced I was going back to Jhelum.

'What, to that shit-hole?' she screamed.

'Yes, to that same shit-hole of a hotel. It's the only bleeding shit-hole that we know about for a hundred miles around here, so we haven't got much choice.'

Reluctantly, she climbed aboard and together – in body if not in spirit – we set off for Jhelum and the delights of the Zelaf Hotel.

Marital relations were more or less restored when we pulled out of Jhelum for the second time. We had no adventurous detours planned that day and were going to stick to the GT Road all the way to 'Pindi. Beyond Dina the road started climbing into the fantastically eroded landscape of the Potwar Plateau, a rugged and rather forbidding badlands that is criss-crossed by ravines and seasonal water courses. At the top of the pass we could look south across the desolate Salt Range, while to the north the snowy heights of the Pir Panjal appeared to float in the sky, their foothills lost in a heat haze.

Spring had finally arrived, even this far north. The fields were carpeted with wild flowers and, as we descended into more open country beyond Gujar Khan, I saw great banyan trees beside the road. Not since Bihar or Uttar Pradesh had I seen such magnificent specimens. But here in northern Pakistan they marched like giants across the countryside. We stopped briefly beside an ancient Buddhist stupa, where the bike was engulfed by a flock of fat-tailed sheep being moved to new pastures by Ghakkar shepherds. Then it was back on the road, which grew into a busy four-lane highway as we approached the twin-city of Rawalpindi-Islamabad.

All I needed to do was to stay on the Grand Trunk Road until it transformed itself into The Mall. For there, right beside the main road, stands Flashman's – the oldest and most unapologetically colonial-style hotel in all of 'Pindi. Across the road is the old cricket ground and the 'Pindi Club, and beyond them the heart of the military cantonment. And to my delight, I discovered right opposite the entrance to Flashman's a perfectly preserved example of the old distance-markers which once littered the subcontinent. Encased in a stuccoed surround with classical pretensions is a tablet bearing the legend GRAND TRUNK ROAD, and below this are given the distances to fifteen different places in Pakistan.

It was just 167 kilometres to Peshawar (the distances are given in kilometres rather than miles), the terminus of the GT Road. If I continued to the Afghan border at Torkham, then there were 220 kilometres to go. But it was the last destination that intrigued me most: Kabul, 393 kilometres. Whoever put up this plaque obviously considered the border no real barrier to the continuation of the Grand Trunk Road.

Though they sit next to each other, Rawalpindi and Islamabad have very different characters. 'Pindi is a bustling, unashamedly commercial place where you can buy just about anything that can be smuggled. The Old City's gaudy bazaars are piled high with televisions and fridges, video recorders and pirated cassettes, all of them imported, few of them duty-paid.

The greatest concentration is around Bara Bazaar, though other smuggled goods such as perfumes, cosmetics and prescription drugs are sold openly all over town. Salesmen make a virtue out of the illicit provenance of their goods. It proves that they are genuine imports rather than locally produced and therefore inferior substitutes. And unless they'd been smuggled how could the salesmen be offering them at such competitive prices?

In British times, much of Rawalpindi's commerce was controlled by Hindus and Sikhs. But from early March 1947 onwards there was open warfare between the communities. On 5 March, a procession of Hindu and Sikh students protesting against the Muslim League's attempt to replace the elected Unionist ministry was attacked. There followed widespread violence in which the well-organised urban Sikhs and Hindus fought it out in the narrow streets around their mohallas.

But outside of town, in the suburbs and rural areas, the more thinly scattered non-Muslim population was defenceless. What happened next was a general massacre during which, according to Indian refugee sources, around seven thousand were killed. The extent of arson and looting within Rawalpindi itself was such that Muslim refugees coming from Delhi were astounded by the devastation.

Down a side street leading into the bazaar area, I saw a dilapidated mandir that had once been the centre of a Hindu temple complex. Telephone wires trailed from its weather-stained and crumbling tower. Obviously it hadn't functioned as a temple for many years; and the only information I could glean about whether any Hindus remain in Rawalpindi was proferred by a Christian taxi-driver. There was still a small community, he said, but they kept a low profile. Although he had lived in 'Pindi all his life and belonged to a minority community, he had never once met a person who admitted to being a Hindu.

If the Old City is given over to buying and selling, Rawalpindi's cantonment is an overgrown garrison town. It is home to the Pakistan Army headquarters, but it lacks the architectural and other graces which distinguish the cantonment area in Lahore. At night the streets are half-deserted and after trawling the area around The Mall for a lively eating place we ended up back where we'd started at Kashmirwala's. Apart from us there were just three diners; but at least we wouldn't have to eat on our own.

The three men at the other table began chatting to us and eventually asked us over to join them. One worked in computers, another in construction, while the third, a Mr Khan, was a civil servant. They were curious about India, since they'd heard only officially vetted information, and were astounded when I told them that in some things – the telephone system being one, the main road network another – Pakistan was more efficient than their big neighbour. 'Of course we'd like to believe we're better than India,' said the computer man, 'but we don't really know.'

'Ah, the United India – that was a great country,' declared Mr Khan, somewhat to my astonishment, for in Pakistan such views aren't far removed from treason. 'Did you ever read Churchill's biography?' he asked, stuffing a morsel of lamb stew into his mouth. 'A great historian,' he opined. 'And in some years' time another historian will write a page or two about what happened in 1947 and a country called East Pakistan, which after twenty-five years became Bangladesh.

'And then,' he continued, 'that same historian will write there was another country called Pakistan, and after fifty years that will be nothing too. It will be subdivided.'

'But we are too small a country to be divided again,' protested the building contractor.

'Ah, just you wait,' said Mr Khan, using his naan to mop up the juices. 'You see, in our country there has never been any real national consensus. We've had a democratic system for years now, but never have the opposition parties been willing to accept the elected government. The two sides are always at daggers drawn. The opposition appeals directly to the people, to stage protests and other direct action. And what do we get? Chaos.

'Look at Karachi – all these factions killing each other. I tell you, until such time as the opposition accept their defeat in an election, until they support the government on decent measures by vote crossing and all that, there will be no real democracy or unity in Pakistan.'

'And what about the corruption?' asked the computer man. 'How do we get rid of that?' I understood he had just failed to land a government contract.

'It happens in India also, doesn't it?' was Mr Khan's riposte. 'Why, only yesterday I was reading about all these high-ranking politicians and ministers in Delhi taking bribes.' And it was true, the Pakistani newspapers had printed gloating reports of the Hawala scandal across the border in India.

'But there is just one thing that puzzles me,' declared Mr Khan. 'The size of these bribes is so very small. In Pakistan you will get nowhere with these sums. Indeed, not until now did I realise you could buy a Hindu politician so cheaply.'

Rawalpindi's cantonment might be quiet, but compared with the new, purpose-built capital up the road it positively throbs with life. After dark, Islamabad becomes a ghost-town. If anyone needs proof that rigorously planned cities are hollow at the core, they should spend time in Islamabad.

Its position, at the foot of the Margala Hills, is admirable. It has been carefully zoned. There is a diplomatic enclave for the foreign missions, a commercial zone, an educational zone, a modern industrial zone and various residential zones – each an island cut off from its neighbours by parkland or scrubland or empty wasteland, which gives the city an unfinished air. Its avenues are broad and tree-lined and seem to go on for ever, but out of office hours they are empty of life. It has pedestrian walkways and parking lots in abundance, most of them chronically underused since the population has not increased as the planners envisioned. Of course, one of the advantages of all these broad streets and empty spaces is that they can be cordonned off by security forces. Such cities pose serious obstacles to rioters and revolutionaries.

If Islamabad has a centre, it is probably the white marble mass of the Shah Faisal Mosque. It was built with Saudi money and claims to be the largest mosque in the world, capable of accommodating a hundred thousand worshippers in its tent-shaped prayer-hall and courtyard – though only a fraction of that number would seem to pray there regularly.

More government buildings and banks are still going up in Islamabad; but I doubt whether it will ever feel like anything other than a self-consciously Islamic version of Brasilia.

Perhaps because there is so little to do, Islamabad is a great talking shop. Politicians and civil servants, journalists and pundits, all those who hang close to the centre of power, have developed political gossip and intrigue into an art form. It is at once their business and their recreation; which suited me fine, because such people were happy to find time to talk to an outsider with an interest in Partition and its legacy.

Once I was plugged into the network I found myself rushing from office to private residence to office again, from the Prime Minister's Secretariat to the Quaid-i-Azam University and then back to the Foreign Ministry. It wasn't long before I detected a certain uniformity in their views. Discussion of Partition itself tended to be brief. It was a historical necessity. Pakistan existed, end of subject. What they wanted to talk about was Kashmir. Here was a live issue that was related directly to what happened in 1947–8. And no matter what topic we were discussing – Mountbatten's role, Nehru's character, the current arms race in South Asia – the conversation always swung back to Kashmir.

'Until the Kashmir issue has been resolved,' I was told at the Ministry of Foreign Affairs, 'other moves towards regional co-operation will be little more than wallpaper.' There had been some progress in other areas, such as reducing tariff barriers between South Asian countries; but as for renewing economic links with India, 'that will remain something of a dream until there is a mutually acceptable settlement in Jammu and Kashmir'.

Pakistan's prodigious spending on defence, a newspaperman explained to me, had to continue because India's 'illegal' occupation of Kashmir posed a threat to Pakistan's security and territorial integrity. And while he deplored the fact that so much of the budget went on arms rather than on education or health, it was difficult to see how that could change while Kashmir remained a burning issue, a symbol of Pakistan's 'dismemberment' in 1948, and a focus for the genuine fears felt by the ordinary Pakistani about their larger and more powerful neighbour.

I can understand this obsession with Kashmir, though only up to a point. The Vale of Kashmir is a verdant and beautiful land. Its population is largely Muslim; and if the principles applied in 1947 to the division of the subcontinent as a whole had been applied also to Kashmir, it would certainly have gone to Pakistan. But at the time, Jammu and Kashmir was not part of the British raj. It was a Princely State, ruled by a Hindu Maharaja; and since this state bordered on both India and Pakistan he technically had the right to accede to either country. A weak and vacillating ruler, he tried to cling onto his independence; but when Muslim troops in the north rebelled and were joined by insurgents who declared 'Azad Kashmir', he threw in his lot with India.

Muslim tribesmen backed by Pakistan were advancing on Srinagar when Pandit Nehru, whose family were originally Kashmiri Hindus, despatched Indian airborne troops to hold the capital. The first Indo-Pak war dragged on until a ceasefire was agreed in December 1948. Since then the *de facto* border has been along the ceasefire line. The United Nations called for the withdrawal of both armies and a plebiscite allowing the Kashmiris to decide their own future, but no such plebiscite has ever been held.

Pakistan went to war again in 1965 in an attempt to take Kashmir by force – again without success. After the third Indo-Pak war, in which Pakistan was badly defeated and lost Bangladesh, Prime Minister Bhutto and Mrs Gandhi signed the Simla Agreement of 1972, which recognised the existing line of control and bound both countries to resolve the dispute through bilateral negotiations. A quarter of a century later and there has been no real progress. 'The Indians stick by their old rule,' a

Pakistani senator told me, 'that possession is nine-tenths of the law, and for them that appears to be good enough.' So, the peace of Kashmir's valleys is still rent by gunfire and explosions as various groups of Muslim 'freedom fighters' take on close to half a million Indian troops and security forces. Westerners seized as hostages are just pawns in this modern equivalent of 'The Great Game'.

After fighting three wars, and half a century's debilitating expenditure on armaments, Pakistan has invested too much simply to give up on Kashmir. And after two days of being lectured on the subject, I was beginning to believe that the Pakistanis' sense of grievance over Kashmir was both genuine and not altogether unjustified. Yet I also suspected that the Kashmir issue has become a 'necessary evil'. It is the one issue on which most Pakistanis are ready to unite; and it provides a wonderful excuse for allowing the military-industrial complex and the handful of feudal families who still run Pakistan to cling onto their privileges. That, I suspect, is one reason why something very like a Cold War still exists within India after fifty years.

Back at Flashman's, after what I thought was the last of these conversations, I discovered that Sarah had already packed up and left. No marital discord this time: we'd arranged that she went ahead to Taxila, an archaeological site some twenty miles further up the GT Road, while I completed my rounds among the talking shops of Islamabad. I was about to set off after her when the hotel manager spotted me. 'There is an urgent message for you,' he shouted. 'It is from the Joint Secretary at the Minister for Kashmir's office. Please call this number immediately.'

I did so only to discover that a meeting had been arranged with the Minister in an hour's time. I agreed to this reluctantly and, swapping leather jacket for blazer-and-tie, headed back up the Murree Road for Islamabad. When I reached the specified block I asked the way. Eventually I was directed to Kashmir House, where an armed guard at the gate told me to wait while he enquired within.

I found it odd that I had to explain the reason for my visit, but after a few minutes I was ushered into the compound. Waiting on the veranda was a reception committee. I was introduced to a profusely bearded gentleman wearing dark glasses and a golden astrakhan cap. 'This is Sardar Muhammad Abdul Qayyum Khan,' I was told, 'Prime Minister of Azad Jammu and Kashmir.'

Hang on a minute, I thought to myself as he treated me to a fierce handshake, this isn't the person I arranged to see. But the private secretary had already fetched a cassette recorder so the interview would be 'on the record'. I could only assume that there had been a change of plan and that instead of seeing the Minister for Kashmir I had been 'upgraded' to the Prime Minister of Azad Kashmir. Anyway, it was too late to back out now.

Once again I was taken through the vexed issue of Kashmir. He began with his own role in the uprising of 1947 when, armed with only country-made weapons, he joined the Jihad and set out from Nila But in Poonch to liberate his fellow-countrymen from the iniquitous rule of the Hindu maharaja and the depredations of his Dogra troops.

Sardar Muhammad Abdul Qayyum Khan vigorously denied he had been aided in this by the newly created Pakistan. 'The charge levelled by Indian propagandists that it was not an indigenous rebellion, that it was infiltration from outside – that is all nonsense.' He was equally adamant that his Government of Azad Kashmir remained to this day wholly separate from the Pakistan Government, even though he has consistently held that a reunified and free Kashmir should join itself to Pakistan. By the end of our talk I was very much aware of the fine line between a 'puppet government' and a 'client state'.

Night had fallen by the time I made it back to Flashman's, and the hotel manager was waiting for me. 'Where have you been, Mr Gregson? Four telephone messages I have taken from Joint Secretary Mr Siddiqi. The Minister has been awaiting your arrival.'

'Oh God!' I bellowed so that heads turned to see what was happening. 'I've been to see the wrong bloody Minister!'

I phoned Mr Siddiqi to apologise. The voice on the other end of the line was highly agitated. 'But you do not understand, the Minister left a full cabinet meeting with the Prime Minister. Even now he is waiting for you. You must come immediately.'

Having made such a mess of things, I could hardly refuse. So I hopped into a taxi and headed back up to Islamabad. I knew that by now Sarah would be imagining I'd had an accident on the road but I had no way of contacting her.

The Minister for Kashmir and Northern Affairs, Muhammad Afzal Khan, was extremely understanding. 'Such an easy mistake to make . . . Now let us get down to business.'

And so I talked through the Kashmir problem for the fifth time that day. The Minister took the struggle for self-determination back to the nineteenth century and the British East India Company's sale of Kashmir, lock, stock and barrel, to the Hindu Maharaja Gulab Singh. It was part of a deliberate policy to divide the Muslim peoples of the North-West, using the Hindu Dogras to act as a buffer state serving strictly British interests.

I was wondering where all this was leading when he declared himself to be a Pukhtun Nationalist, the leader of a separate political party in the North-West Frontier, which had for many years allied itself with Benazir Bhutto's Pakistan People's Party. The British, he told me, were as much to blame for the division of the Pukhtun nation (commonly known as Pathans) by setting up the Durand Line, the international border with Afghanistan that runs right through the middle of Pukhtun territory, as they were for the tragedy in Kashmir. Moreover, if the Pukhtuns had not been divided the problems in Afghanistan would have been settled long ago.

'Nobody,' he informed me, 'has ever subdued the Pukhtuns – not the Britishers, not the Mughals, not even Alexander the Great.' I didn't feel up to contradicting him. Nor did I feel like asking him whether he would include the Pakistan Government as the latest in this long line of rulers who have never effectively ruled over the Pathans.

'Since 1947,' he told me, 'the old imperialism of the British had been taken over by the Indians. As yet these people in Delhi are not reconciled to Partition. They still look to a Greater India. So how can you expect us to have better relations with them, opening up the Wagha Border or allowing them to set up banks in Pakistan?' From his point of view, there could be no thaw in the Cold War with India unless they first gave up Kashmir.

On my third attempt, I managed to get on the bike and leave Flashman's before being summoned to another discussion about Kashmir. Once I cleared Rawalpindi it was pitch-black on the GT Road. The chain mudguards on lorries rattled menacingly in the dark, but at least I hadn't got far to go. Half an hour later I pulled up outside the Archaeological Department's rest-house in Taxila. I was more than three hours late.

Sarah had been convinced that I'd had an accident. Her relief knew no bounds – until, that is, we both noticed a pungent aroma emanating from my rucksack.

'Is that whisky?' I enquired. After the day's madness I needed a stiff drink.

'Of course it's the bloody whisky,' she shouted, 'and it's leaking out of your kitbag.' I dived for the sack, which was already sodden through, and retrieved the bottle of Murree's finest. Only an inch of the stuff remained in the bottom. The rest had seeped all over our clothes or been soaked up by my precious notepads and books. I spread them around the room to dry out, with the result that very soon our quarters stank like a distillery.

There was a knock at the door. 'Madam, food is ready,' announced the grizzled caretaker, poking his nose through the mosquito blinds. I rushed to hide what remained of the whisky while Sarah threw the pile of booze-soaked clothing into the bathroom. But there was no covering up the overpowering odour, and the old caretaker clicked his tongue disapprovingly as he brought in plates of curried chicken and potatoes and roti. As a Muslim and, I assumed, a teetotaller, his nose would be sensitive to the reek of forbidden alcohol. We both felt as though we'd been caught smoking behind the bike-sheds at school.

The essence of distillery lingered early next morning when we tramped off across fields studded with ancient monuments. For Taxila was the capital of the Kingdom of Gandhara, and the remains of ancient civilisations litter the valley floor and surrounding foothills. From the sixth century BC it became the main centre of government and trade in the north-west. Everybody came through here — Persians, Greeks, Parthians, Scythians, Kushans.

Taxila was an eastern satrapy of the Persian Empire until it fell to Alexander the Great's Macedonians. By then a university had already been established, famed throughout the subcontinent for its learning in Sanskrit and medicine, in mathematics and astrology. Alexander himself is said to have engaged here in philosophical discourse with the leading scholars of the day before continuing eastward across the Jhelum River to defeat King Porus and his massed squadrons of war elephants.

Alexander left the subcontinent almost immediately and Taxila entered the sphere of the Mauryan emperors, who ruled from what is now Bihar. The founder of that dynasty, Chandragupta Maurya, extended his Royal Road to link Taxila with his capital at Patalipura; and under Asoka's patronage the Buddhist faith travelled up the road to Gandhara. Of this ancient road there remains no trace, but in the nearby Margalla Pass there is a well-preserved section of the Imperial Road constructed by that other empire-builder who began in Bihar, Sher Shah Suri.

I rode off on the Enfield to gaze at the worn paving stones of the Shahi Road, as it is known in these parts, which are set in a man-made cleft in the pass. The Afghan emperor extended his lines of communication far to the west of his great fort of Rohtas, so that his armies could go out to meet the invader.

Nowadays the old road is used as a short cut by local villagers carrying firewood or worn-out tyres. The modern Grand Trunk Road runs through a broad cutting only two hundred yards away, and the sounds of truck horns carried through the pass to the older route. Standing on top of a hill between the two roads is a granite obelisk erected by 'friends, British and Native', to John Nicholson, whose legendary feats include the relief of Delhi in 1857.

Through this gap in the hills have passed all the great roadways that have bound the subcontinent together for nearly 2,500 years. The paved highway I walked down was a mere five hundred years old; but other roads had crossed these passes from before the dawn of history. That morning I had visited Bhir Mound, centre of Taxila's first city, which flourished from the sixth to the second century BC; I had wandered down the streets of the later city of Sirkap, laid out by the Bactrian Greeks on a grid-plan as rigorous as that applied to modern Islamabad; and I had marvelled at the sculptures combining Greek fluidity of form and Buddhist spirituality – a true marriage of East and West – in Taxila's museum. More than anywhere else on this journey I was made aware of the immense antiquity of the road I was travelling down.

I now stood across the line of advance of countless armies: Persians, Turks, Mongols, Afghans, Mughals, Sikhs, as well as the last of the empire-builders, the British, whose road I had followed from Bengal and whose bitter legacy I was still discovering.

From Taxila the GT Road heads almost due west towards Peshawar. The spring sun shone as we rode through orange and lemon groves that crowded the upper reaches of carefully irrigated valleys.

At Hasan Abdal we bought blood oranges at a wayside market crowded with villagers from the surrounding country-side, many of them Pathans. Among the crowds was a man whose blond hair, green eyes and freckles made me believe for an instant the stories about descendants of Alexander's armies settling in the northern valleys.

Beside the Grand Trunk Road stood a Sikh gurdwara, a centre of pilgrimage associated with Guru Nanak, whose extravagant domes and cupolas were visible from the street. I also spotted what looked like a ruined Hindu temple, but there was no time to investigate. Besides, apart from the annual visitation of Sikh pilgrims from India, Hasan Abdal appears now to be as solidly Muslim as any other small town in Pakistan. And we needed to get back on the road if we were going to reach Peshawar that evening.

But I couldn't resist one last stop before leaving the Punjab behind us. Just where the main road curls down to the River Indus, which for centuries has formed the province's western boundary, I turned left along a side road which leads to Attock Fort. It was this mighty edifice that rendered Rohtas Fort obsolete when it was completed by the Mughal emperor Akbar some forty years later. Entry is forbidden, as the fort is still used by the military and houses a prison. But below its massive walls stands one of the best-preserved caravanserai along the entire length of the Grand Trunk Road. Like so many other monuments along the way, this traveller's hostel was the handiwork of Sher Shah Suri.

I had to argue hard with the military police to gain access to Sher Shah's serai, even though strictly speaking it lies outside the army base. At first they wanted to keep our passports and cameras, but when I refused point-blank they agreed to copying down the passport numbers before waving us through.

I eased the Bullet over a rough path used by shepherds down to the serai. Entering through the east gate I found myself in the middle of a broad courtyard. This rectangular space is enclosed by walls, into which are built arched doorways leading to cells where travellers could lock up their valuables and rest up from the hardships of the road.

That Sher Shah should have built such a substantial rest-house for travellers at the very limits of his domains says a lot about the man. For the last hundred miles he had pushed his great roadway through country he did not fully control; but he understood the importance of good land communications – both for trade and so that his armies could advance swiftly when invasion threatened. Why he chose this spot, where the Indus flows through a narrow gorge, in preference to the older crossing slightly upstream, probably has much to do with its defensive possibilities. Good communications are all very well, but not if they assist the enemy more than your own side. Akbar also realised the defensive advantages of Attock and built his fortress on the heights commanding the river gorge.

Sher Shah envisioned his Imperial Road stretching all the way to Kabul. It was a link between the Afghan Empire he had created in India and the ancestral homeland of the Pathans – the land of Roh, as he called it – from which he continued to recruit warriors to stiffen the resolve of his own armies. He tempted them down from their bare hills with generous grants of land – jagirs in the lush flatlands of the Punjab or the Gangetic plain as extensive, he promised, as the arid lands they had held among the mountains. From the western wall of his serai I could see the first line of those mountains stretching across the horizon.

I found myself wondering: 'What if he hadn't died in an accidental explosion?' Given another ten or twenty years, a ruler of Sher Shah's stature might have unified the entire subcontinent and extended his empire to Afghanistan and beyond. There would have been time for his dynasty to consolidate. And confronted with such a power in the subcontinent, would the European adventurers have made any headway?

But there are already too many 'big-ifs' in history; so taking one last look at the distant mountains and at the Indus surging through the gorge far below, I look my leave of Sher Shah Suri and all his works. Across the river lay the North-West Frontier Province, the most turbulent and to many of its rulers – not least the British – the most fascinating province of all.

14

NORTH-WEST FRONTIER: BROTHERS AND ARMS

We crossed the new road bridge over the Indus and drew up on the far bank. Looking back, the rounded bastions of Attock Fort glowed in the afternoon sun. Further downstream was the village from which boatmen had once ferried travellers across the monsoon-swollen river, while in the dry season a boat-bridge was strung together.

Sarah was just reaching for her camera when a shout rang out.

A policeman was running towards us, wagging his finger in disapproval. 'No pictures,' he yelled. 'Attock Fort, Army property, no pictures. Road bridge, also no pictures.'

I'd met this kind of official paranoia in India, but up to now not in Pakistan. For a nasty moment I thought he was going to try to confiscate the camera. But once the offending object had been put back in its case, the policeman was all smiles and waved us through the border check-point.

To begin with the road curled beside the Landai River, which carries the combined waters of the Kabul and Swat rivers down to their junction with the Indus. Then the surrounding hills opened up and we entered the Vale of Peshawar, a land beloved of the Mughals, its rolling valleys and sparkling streams being excelled in their estimation only by that other valley surrounded by mountains, the Vale of Kashmir.

As we had been travelling north along the Grand Trunk Road we had kept up with the change of seasons, and here in the borderlands it was first spring once more. The raised edges of fields glittered with wild flowers; the willow and the plane trees were just coming into bud; and there was a sharpness in the air carried down from the snow-capped Hindu Kush. A road sign announced that there were only forty miles to Peshawar. I was looking forward to celebrating the end of our journey in style under the ramparts of the Bala Hisar.

The GT Road again broadened out into a four-lane highway and we were going flat out just to keep pace with the local taxis and minibuses – the Pathans seemingly even more addicted to speed than their Punjabi brethren. Then, beyond the garrison town of Nowshera, we ran into a series of road-works.

Even on this unmade surface the faster traffic, private cars and pick-ups converted into taxis, kept overtaking and cutting in at the last minute. I was trying to keep up with the pace, jockeying for position, when the road-works suddenly stopped and we bumped through a succession of muddy potholes and back onto a metalled surface.

I accelerated to get clear of the pack but there was no traction whatsoever between the rear tyre and the road. Instead of speeding up, the bike started to roll from side to side. I struggled to correct the steering, but the back end was swinging around, completely out of control. The next thing I knew the bike was on its side and my head was skidding along the tarmac. Somehow my helmet had got wedged between the handlebars and the road surface.

We were splayed out across the middle of the GT Road. All I could think about was the line of trucks coming up behind us, ready to crush us beneath their huge tyres.

'Get out of here,' I shouted to Sarah, but her leg was trapped beneath the weight of the bike. She was yelling at me, something about a bus coming. With my head pinned to the tarmac I couldn't see much. But she could look backwards and what she saw was a bus bearing down on us.

We were saved by the driver of a private car who deliberately swerved, placing his vehicle in between us and the heavy traffic. The bus's tyres came into my line of vision. I felt the vibration in my bones, waited for the sickening crunch. Nothing came.

The bus driver must have swerved to avoid the car, and in doing so he also steered clear of the fallen bike.

We crawled out from underneath the Bullet and ran for the safety of the roadside. The heavy trucks rumbled past without hitting us. The car driver reversed his vehicle immediately behind the overturned bike, providing a barrier against the onrush of traffic. He then helped me pick up the Enfield and wheel it over to the side of the road.

I was trying to thank him for having saved our lives – incoherently, forgetting even to ask his name. 'It is nothing,' he said. 'Please now check if you are injured.'

Sarah was clutching her left elbow, the side we'd come down on. By some miracle her felt jacket hadn't split open, but underneath it she had gravel burns and bruising.

It was only when I removed my own helmet that I realised how lucky I'd been. The chin guard was deeply scoured. If I hadn't been wearing a full-face helmet I'd have lost half my jaw. I reached for a cigarette when the man who'd stopped his car to help us shouted something. Petrol. The bloody stuff had leaked all over the road.

I put back my lighter and examined the fuel tank. Strange, nothing seemed to be leaking. Then the car driver pointed down the road. 'Benzine,' he shouted.

The whole surface was covered with an amalgam of mud and diesel fuel. A tanker or lorry must have spilled some of its load coming through the bumpy section before rejoining the asphalt road, which would explain why it had felt like a skating rink when I opened up the throttle.

I reassured the driver that neither of us needed to be taken to hospital. 'Very good,' he said. 'But will your machine also be working?'

I looked over the Bullet. The headlight had been smashed, the handlebars were scoured, an indicator was missing. But apart from that there were no obvious signs of damage. I supposed that while I was waltzing down the road we must have lost most of our forward momentum, so that by the time the bike went on its side we'd been travelling quite slowly. I tried the ignition switch and it worked. I walked wearily around to the kick-start. The engine didn't fire on the first try, but the system obviously still functioned.

Sarah was leaning against a tree, dragging on a cigarette. I joined her and asked if she felt up to getting back on the bike. 'Right now it's the last thing I want to do in this world. But, OK, I suppose we've only got another twenty miles to go.'

Half an hour later we limped into Peshawar. The steering felt wobbly as hell and, to tell the truth, so did I. We didn't bother to stop under the ramparts of Bala Hisar Fort; it wasn't exactly the joyous entry I had envisaged.

We'd made it to the end of the Grand Trunk Road – on the map 1,600 miles from where we'd started out in Calcutta, though in fact the mileometer showed the bike had covered almost twice that distance. But the accident down the road had robbed us of any sense of achievement. I felt numb as I pulled into the driveway of Dean's Hotel and cut the engine. A marquee was being erected for a wedding feast or some other celebration. Sarah pulled herself wearily out of the saddle. 'Just thank God,' she said, 'we're still alive.'

You don't need to look at a map to know that Peshawar is a frontier town. It seems to turn its back on the great subcontinent we'd just crossed, looking instead to the north and west, to the defiles of the Khyber Pass and beyond to the vastness of Central Asia. In springtime, the air lacks the torpor of the Indian plains and their perpetual summer.

And the people are different too: Pathans, mostly, big-boned men who stride purposefully towards the Old City, though these days there are many Afghans, fugitives from the endless wars across the border. Among the narrow streets which give off the Chowk you can see Uzbeks and Tajiks from the Far North, making their way to one of the eating houses, adorned with pictures of mujahidin, which cater for their plainer tastes in food.

The first time I arrived in Peshawar I had come by bus from Kabul, and after many weeks among Iranian and Turkic peoples what struck me about this frontier city was its subcontinental flavour. The piles of cumin and turmeric in the spice market, the colonial bungalows in the cantonment and other leftovers of the British raj – even the uniformed policemen – stirred memories of my Indian childhood. The bearded warriors with their bandoliers and Lee Enfield rifles and the women encased from head to food in the burqa I had seen before across the border in Afghanistan. After Herat and Kabul and Kandahar, this city of Peshawar had seemed positively homely.

A quarter of a century and half a dozen wars later, I was back again. But this time I had come from India, and Peshawar now seemed very different from Lahore and the other cities of the plains. Its Central Asian feel has been reinforced by the influx of Afghan refugees since the Soviet invasion of 1979. They have taken over the road transport business almost completely, and now run many of the shops and hotels in the Old City. And, of course, they dominate the most lucrative business of all – smuggling.

The carrying of arms in public has been banned, so you no longer see Kalashnikov-toting tribesmen swaggering through the old town. But the weapons are still there, concealed beneath padded waistcoats and tunics. Anybody who counts for much in this town is always accompanied by armed bodyguards. There is a polite but firm notice in the entrance to the city's only luxury hotel, the Pearl Continental: *Hotel Policy*, it declares, is that *Arms cannot be brought inside the hotel premises. Personal Guards or Gunmen are required to deposit their weapons with the Hotel Security. We seek your co-operation. Management.*

'Nobody has ever subdued the Pukhtuns,' the Minister for Kashmir had told me back in Islamabad – though he didn't add that their legendary independence of spirit had always gone hand in hand with gun culture.

For a hundred years the British Army in India had attempted to pacify the frontier tribesmen. They sent out countless punitive expeditions, built unassailable fortresses, bombed Afridi and Wazir villages from the air; but they had never kept the

Pathans down for long. There developed a certain mutual respect between the protagonists, and from this grew the legend of the North-West Frontier and a highly romanticised image of border warfare. In reality it wasn't pretty at all. British and Indian soldiers wounded in enemy territory would beg their comrades to finish them off, a swift death being infinitely preferable to being left to the tender mercies of Pathan tribesmen or, even worse, their women.

As for the punitive action taken by the British, it grew more terrible as the technology of warfare developed. I'd seen black-and-white newsreels from the 1940s of the RAF bombing defenceless villages to rubble. Even more horrible were photographs showing the damage to Pathan and Baluchi tribesmen caused by the Dum-Dum bullet. A nasty invention if ever there was one, this bullet was first developed at the Dum-Dum munitions factory outside Calcutta and was used extensively on the North-West Frontier. As such, it was a grim connection between the beginning of my journey and its end.

In the 1970s, the old-fashioned, ex-British Army 303 had been the favoured weapon, but for the last two decades the Kalashnikov has been king. I was offered hand-made copies of the classic assault rifle, which are still turned out in the gun workshops of Darra Adam Khel, a township given over completely to gun manufacture and smuggling. There is a continuous racket of bullets being discharged into the air (customers must try out their purchases, after all) and I could have taken my pick of just about anything from a rocket-launcher to a pen-gun. When I asked whether demand had slackened off since the Russian withdrawal from Afghanistan, I was told the different factions of mujahidin kept business booming, though these days the largest market for guns was within Pakistan itself.

That all of this carries on in broad daylight is because Darra lies within the Tribal Territories – a broad swathe of land running alongside the Afghan border which the British never attempted to administer directly, preferring to deal with the tribes through Political Agents. This arrangement was inherited by Pakistan in 1947 and it endures more or less intact to this day. Pakistani law ceases to apply once you cross into Tribal Territory, where it is replaced by decisions of the jirga or council of elders. The right to carry arms is a tradition they will not readily relinquish; and so the gun factories continue to flourish.

Darra may be the main centre of manufacture, but there are shops selling Kalashnikovs right on Peshawar's doorstep. This I discovered by accident when I took the Bullet down the main road west of town. I was looking for Peshawar University, where I'd arranged to meet a woman who'd made a special study of government in the Tribal Areas. But I'd misunderstood the directions and went roaring past the florid frontage of Islamia College, heading towards the Khyber.

The next thing I knew I was in amongst the gun shops of Jamrud Road. As far as I could tell I was still in Peshawar's straggling industrial suburbs. In fact, I had crossed over into Tribal Territory about a hundred yards back. As soon as I pulled off the road a crowd gathered around the bike. An ancient Pathan was telling me I shouldn't be in this place because it was 'off-limits'. A much younger man, comfortably attired in cardigan and kurta pyjama, was beckoning me over to his gun shop. The atmosphere was tense, with the crowd taking sides over whether I had a right to be there or not.

'No problem,' smiled the young man, 'I have protection.' He strolled back to his shop and picked up a Kalashnikov. At that moment someone standing on the roof let off a burst of automatic fire. The locals put their fingers in their ears until the noise was over. It was just another customer trying out the goods.

The young man introduced himself as Mohammad Rafiq. Would I care to look over his wares or maybe even fire off a few rounds myself? I thanked him and explained that I was already late for an appointment. 'No problem,' he replied, 'we have also many pistols, machine-pistols, everything. You want to buy as souvenir?'

I politely turned down his offer, doing my best to make him understand that when I finally flew back to England airport security might not take kindly to the presence of a Smith & Wesson in my luggage, even if I claimed it was just a souvenir of Pakistan. Only my repeated use of the words 'police' and 'customs' eventually persuaded him to give up on a sale.

It was only five minutes' ride back to the university, but I felt as though I'd beamed down from another planet as I entered the modern campus with its orderly avenues, its patches of lawn and its shade trees.

Dr Lal Bahia Ali had an embroidered white headscarf pulled tightly over her hair and fastened under the chin. Although too young to remember Partition herself, she had made a study of how the students of Islamia College – and particularly women students – had played an important role in the final push for Pakistan.

Until very late in the day there wasn't much support for the Muslim League in the North-West Frontier Province. There had been strong opposition to British rule, but for years this had linked itself to the Congress Party, and the provincial elections of 1945 returned a Congress Ministry led by Dr Khan Sahib. The main thrust of the independence movement wanted a Pukhtunistan, autonomy for a Pathan homeland, rather than to join some loosely formulated Pakistan. So the Muslim League had a lot of ground to catch up in NWFP, and enlisted whatever supporters it could, including students, to its campaign of civil disobedience.

'From 1945 onwards,' I was told, 'more and more women became active in the Pakistan movement. Two ladies who were my teachers at Frontier College here in Peshawar, they fought for Pakistan and were respected as freedom fighters. They helped organise processions during the civil disobedience movement. You see, because ladies are very much respected in our society, the Congress government police could not stop them from marching.

'When the Quaid-i-Azam, Mohammad Ali Jinnah, came

here in November 1945, a great number of ladies attended his meetings. Then, when Lord and Lady Mountbatten came to Peshawar in April 1947, so many ladies came out in their burqas to show their support for Pakistan.'

This demonstration had the desired impression on the Mountbattens. The crowds lining the railway embankment by Bala Hisar shouted 'Pakistan Zindabad! Mountbatten Zindabad!' It was just the combination of nationalism and loyalty to appeal to the Viceroy. So the British did little to curb the Muslim League's destabilisation of Dr Khan Sahib's democratically elected government. When a referendum was held just six weeks before Independence the people of the North-West Frontier were given the choice of Pakistan or India – a green card or a red card. By the narrowest of margins the vote went to Pakistan. If there had also been a white card, for an independent Pukhtunistan, the result would almost certainly have been different.

However that may be, the transfer of power was achieved more peacefully in the North-West Frontier Province than elsewhere, as Dr Lal Baha Ali reminded me. 'They sometimes say the Pukhtun people are violent, but in 1947 there was much less violence here than in other provinces. Hindu students at Islamia College were able to continue studying and to graduate up to April of that year. Then the Hindu students were escorted peacefully to the railway station to leave for down-country or to their parents' house. There were no incidents concerning students in any records.

'Whatever other bad things did happen here,' she continued, 'it was in reaction to events happening down-country. And since then the Hindus who stayed behind have been living peacefully here.'

'Are there still Hindus in Peshawar?' I asked. I'd come all the way through Pakistan without meeting a single one.

'Oh, I don't really know,' she replied in confusion. 'I am told some are living in the Old City.'

It has been written a thousand times; but it still bears repeating.

If it had not been for one man, Muhammad Ali Jinnah, Pakistan would not have come into existence on 14 August 1947. What is less often repeated, but is also true, is that if Jinnah had not visited the Frontier in November 1945, then the NWFP might not have ended up joining Pakistan.

The enormous impact of his visit was brought home to me by a veteran Muslim Leaguer, Fida Muhammad Khan. He had been converted to the cause while studying at Aligarh Muslim University. When I'd visited that seat of learning a couple of months earlier, the academics had stressed its non-communal traditions and were wary of discussing its earlier involvement with the Muslim League. Not so Fida Muhammad Khan. 'The Quaid-i-Azam took advantage of that university, where the educated Muslim youth of the entire subcontinent was gathered. They became the mainstay of the Muslim League. From that one place the momentum started, and the students spread this to every nook and cranny of India.

'I myself started training in UP, together with other Muslim League students in our last year at Aligarh,' he told me, his eyes glowing with memories of youthful idealism. 'When I came back here I was a different man. Did I tell you the Quaid-i-Azam visited the Tribal Areas with my father and myself? The authorities said I was just an irresponsible boy who shouldn't be taking the Quaid-i-Azam into dangerous areas. But he knew I was from Aligarh, which was his favourite place. So he said: "A law graduate from Aligarh? Then he must be a responsible boy!"

'There were thousands of tribals assembled to receive him. It was getting dark and there was no electricity, only oil lamps. They were firing guns in the air. I asked him not to get down from the vehicle, but he insisted. You see, they were firing to receive the Quaid-i-Azam. I knew this, but we Pathans are a different people with different customs. He was a man from Bombay; but I tell you, he was a fearless man.

'When the Quaid-i-Azam was invited to the NWFP in 1936, he appeared such a very well-dressed man, and he couldn't speak the common language. So many people said of him "he's not a Muslim, he's a Britisher". But when this same man visited nine years later it was a very different story. The people rushed to see him. He inspired them to join the new Pakistan.'

Fida Muhammad Khan eventually rose to be Governor of the NWFP. But he didn't want to talk of high office or his moves to integrate the tribal areas. Instead, he showed me old photographs of the Quaid-i-Azam with his father up by the Afghan border and told me how, being an inquisitive student, he had once asked Jinnah: 'Do we mean it? Do we really mean Pakistan?'

'I asked this because so many people said he was just negotiating for advantages. To this the Quaid-i-Azam replied: "Yes, we mean it." And he said this with such force and vehemence that a great confidence was created in me. That moment I can never forget.'

Compared with the massive slaughter in the Punjab there was relatively little bloodshed along the North-West Frontier in 1947. One reason for this was that outside of the larger towns the population of Hindus and Sikhs was negligible, so there wasn't a battle for control as in the areas around Lahore and Amritsar. Whatever form of Partition would finally be decided upon – a federation of provinces or the nation state of Pakistan – the frontier Pathans were confident they would have Muslim rule. This absence of fear meant there were far fewer killings.

The non-Muslims belonged mainly to business and trading communities, so there wasn't that same attachment to the land which made Sikh and Hindu Jat cultivators in the Punjab stay on until it was too late. There wasn't the same violence or sudden exodus; but the non-Muslims of the NWFP were nonetheless made to feel unwelcome in the new Pakistan. Arson and other attacks against their property – especially that of Hindu moneylenders who had held rural Pathans in their thrall – were commonplace. And refugees from the North-West had to make their way down the corridor through the Punjab, where trains and road convoys were often attacked by local Muslims.

Peshawar itself contains many remains that show the city once had a thriving Hindu community. The old Panch Tirath, or Five Holy Places, a grouping of sacred tanks where Hindus used to bathe and carry out cremations, had legendary links with the Pandava brothers, whose victory at Kurukshetra is celebrated in the *Mahabharata*. It had been a famous landmark beside the GT Road; but after Partition its artificial lakes were turned into a fisheries centre.

Then there is the Gor Khatri, a place holy to Hindus, Sikhs and, even earlier on, to Buddhists, who knew it as the 'Tower of the Buddha's Bowl' on account of the sacred relic that was housed there. And on a more secular level, there is Sethi Street, home of the great business dynasty of that name, which controlled much of the trade across the passes to Central Asia, China and Russia. A hundi or letter of credit issued by the Sethis was reputed to be negotiable anywhere from Balkh to Bengal.

If a Hindu community still existed in Peshawar, I reckoned this was as likely a place as any to seek them out. But the intensely Muslim character of the Old City discourages questions such as 'Do you happen to know if there's a Hindu temple around here?' The unsmiling Pathan advancing towards you might interpret this line of questioning as a deadly insult, while the women were invisible beneath their burqas.

Sarah wore baggy trousers and wrapped a scarf around her head whenever she went into the Old City. Her modesty thus preserved, she had a fine time among the bazaars, pricing lapis lazuli from Afghanistan, Turcoman camel bags, fragments of pottery which the salesmen claimed were Gandharan. 'Ever since we've been on that motorbike,' she complained, 'it's been impossible to do any serious shopping. You always say "there's not enough space" or "it's too fragile". Well, now we've made it to Peshawar I'm going to catch up for lost time.'

Our progress through the Old City was slow, requiring as it did much sitting on cushions and drinking of green tea while the process of inspection and bargaining took its normal, unhurried course. By the time we had passed through the Andarshar Bazaar, done the rounds of the Afghan traders in

Shinwari Plaza, examined the copper- and brass-ware on Qissa Khawani – the old 'Story-tellers' Bazaar' where travellers' tales were once told – and discussed the various qualities of Astrakhan lambskins below Cunningham Clock Tower, the afternoon was almost spent. As we walked up Sethi Street, past the tall mansions with their finely carved wooden balconies and screens, I tried asking shopkeepers whether they knew of a Hindu temple nearby. Some looked at me as though I were a madman; others simply shook their heads.

At the top of Sethi Street we passed through a massive but crumbling Mughal gateway into the Gor Khatri. The site had been transformed into a majestic caravanserai by a daughter of the Emperor Shah Jahan. A second gate stood opposite the one we had entered by, and it was obvious that this had once been a major stopover for merchants on the road to Kabul and points north. But the vast central courtyard has been encroached upon by government offices, and the serai's eastern wall has served as a garage for the city's fire brigade since the early 1900s.

In one corner there is a Sikh temple dating back to the times when the Gor Khatri was used as the residence of the Sikh Governor of the frontier region, and beside this is a small tank. But the temple was locked and there was nobody about, so I decided to give up for the day. 'Why don't you ask Joseph?' Sarah suggested. 'He might be able to help. There are a couple of shops in the bazaar I want to go back to. I'll meet you at Joseph's in an hour or so.'

Just about every foreign correspondent, arms dealer, aid worker or cricketer who has been through Peshawar knows Joseph. If they don't know him by name, they've probably bought a drink off him. For Joseph is the only public bartender in Pakistan, and has been, he says, for nearly twenty years. And while the starkly lit room over which he presides on the top floor of the Pearl Continental is hardly the cosiest of snugs – there are dire warnings against introducing Muslims on the door and you have to fill in an application for a liquor licence before being served –

it is the only place in the Islamic Republic where visitors can drink outside the privacy of their hotel bedroom.

Joseph's prime qualification is that he's a Christian. His family are devout Catholics and his daughter has entered a convent in Rawalpindi. 'We have all been Christian since my grandfather's time,' he told me. 'Before that we were Sikhs.'

His father was in the army and had stayed on after Partition. But his elder sister had been married and lived in East Punjab. He'd visited her in India twelve years earlier; but when he was subsequently told she was dying he couldn't go and see her because he was unable to get a visa. 'It was the same when my mother and father expired,' he told me. 'Nobody could come from India. This problem with the border is only governments' doing. The people of Pakistan and India would like to come and go more freely. They have very much the same culture. They like to mix together.'

He wasn't able to help me about the Hindu community. 'They are there in the Old City, but I don't know the place exactly.' But he had personal experience of what happens when Muslim–Hindu anger boils over. 'At the time when the Babri Masjid was destroyed in India,' he told me, 'some of the mullahs here became very angry and led a procession to our churches. These people started stoning our churches; so we Christians made our own procession. There was a clash and they broke the street lights and burned two buses. Then the police arrived and surrounded us Christians and our churches, to protect us.

'Why they do this against us I do not know. We have nothing to do with India. We are Pakistanis, just like they are. But sometimes these tensions arise and as a precaution we must keep something in the house to defend ourselves.'

At this point Sarah waltzed into Joseph's bar with the smuggest of smiles across her face. 'I think I've found what you're looking for,' she announced, before ordering herself a large gin. 'It's down a side-street in the Old City. It's painted in all these pinks and reds – definitely un-Islamic colours. And there was this music which sounded rather like a Hindu puja coming from inside.'

'Do you think you can find it again?' I asked, pulling out some rupees to pay for the drinks.

'I think so,' she replied teasingly. 'It's near a fish market. But before we go anywhere I'm going to finish this. You'll just have to wait. Because without me you'll never find it.'

She was right about that. After nightfall the narrow lanes twisting through the Old City seemed doubly confusing. We had to backtrack a couple of times to a certain shop or crossroads she remembered. But once she found the fish market it was like watching a hound working the scent. Two minutes later she pointed down what looked like a cul-de-sac.

'It's down there, the big building on the left.' I peered through the darkness. It didn't look like a Hindu temple to me. In fact it didn't look that different from the other tall houses lining the alleyway, apart from its brightly painted gateway and sills.

I pushed at a small hinged section of door and stooped to peer inside. All I could see was a plain assembly hall which might be used for any kind of meeting. But immediately I knew a Hindu temple lay within. The whiff of incense, the unmistakable tinkling of a puja bell – they said it all.

To enter, I had to duck under a door sill so low that I ended up on my hands and knees. Straightening up I found myself confronted by forty pairs of curious eyes. The entire congregation had turned to see who was blundering into their sanctum. A doorkeeper led me into a small cubicle where I was instructed to remove my shoes. That I was expecting; but when they produced a white skull-cap for me I became a little confused. This requirement of covering the head seemed more Muslim than Hindu in character.

Sarah was now clambering through the low doorway. Her headscarf was in keeping with the way most of the women in the congregation were dressed. They and the younger children sat apart from the men; but their faces were unveiled.

I was introduced to a temple official called Pandit Jagdish Lal who told me this was a Durga temple and that they were followers of Baba Sri Pir Rathanath. The mixture of the Hindu honorifics and pir, the Muslim term for a saint, was striking. This Pir Rathanath, I was told, had lived twelve hundred years ago and was the first in a long line of their gurus. Originally they had come from Afghanistan, moving from Ghazni to Kabul and then on to Peshawar. When Pakistan came into being in 1947, their twenty-ninth guru left for Delhi and had never been back. He had died twenty years previously and their sect was now governed by the thirtieth guru, who had built many temples in India. But the present guru had never visited this remnant of Hindus who had stayed on in Peshawar.

The Pandit was unshaven, but most of the men sported moustaches and in their manner of dress – the kurta pyjama and waistcoat – were scarcely distinguishable from the Muslims among whom they lived. Their low chanting sounded like a form of Pashtu studded with Sanskrit. Was this the language, I wondered, of the ancient Hindu and Buddhist communities of Afghanistan from before the time of that country's conversion to Islam? If their first guru lived twelve hundred years ago, this community traced its origins back to the times when Hindu and Muslim rulers were still contesting possession of Afghanistan. Or was it a more recent amalgam, the result of having been isolated for so long from developments in the Hindu heartlands of India?

I was invited to look around the temple. The walls were painted in green and pink, with alcoves decorated in brightly coloured geometric patterns. Upstairs was a shrine to their gurus filled with gilt-framed portraits – the older ones represented in pen-and-ink, the more recent by photographs retouched and coloured by hand. With their full beards, their turbans and darkly penetrating eyes, this succession of Hindu pirs were unlike any portraits of gurus I'd ever seen. To my eyes, they looked like wild Afghans; though there was one whose closed eyes and blissed-out expression reminded me of a certain sadhu I had encountered by the sacred tank at Kurukshetra.

'Peshawar was once a city of temples,' said Shakeel Chander, 'but most were closed down after Partition.' He wore the aid officials' standard hot-weather gear of a Le Croc sports shirt and well-cut cotton trousers. Previously he had practised as an advocate, but he now worked as office manager for the European Union's delegation in Peshawar, co-ordinating various relief agencies' work with the Afghan refugees.

His tall and narrow house across the way from the temple was thoroughly traditional, with lots of wood-panelled rooms on slightly different levels. 'While you are in Peshawar,' he said, 'you really should go and see the refugee camps. They are still there after so many years.'

His young wife bustled about, plumping up cushions and bringing in milky tea and biscuits. Without veil or head-covering, her long hair plaited behind, she looked a model of Hindu motherhood. But when she went out shopping she covered her face, as did all Hindu women.

Shakeel was telling me there were less than fifty Hindu families in the Old City and that they all came to this main temple. 'Most of the community left after 1947. My own family was planning to leave. All my uncles migrated to India, but my father stayed in Peshawar. Now we are the only members of my family here.'

It was a close-knit community, one turned in upon itself after half a century of almost complete isolation. Some of the leading families, including the Sethi trading dynasty, had converted to Islam. 'Nowadays the great majority of Hindus here in Pakistan are from down south, from Sind. But they never come up this way.

'We generally keep a low profile. For example, we Hindus don't go about shopping during Ramadan as that might anger the Muslims. But personal relations are very good. I have four old classmates, all of them Muslims, who are good friends to me.'

He confirmed what I had already heard, that there had been relatively little bloodshed in the North-West Frontier Province during Partition. 'I think that is part of the religious tradition here; the people are more tolerant than in other parts. After

Partition, when most of the Hindus left, they helped us and were very co-operative.'

I asked him if there had been any trouble after the Babri Mosque was demolished. 'There were problems at that time, it's true, because Muslim people all over the world were outraged about this. The Government of Pakistan made a resolution protesting about it. Here in Peshawar there were demonstrations, but the crowds did not attack the Hindu community. In other cities there were attacks on temples. In Lahore there was one near Ravi Road that was demolished, and a small one in Rawalpindi. But here in Peshawar there were no such problems.'

Before leaving his house, Shakeel insisted on giving me the names of people I could contact about the Afghan refugee camps. 'What happened in 1947 is all past,' he said. 'It is this refugee problem which most concerns us in Peshawar these days.'

We returned briefly to the temple to listen to the end of the puja. The chanting had ceased and the temple priest was conducting some kind of sermon. In form, at least, it sounded not so very different from the manner in which a mullah addresses the faithful.

When the puja ended we crawled through the low portal and out into the street. I'd forgotten to hand back my skull-cap and one of the worshippers told me to wait while he returned it to the temple guardian. His name was Inder Prakash and he was one of Shakeel's cousins. Half-way through this conversation he broke off suddenly and crossed the street to embrace a friend of his in the traditional Islamic fashion. 'This is my friend Muhammad Qasim,' he announced, 'and he is like a brother to me. He invites you to take tea in his house. It is just nearby.'

Yet more tea . . . On the other hand, I was curious about these two friends, the one Hindu, the other Muslim. And his house was only two doorways down from the temple. So, removing our shoes as we entered, we sat down to tea – clear this time, with plenty of sugar.

Muhammad Qasim also practised the law. He told me that this five-storey house had been built by a Hindu in 1929. 'In those times, all the houses in this street were lived in by Hindus. Then in 1947–8 the Hindu family left and this house was granted to Muslim refugees from India for just a small fee. My own family bought it from them twenty-five years past, and now my parents and unmarried sisters are also living here.'

The door opened and a child ran into the room. 'This is my son Ali,' said Muhammad Qasim. 'He is four years old.'

Young Ali had dark curly locks and wore a pristine white jumper over his pyjamas. To begin with he was shy, hiding his head in his father's arms. 'My sister and my parents help, but I alone am responsible for his upbringing. His mother died after giving birth. It was from renal failure.'

An expression of deep sorrow, forcefully contained, passed across Muhammad's face. Kidney failure. Something that probably could have been sorted out in the West, but not here in Pakistan.

While Muhammad talked quietly with his son, telling him not to be so shy about the strange guests, Inder was telling me about the Hindu community in Peshawar. There were, he said, perhaps 150 Hindu houses in the cantonment area, served by four temples, though these were small and deliberately inconspicuous. And he told me about their first guru, Baba Pir Rathanath, and how originally he'd been a prince but had become a wandering ascetic, preaching to the people and founding new places of worship.

I learned that the mosque in which Muhammad prayed was very close to the temple. They coexisted, side by side, as they had for nearly a thousand years before Partition. 'This Inder is my brother,' Muhammad said, putting an arm around the Hindu's shoulder. 'We Muslims go to their meetings and he comes to our meetings. In this city there is no problem for Hindus. With us here they are totally safe.'

I looked at the pair of them with their same neatly trimmed moustaches, their same style of dress, and decided that they could almost have passed as brothers. I felt moved by

Muhammad's protective attitude to Inder, and Inder's trust in Muhammad. And I thought that in all of my journey across the subcontinent I had not seen anything quite like it.

I had heard many stories of how, amidst the communal frenzy of Partition, Hindus had taken Muslims into their houses and Muslims had protected Hindus. I knew that these bonds of friendship stretching across the communal divide still exist, that they could be multiplied many thousands of times over in just about every city I'd passed through. But by their very nature these are private, at times even secretive, relationships. There is nobody to sing their praises, no vested interest, no political party or religious leader, that particularly wants to encourage them.

Such friendships represent a victory of personal over institutional values, of common humanity over divisive doctrines. To discover this where I had least been expecting to, in the most Muslim province of all, made it the more poignant. For these Hindus of Peshawar are among the most isolated minorities in the subcontinent, separated both from their guru in India and their ancient roots in Afghanistan. For generations they have lived in the shadow of the Hindu Kush – whose name means the 'Hindu Killer' mountains – and they survive on the basis of trust, the heartfelt belief that their Muslim brothers such as Muhammad will protect them. It was like finding a garden in the middle of the desert.

EPILOGUE:
EVERY BULLET HAS ITS BILLET

I had come to the end of the line. In Peshawar the GT Road loops around the cantonment area and turns back on itself. From this, the north-western terminus, there was only one way to go. That was back the way I'd come, to Rawalpindi and Lahore, and on to India.

And yet the road had not always ended here. In the days of the Grand Mughals their Imperial Road had continued on to Kabul. Sher Shah had dreamed of such a road. Akbar's and Jahangir's engineers made it a reality.

But with the civil war in Afghanistan going from bad to worse there was no way that we could make it overland to Kabul. Continuing as far as the Afghan border was a possibility. That route climbed up through the Khyber Pass. Officially it was off-limits to foreigners, but after badgering the authorities for several days a special permit was granted.

Except I couldn't take the Bullet, because the permit was granted only on condition that we were accompanied by two armed guards. 'How can they protect you on a motorcycle?' an official demanded. 'There have been many cases of kidnapping, young children taken for ransom. We cannot have this happening to you.'

In some ways I was relieved. The bike was not well. Apart from the crash damage, the engine wasn't firing properly on the low-lead petrol available in Pakistan. Every thirty miles or so I'd been having to stop and clean up the spark plug. The prospect of a breakdown in Tribal Territories wasn't appealing.

So we went up the Khyber under armed escort. It's hard to imagine a more forbidding place with its bare mountains, Kalashnikov-toting tribesmen and isolated hill-forts from which the British and now the Pakistani army have attempted to enforce some measure of control. We continued to the Afghan border, ignoring warning signs that 'By Order of Government Entry of Foreigners is Prohibited Beyond This Point'. What constitutes a 'foreigner' in these parts is open to dispute. Pathans from both sides of the border cross over with impunity.

The main road crossing at Torkham was crowded with trucks and buses going in both directions. The volume of human and goods traffic was in stark contrast to the Wagha border with India. There were thousands in transit, the men uniformly bearded, the women in burqaas. Most of them were Afghan refugees. The money-changers sat with huge piles of banknotes in front of them – US dollars, Pakistani rupees, rapidly devaluing Afghanis. A young boy was carrying a used rocket casing into Pakistan. Such are the exports of war-torn Afghanistan.

We climbed a hill and looked over the barbed-wire into another country intent on destroying itself. Some clearly profit from this state of anarchy. Just across the border was a truck-park filled with shiny new containers. I wondered how the hell they'd got to the top of the Khyber Pass.

'We call this place mini-Dubai,' a Pakistani told me. He explained how tax-free goods are flown into Afghanistan by Russian aircrews. The main point of entry was Jalalabad, further up the road towards Kabul. The containers were being unloaded for onward transport into Pakistan – television sets, cosmetics, you name it. The more valuable goods would be smuggled over the border, naturally. One of the trucks was being escorted by mujahidin aboard a Russian armoured personnel carrier. 'This truck must be carrying valuable goods,' was the Pakistani's comment.

I asked what he thought was on board. Drugs? Banknotes? Weaponry?

'Who can know these things?' he replied, and raised his eyes towards the storm-clouds gathering further up the valley.

I took the hint. In a place such as Torkham there are some questions you don't ask. The traffic in illicit goods was a no-go area. But the human traffic was a lot safer and, from my perspective, much more interesting.

Most of the people crossing the border were Afghan refugees. All the way through India and Pakistan I'd been talking to refugees from an earlier conflict. I'd visited some of the camps they'd stayed in, travelled the same roads they had fled down. But after the brief cataclysm of Partition they had settled down in their adopted country and merged more or less successfully into the society around them. Not so the Afghan refugees along the North-West Frontier.

More than fifteen years after the Soviet invasion of their homeland, the Afghan refugee camps across the border in Pakistan are still there. The Russians may have been sent packing; the Communist threat dissolved into thin air. Yet as long as the fighting continues in Afghanistan, the refugee problem will remain.

Before leaving Peshawar I looked around two of the big camps off the Jamrud Road. Townships would be a better description, for the refugees have built houses of dried mud in the Afghan fashion; or ghettoes, since their presence is resented by local people, who see them taking their jobs. What is very apparent is that these 'camps' are here to stay, even though since the Russian withdrawal the United Nations and most of the voluntary agencies have cut their funding, leaving the host country, Pakistan, to pick up the slack.

We were shown around Nasir Bagh Camp by Muhammad Younas Khan, who has the unenviable job of administering the 200,000 Afghan refugees in and around Peshawar. The people in Nasir Bagh had mostly worked for the Soviet-sponsored regime. For them, going back to Afghanistan was not an option and they were treated as collaborators by other refugee groups. There were former engineers and doctors and army commanders among them; but they couldn't find work in Pakistan and were drifting into penury. These people really have nowhere to go. The feeling of hopelessness was overwhelming.

Other refugees are being encouraged to return. Food and fuel distribution in the camps has stopped. But the Afghans won't leave while there is still fighting in their homeland. 'Here they have schools and electricity and health services,' explained Younas Khan, 'even if nowadays they have to pay for them. Over there, they say they have none of these things. And worst of all, they have no security against the warlords.'

Whenever the civil war inside Afghanistan intensifies the population in the camps rises towards three million. When the fighting eases it comes down to around half that level. Somewhere inside some UN agency there is probably an accounting system which works out how many 'refugee years' have been generated by a given conflict. For Afghanistan the grand total would be around 30 million and rising. In other words, roughly the same number of 'refugee years' caused by the division of India in 1947. So, although Partition involved far more people, at least it was resolved relatively quickly. With the Afghan refugees there's still no end in sight.

I had planned to ride the Bullet back to India. But the bike was sick and I was running out of both time and money. Sarah wasn't keen on another two or three days' ride back through Pakistan, either. So I took the easy way out. I booked tickets for both of us and the bike on the overnight train to Lahore. With luck we'd be back in Amritsar, at Mrs Bhandari's, the following evening.

The next morning, I took the Canal Road from Lahore, the back route to the border. The engine was misfiring badly. As we crawled into the Pakistan border post at Wagha, the Bullet made one last splutter and fell silent. Sarah went ahead to deal with the paperwork while I pushed the bike into the shade. The seasons had turned: it was hotter now and there was a riot of flowers in front of the customs shed – just as we'd been promised when we entered Pakistan.

It took barely ten minutes for the carnet and passports to be stamped. Sarah went ahead to the border on foot, leaving me to sort out the bike. I tried cleaning the blackened spark plug, but the engine still wouldn't fire. So I hauled the Bullet off its stand and pushed it past the Pakistani border guard and out into no-man's-land.

The loaded bike was heavy and I was pouring sweat. About half-way across I paused for breath. *Long Live Pakistan*, proclaimed the gateway behind me. *Welcome to India, the World's Largest Democracy*, declared the one ahead. And silently, the salt-sweat stinging my eyes, I cursed this border by every name under the sun.

It had been engendered out of fear and hatred and confusion. Its birth-pangs were horrific. And even now, fifty years on, there remained a residue of hostility – both between India and Pakistan, and between the Hindu, Muslim and Sikh communities within India. I hadn't needed to seek it out; it was there, lying in wait for the traveller.

I thought of the millions of refugees who had used this same border in 1947 to cross over into India or Pakistan and for a moment I felt like saying: 'A curse on both your houses.'

But that was a momentary aberration. Because for India I have the deepest affection and respect. It has remained, as the notice above me proclaimed, the most populous democracy in the world for almost all of fifty years. In food production and healthcare and education it has made enormous strides. The enduring legacy of Partition is only one of a thousand strands.

Pakistan, the country I'd just left, has had a much patchier history as a democracy. Since I was last there, Muslim fundamentalists have marched on Islamabad, the military intervened, and Benazir Bhutto's government has been dismissed on grounds of ineptitude and corruption, to be replaced first by President's Rule and then, after an election in which disillusioned voters stayed away in droves, by another Nawaz Sharif administration. If anything, it faces an even greater task than India in curbing government corruption and feudalism. But then, back in 1947, forging a nation state out of five of the more backward provinces on the periphery of the subcontinent was a herculean task. The new Pakistan succeeded in doing so, and for fifty years has gone its own way. It has forged new links within the Islamic World, with the Arabian peninsula and Central Asia. And, as the absence of traffic at this border crossing confirmed, it has turned its back resolutely on India.

It may well be that a united India, organised along fairly loose, federal lines, would have benefited the peoples of the subcontinent more than dividing it into mutually antagonistic nation states. But such visions of how things might have been – the age-old unity of the subcontinent carried forward into self-rule, the long-sought-after goal of freedom realised without so much senseless slaughter – these are just pipe-dreams. Partition happened, and my own forebears, Englishmen of my father's generation, had pushed it through to its dreadful conclusion. When 'Divide and Quit' became official policy, all that was left was 'making the best out of a bad job'. At least, that's how they saw it.

Back then there was a popular expression doing the rounds, that 'when the British finally quit India, all they'll leave is a pile of empty beer bottles and the GT Road'. Since I'd just travelled the length of the GT Road and added a few more bottles to the pile, that much I knew was true. But I also knew there were other things – India's parliamentary and judicial system, its military traditions, the use of English as a *lingua franca*, even the original design of the Enfield Bullet – that drew on two centuries of British rule.

There was something else the British left behind, for which I had developed an intense loathing – the dead-weight of bureaucracy. What's more, I was about to encounter it again in all its illogical inflexibility. Up ahead I could see the squat bunker which housed the Government of India's immigration and customs service, Attari Road.

'Good to see you again,' I said to the same customs official who had 'processed' the bike's papers on the way out. He took the carnet without a word and studied it for some minutes before peering at me over his thick-rimmed spectacles.

'I see this vehicle has been exported to Pakistan,' he began. 'Now you must be paying import duty to bring this said vehicle into India.'

It took two hours' of heated argument before we could convince him, his colleague, his superior and his superior's superior that we had simply visited Pakistan and returned. Since the bike was made in India, registered and taxed in India and was under Indian ownership, how could we be importing it?

'But there is no precedent,' he said, confirming how little Indian traffic crosses the border. 'If you keep insisting like this,' he complained, 'we will be losing our jobs.' His colleagues then proceeded to justify their employment by searching the bike – side-panniers, petrol tank, the lot. Not once but twice.

I used some of the time cleaning up the spark plug and tweaking the carburettor. Sarah hitched a ride into Amritsar with a bus carrying English cricket supporters. 'To make sure there's still a room at Mrs Bhandari's,' she told me, though I knew she'd had enough of riding pillion on a juddering and misfiring motorcycle.

A sensible decision, as it was growing dark by the time I cleared customs. I hit the starter pedal; the engine fired first time. 'Obviously she's happy to be back in India,' I thought, as I pointed the Bullet down the dead-straight road towards Amritsar.

There was no traffic about and for once I had the luxury of reflection rather than having to concentrate single-mindedly on the road. Memories of the early stages of my journey flashed up – the pilgrims taking their dip at the sangam, the three old men in the Jama Masjid, the Sikh trucker who offered to take me to Kashmir. The older generation had looked back to Partition, often with bitterness; the younger were more intent on getting on in life, whether it was making money or teaching or voluntary work. Communal strife, they argued, was a thing of the past.

Fragments of the journey were still rushing through my brain like newsreel clippings when I realised the bike was running away with me. I eased back the throttle but the revs kept climbing.

Something was seriously wrong. Either the throttle cable had worked loose or the carburettor was jammed open. The only way to lose speed was by pulling intermittently on the brakes and shifting down through the gears. But each time the engine note kept on rising and the bike began accelerating again, so I was forced to cut the ignition and freewheel to a stop.

The street lights of Amritsar lit up the horizon, but it was inky dark by the side of the road and I had no torch. Not the best conditions for a spot of 'trouble-shooting'. I tightened the cable and poked around in the dark, trying to adjust the carburettor and timing screw. But while the bike started up first time, I only made it another mile up the road before the motor was howling like a banshee and I had to switch off the ignition again.

Earlier on I'd have been tempted to kick that uncontrollable lump of metal. After all, it did seem intent on killing me. But now I just hunkered down beside it and tried to work out what was wrong. It's the Bullet's Revenge, I thought, revenge for all the maltreatment I've put it through. But with a little patience and perseverance, maybe we'll sort out this problem and cover those last few miles together.

It was nearly an hour later that we roared through the gates of Mrs Bhandari's Guest House. Sarah was sitting out on the lawn, drinking the once cold beer she'd ordered for me.

'So what kept you this time?' she enquired.

We parted, the Bullet and I, in Amritsar. The bike went by train back to Madras; Sarah and I by plane back to England.

Waiting for me at home among the pile of unwanted mailshots and bills was a letter from my father. Inside was a clipping from an old newspaper he'd dug up. It had been printed in 1908, the fiftieth anniversary of the relief of Lucknow and the end of what Indians know as the First War of Independence and the British as the Indian Mutiny.

The original letter had been written from the 'Camp before Lucknow', 7 March 1858, by one Corporal H. Gregson, then serving in a native company of sappers. According to my father's reckoning, he must have been my great-great-granduncle.

My father, also an H. Gregson, had himself enlisted with the Madras Sappers and Miners for the duration of the Second World War, but before unearthing this letter he had no idea of this earlier Sapper Gregson's existence.

I read through this curiosity of a letter. Much of it was about pay and conditions. Each month, he calculated, he earned 63 rupees − or £6 6/- in English money. 'I have every comfort a man can require,' he bragged to his stay-at-home brother. 'Provisions are very cheap; you can get a sheep for two shillings, and all other things in proportion.'

His report of the fighting is coldly factual. 'We move camp nearly every day nearer to Lucknow,' he wrote, 'as we drive the enemy in. Our column had a hard day's fighting yesterday; we drove the enemy over six miles of the country like chaff before the wind. I found one of the enemy in a tree as we advanced, and one of the cavalry shot him, for we show no quarter.' Nor did he have any doubts about the rightness of what he was doing. 'You may see in the papers about the crimes committed here by the Sepoys, but I could not have believed the statements if I had not witnessed some of the atrocities. I am now a long way up the country; all the way there is nothing but destruction.'

Then he used a phrase which stopped me in my tracks. 'I am quite happy among the row of cannon and musketry,' he asserted, because 'I believe that every bullet has its billet, and if I am to be shot it is the will of God.'

Every bullet has its billet . . . A solidly Protestant belief that all things are predestined, that whether he lived or died was already preordained. Not so very different, perhaps, from the Will of Allah being invoked in the opposing camp. No room for self-doubt here.

It made me wonder whether I'd inherited something of that same, grim fatalism. For what had kept me going all the way up the Grand Trunk Road was a sense of acceptance. If my number's up, then so be it. Otherwise I'd probably have gone crazy from fear and frustration. But whether this runs in the blood or comes from my Indian upbringing, I can't tell. The subcontinent breeds many strains of fatalism which can make life just about bearable for the downtrodden masses. It stands in the way of sudden change. But when change is enforced from above, as in 1947, that fatalism becomes a desperation which turns cowards and false-heroes into bullies, murderers and victims. That much I'd learned following Partition's trail through India and Pakistan.

I was reunited with the Bullet once again, albeit briefly. The following winter Sarah and I flew out to Madras, where I was to attend a press conference. Enfield had agreed to lend me a Bullet to try out a motorcycle tour of South India they'd started, but they didn't specify which machine it would be.

That first morning back in India I heard the low, thumping exhaust note of a Bullet coming up the drive. An unmistakable sound. And there *she* was: the Bitch, aka one silver-grey Royal Enfield 500 cc Bullet, registration no. TN02B5137, chassis and engine no. 5B5-5227N.

No sooner had the mechanic who'd delivered her dismounted than I was all over that machine. The scratched paintwork on the front fork where the bus had reversed into us was still there. The gold lettering along the tank hadn't been retouched, so it still read ENFI – the last three letters having worn off long ago, in Bihar, when I had to grip the tank with my knees to stay on while riding through all the potholes. The headlight frame retained the scars of our crash outside Peshawar.

I patted her and peered at the mileometer. Someone had notched up another 6,000 kilometres. (I later learned she'd been used as a demonstration model and had just returned from a trip to Delhi with a police officer.) Some of the chrome-work showed signs of the monsoon season. But I couldn't care less. We were reunited and would be heading out on the road once more.

The mechanic mentioned that the tank was almost empty. If I gave him the money he'd fill up at a petrol station nearby. I remembered the humiliation of running out of fuel at the 'flagging off' ceremony in Calcutta and handed over a wad of rupees. Besides, I needed to stay put. Enfield's marketing man, Mr Shankar, was coming round to see that everything was OK. I sat back and waited.

But Sarah was worried about something. 'I've a bad feeling about this trip,' she said. 'After making it safely up the GT Road, it would be bloody stupid to crash the bike tootling around South Indian temple-towns.' And that got me worrying: for Sarah has many times before demonstrated a certain prescience, or at least an instinct for impending trouble. Even her best friends know her affectionately as 'The Witch'.

Forty minutes later the mechanic reappeared dripping blood. There had been an accident at the traffic lights. The mechanic's right hand was badly grazed, but it was his toes that concerned me most. He'd been wearing open sandals, and blood mixed with grit was congealing around deep cuts. I told him to see a doctor or at least to get his foot washed with disinfectant and properly dressed. He returned minutes later with some cotton wool wrapped around his toes and insisted on showing me the bike there and then. I think he was as worried about keeping his job as about keeping his full complement of toes.

We trailed down to the main road, the mechanic babbling about how this was the first time in his life he'd ever had a biking accident. The Bullet had already been loaded onto a handcart. She was a real mess. The front end had been stoved in, both forks bent, the headlight and control cables were hanging loose like mechanical marionettes, and the front brake's disc was cracked clean in two. The mudguards, spokes and exhaust pipe had also been damaged. There was no way I would be going anywhere on that twisted heap of metal.

And I very nearly went completely ape-shit. Something I'd become attached to – even if it was just a machine – had been destroyed. And for this to happen at our emotional reunion . . . But then I looked at the poor, bloody mechanic and the misery on his face. He was still in a state of physical shock, fearful for his job and future livelihood. I had to control myself.

Mr Shankar arrived while the mechanic was away getting his wounds dressed. He knew nothing of what had just happened.

'You have seen the Bullet?' beamed Mr Shankar.

'Briefly,' I replied.

'Is it not wonderful?' he continued. 'Actually the same vehicle you took up the GT Road.'

'It was a wonderful moment, Mr Shankar . . . but there has been this accident.'

'Accident?' he said, his smile now gone. 'Not serious, I hope.'

Poor Mr Shankar. Everything he touched seemed to turn to dust. Certainly his pleasure in having engineered my reunion with the Bullet vanished when I showed him the wrecked bike. The mechanic was there, fearful of this representative of management. It was up to me to avert the hand of calamity.

'It really doesn't matter, Mr Shankar,' I began.

'Nonsense, nonsense. If you agree to delay your departure by one day, I'm sure we can arrange for this to be repaired.'

As usual, he was being over-optimistic. That bike required several weeks, if not months, of skilled labour to be put back together again. Eventually it was decided to lend me another Bullet, a 350 cc model, and on this Sarah and I rattled our way around the temple-towns of South India. The bike behaved well; but it wasn't the same as being on the Bitch.

When I saw the mangled machine being towed away on the handcart I thought it was the last I'd see of her. *Every bullet has its billet* . . . Mine, I thought, had found its billet in the Great Junkyard in the Sky.

But I should have known better, at least in India. Right now, in some mechanic's shop outside Madras, a Bullet bearing the registration plate TN02B5137 is being patiently reassembled.

Machines you can mend. Not so people who have lost their loved ones, their homes, their livelihoods. Then the wounds lie festering beneath the surface for decades. In the Indian subcontinent they're still there; and sporadically they break open again in another bout of communal bloodletting. Either that or more sabre-rattling between India and Pakistan.

Communalism is by no means a spent force, and the sense of dissatisfaction I encountered among ordinary people in both countries, against corruption in government and the privileges enjoyed by others, may yet break the bounds of habitual self-restraint. Maybe reform will come from within. If not, I fear there will be more bullets and refugees flying up and down the Grand Trunk Road.

GLOSSARY

Amir Muslim nobleman
Anna Coinage, worth one sixteenth of a rupee
Apsara Heavenly nymph
Ashram Spiritual retreat
Ayah Nanny
Azan Muslim call to prayer
Baba Old man
Babu A clerk or office workers, esp. in Bengal
Bagh Garden
Bania A merchant caste
Baksheesh A tip, offering or bribe
Beg A Muslim nobleman or warlord
Begum Muslim princess
Bhai Brother
Bhavan House or building
Brahmin The caste of priests, the highest of the four main
    Hindu castes
Bund Dam or embankment
Burqua All-enveloping dress for Muslim women
Bustee Slum or squatter settlement
Cantonment Planned military or civil area in a town, where
    the European population lived
Caravanserai A resting place for travellers, usually a courtyard
    with rooms around it
Chai Tea
Charpoy A wooden-framed string bed

Chhatri Umbrella-shaped dome or pavilion

Chowk A square or open space in a city where markets can be held

Chowkidar Nightwatchman or guard

Crore Ten million

Dacoit Bandit

Dal A stew made with lentils or split-peas

Darshan Viewing of a Hindu deity

Dhaba Wayside eating place, trucker's rest-stop

Dharma Divinely sanctioned Hindu law; moral or religious duty

Dhobi Laundryman

Dhoti Tucked-up loincloth worn by men

Dhooli A simple palanquin, a chair carried on a pole by two bearers

Dirwan Gatekeeper or watchman

Doab Fertile agricultural plains in Northern India

Dom An 'untouchable' caste entrusted with cremating the dead

Ekka A one-horse carriage

Ghat A bank, usually stepped, leading to a river or tank where ritual bathing or cremations take place

Ghatia Assistant at ritual bathing

Godown Warehouse

Goonda Hired thug, criminal

Gurdwara Sikh religious complex, usually with a temple or shrine

Haj Muslim pilgrimage to Mecca

Haji One who had been on the Haj

Hartal General strike

Haveli Old townhouse, usually around a courtyard

Hookah Water pipe for smoking tobacco

Id-ul-Fitr (also *Eid-ul-Fitr*) Muslim feast which marks the end of Ramadan

Imam Muslim religious leader

Imambara Tomb of a Muslim holy man or focus of the Muharram procession

Inshallah God willing

Jagir Grant of land, usually for military service

Jat Caste of farmers, land–owning cultivators

-ji Honorific added to names, as in Gandhiji

Khana Food, a meal

Kirpan Sikh ceremonial sabre or dagger

Kos The Mughal measurement for distances, between two
  and three English miles

Kshatriya The warrior caste

Kumbh(a) A pot

Kurta Loose shirt worn in the Punjab and North India

Lakh A hundred thousand

Lathi Bamboo staff, often strengthened with iron rings

Lingam Siva represented by the phallus

Lungi Loosely wrapped loincloth

Madrasa Islamic school or college, often attached to a
  mosque

Mahabharata Ancient Sanskrit epic poem, concerning the
  battle between the Pandavas and the Kauravas, later
  incorporating the *Bhagavad-Gita*

Maharaja King or prince (lit. Great Ruler)

Maidan An open park or grassy area within a town

Makar Sankranti Holiday, usually held in January

Mali Gardener

Mandir Temple

Mantra Sacred chant used in meditation

Margh Wide roadway

Masala Spicy

Masjid Mosque

Maulana Muslim scholar or official in a mosque

Maya Illusion

Mela Usually a Hindu religious festival, though also a secular
  fair

Memsahib Married European woman, mistress of the house

Minar Tower or column

Mohalla An enclosed subdivision or ward of a city, often
  entered by a single gate

Muezzin Mosque official who calls the Muslim faithful to prayer

Muharram Muslim period of mourning for Hasan and Hussain

Mullah Muslim religious teacher

Naan A large flat bread typical of North India and Pakistan

Nandi Figure of a sacred bull, Siva's vehicle and a symbol of fertility

Nawab Prince or ruler, usually Muslim

Paan Folded leaf stuffed with betel nut, lime and spices, eaten to aid the digestion

Pahari A person from the hills, or object typical of hillmen

Pakora Vegetables or cheese coated in batter and deep-fried

Pandit Brahmin sage or scholar, also used as a reverential title as in Pandit Nehru

Parsi Zoroastrians, originally from Persia

Peepul (pipal) The tree species (*Ficus religiosa*) associated with the Buddha's Enlightenment, also known as the Bo or Bodhi tree

Peon Messenger or servant

Pir Muslim holy man or spirit

Prasad Consecrated temple food, sometimes distributed to worshippers

Puja Hindu prayers, ritual offerings to the gods

Pukka Proper, solidly built

Purdah Seclusion of Muslim women from public view

Raj Rule or government

Raja King or ruler

Rajput Member of the Kshatriya or warrior caste, also used to denote princes

Ramadan Muslim month of fasting

Ramayana Epic poem, originally in Sanskrit, recounting how Lord Ram rescued his wife Sita

Sadhu Hindu holy man, often an ascetic or mendicant

Sahib Respectful term of address, previously used to denote Europeans

Sangam Confluence of two or more rivers

Sanyasi Wandering ascetic

Sepoy Indian soldier, equivalent to private; previously a native soldier of the British Indian army

Saivite Devoted to Siva

Shalwar kameez Long tunic and matching loose trousers worn mainly by girls in India, and by both men and women in Pakistan

Sharia Muslim theological law

Shikhara Curved tower or spire of a Hindu temple

Sri Honorific title

Sudra Lowest of the four main Hindu castes

Swaraj Self-rule

Tamasha Celebratory spectacle

Tandoor(i) Clay oven used in the Punjab, the North Indian style of cooking

Tank An artificial lake or reservoir

Tempo A large three-wheeler vehicle

Thakur One of the higher Hindu castes

Tik hai OK

Tirthankara The twenty-four gurus or saviours worshipped by the Jains

Tonga Two-wheeled pony carriage

Wallah Man, fellow, as in rickshaw-wallah

Yadav A Hindu caste group

Zamindar(i) Feudal landlord

Zindabad Muslim victory cry

ACKNOWLEDGEMENTS

In journeying across the Indian subcontinent I met, literally, thousands of people who helped out in some way. To those not mentioned in this brief list, my thanks go none the less.

I am especially grateful to Christopher Sinclair-Stevenson, for treating me to a true publisher's lunch and for believing in the idea behind this book; my agent Derek Johns of A. P. Watt, for his unswerving support; my editor, Roger Cazalet; Tyrel Broadbent, for his comments on the manuscript, his paintings of scenes along the Grand Trunk Road, and for instructing me in motorcycle lore; and Margaret Neller of the AA, 'St Margaret of Basingstoke', for organising an international carnet in record time, thereby allowing the bike to enter Pakistan.

In Madras, Praveen Purang of Royal Enfield Motors, who agreed to lend me the Bullet, and all the Enfield managers, agents and mechanics who helped keep the show on the road; also Rabi Rajaratnam who put us up at the Madras Gymkhana Club when there was no room to be had at any inn.

In Calcutta, Jahar and Roma Sengupta, for their unfailing hospitality; and, among the many people who proffered advice or reached back into their own memories of Partition, Professor Amales Tripathi, Bobby Mazumdar, Arun Ghosh, C. R. Irani of the *Statesman*, Bob and Anne Wright, Mrs Malabika Sardar, Mr and Mrs McDonald D'Silva, Professor N. K. Pal, P. T. Basu and Bhaskar Ghose; and Ajoy John for arranging access to the *Statesman*'s archives.

Of the many people along the road I must thank Misri Lal Ram, a brilliant driver and a steadying presence during the first part of the journey; A. K. Banerjee and Majid H. Khan of the Hotel de Paris, Varanasi; Mrs Santosh Mahendrajit Singh of The Attic, and Sunil

Rashtogi and his family in Kanpur, A. K. Singh and family of Etah; Dr R. P. Singh and Professor Nooral Hasan Khan at the Aligarh Muslim University.

In Delhi, Jonathon Bond and Jigme, for the warmest of welcomes; and for their advice and insights, President Shankar Dayal Sharma, Milon Bannerji, Sri Natwar Singh, Mark Tully, John Lall, Pran Chopra, Rahat Hasan at the British High Commission, and Belinda Wright; also Brigadier R. K. Bose of the Delhi Gymkhana Club, and Mirza Wahi Ali Khan for translating from Urdu in the Jama Masjid. In the Punjab, Satindar Singh Oberoi, a trucker who unravelled some of the mysteries of Indian road habits; Amajit Singh who smoothed my way at the Golden Temple; Professor Jargtar Singh Grewal and Professor H. K. Puri of the Guru Nanek University, Amristar; M. P. Agarwal, for looking after the bike and his wife for cooking a delicious Punjabi meal; and Mrs Bhandari and all her patient staff.

In Pakistan, Fakir Syed Aijazuddin, British Honorary Consul in Lahore, for his hospitality and thought-provoking essays; Dr Saifur Rahman Dar of the Lahore Museum; and Lt.-Col. Muhammad Kamran Khan Dotani of the Punjab Club, for sharing his forthright views and showing me his magnificent aviary. In Rawalpindi-Islamabad, Dr Riaz Ahmad, for his biography of Jinnah and his historical insights; also Noor Saghir Khan, Khalid Ali, Senator Shafqat Mahmood, Shahryar Rashed, and Tim Hitchens of the British High Commission.

At Taxila, the Archaeological Museum's curator, Sarwait Baig; and in Peshawar, Professor Farzand Ali Durrani, Vice-Chancellor of Peshawar University; Fida Mohammad Khan; Syed Hassan Gillani, Editor of *Al Jamiat-e-Sarghad*; Asif Khan, Pushtu film star, for standing us a meal at Salatin's, free entry to his film *The Brothers Kalashnikhov*, and later a guided tour of Evergreen Studios; Abdul Haq of the British Council; Shakeel Chander; Nasser Ahmad and his son, Dauqueer Ahmad, for accompanying us up the Khyber Pass together with bodyguards Momin Khan and Zar Khan; and Muhammad Younas Khan for taking me into the Afghan refugee camps.

And above all my wife, Sarah Woodward, for hanging in there.